KT-362-381

'Well paced, well written . . . insistently filmic'
Will Self, *Evening Standard*

'Strong and gripping . . . cunningly wrought and forceful'
Independent

'Raw, twitching . . . Willocks has an uncanny ear for the
rhythms of US prison slang . . . not since Seth Morgan's
Homeboy has doing bird been captured with such
metaphorical flourish. There is a philosophical
depth to the novel.'
Sunday Independent

'This book should carry a warning: don't bother reading
if you're afraid of being unable to put it down before the
final page . . . a compelling, nightmarish canvas,
marvellously painted . . . *Green River Rising* has the
sure touch of a real craftsman.'
Publishing News

Also by Tim Willocks

Bad City Blues
Bloodstained Kings
The Religion

GREEN RIVER RISING

Tim Willocks was born in Stalybridge, Cheshire, in 1957 and
studied medicine at University College Hospital Medical
School. He is the author of *Bad City Blues*, *Bloodstained Kings*
and *The Religion*.

Praise for *Green River Rising*

'*Green River Rising* is a stunner – and may be the best
prison novel ever. This is a book of dark alchemy:
turbulent milieu, brilliantly etched characters, pure
adrenaline-fuelled narrative – richly sustained and stylishly
realised. Tim Willocks has crafted a superbly contained
trip to hell that I urge you all to sign on for.'
James Ellroy

'*Green River Rising* really is a phenomenal piece of
fiction . . . one of the most illuminating guided tours of the
male psyche since *Tristram Shandy* was published'
Sunday Telegraph

'The best thriller since *The Silence of the Lambs . . . Green
River Rising* is a brilliant entertainment . . . a powerful
novel that will shock, and sell'
Daily Telegraph

'Succeeds in gripping from the start and holding to the
end' *Arena*

'Undeniably exciting and well-told'
Daily Mail

GREEN RIVER RISING

TIM WILLOCKS

arrow books

Published in the United Kingdom by Arrow Books in 2007

1 3 5 7 9 10 8 6 4 2

Copyright © Tim Willocks, 1994

Tim Willocks has asserted his right under the Copyright, Designs and Patents Act, 1988, to be identified as the author of this work.

First published in Great Britain by Jonathan Cape in 1994
First published in Great Britain in paperback by Arrow Books in 1995

Arrow Books
The Random House Group Limited
20 Vauxhall Bridge Road, London SW1V 2SA

www.randomhouse.co.uk

Addresses for companies within The Random House Group Limited can be found at:
www.randomhouse.co.uk/offices.htm

The Random House Group Limited Reg. No. 954009

A CIP catalogue record for this book
is available from the British Library

ISBN 9780099509486

Typeset by Palimpsest Book Production Limited, Grangemouth, Stirlingshire

Printed by Cox & Wyman Ltd, Reading, Berkshire

Dedicated to

JOSEPH ROY WILLOCKS

*Who took me to the pictures, and taught me how
to show a manly bearing.*

'I have been studying how I may compare this prison where I live unto the world.'

Richard II
William Shakespeare

THE WORD

'Imagine darkness, if you will, and in that darkness bars of steel encrusted with the rust and filth of ages. The bars are set in blocks of granite rock as ancient as the hills in which time forged them, and stacked above and mortared fast are yet another hundred feet and more, of granite, block on block.

'Between these bars and through this subterranean wall flows an effluvium, the sewage foamed with scum of twenty-five hundred desperate men, and of countless thousands more before them.

'Breathe this infernal air. Taste it. For it is the smell and taste of punishment, raw and pure, and this dissolving slag contains the paradox of a tortured and incomparable race. Here that race must find their home, their final blind communion with insatiable and uninhibited waste, the waste that is the destiny of all. This sewer in the bowels of a monstrous gaol, this sewer in the sewer of the world, is where necessity ends and possibility begins: in the glory and the pain of utter loss.

'This is The Green River.

'And this is the tale of its rising.'

PROLOGUE

THE VALLEY

A MILLION MAN-YEARS of confinement had burnished the surface of the granite flags to a greasy smoothness ingrained deeply with filth and despair. As Warden John Campbell Hobbes crunched along the central walkway of B block he could feel in his bones the imprint of generations of shuffling feet. In his throat he could taste the corruption of stale sweat and infected phlegm, the commingled vapours of nicotine and hashish. Here was the impacted stink of human waste and pain, concentrated, hyper-distilled and stored for decades beneath the high glass roof which rose in a great vault above the triple-stacked tiers of the teeming cell block. This was where men were sent to kneel and where those who didn't want to learned the way.

Somewhere on the planet there were worse places in which to spend time – much worse – but none of them were located in these United States. This was the best that civilisation could do: a civilisation which Hobbes had watched crumble before his eyes and which he now despised with all the contempt his prodigious intellect could muster. The steel cleats on his wingtips struck a relentless beat against the flagstones as he walked and somehow the sound put him in mind of his duty. That duty, that *policy*, was to discipline and punish and Hobbes had pursued it as diligently as any man could. Yet today he would turn his back on it. Today he would pursue that policy by other means.

Today John Campbell Hobbes would shatter the jewel of discipline with the hammer and chisel of war.

Three paces behind Hobbes strode a phalanx of six guards in full riot gear: helmets and visors, Kevlar body armour, nightsticks, perspex shields and Mace. The public address system – eight loudspeakers mounted above the rear gate sally-port – played a military tattoo of drums and pipes to which Hobbes and his men swung along in time. The drums filled Hobbes's limbs with a power without measure and drowned the murmurs of the convicts herded out onto the overhanging gantries. They hated him, blindly and without understanding, and though in the past it had tormented him today he welcomed their hate.

Stone. Drums. Punishment. Power.

Discipline was all.

Hobbes was all.

By other means.

There was a pause in the raging momentum of his thoughts. Hobbes checked himself, checked the writhing coils of his mind for any trace of error, hubris or doubt. He found none. It was so. A universe could only be reshaped by the unleashing of cataclysmic and unpredictable forces. The great physicist had been wrong: God did indeed play with dice. And in the grim and shabby universe that was Green River State Penitentiary John Campbell Hobbes was God himself.

The Penitentiary had been designed by an English architect named Cornelius Clunes in an age when it had still been possible to combine philosophy, art and engineering in a single fabulous endeavour. Commissioned in 1876 by the governor of Texas, Clunes had set out to create a prison in which every brick was imbued with the notion of a power both visible and unverifiable. No dark dungeon was this. No squat, brutal box. Green River was a hymn to the disciplinary properties of light.

From a cylindrical core capped by a great glass dome four cell-blocks and two work blocks radiated away at sixty degree intervals like spokes from the hub of a giant wheel. Beneath the dome was a central watchtower from which a spectator could enjoy a clear view down the central walkway of all four cellblocks. The block roofs were mounted on smooth granite walls that overhung the top tier of cells by twenty feet. The kingposts, tie beams and rafters of the roof were constructed of wrought iron and covered with extravagant sheets of thick green glass. Through the glass streamed the all-seeing light of God: a permanent surveillance that induced in the cowering inmate a state of conscious and permanent visibility, and ensured the automatic functioning of power. Looking outside from the window of his cell the convict could see the encircling walls with their resident riflemen; from the bars of his door he saw the central observation tower with its cameras and guards. At night his cell was illuminated by a dim green bulb and the walls and walkways by spot-lights. A man entering Green River said goodbye to darkness for the duration of his stay. Darkness permitted at least the illusion of privacy and invisibility, places where a man might try to reconstruct some sense of his own individual existence. Light was discipline, darkness was freedom. Because the inmate was constantly visible he could never be sure whether he was being spied upon or not and thus became his own warder, perpetually watching himself on his jailer's behalf. Green River was an architecture of power built upon the paranoid fantasies of the guilty.

Here in cellblock B was the Valley of the Long Distance Runners. Such, at least, was the name given to them by their leader, Reuben Wilson. All the inmates on B were black. There was no official segregation policy but in an environment saturated with danger and fear men naturally drew together in tribal groups and in the interests of an uneasy peace Hobbes and his guards allowed it. C block was Black and Latino; A block was mixed Latino and white; D was exclusively white. An antagonistic juxtaposition of hostile forces waiting to be unleashed. War being mankind's natural state, peace was only ever a prelude and a preparation. As Hobbes walked down the valley past a seething crowd of sullen, sweating faces the only quality he was able to identify in their eyes was a virulent nihilism born of prolonged and mindless suffering.

At the far end of the block – and within easy distance of the sallyport to the yard – stood a microphone on a raised dais. As he approached the dais Hobbes felt rivulets of sweat running down his neck into his shirt, and from his brow into his eyes. He resisted the urge to wipe his face. Cornelius Clunes had invented his masterpiece in the damp and gloom of Victorian London. An unforeseen effect of his iron and glass extravaganza, when realised in the sub-tropical climate of East Texas, was to turn the prison into a giant greenhouse which captured the rays of the sun and deposited their energy in the sweltering bodies of the imprisoned. In the old days the conditions were so appalling that the prison population was regularly decimated by outbreaks of cholera, typhoid and yellow fever. During these episodes the prison had been turned over to its inmates and food dropped in from the walls until the contagion burned itself out. Because the prisoners took it upon themselves to do what the authorities had dared not – and slaughtered wholesale those showing signs of infection – an outbreak of disease in those days had produced a spasm of violence so extreme as to be beyond even Hobbes's imagination.

After the Second World War the prison had been closed with the opening of a hygienic modern penitentiary north of Houston, but in the Sixties a soaring crime rate, air-conditioning and the singular vision of John Campbell Hobbes had brought Green

River back to life. Green River, he felt, was *his*. His universe. A superb instrument, the panoptic machine, established on the edge of society and through which the deviant but still human elements of that society would be disciplined, punished and divested of their capacity for antisocial acts before being returned to civil life. An endeavour, no one could deny, of unquestionable nobility. But over the past twenty years Hobbes had seen his instrument turn – slowly at first, then uncontrollably – into a foul zoo that mocked his original intention. His presentations to the State Bureau of Corrections had been ridiculed by some, admired (if secretly) by others, and rejected by all as politically unworkable. Very well. The time had come at last to show them the consequences of their blindness. Hobbes reached the dais and climbed up behind the microphone.

The sound of pipes and drums stopped abruptly.

The block was never silent. Never. But for a moment, in the sudden aftermath of the music, the great stacks of cramped cells seemed almost quiet.

Hobbes drew in a deep breath, swelling his chest and squaring his shoulders. Below the dais, in a shallow V formation, stood his guards. Beyond them towered the steep cage-lined walls, the cages giving way to granite blocks, the blocks in their turn to iron and glass, the iron and glass to the glare of the sun. The convicts had been rousted from their cells and stood smoking and scratching their private parts as they leaned over the safety rails running along the catwalks. Few of them wore the regulation issue denims without some form of additional decoration. Many were naked to the waist. Pitiable gestures of defiance. Defiant or not Hobbes had their attention now, if only because his impromptu 'State Of The Union' addresses represented a welcome novelty in the unbroken tedium of their lives. As he stood there before them, broad and craggy, bald, black-suited, face of bitter stone, the almost-quiet evolved into a growing rumble from the crowd. At first it was just belly and throat sounds, preverbal growls of raw anger, as if the five hundred men were a single organism. Then out of that formless rage came shouts. In the overheated air, thick with the smell of perspiring bodies, the words seemed to tumble towards Hobbes in slow motion.

'Hey, Warden! Yo' mama like to take it in the ass!'

The voice came from the third tier and was followed by a gust of laughter. With slow movements Hobbes took a white handkerchief from his pocket and mopped his brow in silence.

'She tol' me that's the way you all like to stick it to her but your meat just way too small.'

More laughter. From the second level came a shout of *'Warden Teeny Meat!'* Hobbes still did not speak. He folded his handkerchief and let the noise build further. The cavernous space around him filled with waving arms and shaking fists, gaping pink mouths, jaundiced eyes smeared with broken blood vessels, yellow teeth parted in bigotry. When Hobbes could no longer make out any individual sounds in the storm of abuse he leaned forward over the mike.

'I pity you all.'

Hobbes spoke softly, letting the amplifiers give volume to his words. The noise from the cells subsided. Despite their rage they wanted to hear him. Hobbes lingered and looked up at the tiers, stopping here and there to pick out an individual face. He nodded to himself as if in sorrow and spoke again.

'Lower than animals.'

'Fuck you!'

'Yes!' Hobbes snapped his head towards the shout. 'Confined to your cages without knowing why! Pathetic scapegoats for a world you lack the basic intelligence to understand!'

Hobbes felt his voice rising in pitch. He brought it down again.

'You may imagine that you are here to be punished: for

your miserable acts of depravity and violence; for the bestial rapes and killings that you boast of in your filthy holes. Wrong.'

Hobbes dropped his voice a tone.

'Quite wrong.'

He made them wait and they waited.

'Your lives are far too worthless to justify the existence of a machine of this ingenuity. Alternatively, you may think you are here as a deterrence – to yourselves and others. Wrong again. No one cares that you choose to slaughter, rape and poison each other in your stinking ghettoes. Personally I applaud such behaviour.'

So far his speech had been received in relative silence. Now a murmur of anger rippled along the catwalks. Hobbes gave them a grim smile.

'I know that there are innocent men amongst you.' He said this without sarcasm. 'Oh yes. Truly innocent. Victims of a knowing and outrageous injustice.'

Another murmur, this time louder. Hobbes injected more feeling into his voice.

'And I accept that in the wider scheme of things you are all victims of that same knowing and outrageous injustice. That, my friends, is why you are here.'

As the truth of his words sank into minds dulled by deprivation the growling grew louder still and Hobbes raised his voice to a shout.

'Your true function, if you would know it, is to provide a caste of sub-human scum whom society can despise and fear and hate. Listen to me. *Listen!*'

Hobbes glanced up to the second tier and amongst the yelling faces picked out Reuben Wilson, a lean, pale black in his thirties who watched him with a quiet stare. Hobbes held Wilson's gaze and waited. Wilson made a gesture with his hand. As if by magic the cons in Wilson's vicinity fell silent, a silence which spread in seconds to encompass the whole block. Hobbes was impressed but not surprised. He nodded to Wilson and continued, speaking slowly so that they would understand what he was saying.

'You exist – purely and simply – to provide a filth drain, a septic tank into which the rest of us can excrete our own malice and cruelty, our lust for vengeance, our dark unspoken fantasies of violence and greed. Your pain is essential to the smooth functioning of civilisation. But do not flatter yourselves. Your individual crimes – no matter how shocking – have no meaning whatsoever. All that is required is that you be here, innocent or guilty, good and bad alike. You are a pot to be shat in – that and nothing more. Understand that. And know that I understand it too. And as you lie weeping in your cells I want you to reflect on this: that just by being here you are doing excellent service – a good job – for the society you so despise.'

There followed a long pause as they struggled to take in the full meaning of what had been said. Hobbes watched, gripped by the mass personality of the crowd. Somehow they would all get it at once. The crowd murmured and sighed. A live current leapt back and forth between the tiers.

Suddenly, in a single impulse, five hundred men exploded with rage. A torrent of obscenity, of bellowing throats and stomping feet and shaking fists, swept like gale-driven waves through the cellblock and broke against the pillar of rock that was John Campbell Hobbes. Below him the line of guards shifted nervously, shuffling closer together and fingering their Mace. A single faltering step would precipitate violence. Yet as a surge of adrenaline charged through his central nervous system and verified as nothing else could the certainty of his bold design, Hobbes knew no fear. He bellowed into the microphone.

'Now return to your cells.'

The order was ignored, as Hobbes knew it would be. From

the line of guards Captain Bill Cletus turned and looked up at him. His florid features were composed and steady. Hobbes nodded and Cletus bent his head and spoke into a radio clipped to his lapel. The steel door of the sallyport behind Hobbes rumbled open and a second squad of sixteen guards charged into the block. Round their necks hung gas masks. Four of them carried tear gas launchers which they trained on the bristling tiers. The rest held riot guns at port arms. When the guards were in place Hobbes spoke again, his limbs humming.

'Return to your cells. Further disobedience will invite needless punishment.'

From the second tier a dark object flew down towards Hobbes. Though he saw it coming he made no attempt to avoid it. The object struck him on the shoulder, clung on for a second, then dropped to the dais at his feet. The rage of the inmates subsided into curiosity. Hobbes glanced up to the second level then turned to Bill Cletus.

'Wilson,' said Hobbes.

Cletus and four of his men clattered up the steel staircase towards the second floor walkway. At the top of the stairs an obese convict – a double rapist named Dixon – deliberately half-blocked their way. Cletus hosed him down with Mace. As Dixon staggered back into the wall, blinded and wheezing, Cletus stepped past him onto the walkway. The two guards following Cletus fell on Dixon like woodcutters, slashing him to his knees with their nightsticks. When he was bleeding and broken to their satisfaction they jacked his arms up behind his back, hauled him to his feet and bundled him violently, face down, into a toilet at the back of a vacant cell.

Wilson, light on his feet as a dancer, held his fists cocked in front of him. From the dais Hobbes saw the expression on his face as Cletus and his men closed in. Wilson was an ex-number one contender for the middleweight championship of the world and the young bloods from the ghettoes who had never achieved more than the successful robbery of a convenience store worshipped him. In truth Hobbes had the highest respect for Wilson. What's more Wilson had spent eight years inside for a crime he hadn't committed. As the guards stalked him along the catwalk Wilson glanced down through the rails of the walkway and saw Hobbes watching him. Again they held each other's eyes and in that moment Wilson calculated the consequences for the prisoners of his resisting. He dropped his guard and stood up straight in front of Cletus.

'Wasn't me, Captain,' said Wilson.

Cletus rammed the tip of his stick into Wilson's belly then lashed him across the side of the head with the butt end. Wilson rolled with the blows, spinning into the safety rail as the guards seized him from behind. With as much force as possible they cuffed his arms behind his back and manhandled him down the stairs. Hobbes noted that no one intervened on Wilson's behalf.

The block was quiet except for the sound of Wilson and the guards clattering down the steel stair and of Dixon coughing and whimpering in his cell. Hobbes surveyed the inmates. A pall of helplessness and shame had fallen over them. The guards dragged Wilson in front of the dais and let go his arms. Wilson swayed for a moment as if he might fall, then steadied himself. He stared at Hobbes without blinking.

Hobbes turned away to examine, for the first time, the object that struck him on the shoulder. It was a human turd, now broken into two pieces. Hobbes bent down and picked up the larger piece between his finger and thumb. He paused, still bent, and looked briefly into Wilson's eyes. The boxer understood: but could do nothing. Hobbes stood up. He raised the turd high above his head, displaying it to the prisoners. A murmur ran amongst them. When he was sure they knew what he was holding he stepped up to the microphone.

'This is what you are.'

All attention was on him. Deliberately, and with the appearance of relish, Hobbes took the turd into the palm of his hand and squashed it in his fist.

A subdued exhalation of disgust, a 'Jesus' muttered under five hundred breaths, rose up towards the glass vault of the roof. Hobbes turned away from the tiers and looked down at Wilson. Wilson licked blood from his lips and swallowed.

'You any idea what you're doin'?' said Wilson.

Hobbes held his dark eyes for a full ten seconds. Wilson was too intelligent to be left on the block. He could not be allowed to thwart Hobbes's design. It was unjust but necessary: Wilson would have to go to segregation. Hobbes nodded to Cletus.

'Take him to the hole.'

The guards yanked Wilson away and shuffled him out through the rear door into the yard. His fellow inmates watched him go in silence. Hobbes returned to the microphone.

'You will now return to your cells. All work, yard and visiting privileges are suspended indefinitely. In other words: total lockdown.'

In the vacuum left by Wilson's abduction they took this with relative silence.

'And while you have twenty-four empty hours a day in which to occupy your minds, think on this:'

Hobbes raised his soiled hand, palm open towards them.

'I can wash this clean in thirty seconds. But you will be niggers for the rest of your lives.'

Hobbes turned on his heel, stepped down from the rear of the dais and walked out into the yard.

Out in the open air he realised that his heart was racing and his breathing was rapid. The address had gone better than he dared hope. He pulled out the handkerchief and wiped his hand. As he did so he saw Bill Cletus staring at him. On a gut level

Cletus understood the workings of the prison better than anyone except Hobbes. But he did not have Hobbes's mind. Nor did he have his will. Hobbes glanced up at the sky. The glare of the sun was intense. He looked back at Cletus.

'From tomorrow,' said Hobbes, 'I want the air-conditioning system of B block turned off.'

Cletus blinked. 'And the lockdown?'

'Indefinite, as I said.'

'There'll be blood,' said Cletus.

Cletus almost doubled his salary with the contraband he smuggled in for Neville Agry, the Lifer crew chief of D block. Hobbes knew this. He considered reminding the captain but decided that at this point it wasn't necessary.

Hobbes said, 'Whatever the consequences of my orders, Captain, your only duty is to obey them.'

Cletus took a step backwards and saluted.

'Yes, sir,' he said.

Hobbes nodded, then turned and walked away across the yard. For the first time in longer than he could remember his conscience was at ease with itself. He was doing what needed to be done. Someone, at last, was doing what needed to be done. It would be ugly. But it was necessary. The temperature was set to rise and the defining hour would follow. Hobbes folded the handkerchief into his pocket and started back across the yard towards his tower.

PART I

THE RISING

ONE

An hour before the 0700 first lock and count Dr Ray Klein opened his eyes and thought about the seagulls wheeling high above the outside walls. Or rather he imagined the gulls. As likely as not there were none. If Klein himself had been a gull he would've damn sure given this squalid grey shithole a wide berth. There had to be better garbage elsewhere. And if, by chance, the biggest flock of carrion in the history of East Texas was out there – as big and loud and hungry as you please, and wheeling for all they were worth – then Ray Klein would never have heard them above the constant murmur of five-hundred-and-sixty-some convicts as they tossed and grunted and snored in their narrow bunks.

Klein blinked and reminded himself that he was an asshole.

Freewheeling birds were a stupid image for a convict to hold in his mind for they brought not a shred of comfort. Yet Klein thought about them just the same, partly because he was an obdurate son of a bitch, and partly because he had not yet conquered his lifelong compulsion to do exactly those things that kept comfort beyond his reach. In this respect he had much in common with his fellow inmates. But unlike them Ray Klein, on this day, had another reason for letting the birds fly about the imaginary dawn landscape of his mind:

after three years hard time there was a chance – a *chance* – that the bastards who ran this goddamn place were finally going to let him go free. Klein exterminated the birds inside his head and swung his legs over the side of the bunk.

As he stood up the stone flags were cool and dense against the soles of his feet. He squeezed the flags with his toes, then bent forward in the dim green aura of the night light and placed both palms flat on the floor, squeezing the stale blood out of his hamstrings and spine. He didn't really want to stand up in the semi-darkness and stretch his body. He hated it. He wanted to spend another hour in oblivion, roaming the dreamy interior of his skull where the space contained therein was as vast as the universe itself and considerably less painful. Yet he spent another ten minutes in a variety of painful contortions. He had long ago taken into his heart the words of William James:

'. . . be systematically ascetic or heroic in little unnecessary points, do every day something for no other reason
than that you would rather not do it, so that when the
hour of dire need draws nigh, it may find you not unnerved
and untrained to stand the test . . .'

So Ray Klein finished his stretching and knelt down, sitting back on his heels with his palms resting on his thighs. Even after all these years this part still made him feel kind of cool. Cool wasn't a quality he readily associated with his own person-ality and so on these rare occasions he allowed himself to feel it. He closed his eyes and inhaled sharply through his nostrils.

This was as quiet as it ever got in cellblock D and it was Klein's Jamesian habit, every day, to get up earlier than he needed to and pretend that the hour was his own. He began with the *mokso* – the focused breathing to clear his mind – then went on to practise karate until the bell roused the rest of the block to the sullen and paranoid level of consciousness that, in Green River, passed for human existence.

Klein's second tier cell was eight feet by six. He made all the karate moves – the kicks, turns, blocks and punches – in slow motion, his muscles densely bunched with maximum tension. This made great demands on his strength, balance and control, attributes with which he was not naturally over-endowed, and after three years he was able to complete his routine in near silence, without panting for air, without breaking any toes and without falling over. Today he practised the kata *Gojushiho sho*.

This daily ritual helped to drain off the anger that the prison pumped into his blood. It neutralised the poison and kept him strong, kept him calm, kept him bound apart from all the rest; kept cold and hard the steelwork and ice he had constructed around his soul.

Since his plunge from grace this architecture had proved a necessary blessing. In the River a soul was a dangerous handicap, a personal torture chamber only to be visited by masochists and fools. Klein had been both in his time but now he knew better. Strangely enough the discipline and self-denial had come to him more easily than it had to most inmates, for his profession had prepared him for it. He had spent much of his adult life steeling himself. As an intern and as a resident and as a chief resident, he had steeled himself. He had hardened his heart against himself; against the endless hours on duty, against the intolerable and yet endurable lack of sleep; against alternating fourteen and twenty-four hour days, year upon year; against the pressure and the fear of making a mistake and killing or disabling a patient; against the horror of mutilated bodies and the naked grief of the bereaved; against the endless stream of examinations; against failure; against the unique dread of telling a man he was going to die or a mother that her child was already dead; against the pain he inflicted on himself and the pain he inflicted on others. Needles, scalpels, amputations, toxic drugs. Through all this and more – and this he shared with his colleagues for he was nothing special – Klein had steeled himself. So that by the time his life collapsed around him and he was sent up to the River he had only needed to add a little ice to the steel and then he'd been ready.

On the street Klein had been an orthopaedic surgeon.

Now he was a convicted rapist serving his time.

Today he might be set free.

And if he was set free he would have to steel himself again: to a future as featureless and implacable as the granite wall of his cell.

Klein turned in the narrow space and inflicted an elbow-strike-to-the-face/throat-lock/head-butt combination on an imaginary enemy standing just inside the steel bars of his door. The imaginary enemy's face collapsed and his body went limp as Klein strangled him. You're the shotokan warrior, he told himself, you hope for nothing, you need no one, you are free. He smiled and wiped sweat from his eyes.

Klein had been a student of karate since his college days and nothing else had sustained him more dependably through the years of his medical training. At first, when he'd carried on his habitual morning routine in the River, Klein had felt kind of an idiot posturing this way and that in his cell. The inmates of neighbouring cells, in trying to explain the soft grunting noises he made, had accused him of jerking off, of threading a blunt instrument up his own anus, of unlubricated self-catheterisation and other lone perversions both dangerous and obscure. At the time telling them he was practising karate had seemed even more shameful than jerking off – and in addition much more likely to get him his face cut off – and he had stopped. But he'd argued to himself that if he was going to survive in here he had to keep just a little something for himself, and somehow – whether it made him an idiot or not – karate was it. So Klein had resumed his morning practice and before the mocking voices of his neighbours had become intolerable Myron Pinkley had stolen Klein's dessert – lime flavoured jello – in the mess hall.

Ultimately, the brain damage Pinkley sustained proved irreversible and he was born again and joined the Jesus Army. The only tears shed over this incident fell from the eyes of Pinkley's mother, who wept for joy at her son's spiritual redemption. And Klein's neighbours had stopped asking what went on in his cell at each day's dawning, because they all understood thereafter that it wasn't any business of theirs.

The hammering of the bell and the bellowing of sour-faced guards marked the end of Klein's routine. Soaked in sweat, he wiped his face on a dirty shirt and stood at the front of his cell. There were six lock and counts every day and the first began when the lights came up and the cellblock lumbered awake with a cacophony of coughs and hawked phlegm, of muttered obscenities and loud complaints about the stench of farting cell mates. Then came the mounting redneck blare of radios and cassette decks, and the shouts of the guards, ritually made and ritually ignored, to turn the goddamn music down. Finally came the count itself, the sullen litany echoing back and forth across the tiers as each man, six times a day, proclaimed his identity as a state-given number.

A Cuban screw named Sandoval appeared beyond the bars of Ray Klein's door.

'Eighty-eight-four-one-nine, Klein,' said Klein.

Sandoval nodded without speaking, checked his list, moved on.

Klein's feet slapped the sweat-spattered stone as he walked to the back of his cell. He pulled back the hanging blanket that covered the toilet and took a piss. The cell had been built for one man and since he had accumulated enough wealth to afford it Klein had lived there alone. Most of the single cells held two men and the doubles four. Everything had to be paid for and living space was expensive. The private medical practice Klein had established in the prison had made him wealthy enough to afford it. There were rich and poor in here just as there were in any society and like anywhere else the ability to buy special medical treatment was seized upon as a badge of social power. Klein washed himself down at the sink and dried himself on a large bath towel, another luxury item. By the time he'd finished he was again drenched in sweat, such was the humidity in the cellblock and the heat of his engorged muscles. He delayed dragging on his denims until his sweat had evaporated some into the stagnant air. He stood naked before his shaving mirror, the drone of his electric razor blending with that of hundreds of others. Blades were forbidden. On the lower edge of the mirror was a strip of grubby white adhesive tape. Written on the tape in black ink, where he could see them every morning and remind himself, were the words:

NOT MY FUCKING BUSINESS

This aphorism was the top and bottom of the moral, political and philosophical system whose mastery was necessary to survival in Green River State Penitentiary. Its importance had been impressed on Klein early on by Frogman Coley, the trustee superintendent of the prison infirmary. Klein had asked Coley how it was that one of the patients recovering on the ward had come to have both his testicles severed and inserted into his own rectum. And Coley had gripped Klein's shirt-front and told him:

'You don' ever wanna know, whitefish. You don' ever wanna find out 'bout nothin' goes down in here. You do, you don' stick your pecker in. Anywhere. Look, say one day you passin' the shower room, you hear a guy bein' cut, or he gettin' his ass raped. Maybe he's your friend. Your best friend. Maybe you like to be in there yo'self, gettin' some. Or maybe like this po' sucker here they takin' his balls off with a blunt razor and you can hear him screamin' through the washrag they stuck down his throat. Walk on by, brother, cause there always a reason for it you don' know about. An' even if they ain't no reason at all, it's not your fucken bidness.'

And on a couple of occasions – rare but indelible – Klein had witnessed atrocities and heard the screams of pain. And he had indeed walked on by. In fact it had been easy. The words on the tape caught his eyes once more: NOT MY FUCKING BUSINESS. Klein switched off his razor. Flushed as he was with the energy of his karate routine it was easy to feel ballsy and tough. He wondered how he would feel when he got out on the street again; if he got out. The middle-class world he'd left behind would be an alien landscape, the bland, narcis-sistic and ill-informed chatter even more of an irritant than it always had been. He warned himself again not to set himself up for a fall: he was still a convict. Until they released him that's all he was.

He pulled on his regulation denims: long-sleeved shirt with two breast pockets, pants, a canvas belt. As he sat on his bunk and tied the laces of his training shoes a sudden rumble arose from all around him and climaxed in a teeth-jarring crash that echoed back down from the vaulted glass roof. The first count was complete, the machine was satisfied for another hour, and the one hundred and eighty steel doors of D block thundered open in electronic unison. After breakfast Klein and the other inmates would trail back to their cells and the screws would lock them in again for the second count. Then they would be released again for morning work detail.

Klein stood up. Men heavy with sleep, their shoulders caved forward with the torpor of those whose day promised nothing but more of the same, trudged past the open door of his cell.

None of them was curious enough to look in, none of them cared to call out a greeting to him nor he to them. It was too early, and they were too recently abducted from the peace of nightmare or dream. Men whose future was behind them. If Klein didn't get the result he hoped for today, if the parole board refused his suit, Klein too would . . .

He stopped the thought dead and told himself he was a fool for shackling himself with hope. He reminded himself he had nowhere to go but down, that the sanctimonious jerks on the parole board had seen the contempt radiating from his eyes and had decided to keep him caged for another year, or two or even five. He told himself again, for the thousandth time: This is now. There is no past. There is no after. There is no outside. There is no beyond. This is where you are. And all that you are and all that you may be is what you are in this moment. That and nothing more. Now go get your breakfast.

Klein stepped out on to the walkway, walked along the tier and clattered down the spiral stair. As he reached ground tier Nev Agry passed him, walking towards the main gate sally. Agry was four inches shorter than Klein and about ten pounds heavier. His bulk was invested with the charisma of the tried and tested psychopath and his potency enshrouded him like a forcefield. He was the barn boss of D block and the strongest of the white Lifer crew chiefs. Klein had treated Agry a number of times, for minor ailments and a series of recurrent chest infections resulting from three packs of Luckies a day. Klein was also good friends with Agry's wife, Claudine, but she was back on B block where she'd undergone another involuntary change of gender and, as plain Claude, was sweating it out under the lockdown. Agry nodded to Klein as he passed and headed off for the mess hall with Tony Shockner at his shoulder. A nod from Agry was considered a great privilege but the only privilege Klein wanted now was parole. At ten-thirty this morning he would find out from Warden Hobbes whether it was his or not.

Klein could tell it was going to be a long day. So he shrugged and braced himself for whatever it had in store and joined the long line of futureless men as they filed through the gate towards the mess hall.

TWO

In the prison infirmary Reuben Wilson reached for the small trapeze hanging over his head and hauled himself into a sitting position. He gritted his teeth against the pain in his belly. In fact the pain wasn't that much to speak of. His teeth were gritted because he was scared that the stitches holding his abdomen together would burst apart and empty his entrails into his lap. Frog Coley, the motherfucker, had told him he'd seen it happen more than a time or two, and boy had those suckers screamed. It was thirteen days since Wilson's ruptured spleen had been removed and Ray Klein had assured him that unless he took a kick in the gut – or tried to kick someone else's – the wound would hold firm. Wilson believed Klein; but he believed Coley's stories too so he was cautious just the same.

To Wilson's mind the infirmary was the grimmest building in the whole fucking joint – and Wilson was a man who'd done his share and more in Segregation. It had taken him a while to understand why. The tiled magnolia-painted walls of Travis Ward were discoloured with nicotine and age, yet it was brighter and cooler than the Valley. Also Wilson preferred the odour of disinfectant to the mixture of sweat, piss and semen that clung to every stacked inch of the tiers. And despite the constant rustle of coughs and wheezes from the lungs of the dying it was quiet on the ward – tranquil, even – compared to the ceaseless clamour of B block. No, the grimness of the infirmary, he'd come to realise, lay elsewhere: in the white steel grate that divided the ward into two twelve bed sections; in the bars embedded in the thick reinforced glass of the windows; and in the guys dying of Aids in so many of the beds. The conjunction of the bars with the gaunt figures embodied Wilson's – and every man's – darkest dread: of dying on this side of the wall. When living in chains became a commonplace, dying in chains became the final bitter defeat. And, as Wilson had seen, these guys had plenty of time to think about it.

A broadside of membrane-ripping coughs erupted from the other side of the ward, the kind that made Wilson's chest ache just to hear them. Wilson looked up. In the bed opposite the spectral form of Greg Garvey had slipped down from his pillows so that he was almost flat on his back. Too weak to drag himself upright, or even to roll over onto his side, Garvey tried feebly to spit out a cupful of infected phlegm. Half of it hung from his lips in a green mucoid mesh that stuck to his chin and neck. The rest clung to the insides of his throat and set him coughing again: racking spasms that scraped away the last of his strength.

Garvey was a white junkie serving two-to-ten for wounding a convenience store owner in a robbery. He was twenty-three years old.

'Shut the fuck up, Garvey, you stinking faggot.'

The shrill voice belonged to Gimp Cotton, a murderer whose thin face was covered with a lacework of blue-black self-inflicted tattoos. When Garvey fell into another, weaker, paroxysm Cotton threw back the sheets and hobbled to his feet. His left leg was in a cast. Cotton had sawed through his Achilles tendon – for the third time in five years – in order to take a vacation from C block. He limped across the aisle towards Garvey.

'If nobody else wantsa deal with these goddamn Aids fuckers, I will,' shrieked Cotton. His face shone with the satisfaction of mindless hate. Reuben Wilson knew this hate, this mindlessness, for it was his life.

'Leave him alone, Gimp,' warned Wilson.

Gimp turned on Wilson. His tattooed face writhed with malice. 'He's been coughing that shit on us straight guys all night long. It ain't right.'

'You can't catch nothing from a cough,' said Wilson. 'Klein said so.'

Cotton paused at the head of Garvey's bed, supporting himself with his left hand against the wall. He looked at Wilson.

'Bullshit. That short-timing bastard'd tell us anything.' He squinted at the melting tallow of Garvey's face. 'I'm gonna get rid of him.'

With his right hand Cotton grabbed a pillow.

'I said leave him alone.'

Wilson leaned forward in his bed, his voice big with menace. His stitched belly contracted with the effort. For an instant Wilson saw the entrails tumbling into his lap, heard the sound of his own screams. Wilson had never screamed in his life. It wasn't something he was keen to check out. His hand flew to his wound: it was fine. He leaned back and saw Cotton watching him, looking smugly at the hand cradling his stomach. Wilson's guts contracted again, this time with humiliation.

Cotton said, 'I'm doin' us all a favour. Including him, the poor fuck.'

Cotton crammed the pillow over Garvey's face, then leaned forward with all his weight. After a long pause a thin hand rose from the damp sheets to paw at Cotton's wrist.

Wilson dragged his own sheets aside and clambered down from the high mattress. He hadn't exercised as much as he'd been told to and his legs felt like jelly. He steadied himself on the bedstead and asked himself just what the fuck he planned to do when he got across the room. Normally the Gimp would've soiled his shitstained skivvies if Wilson so much as looked at him, but the tattooed killer knew what Klein said about the stitches. The thin hand clawing at Gimp's wrist gave up and fell back onto the bed.

'Cotton,' said Wilson, 'you get back in the population I'll have your fucking lips cut off.'

'Kiss my ass, coon.'

There was a clang as a steel door was slammed in anger. A bass voice shook the room with outrage.

'Jesus Christ!'

Earl 'Frogman' Coley was five feet eight inches tall and weighed two hundred and thirty pounds. His skin was a lustrous, bituminous black and his skull was a huge and craggy rock, softened only in its lower regions by the fat of his neck and jowls. Twenty-three years ago he'd been a sharecropper in the East Texas wetlands round Nacogdoches, with a wife, four kids and a mule. One day he found two white teenagers pouring drain cleaner into the mule's eyes while it was tethered to a fence post. Coley took a rope hackamore and gave the boys the thrashing they deserved and sent them on their way. But niggers raise their hands to white boys at their peril, and the county court found Coley guilty of child abuse and attempted murder and sent him down for ten years to life. He hadn't seen his wife in seventeen years nor any of his children for twelve. For a decade-and-a-half past Earl Coley had been the superintendant of the prison infirmary.

Now Coley charged down the centre aisle of the ward, rolling up the sleeves of his whites. Cotton let go of the pillow over Garvey's face and hobbled back across the ward, his tattoos stretched tight across his cheekbones with panic. As Cotton reached his bed Coley grabbed an aluminium water jug from the table and punched it into Cotton's face. Even Wilson, with fifteen years in the ring behind him, flinched at the clank of the impact. Cotton spun and sprawled face down on the mattress, whimpering as he shielded his head with his arms and elbows. For a moment Coley stood over him, shaking with rage, murder in his eyes. With an effort he glanced across at Garvey. The junkie wasn't moving. Coley dropped the water jug dented with the imprint of Cotton's face, and hurried across the ward.

Coley tore the pillow from Garvey's head then slid both his arms under his limp body. He rolled him over onto his side. Garvey was just barely breathing. Coley reached a finger into his mouth and raked out a clotted skein of infected mucus. Garvey emitted a feeble rattle. Coley looked over his shoulder at Wilson.

'Hand me that sucker, man.' Coley pointed at a plastic contraption with two flexible tubes that hung from a wooden box at the foot of the bed. 'That plastic shit, there. Quick.'

Wilson strode forward but his legs betrayed him, just turned to spaghetti underneath him. He grabbed the rail at the bottom of his bed. He felt ashamed. At least he managed not to clutch his stomach the way he wanted to. He looked at Coley for help.

'Fighters,' said Coley, with contempt. 'Outside the ring you just a bunch of drippin' pussies.'

A flame of anger pushed Wilson across the ward at near-normal pace. He snatched the suction pack from the box and handed it to Coley. Coley put one of the tubes between his lips and sucked; the other he slipped down Garvey's throat, siphoning the mucus into the plastic container. Wilson, squeamish, yet in awe of Coley's expertise, watched. By the time Coley had finished Garvey's breathing was back to the shallow gasp that for him counted as normal. Coley rolled him onto his back again then lifted him into a sitting position.

'Fix them pillows,' said Coley.

Wilson hesitated again, this time not for fear but for pride. In the Valley he was lord of life and death. No one spoke to him this way.

Coley stared at him. 'You ready to go back to B block?'

Wilson squinted at him. It was a long time since he'd been both insulted and threatened before breakfast. Words crossed his mind: People had their tongues cut out for less than that, Old Man. Could Coley read the essence of the thought in Wilson's eyes? Wilson couldn't read Coley's eyes at all. Here Coley was lord. Wilson reached over, not caring any longer if his guts fell out over Coley's big flat feet, and stacked the pillows behind Garvey's shoulders. When Coley was satisfied that the dying man was comfortable he turned his hooded eyes back on Wilson.

'You didn' give me no answer.'

'You mean 'bout going back to the Valley?' said Wilson. Coley nodded.

You must be fucking kidding, man, thought Wilson. Coley's massive face confronted him with silence. The crack about drippin' pussies returned to Wilson's mind. He swallowed.

'I ain't due back on the block. I got ten days' punishment in the hole to serve out,' said Wilson. 'But if you say so I'll go.'

Coley looked at him gravely. Something in his eyes changed.

'I know it ain't right,' said Coley, 'but I got sick men down below sleepin' on camp beds.'

'I'll be glad to get away from the Gimp,' said Wilson.

'You can stay a couple more days, long as you get some exercise.'

Coley looked across the room and saw Cotton watching and listening with his ballooning face cradled in his hand.

Coley smiled. 'You go back this afternoon, Gimp. Cast and all.'

'You fat nigger fuck. You caved my face in. You gonna pay for this.'

Coley crossed the room with the speed and momentum of a linebacker. As Cotton scrambled away Coley grabbed a fistful of skin and hair from Cotton's scrawny chest. He half-lifted him from the bed. Cotton screamed.

'You touch any of my people again, you find out just how small a shit the medical examiner gives 'bout what's in them plastic bags we send him.'

Cotton squirmed free and crawled to the far side of the bed where he curled whimpering with pain. Coley turned back to Wilson.

'I need some help with the breakfasts.'

Wilson said, 'Sure.'

Coley smiled. 'Help you get that belly back in shape.'

Coley turned and lumbered down the ward towards the gate.

Reuben Wilson, warlord of B block and feeling obscurely privileged by the Frogman's smile, stepped into the aisle and followed him as fast as he dared.

THREE

UNDER NORMAL CIRCUMSTANCES Henry Abbott had a particular fondness for oatmeal. His grandfather, who had ridden with Colonel Chivington at Sand Creek, had eaten oatmeal every day of his life and had lived to be ninety-three years old. Now the experts had announced that it was good for the heart and circulation, and the secret was out. Abbott did not object to this, but the oatmeal sitting in front of him on the mess hall table was not good. Abbott knew. He pushed the plastic bowl away untouched. This oatmeal was full of ground glass.

From his shirt pocket Abbott took a cheap notebook purchased in the prison store and a black Sheaffer fountain pen with a gold nib. The pen was the only object Abbott possessed that wasn't prison issue. He opened the notebook to a fresh page and wrote today's number in green ink: '3083' then beneath it: 'Oatmeal not good – full of ground glass.'

The powdered eggs, on the other hand, Abbott found acceptable. He put his pen and book away, laced the eggs with ketchup and shovelled the mixture into his mouth with a plastic spoon. Things didn't taste so good off plastic. Like coffee from a styrofoam cup. In the canteen everything was plastic and Abbott hated it. Now they had put plastic in his face too – packed it tight under his cheekbones to make it harder to smile, and down inside the canals of his teeth to make it harder to chew, and in and around the angles of his jaws and under the root of his tongue to make it harder to speak. They'd injected the plasticating chemicals into his left buttock yesterday morning. Now, twenty-four hours later, the chemicals had been processed by the liver while he slept and had worked their way into his face – as they were designed to do – and plastified so that he couldn't smile so good or talk so good and had to work hard at chewing and swallowing the rubbery breakfast eggs. Most of all, the chemicals placed a shroud of freezing fog around The Word so that its voice became muffled and distant. Yet despite the icy shroud The Word was always there: beyond him, about him, above him. At The Word's suggestion he had already documented the plastication in his book for the benefit of future generations, yet he rarely felt that his notes did The Word justice. Despite his continued failure as a scribe Abbott tried. After all, they would have silenced The Word forever if they could. And Abbott suspected it was this very motive that had compelled them to put ground glass in his oatmeal.

The Word knew and only The Word. And they knew it. And they would go to any lengths to prevent The Word's knowledge from getting out. If the oatmeal failed to make Abbott's inner organs bleed – and fail it would because he had been warned not to eat it – then the plastic in his face, distorting his speech, would ensure that no one would believe him. Abbott couldn't quell a certain admiration: they certainly knew their business. And yet they would fail, for The Word would be heard, at least by one. By him if by no one else. By Henry Abbott.

The canteen was busy, as Abbott had observed it always was at certain times of the day. Breakfast was one such time. The inmates queued up at a row of metal tubs. The tubs were suspended in a pool of hot water secretly concealed – as so much else was secret and concealed – behind a polished steel partition. Behind the tubs the cooks ladled luke-warm food into the plastic trays held out by the inmates. The cook who had laced Abbott's oatmeal with glass had been very quick: a wink to his partner, a smile at Abbott – he hadn't smiled at anyone else – and while the smile distracted him, the powdered glass: released from a concealed pouch up the cook's sleeve. Before Abbott had been quick enough to actually see the glass it had dispersed, invisible and deadly, into his breakfast oatmeal.

Close, but no cigar.

Abbott looked up from his eggs and saw Doctor Ray Klein walking towards him between the rows of noisy, crowded tables. Abbott, as usual, had a table to himself. This wasn't something that he chose or even wanted; it was just the way of things. The Doctor carried over his tray and sat down facing him. The Doctor was just under six feet tall and yet the top of his head was barely level with Abbott's collar bone. The Doctor looked up. His face was lean and behind the bones Abbott felt the flames of a pale, pentecostal fire that burned without warming and consumed without replenishing the Doctor's spirit.

The Doctor said: 'Morning, Henry.'

Abbott wiped his mouth on the back of his sleeve. 'Good morning, Doctor Klein.'

Abbott's voice sounded strange even to his own ears. No wonder. Plastication of the vocal chords. He held out his hand and the Doctor shook it. The Doctor's hand felt small and Abbott was careful to be gentle. No one else ever shook Abbott's hand. He did not know why. And no one else called the Doctor, 'Doctor Klein'. It was possible that that accounted for the handshake, but Abbott wasn't sure. It remained mysterious; and yet Abbott knew that it was of significance.

'You're not eating your oatmeal,' said the Doctor.

The Doctor saw things. He observed more than most –
but not everything. Abbott saw some things the Doctor did
not. Since vice-versa was also the case that was to be expected.
It was something they shared: and so even when the Doctor
missed the incredibly obvious Abbott was there to point it
out, and the Doctor accepted Abbott's judgement as, of course,
Abbott accepted his. It was mutual, then. And good.

'You're right,' said Abbott. 'It's full of powdered glass.'

The Doctor flashed him a look grave with concern. Abbott
nodded. The Doctor pushed his own bowl towards him. 'This
one's okay,' he said. 'Take it.'

Abbott hesitated. 'You'll be hungry. I can't.'

'You're a big man,' said the Doctor. 'You work hard. You
need it more than I do.'

Abbott nodded. As usual the Doctor's logic was irrefutable.
Abbott took the bowl of congealed cereal and started to eat.
As he ate he scanned the room with his eyes, without moving
his head. He considered mentioning the plastic in his face but
the Doctor would only worry – that was the kind of man he
was – and there were more important things to discuss.
Between bites he held his hand in front of his lips and spoke
from the side of his mouth.

'Don't look at me,' said Abbott. 'I have something to tell
you.'

The Doctor concentrated on his eggs. 'Go ahead.'

'I've detected a vibe. An irruption.' Abbott took a swallow
of his oatmeal.

'An irruption,' said the Doctor.

Abbott nodded. 'Someone is going to die.'

The Doctor nodded back without looking at him. 'You?'
he said.

'They tried but I was too quick for them,' replied Abbott.
'Yesterday they added a plasticating compound to my injection to try to stop me talking. Today, powdered glass.' He

paused while two inmates, Bialmann and Crawford, walked by the table. Abbott risked a look into the Doctor's eyes. 'It's incredibly obvious, isn't it?'

The Doctor nodded. 'Then who's the target?'

'I don't know yet, but I recommend you stay away from Nev Agry and his people.'

'Sounds like good advice,' said the Doctor.

Abbott wondered if the Doctor truly understood the risks involved. How could he, without The Word? Abbott resolved to be vigilant on his behalf. The oatmeal was finished. Abbott sipped his coffee. It was cold.

'I advise', he said, 'that you keep to your cell. To be absolutely safe, avoid all contact.' He lowered his voice. 'Especially with the coloureds.'

'I have to go to the infirmary,' said the Doctor.

Of course. Abbott understood perfectly. They needed him there.

'And I have an appointment with Warden Hobbes.'

'Be careful,' said Abbott. 'Warden Hobbes is a dangerous man.'

The Doctor stood up and put his hand on Abbott's shoulder. He squeezed firmly. For a moment Abbott felt the plastic in his face soften.

'You too,' said the Doctor.

Abbott looked up at him through the sense of softness now permeating his throat and liver. The Doctor's eyes were a pale blue, with a core of fierceness at their centre wherein burned the wasting fire.

The Doctor said: 'If you have anything else to tell me, any worries, I want you to come find me and tell me. Okay, Henry?'

Abbott rolled his jaws. The plastic was hardly noticeable now. 'I understand.'

The Doctor gave Abbott's shoulder another squeeze and then was gone. As Abbott watched him disappear he caught sight of Nev Agry sitting at a table with Crawford and Bialmann. Obvious. Incredibly so. Agry normally held court, if he showed in the canteen at all, with his lieutenants – killers like Tony Shockner. Crawford and Bialmann were short timers, embezzlers, nobodies. Just being near Agry took them so close to pissing their pants they could hardly get their plastic spoons to their mouths. And there was Nev Agry, sitting back and smiling like he was just a regular guy.

And smoking with his left hand.

Abbott got up, took his tray to the garbage chute, emptied it, then headed out towards the rear gate sally without appearing to be in a hurry. As he left his tray he saw a guard – Perkins? Abbott couldn't remember – walk over to Agry's table and whisper in Agry's ear. Abbott turned away. He walked faster as he felt Agry's eyes drilling malevolent tunnels into the back of his head, as if attempting to scan the information concealed in his mind, as if trying to read the lips of The Word itself, shrouded in mystery. Abbott stopped as a sudden piece of knowledge was revealed to him.

Nev Agry normally smoked with his right hand.

And the guard, Perkins, worked on B block, with the coloureds.

Incredibly obvious.

Suddenly Abbott's vibe was stronger than ever, an overwhelming sense of pure irruption, a deep hum emanating from the nameless chaos over which only The Word held sway.

And Abbott wondered: Will The Doctor Be Safe?

The question repeated itself again. And then again. He reached for his notebook to record it but the emanating hum suddenly became a chorus which filled the air about his head with a chant – a dance, a prayer – of deepest profundity: We Need Him.

We need him.

We need him.

Abbott blundered through a row of men, upsetting their trays, his ringing ears deaf to their oaths, and he ran, ungainly and huge, out of the babbling mess hall, down the stairs and still down, and down again, striving towards the darkness and the damp where he knew The Word would give him sanctuary. Where he knew he would be safe.

For a while.

FOUR

By the time second lock and count was over a sharpening edge of nervous tension had scraped away the insides of Klein's viscera. Up there in his castle-keep above the main gates Hobbes had the result of Klein's parole board review sitting on his desk. Klein checked his watch again: in ninety-four minutes he would get the verdict. His time left in the River might be numbered in hours; but it could just as easily be years. The parole system was a rack on which they kept most every con in the joint – even the two-hundred-and-twenty-year-men and triple lifers – stretched and silently screaming. They gave you ten minutes to kiss their ass in exactly the way they wanted you to. Do it right and you were a little tweety bird fluttering off into the wide blue yonder. Show the wrong attitude, or catch them on a bad day, or at a time when over-crowding wasn't on the agenda, or when there was a law 'n order election campaign for state governor under way, and they'd throw you back under the grinding wheels for another year or more. At his last year's review they'd turned Klein down.

He pushed the issue to the back of his mind but it was hard to keep it there. He'd pushed a lot of things to the back of his mind during his imprisonment. As his meeting with Hobbes loomed before him they had started to elbow their way back into his consciousness.

Deputy Prosecuting Attorney Henrietta Noades, for one, the prim, bespectacled bitch whose eyes had gleamed with unmistakable pleasure as the judge had sent him up for five to ten. Credited with bringing in the women voters in time for her boss's re-election, she'd been promoted on the back of Klein's conviction. For another there was the smoking rubble of his career. He'd never been any kind of academic hotshot; he'd never sought the stratosphere. Working in the public hospital in Galveston where he was relatively free of medical politics and could concentrate his energies on honing his skills and doing his job was all he'd wanted. That and his house with its view of the Gulf and his sailboat. All that was gone now and Klein was long past the futility of mourning its passing. Or so, at least, he told himself.

The fact was that deep inside the ice around his heart was an unlanced abscess of pain: the thought that he would never be allowed to return to the work for which he had sacrificed so much. Klein was a rapist. The law said so and the law had no taste for the ambiguities of human life. Klein was not guilty of the offence for which he had been sentenced. He was guilty of greater, more commonplace crimes – of selfishness and cruelty and stupidity – but not of that one. He had hurt a woman he'd once loved more than life, a woman whose name he no longer allowed into his consciousness. He'd hurt her more deeply than he could have imagined – that is, as deeply as he himself had been hurt, if he'd let himself feel it – and she had punished him savagely. And then she'd punished him again, more savagely still. But a man took whatever fate threw at him and he dealt with it. The way that he did so was the only true measure of himself that he had.

Klein reminded himself from time to time that for the first half of his three-score-and-ten, before he'd lost his way, fate had treated him well. He hadn't fallen from the womb into some parched and desolate field in the Horn of Africa or into a toilet in some freezing tenement block. Nature had given him a decent brain and a strong body. His mother had raised him to love the written word and his father to lay a hand on no one and yet to take no man's insult without exacting a due and dispassionate revenge.

No, fate had not cheated him. Though much had been taken, much endured, or at least he hoped so. His father had not lived to see Klein's fall and Klein was glad. He was glad he had not had to witness the pain it would have caused him. His father would have walked with him arm in arm to the electric chair – innocent or guilty – if it had ever come to that. He would have stood by him, for he'd been forged in more generous, less ambiguous times. But no man could escape his own moment in history. These were the mean times and Klein was part of them.

Five years to ten in the Green River Pen.

Klein reflected that 'rapist' wasn't a word that had much of a ring to it. Armed robber, drug-dealer, even murderer, were somewhat more respectable. In the River, hardly a bastion of feminist man, the word that had been scrawled across his life meant little. Out in the world – well, he would find out when he found out. One thing was for sure: he didn't intend to whimper around trying to explain or justify or excuse. He would take each day as it came. He was scared of the future, he wasn't fool enough to deny that, but he would meet it. He did not know what lay beyond the prison gates. He did not know and he did not ask. The future was a black hole and he allowed himself no dreams or hopes for what it might contain. No more castles made of sand. He knew how to live without them. The River had given him that much and that at least could not be taken away.

Klein left his cell and made his way down the spiral staircase of D block for the second time that morning. He passed through the main gate into the atrium and turned past the watchtower and down the corridor of the General Purposes wing towards the main exit door. As he walked he diverted his mind from his own maudlin thoughts by recalling Henry Abbott's warning at breakfast. He wondered what undercurrents the big man had picked up on.

The River contained a population of unusually paranoid men – convicted criminals – who were trapped against their will in a world where paranoia was the basic currency of existence for inmates and jailers alike. Here even the calmest and most trusting of souls was haunted day and night by suspicion and fear. This was the only rational reaction to the prevailing conditions. Beyond these rational paranoids, of whom Klein was one, were another group: the clinically insane. Henry Abbott was a standout member of the latter and by and large he was avoided and ignored by sane and insane alike. Most everyone was content to write him off as a retard. But Klein knew that while the schizophrenic mind invested innocent phenomena with grossly delusional meanings, such a mind could also be abnormally sensitive to the actual, if unspoken, emotions of the people around it. The old joke about 'just because you're paranoid doesn't mean they aren't out to get you' had some truth to it. So with his overdeveloped, lopsided awareness – his psychotically tuned antennae – Abbott sometimes sensed real currents that Klein was unaware of.

Nine years before, on a balmy New Year's evening in the hill country west of Langtry, Henry Abbott had taken a heavy ball-peen hammer and with a single blow each killed all five members of his family – wife, three daughters and mother – as they slept in their beds. He'd then set fire to the house. The state troopers had found him standing in the yard watching it burn whilst singing a hymn that none of the troopers recognised. Up until that time Abbott had been a devoted husband, father and son, noted only for being – very probably – the most gargantuan teacher of high school English ever seen in a state that prided itself on the size of its menfolk. The only explanation Abbott ever offered for his crime was that '. . . the fires of Orc, that once did blaze with the smoke of a burning city, have been extinguished with the blood of the daughters of Urizen.' A number of interpretations of this statement had been offered to the court by expert psychiatric witnesses but none of them were ever authenticated by Abbott himself. At no moment during the trial did any one, least of all the jury, doubt that Abbott had been afflicted by a catastrophic psychosis and had acted without legal responsibility for his actions. Yet they'd brought in a unanimous verdict that he was legally sane and therefore fit to receive the five consecutive life sentences handed down to him by the judge. This was because the jury knew that the psychiatric services offered by the state for the treatment and care of the criminally insane were so primitive and inept that a legally insane Abbott might well have been out on the street within a few years, if indeed he did not escape within hours. Instead of receiving the clinical assessment and treatment he needed, Abbott had been banished to Green River.

Once inside the River Abbott had entered a nightmare more merciless than any his psychotic imagination could ever have constructed. Feared and therefore hated, he was subjected to those special bigotries and punishments that are the usual lot of the mentally ill but amplified – as were all bigotries in the River – by many degrees of magnitude. He was insulted, he was shunned, he was cheated. He was deceived, robbed and exploited. Most of all he was isolated. He was six feet and seven inches tall and could carry an engine block the length of the machine shop without panting. Perhaps, if he hadn't been so big, or so crazy, he would have been able to create some innocuous niche in which to function and exist. Others did. But Abbott couldn't. If he wasn't a target he was a hole in the air. Within the larger glass and steel cage of the penitentiary he was trapped inside his own personal architecture of psychic pain: a cycle of isolation, psychosis, segregation, drugs, oblivion, neglect, more isolation, more neglect and more psychosis. Savagely punished from both within and without, Henry Abbott lived beneath the underdogs.

And yet Klein owed him. During those first weeks in D block Klein had recognised the ability of the prison to turn a man's personality upside down. He felt the fear and deprivation perverting his thinking, warping his reason. NOT MY FUCKING BUSINESS. In the relative quiet after lights out he would lie listening as the sounds of stifled weeping drifted through the bars. But that wasn't his business. Sometimes the sounds, shameful and small, were his own. Even then it wasn't his fucking business. Nor anyone else's. The penitents of Green River were there to witness and endure extremes of misery without feeling a shred of pity, particularly for themselves. Pity in general was weakness and therefore dangerous and immoral. Self-pity was an evil bordering on perversion. So like the rest of them Klein, who wanted to live and survive and one day to leave, stifled the sounds of his own pain and ignored those of others.

But one night – just seven weeks into Klein's sentence – the voice of Henry Abbott had not been stifled.

'*Hello?*'

The word had pealed around the stacked tiers of cells, echoing through the nightmares of light and heavy sleepers alike as if a damned and phantom soul were calling from the far side of creation. By the green cell light Klein read his watch at 2.03 a.m. A chill ran through his entrails as the word rang out again.

'*Hello?*'

And again.

'*Hello?*'

And again.

'*Hello?*'

With each repetition the nature of the question changed and became more harrowing, more desperate, as if the whole vocabulary of this wounded creature had been stripped down to that single word. Is there anyone there? What do you want? Tell me. *Tell me*. Leave me alone. *Leave me*. Please, leave me. Please, let me die. Please. Let me die.

In Abbott's cries Klein recognised the vocalised half of the harrowing dialogue – by turns raging, threatening, pleading and cowed – that the psychotic person conducts with the torturer within himself. Klein had heard the half-dialogue before, in the chaos of the emergency room, but never from the same side of the fence. In cellblock D the only attention Abbott provoked was a chorus of death threats and obscenities that blended in with and exaggerated those already raging inside his skull.

'You're dead, booby!'

'I'm gonna cut your fucking dick off.'

'Shut the fuck up.'

'I'm warnin' you, Abbott, you long sackashit.'

'Go kill yourself.'

'Yeah, go kill yourfuckenself.'

It was an unpleasant scene. But it wasn't Klein's business and he ignored it. Or to be more accurate, he ignored Henry Abbott, and after they tired of their shouts being ignored so did the rest of the inmates.

Two days later Abbott had still not been out of his cell. He had taken no food or drink, and had still found no more words with which to communicate.

'Hello?'

'Hello?'

On the third night he subsided into a fragile and terror-stricken silence. When he was loud the hacks had been reluctant to risk dragging him down to the hole for fear of one of them losing an arm or an eye, but when the bellowing of inmates complaining about the smell got angry enough, and became an excuse for throwing burning rolls of toilet paper from the tiers, Captain Cletus turned up and gave the order to roust Abbott out.

When Klein saw them running a fire hose along the catwalk towards Abbott's cell he realised that 'NOT MY FUCKING BUSINESS' wasn't going to see him through his time here after all. You couldn't stop them taking most of what you were, but you could stop them taking it all. In the end just exactly how much was still up to you. Exactly how much was the only choice you had left. During the three days in which Klein had left Abbott to suffer, he'd begun to feel himself dying. This wasn't a metaphysical fancy. It was a real thing that he felt in his body – as a rotting feeling in his guts, an ache in his pelvis and spine, a tightening band that cut into his brain. When he saw the fire hoses he knew that they would wash Ray Klein away along with the excrement smeared over the inside of Abbott's cell. The burden on him was the burden of knowledge, his medical knowledge, and with that knowledge, obligation.

Klein had called Cletus to his cell and asked permission to go in and talk with Abbott. After a long pause Cletus had said, 'You wouldn't be too smart a son-of-bitch for your own good would you, Klein?'

'I hope I am not, Captain, sir,' replied Klein.

'Get yourself killed on my watch I'll have paperwork coming out of my ass for weeks.'

'I could just do with some sleep,' said Klein.

Cletus considered him. 'Okay, Klein. But it's your neck.'

Across the front of the stacked tiers there was a stir, a flurry of talk, a movement of faces to cell doors, of hands gripping the bars and ears pressed between them as the realisation spread that the new guy Klein was going to go in there with the booby. Abbott, when steady, had the strength of three; when insane the strength of five; and they all knew that crazies didn't feel pain. Why the year before last one of them had sawed off his own cock and balls with a broken shaving mirror without making a fucking sound. Klein was a mad fuck himself to even think of it. A short timer who didn't know the score. That fucker Abbott had the strength of six guys, maybe seven. Guy's a fucking giant, a freak for Chrissakes.

Abbott the giant sat crouched in a corner of his cell, covered in filth and mumbling incoherently while he picked at a sore on his face. Terror imparts to sweat and excreta a smell all its own – rank, thin, shaming. It drives men away because it evokes from the most primitive lobe of the brain the memory of the original helplessness and terror from which they all have come, their common origin as victims. Klein, mastering the urge to vomit and run, stood on the threshold of the cell door and introduced himself.

'Hi, Henry. I'm Ray Klein.'

When Abbott made no reply Klein stepped inside and sat down on the bunk. A moment later the cell door thundered shut behind him.

Klein spent the whole night on Abbott's bunk, saying nothing. He ignored the obscence catcalls and shouts from neighbouring cells and just sat in silence, acclimatising to the stench and trying to find a centre within himself that felt safe and that Abbott too might recognize and therein find some comfort. At some point in the early hours Klein fell asleep. When Klein woke up to the bell at first lock and count, his head was pillowed on Abbott's shoulder and the big convict's arm was wrapped around him.

That day Abbott accompanied Klein, without violence or persuasion, to a cell in the segregation block – the hole – and started on the drug regime that Klein recommended. Locking a man in the hole and giving him major tranquillisers wasn't

Klein's idea of a good time, but he was allowed to see Abbott four times a day, no one got hurt, and Abbott had gradually recovered. Now he was on two-weekly intramuscular depot injections of slowrelease phenothiazines to control his symptoms – the plastic in his face that made it hard to talk and smile.

Abbott never quite made it to normality but he got by. Dennis Terry gave him a job in the sewers that no one else wanted and on the occasions he went crazy again it was Klein who was asked to talk him out and take him to the hole, with which Abbott peaceably complied. But there was one time that Abbott had gone to the hole when he wasn't crazy, when it had come down to Klein to stake out the other boundary of his life in Green River.

Myron Pinkley was a petulant, self-centred twenty-one-year-old sociopath with beefy shoulders and a bullet head who'd killed three strangers at a campsite in Big Bend National Park whilst on a mindless sex and murder spree with his girlfriend. Pinkley hovered sycophantically around the fringes of the Agry crew without any real hope of getting in and he was generally regarded as the kind of pain in the ass jerk-off who would one day kill someone in front of a guard and spend the rest of his days in seg. One day – at a Sunday lunchtime not long after Klein had first drawn attention to himself by helping Abbott – Myron Pinkley had stolen Klein's dessert.

Klein sat with dozens of eyes on him while his guts turned to lava. The stinking little square of bottle-green jello that Pinkley shovelled into his mouth with his fingers wasn't worth a shit to man nor beast, but the gelatine block represented dignity, respect, power. For Klein it was still too soon, the values of this world still too alien for him to understand. To stop Pinkley would've required a violent scene and its consequences. The worthlessness of the jello was so extreme, the price of retrieving it so absurdly out of proportion to its value, that Klein hadn't been able to bring himself to do anything.

He just sat there blushing and trying to control his bladder while Pinkley sucked his fingers clean, grinned and walked away with his chest puffed out like a turkey. Klein passed the day in a torment. All the advice he received was to the effect that if he let Pinkley get away with it he was fucked. The evening of that same day Pinkley took Klein's chocolate pudding. This time Henry Abbott was sitting alone at the next table.

Abbott lumbered over and grabbed Pinkley's hand and Pinkley punched him in the mouth. Abbott didn't flinch and just stood there holding onto the hand. After a few seconds Pinkley's face began to fold in on itself with pain. When he tried for Abbott's eyes with his free hand Abbott squeezed harder and Pinkley fell screaming to his knees. Three guards, then four, then five, were unable to get Abbott to release Pinkley's hand. They threatened him, they kicked him and they bludgeoned him about the head. But Abbott silently refused to let go. Eventually they manhandled him to seg, Abbott dragging the shrieking Pinkley along the floor behind him like a recalcitrant teddy bear. When three hours later Abbott still hadn't let go of the hand, they put him under with first twenty and then seventy, and then one hundred and eighty milligrams of intravenous valium.

Pinkley lost his right thumb and index finger, hardly much better than losing the whole arm. He also lost credibility. Word got round that he had a shiv with Abbott's name on it for when Abbott got out of the hole. Big though he was Abbott would be a sitting target. The prevailing mood was that Klein ought to do something about it.

When he came down to it the problem was easy. Everything Klein had done since entering the River had been accompanied by a profound sense of helplessness and fear – taking a shower, pissing in the latrine, going to the gym, talking to a guard, not talking to a guard, choosing a table in the chow hall, who to nod hello to, who not. Every action no matter how insignificant carried a question with it: what will happen and who might I offend if I do this? Can I speak with a Latino, can I afford not to hate the Blacks, can I state a preference for Muddy Waters over Willie Nelson without getting my tongue cut out? Is it really this bad? He could never tell for sure. The terror and uncertainty were fuelled by a mixture of fantasy, rumour and brutal reality. Finally enacting a piece of reality of his own was a relief. Klein purchased a six-inch nail from a man out of carpentry and a short length of broom handle from a Cuban cleaner. He drove the nail through the wood like a corkscrew. Then, finding Pinkley in the rear of the kitchens where, with his disabled arm, he'd fallen to the humiliating job of emptying slops, Klein punched the nail through the side of Myron's head, just behind the temple.

When Fenton, the head chef, found Pinkley an hour later the young convict was still emptying slops as if nothing had happened, with four inches of galvanised iron piercing his frontal lobes.

Pinkley survived the repair of his middle meningeal artery with no memory of his accident, to which there were no witnesses. Nothing was ever proven or even seriously investigated. Nev Agry, a couple of days later, had bent down by Klein's ear just as he was about to tuck into his chocolate pudding and told him, 'Nice work, Doc.'

Captain Bill Cletus had taken him to one side. 'Understand me, Klein, you fucken smart ass. Don't let this thing go to your head.'

If Klein's conscience had ever asked him if a crippled arm and permanent brain damage wasn't too severe a retribution for stealing four ounces of lime-flavoured jello, its voice was drowned by the shouts of triumph and glee from every fibre in his body. As if by magic a substantial wedge of fear disappeared from his life. For the first time he found himself able to piss in the latrine whilst standing between two lifers. He assuaged any guilt he might have felt with the fact that Pinkley emerged from the affair with an altered personality which, even his mother agreed, was an immense improvement on the one that his creator had given him. Docile, obedient, almost irritatingly pleasant, Pinkley joined the Jesus Army – 'LOVE FAITH POWER' – continued slopping out in the kitchens – a labour he was happy to offer up to God – and spent an hour twice a day in chapel redeeming his soul. If Pinkley had died – and the nail might have killed him – maybe Klein's conscience would've given him a harder time than it did, but hell, he'd had a fair notion of just how much the frontal lobes could take and anyway, all that counted in the end was that for ever after his desserts were his own to dispose of as he chose. His habit was always to give his jello away.

Klein's thoughts returned to the present as he approached the inner gate of the General Purposes wing and saw the guard – Kracowicz – scowling at the prisoners walking past him. As Klein drew level Kracowicz pulled a Latino from the line for a body search.

The corridor of General Purposes, because it was built of regular floors and rooms rather than towering stacks of cages, was less oppressive than the cellblocks. Above your head as you walked – and only a few feet above at that – was a real ceiling instead of the damned glass roof. The wing as you passed down it contained the library, the chapel, two rooms where the ludicrous group therapy sessions so beloved of the parole board took place, and the gym. The gym was an ongoing source of conflict between the boxers, who saw it as theirs by right, and the basketball players who had a concrete court outside but coveted the gym's sprung wooden floor. As Klein walked by he avoided – by unthinking reflex now – bumping shoulders with anyone who might take it as an excuse to start a fight.

At the outer gate the guard Grierson stood under the air-conditioning vent sweating lightly into his khaki uniform. Klein was rarely frisked and even more rarely was he frisked thoroughly. A decent search by practised hands, taking into account the sullen and reluctant compliance of the inmate and the ingenuity lavished upon methods of concealment, took five to seven minutes. Pockets emptied, collars, cuffs and seams fingered for inserts, shoes off, toes opened, genitals lifted, unsavoury buttocks spread apart. It was a tedious and unfulfilling task. Most such searches unearthed contraband too trivial to command more than mild punishment – a tooth-pick joint cost you telephone privileges for a week – and discretion calls varied widely depending on the anality of the guard in question. The resources to search every con every day at every gate were far beyond Green River's means. There were metal detectors at every gate but they were twenty years old, easily fused when necessary and often out of order awaiting repair by Dennis Terry's maintenance crew. Grierson nodded at Klein and waved him by.

Outside the sun was high and bright in a blue-white sky and after the mixed effusions that permeated the interior of the prison the air in the yard was sweet. To his left, between General Purposes and D block and surrounded by high steel mesh, was the white muscle yard where the cons, particularly the meatbags from Grauerholz's clique, pumped iron. Since Myron Pinkley got religion Klein had been allowed to work out three times a week amongst the twenty-inch arms. To his right, between the gym and B block, was where the blacks pumped up. Klein had only strayed onto that turf twice, on each occasion by invitation when someone had let slip a two hundred pound barbell and collapsed their thorax.

Klein walked along the concrete path that led to the main gates proper: an arched tunnel sandwiched between two pairs of giant oak doors studded with wrought iron. Between these inner and outer doors was a third, of Pittsburg steel, that was operated electronically. A vaunting granite wall built in symmetry with the six spokes of the main prison formed a huge stone hexagon sealing in two thousand eight hundred inmates and their keepers. The foot of the wall, it was said, lay buried dozens of feet below the earth so that no man could tunnel his way out. On the rim of the great wall were two banks of razor wire that always reflected the same dull grey no matter how bright the sun. At regular intervals around the wall riflemen in watchtowers cradled M16s and kept a bored eye on the yards and workshops below.

Above the main gates rose a thick, squat turret that somehow managed to combine elegance and brutality in equal measure. Inside the turret Warden Hobbes lorded it over his delinquent charges. The elaborate architecture spoke with the massive confidence of another age and as a relic it was awesome – even beautiful – but to Klein it was a shitheap of misery for which he could find neither respect nor admiration. Under the gaze of the nearest rifleman Klein turned away from the gates. That afternoon he would hold his private clinic in the underground room he rented from Dennis Terry and whose security was guaranteed by Nev Agry. There a stream of convicts would visit him with their ailments and infections, and pay him in cigarettes, porn mags, prison scrip, cash dollars, or whatever other coin Klein decided was acceptable. Now he rounded a corner in the maze of wire mesh and headed towards the infirmary where he spent each morning.

The hospital was a two-storey structure built in the lee of the south-west wall. Klein ran through the week's schedule in his head: Juliette Devlin wouldn't be there today. With the visit to Hobbes on his mind he wasn't too sorry, though he always looked forward to her visits. He recalled that she'd bullshitted him into making a bet on tonight's game between the Lakers and the Knicks. He had wagered a carton of

Winstons against two new pairs of Calvin Klein underpants
that the Knicks wouldn't lose by more than six points. As the
underwear manufactured by his more glamorous namesake
was an unheard-of luxury Klein thought this represented good
odds. He jogged up the steps to the infirmary and through
the big double doors which in daylight were usually wedged
open. On duty at the second door, a barred gate, was the
Korean guard, Sung. As Sung took him through and unlocked
the third door, of plate steel, to let him into the wards Klein
wished him good morning and as usual Sung did not reply.
Sung had travelled halfway round the world to guard a bunch
of killers in Texas and maybe didn't see the sense in wishing
them good anything. Klein went down the corridor past the
dispensary and into the sick bay office. The office had been
painted mustard yellow fifteen years before as if to remind
the sick and their keepers that they weren't there to have a
good time. The yellow paint now bubbled and peeled from
the sagging plaster of the ceiling. Klein grabbed a white coat
and a handful of lab reports and headed down to Crockett
ward. When he got there Frogman Coley raised his great
grizzled head from examining a patient and walked down the
aisle towards him. A stethoscope was slung from the nape of
his neck and he wore rubber gloves.

'What's new, chief?' said Klein.

'Lopez is still shitting what blood he's got left in him. See
what you think. I reckon his Mama should be warned. She
knows Vinnie don't wanna see her, but she said she wanted
to know.'

'Sure.'

'I think Reiner's got PCP. Deano Baines's haemoglobin is
up. And the Gimp tried to kill Garvey with a pillow.'

'He still alive?'

Coley raised an eyebrow.

'I mean the Gimp,' said Klein.

Coley nodded grimly. 'Let's check these mothers out.'

Coley snapped his gloves off, rolling them inside out, one into the other so that his skin didn't touch the outer surface and get contaminated. It was a habit he'd picked up from Klein and Klein enjoyed seeing him do it. Coley tossed the gloves into a waste bin and followed Klein to the foot of the first bed.

Klein sometimes thought of Green River as a Russian doll carved from increasingly dense layers of horror. At the centre of the doll was a black void called Aids. It wasn't a topic with which Klein had previously been well-acquainted but in here he had learned.

No one knew what proportion of the population was infected with HIV but it was high. Large numbers of inmates had abused IV drugs on the outside and many had brought the virus in with them. Once inside continued addiction, the sharing of syringes and injection works, dangerous sex and a lot of spilled blood combined to raise the prevalence even higher. In the outside world Aids had provoked safe and sober men with fat salaries, good educations and faithful wives to acts of stupendous incompetence and bigotry. To Klein's mind they had no excuse. In Green River things were different. In Green River the fear of contagion was so intense that it had disappeared from the surface of life – taboo, forbidden, un-mentionable – and churned instead through dark cisterns hidden within the mind of every man. The infirmary was swamped with cases. Ray Klein and Earl Coley bore the brunt.

Their fight was with a menagerie of microscopic forms which struggled for life in the bodies of the infected, as the men them-selves did struggle in the world, in the prison and here at the last ditch, in Crockett ward. *Candida albicans*, *Mycobacterium tuber-culosis*, *Haemophilus influenzae*, *Mycobacterium avium*, *Streptococcus pneumoniae*, *pneumocystis carinii*, *Salmonella*, central nervous system toxoplasmosis, cryptococcal meningitis, cytomegalovirus retinitis, multifocal leukoencephalopathy, large-cell lymphoma, and who knew what else besides: a festival of pyogenesis and neoplasia to make God himself wonder at the fecundity of his own imagination. And at the mad defiance pitched against him by these foolish men.

Their morning round followed a routine. They approached each patient together and Coley – who hadn't left the building in many years – described any overnight developments. Klein showed Coley the few lab reports they were able to afford, and if necessary explained their significance. Coley then methodically examined the patient, going through each system in turn as Klein had taught him. Watching Coley's hands at work – hands born to pick cotton and plough stony fields – was always a good moment for Klein. A moment of reprieve. During the past three years Klein had taught Coley most clinical medicine worth knowing and Coley had been a sponge, soaking up knowledge with a passion that Klein had envied. In Klein's mind there was no doubt: the black sharecropper had the gift of hands. Coley was a great natural physician. Bodies spoke their pain into his fingertips and he heard them. Klein had met a few such men in his profession and had always marvelled to see them work but there were not many, and much as he would like to he did not count himself amongst them. Klein had never said any of this to Coley, never expressed his admiration and pride, for fear of mutual embarrassment. He had never felt at home with California-style statements of friendship, love and mutuality and the River didn't seem like a good place to start. Yet before he left he would like to tell Coley. Maybe that would be soon. Maybe this very day. A clatter of metal on stone rang from the end of the ward and Klein put thoughts of freedom from his mind.

Vinnie Lopez lay staring at the ceiling in a congealed mass of soiled sheets. An IV line in his left arm delivered dextro-saline with added potassium. On the floor by his bed was a stainless steel bedpan that Lopez had tried to grab from the bedside table and had dropped. Lacking the strength to reach for it he lay in the mess with his fists clenched by his sides, his face a mask of shame and humiliation.

Coley said to Klein, 'Go get some clean linen.'

Klein walked quickly to the linen closet at the end of the room. He accepted Coley's orders to perform basic tasks in the hospital without question, and they were many. Without this distribution of power Klein would never have been able to use or pass on any of his knowledge. Coley had run the infirmary for sixteen years before Klein had showed up and if he stayed alive he would be running it sixteen years after Klein left. Coley was the wagonmaster. When Klein got back to the bed Coley had taken down the drip bag, which was empty.

'This one's through. He's getting one every eight hours. You reckon that's still enough?'

Klein nodded, his eyes on Lopez, and Coley disappeared. Klein put the sheets down and drew a screen around the bed. He fetched a bowl of hot water, slipped on a pair of rubber gloves, and washed Lopez from his neck to his knees. In six months the Mexican had declined from being Reuben Wilson's sparring partner to a ninety-five-pound bag of bones. His $CD_4 + T$ lymphocyte count had dropped below 150 and his bowel was infected with a campylobacter organism which had proved resistant to antibiotic therapy. Or at least to those drugs that were available to them. There were newer, more powerful preparations, so Klein had read, but they cost more than they could afford. The chronic bloody diarrhoea had depleted Lopez's potassium and protein reserves, and caused an anaemia that was getting worse by the day. In addition, his mouth and oesophagus were inflamed with candidiasis.

The necessary blood transfusions, like the drugs, had to be requisitioned by Bahr, the official prison doctor, but Bahr didn't see the point. Bahr was a local internist who dropped by four times a week, stayed for an hour – all the letter of his contract demanded – and before heading off to the golf course told them to send anything they couldn't handle to the emergency room at the County hospital. His attitude was to lay heavy doses of sedatives on the Aids guys and let them die in peace. Klein despised Bahr, not because this policy was unreasonable or in-humane, but because it was primarily designed to cut down Bahr's workload. Bahr collected a good fee from the Bureau of Corrections for his hour or two a week – money better spent on drugs and supplies. But Bahr wielded power. If he'd been so inclined he could have had Klein and Coley removed from the hospital for good. In fact they regularly broke so many prison regulations in there they could have been sent to seg for years. So they kissed Bahr's ass, kept most problems to themselves and only called him out of hours when there was a death to be certified, to which duty, another generous fee being involved, Bahr had never been known to object.

As regards Bahr's Aids policy, Klein and Coley had decided that it was up to the guys who were doing the dying. If a man wanted to fight, they would fight with him. By the time they reached the infirmary a lot of them had been ill for as long as they could be without letting anyone else know it. These were men who were used to bad news, who'd been taking it and giving it all their lives, but dying of Aids in the prison infirmary was the one end-of-the-line they didn't want to deal with. In Green River the appearance of toughness was cultiv-ated with religious fervour. They all accepted the day-in, day-out fear of a shiv in the back, most of them had stared down the barrel of a .38 in their time, and all would at least have tried to spit in the warden's eye as he walked them to the electric chair should that have been their fate. But a lingering death behind steel bars by this disease – *the* disease, the faggot disease – was, in the eyes of the population, as low as a man could fall.

Consequently most guys opted for the tranquillisers and, Klein thought, why the fuck not? Sometimes he felt that life was given a value it didn't deserve anyhow. People lived and died; who gave a shit about the timing except those who were left behind to grieve? And grief belonged to the griever not the dead. Klein hoped that when his time came he would have the sense to finish it quick and clean, because the final result was never in doubt and what was the point of fighting it?

But Vinnie Lopez was one of the fighters. A boxer. As Klein bundled the soiled undersheet into a plastic bag he glanced into Lopez's fevered eyes and saw the fiery defiance of terminal despair. For a second the steelwork and ice round Klein's heart was shaken. Forbidden emotions assailed him. Before they could weaken him, before he could name them, Klein turned away. He snapped off his rubber gloves, bagged them and put on a clean pair. He shook out a fresh sheet. He avoided those dangerous eyes. He rolled Lopez to one edge of the bed and spread the sheet beneath him. As Klein rolled him back onto the sheet, the kid's face crumpled.

Tears fell down Lopez's cheeks. He hid his face in the crook of his elbow and squirmed onto his side so that his back was turned to Klein. To Klein's knowledge, no one had ever seen Lopez cry before.

Klein's guts knotted inside him. Lopez, who boasted four slayings as leader of a San Antonio street gang and was taken seriously even in here, now looked like an eight-year-old child. Klein shook out the top sheet over the bed and let it drift gently down over Lopez's clenched figure. Klein knew that sometimes a man preferred to be alone with his pain and shame; yet sometimes that was an excuse for not trying. At that moment Klein found it hard to know. As he tucked the sheet in he shoved thought from his mind and listened to his guts. He straightened up.

'Vinnie,' said Klein.

Lopez spoke from behind his elbow. 'Go 'way, man.'

Klein sat on the chair by the bed. Lopez's back was hunched towards him under the sheet. Klein rested his hand lightly on Vinnie's shoulder and felt him tighten up even more. He kept the hand there. After a moment Vinnie's body relaxed just a little. Klein suddenly wished he had some Spanish.

'Vinnie,' he said. 'You can tell me to fuck off after this if you want to, but this is mine and Coley's outfit and you've got to understand the way things are in here. The way things are is that there's no shame in tears, or in shit, or in the sickness infecting your body. Not in here. You understand?'

The thin body under his hand shook with grief.

'If I was sick maybe you'd do the same for me,' said Klein.

Lopez turned on him. His eyes were hot with anger and contempt. Klein let his hand fall away.

'I would spit on you,' said Lopez.

Klein held his eyes for what felt like a long time, then shook his head.

'No,' said Klein, quietly. 'You spit on yourself.'

The contempt in Vinnie's eyes dissolved into raw grief. His face trembled and he started to turn away again. Klein put his hand back on his shoulder and stopped him.

'Die like a man, Vinnie.'

Vinnie stared at him, bewildered, his lips trembling. His voice was a whisper. 'I want to.' He struggled for his tears not to return. 'Tha's all I want. Tha's all, man. Tha's all.'

Klein swallowed thickly. 'This is how men die.'

Vinnie shook his head for it not to be true. Klein nodded.

'It's easy to feel like a man with your foot on someone's throat,' said Klein. 'It's a good feeling, I know. To hold onto your pride when you're lying in your own shit is something else. That feeling I don't know. Maybe I could never find it even if I tried. But the man who could – the man who could find his pride and feel it and hold onto it – he would be a great man.'

This time the tears came back to Vinnie's eyes and he clenched them shut. With an effort he looked up at Klein. 'I'm frightened, man,' he said.

'I know, Vinnie.' Klein took his hand.

'I'm frightened.' Lopez started sobbing softly.

Klein sat there in silence and let the ache that was as big as the world fill his chest. For he had learned that any comforting words he might have mustered would have been for himself, and not for Vinnie. There was no comfort in rotting to death at twenty-two. For a second the steelworks and ice collapsed entire and Klein was possessed of a need, terrifying in its force, to cast some spell which made them all healthy. And happy and rich and free. And himself with them. And with that he was suddenly afraid that his parole application would be successful, and maybe understood why he had blown them out at his last year's review: if they let him go he would lose all this too. Here he was still a doctor; out there he would be a bum. For a moment he wanted to go and break a chair over Captain Cletus's head and get himself sent to seg. The moment passed. Instead he cleared his mind and held onto Vinnie's hand and listened in silence to the wasted lungs heaving quietly under the sheet. After what seemed like hours but was only a few minutes, Vinnie fell limp and quiet. A voice growled out from a few yards the other side of the curtain.

'Put that fucker out, Deano, we got oxygen in here. I tol' you before: you fit enough to smoke you fit enough to drag yo' worthless ass down the TV room. We don't want to inhale your shit in here.'

Lopez stiffened and scrubbed his face with a handful of sheet. 'I don't want the Frogman to see me this way,' he said.

'Sure.' Like most everyone else Vinnie held Coley in awe. Klein nodded and stood up. 'I'll see you later.'

He picked up the laundry bag and paused by the screen curtains. 'Vinnie, I want you to do something for me.'

Vinnie looked up at him.

Klein said, 'Let me invite your mother for a visit.'

Vinnie turned away.

Klein said, 'Think on it. Think on what we talked about.'

As Klein reached for the curtain Lopez said, 'Klein.'

Klein looked over his shoulder. After a pause Lopez nodded.

Klein nodded back. 'Thanks, Vinnie.'

He slipped out between the screens and intercepted Earl Coley on his way in.

'Vinnie needs some time on his own,' said Klein.

Coley glanced at the screens then back at Klein. He hefted the bag of IV fluid in his hand. 'Guess this can wait till later.'

'Thanks,' said Klein.

Coley looked at his watch. 'Thought you had an appointment with great God Almighty, find out how sweet you sucked them stubby white dicks on the parole board.' He showed his watch to Klein.

Ten thirty-five.

Hobbes was waiting.

'Balls,' said Klein.

Klein dragged his white coat down over his shoulders and started at a run for the door.

FIVE

'KNEEL DOWN, NIGGER.'

Stokely's hoarse whisper was loud against her ear.

'I don't wanna have to look at your muthafucken face.'

Sour breath drifted into her nostrils, then the rank, ruttish smell of Stokely's cock as he hefted it free of his shorts. Above the sound of Stokely's voice Ice T injected heavy vocal menace into a war song blaring from the tape deck.

'Make it quiet too. Like I tol' you befo', this gets out I cut yo' black faggot dick off and shove it up your ass.'

There was a lot of talk, in the River, of cutting, ripping and stomping, most of it bullshit. When it came from Stokely Johnson you took it seriously. No one had forgotten what Johnson had done to Midge Midgely's nuts. With the top of her head pressed into the thin pillow, her weight on her elbows, Claudine took some deep breaths and relaxed her thorax and abdomen. The smell of sour breath was replaced by that of latex, its clinical odour contrasting sharply with the hot, rank air as Stokely struggled with a condom.

'Shit, man. I hate these muthafuckas.'

Claudine waited. A moment later, when she felt the tip of his sudden raw hard-on between her buttocks, she inhaled deeply and bore down, as if she were attempting a rock hard shit. Stokely slid in with a muffled exhalation of satisfaction. Suddenly his voice was soft.

'Sweet,' said Stokely.

The cell was hot and moist and reeked with the smell of hashish, rectal mucus and sperm. This was the cooler part of the day, before the sun got high enough to bear down directly on the glass roof of the block. Apart from meals three times a day they'd been confined to their cells for two weeks. For the last ten days there'd been no airconditioning. Broken down, the screws had told them, awaiting repair. By mid-afternoon the temperature would be over a hundred and saturated with the sweat and breath of half a thousand men packed into cells built to house three hundred. In some ways Claudine welcomed the heat. It induced a sense of lassitude and inner deadness that made submitting to Stokely's assaults easier to bear.

'Baby,' said Stokely.

He caressed her scalp and she wondered what pictures were going through his mind and whose muthafucken face he did want to look at. It was said that Stokely had a woman somewhere in California, maybe Bakersfield, and two kids. Sons. Stoke was a long way from home.

'Baby,' said Stokely again.

His hands gripped her waist, strong but no longer brutal, the hands of a man who in his heart wanted to hold and take care of a woman, and be held in his turn by the gaze of a woman who saw him for who he was and wanted him just the same. Sadness squeezed Claudine's insides and she wished Stokely's lovemaking hadn't betrayed him that way. Then it would've been easier to hate him.

She wished suddenly that she had all her hair back, long and lustrous with oil. As a woman she'd found it easier to hate. And easier to comply. Easier to believe that Nev Agry's brutal shunting fucks were all she deserved. Her transfer back to B block and the black population where she'd first started out had plunged her into confusion. She didn't know who she was any more.

As Agry's wife Claudine had been, by universal consent, a beautiful woman. Agry had bought her clothes, perfumes, a real Ladyshaver for her legs. Silk camisoles. Red nail polish. And her hair had hung halfway to her waist. Agry had called her – without irony – his queen. Swift and appalling punishment awaited anyone rash enough to threaten the illusion she and Agry had created. Agry had given her a white wedding right there in D block – the most extravagant party in the prison's history – with gifts from the other crew chiefs, bridesmaids, and a three-tier cake with their names entwined on top. A convict from A who was a licensed minister out of Oklahoma City had performed the ceremony. Everyone understood: no insults, no fag jokes, no sniggers or insinuations. To be the object of envy and lust was acceptable – that, after all, was a woman's right – but no hint, no rumour, no whisper of the fact that beneath her dress hung a cock and balls was allowed to pass without violent retribution. Even the screws understood. After four years Claudine's awareness of her true gender had disappeared into some obscure recess of her mind – like an immigrant forgetting his native tongue. Pitching her voice an octave higher, her feminine gestures and flirtatious glances, the way she held a coffee cup or smoked a cigarette, all became second nature. She was Claudine Agry. Nev Agry had purchased her transfer to his luxury four-man cell for an undisclosed sum, believed to amount to an ounce of quality cocaine and a case of Maker's Mark. Now she was back where she started, on B block.

No one knew it, especially not Agry, but she'd requested the transfer herself for reasons too dangerous to reveal. If Agry discovered the truth before she was out of here she was dead.

On her return to B block she – he – had cropped her hair off, cut her nails, scrubbed her face, exchanged her silk for prison denim, her body lotions for sweat. Claudine Agry – tall, slim, elegant – had turned back into Claude Toussaint – skinny, boyish, clumsy. The queen of cellblock D was now a less-than-zero ex-crack dealer – a nigger despised by niggers for sucking the whiteman's cock. She was a he again but it was too soon for it to make sense.

Claudine's thoughts returned to the present as Stokely's fucking got faster and deeper. She gripped the sheet in her fingers. Stokely ejaculated, smoothly and without violence, and paused for a moment with his weight resting on big fists placed on either side of her head. His sweat dripped down onto her back in big warm splats. The pause lengthened and Claudine feared its end. It came with Stokely's rough, contemptuous withdrawal and she jerked away with a loud grunt as her pelvic muscles went into a painful spasm.

'Shut it, bitch.'

The softness in Stokely's tone had gone until next time. Now his voice was filled with the self-loathing he couldn't contain within himself.

'Look at me,' ordered Stokely.

Claudine kept her face turned away. 'Give me a break, man, shit.'

Stokely pitched her over onto her back and she rolled into a ball, arms over her head, knees pulled up to her chest. Stokely slipped his hand over her mouth and punched her in the ribs. She grunted against the fingers clamped over her face. When she heaved in a lungful of air she smelled the stink of rubber on his hand. Stokely let go and stood up. He walked to the back of the cell and flushed away the condom. As Claudine rubbed her ribs and Stokely took a piss she reminded herself that if Hobbes kept his word she wouldn't have to take it for too much longer.

Hobbes had promised Claudine that if she stopped dressing and acting like a woman the parole board, upon his recommendation, would look favourably on her upcoming review. Hobbes had pointed out that the members of the board could hardly be expected to release a man who turned up with long red-painted nails and lipstick and fluttered his false eyelashes at every question. Claudine, in her turn, had pointed out that she had no choice: Nev Agry would've had her killed on her way back across the yard. Hobbes had guaranteed her safety – but only if she transferred to B block. Claudine had been unconvinced. Even seg wasn't safe from Agry. Then Hobbes had told her about the lockdown. Not even Agry could get to her there. And by the time the lockdown was over she would be paroled. There was still a risk, of course, but if Claude wanted to take it Hobbes would make the arrangements.

And for a moment Claudine had become Claude again and he had known that it was worth it. Worth anything to spend some time walking round the Quarter again. She – no, Goddamnit, *he* – would stand and breathe the gas fumes on Bourbon Street and feel his cock grow hard as he watched them long-legged bitches in short skirts strut by on their high heels. Then he'd go take a stool in Alfonso's and drink One Hundred Pipers through a straw. Yeah. With a big roll of twenties in his pocket. He wondered if any of the bitches would remember him. He hadn't been blown in a long time.

So Claude had said yes to Hobbes and here he was, with his new cell mate fucking him in the ass.

He. His. Him. He was getting there.

'Get dressed,' said Stokely.

The violence in Stokely's voice had peaked and subsided back to its normal growl. The splashing of water came from the back of the cramped cell as he washed himself down. The Ice T album came to an end and the tape deck snapped off. From down the block came the sound of someone chording a guitar and singing an Albert Collins number. Claude swung onto the edge of his bunk and reached for his pants. His. He needed an urgent shit but Stokely's heavily muscled frame still occupied the tiny bathroom area.

'Wilson should be back soon,' said Claude.

Stokely turned from the sink and wiped water from his face with a white towel turned grey with use. 'You tryin' to say somethin'?'

'No.' Claude wished he hadn't spoken.

'You think I can't run things right while he's away?'

'I didn't say no such thing,' said Claude.

Stokely threw the towel down and walked over to where he could tower over Claude and make him cringe. Claude cringed.

'Wilson took you in 'cause you a disgrace to the brothers and he want to show them ofay muthafuckas we big enough to have you back.' He clenched his right fist. 'Cause we solid, man, you unnerstand? This is the Valley of the Long Distance Runners. The hangin' tree's still standin' out there and one of these days we gonna turn the fucking sky red – but while we in here we cut it together. Otherwise we nothin'.'

'That's why I came back,' said Claude.

'Bullshit.' Stokely stuck his finger in Claude's face. The smell of rubber still lingered. 'You usin' us. I don't know how but you usin' us.'

'I need a shit,' said Claude. He tried to stand up. Stokely put a hand on his chest and shoved him down.

'You usin' us like you used that Agry muthafucka.'

He couldn't tell which part of him spoke, Claude or Claudine, but suddenly he was brave with anger. 'Agry took from me same thing you take. What's the difference, Stokely?'

He twisted the last word as it left his tongue, camped it up high and shoved it into Stokely's ass. Then regretted it. Stokely took a half-step backwards and clubbed him with his fist, backhanded across the mouth. Claude tasted blood. A big hand closed round his throat. Stokely lifted him off the bunk until their faces were two inches apart.

'You talk back to me when you prove you a man again. Till then yo' faggot ass is mine. Now go take yo' shit, Claudine.'

Stokely let go of her and backed off. When she stopped coughing she went over to the pot, dropped her pants and sat down.

She. Her. Claudine. Fuck this, man. Get it together.

He wondered if Wilson would ever let him see Klein again. He wanted to talk with him. There was no one else he trusted. And even if there had been they wouldn't have wanted to listen. His bowels lurched and gurgled beneath him. From the other side of the curtain he heard Stokely bellow with disgust.

'Jesus Christ. You come out of there I'm going to fuck you up good, you bitch.'

Claude sighed and reached for the toilet roll. He liked being back on B block. He really did. As he wiped his ass he let his mind drift back to those long-legged bitches in their high heels and short skirts – and prayed he'd make it back to Bourbon Street before Nev Agry made it back to him.

SIX

SINCE THE SECOND lock and count Nev Agry had lain pros-
trate and alone on his bed, lighting one Lucky Strike after
another, each from the butt of the last, whilst his body trembled with pain.

His eyes were wide but the ceiling of his cell did not register
in his brain. Instead he saw Claudine. Her face. Her lips. Her
skin. Her long, immaculate thighs. Then a picture, porno-
graphic, too repulsive to behold, flashed before him and a
bolt of nausea pierced his guts. He sat up and dug blunt,
savage fingers into his eyes until the blackness before his retinas
danced with flashing light. The picture disappeared. He
calmed. He realised that the tape deck was playing Bob Wills
and the Texas Playboys singing 'San Antonio Rose'. Agry did
not consider himself an overly sentimental kind of guy but
rarely did 'San Antonio Rose' fail to throw a tightener round
his throat. Right now it brought him close to tears.

> It was there I found, beside the Alamo,
> Enchantment strange as the blue up above.
> A moonlit path, that only she would know,
> Still hears my broken song of love . . .

Agry reached over and snapped off the cassette. The time for tears would come – his tears, the tears of others – but not right now. Nor was it yet time to eradicate the vile pictures that Perkins had seeded in his mind for only blood would wash them away. But soon, he promised himself, soon. Perkins, the white screw from B block that Agry kept in his pocket, had confirmed the truth that Agry had known in his water for some time.

The stinking black nigger scumdog Stokely Johnson was fucking his Claudine in a regular and anal fashion.

Again: the picture. Blurred bodies. Slow motion. Humping thighs. Black skin. Sweat.

Agry's stomach rolled and tumbled. He ground his teeth against scalding bile and the breakfast eggs he had not been able to digest. He swallowed. He hauled himself to his feet. The walls shifted about him. The Lucky Strike clenched in his fist burned into the web of his fingers and he looked down. He saw the red tip of burning tobacco scorching his skin. He smelt the burning hairs. Yet the pain seemed far distant. He reached out for it, called it in. Suddenly it was there: stinging and bright. His hand jerked and unclenched itself. The butt fell to the floor. Slowly, Agry's head cleared of pain and doubt. He'd made his plans. The Warden had had the gall to warn him off, as if the old fool believed he really ran this joint. Well, Nev Agry would show him different. He'd weighed the cost and the consequences and he was ready to pay. He was ready to make them all pay. Agry trod on the butt and stripped off his shirt. It was time to bring Claudine back home.

Now that Claudine had gone Nev Agry lived alone in a four-man cell at the far end of ground tier, cellblock D, in the style befitting the most powerful of the Lifer crew chiefs. Colour TV and VCR. Porn video collection, hi-fi, an orthopaedic mattress on the bed, a wooden seat on his toilet. A refrigerator. A four-speed electric fan. The door of his cell was covered by a muslin sheet. The sheet gave him privacy but displayed the silhouette of anyone who stood beyond it. And at all times in the next cell were at least two of his men prepared to take any blade or bullet meant for him.

Agry was of medium height and suffered frontal balding, a fact his short cropped hair made no effort to conceal. The skin of his body was church-candle white and lightly coated with blond hairs. He was naturally thick-set and heavily muscled, though not cut like those faggot body builders. His forearms were like hams, the left one sporting a US Marine Corps death's head tattoo and the motto 'Death Before Dishonor'. From his medicine chest he took a number of bottles and in turn swallowed a Megavitamin, some ginseng, a gram of vitamin C, and a handful each of fish protein and dessicated liver tablets. He swilled his gullet clear with cold mineral water. Evian. He didn't know if any of this shit did him any good, and it was expensive, but he reckoned he needed all the help he could get. In his cell were no illicit drugs of any kind. His men carried these for him as he needed them, usually for sex, much less frequently for acts of violence. Agry hadn't had sex for what felt like a long time. Two fucking weeks. As he put the bottle of water away he noted that he was now possessed of a deep sense of calm. The calm confirmed as nothing else could that what he had set in motion was the only right thing to do.

Agry lifted his mattress and pulled out his body armour. The homemade vest promised protection against shanks and razors: two layers of leather sealed together with epoxy resin. Embedded in the resin was a sheet of fine-mesh steel wire. He slipped his head through the hole in the centre so that the vest covered his torso back and front, and tied it in place with thongs at either side. The leather against his skin felt like war. He put his shirt back on, buttoned it to the neck and tucked it into his pants.

Semper fucking fidelis.

From beyond the curtain came a discreet cough. Agry said, 'Come on in, Tony.'

The sheet parted and Tony Shockner walked in. Tall, rangy, twenty-nine years old and wearing wire-rimmed prison issue glasses, Shockner had the look of a Midwestern basketball coach. He was serving one hundred and eighty years for murder and armed robbery. He had executed two men in Green River on Agry's say-so. Agry knew him to be intelligent – more so than Agry, he admitted it – and good at taking orders. If he was the man who would be king – and Agry did not think so – he concealed his ambition real well. Now he stood inside the curtain with his arms long and loose by his sides. He nodded to Agry.

'Boss,' he said.

'You got something for me?' said Agry.

Shockner put his hand in his pocket and drew out a cutthroat razor. As a rule Agry did not carry weapons – an automatic ten days in the hole – and did not keep them in his cell. With his crew around him he had no need to. Now he took the razor from Shockner and opened it. He laid it lightly against his forearm and shaved off a patch of hair. He nodded. Shockner reached in his pocket again and produced a small plastic drum that once contained raw gland tablets.

'You wanted this too,' said Shockner.

Agry twisted the cap off the drum. It was three-quarters full of powdered sulphate. Agry shovelled a small pyramid onto the tip of the razor and snorted mightily up his left nostril. Good. Agry held cocaine in contempt as a popsicle drug for yuppies and niggers. God knew, as did Agry, that the Marines fought three major wars on speed and it hadn't let them down. Him neither. To his regret he'd never seen action with the Corps, having spent most of his service time in the brig pending a dishonourable discharge. Now he would prove, at least to himself, that in battle he would have been worthy of wearing their colours. He took a second snort of sulphate then capped the drum and handed it back to Shockner.

'Help yourself and see it gets passed round,' said Agry.

Shockner tossed the drum in his hand and pursed his lips. Behind the wire rims his eyes were troubled.

'Something wrong?' asked Agry.

Shockner shrugged. 'Nerves, I guess.'

Agry pointed at the drum with the razor. 'That'll give you all the nerves you want and get rid of the ones you don't.'

'You sure they'll go for it?' asked Shockner.

'Who?'

'DuBois and the others.'

'This ain't no fucken democracy, Tony.'

Shockner nodded. 'Well they're waiting for us.'

'Good.'

Agry turned to examine himself in the mirror. The grey eyes staring back were bright. Bitter liquid trickled down the back of his throat. He sniffed and swallowed. The sulphate was already a night train powering through the darker reaches of his nervous system. Semper fucking fi, man. He donned a pair of Ray Ban aviators and turned back to Shockner.

'Let's go.'

Agry and Shockner walked past the circular stairway from the third tier and out through the block gate and guard station into the central atrium. In the open top of the three-storey watchtower a guard – the old timer, Burroughs – lounged against one of the oak stanchions supporting the tower roof and picked his nose. The tower was a hexagonal cylinder of stone and wood with sheet steel reinforcing on and around the doors. From the first two storeys smoked plexiglass windows looked out on the central walkway of each of the six blocks. The ground floor of the watchtower contained the main watch command centre. Agry pictured the scene within: two guards dozing in front of a bank of black and white TV screens whose pictures changed every five seconds from one video camera to another. As did the guards, in their hearts, Agry knew that the screens were an exercise in futility. There was constant movement within the River: two and a half thousand men had to be fed, watered, exercised, clothed, laundered and provided with work. In addition the prison was vast and labyrinthine. The guards' pitiful cameras covered only a small proportion of its total area and none of its darker reaches at all.

The basement of the guard tower housed a communications centre, now twenty years old and more, which was linked by cables running under General Purposes to the main gate reception complex. Alongside the video screens was the master control panel for the cell doors and block gates. From here the cells could be opened either individually or in whole tiers. At the gate to each cellblock was a smaller office from which alternative control of the doors was available, but which could be overridden if necessary by tower command. Agry knew it all and it was all in hand.

As Agry and Shockner turned right, away from the tower and into the mess hall, they hit the stink of spoiled food and old grease. The mess hall was quiet, empty except for those dozen or so inmates half-heartedly swabbing the floors and clearing the formica-topped tables ready for lunch. Agry cut behind the serving counters into the kitchen, into the blast of heat from the rows of blackened cooking ranges and stainless steel cauldrons. Here there was a frenzy of activity, with men in stained whites, mostly Mexicans and other ethnic losers, sweating violently over their work and trying to ignore the shrieking of Fenton, the head chef.

'Rice, cocksucker! *Rice! Arroz! Comprendo?*'

Fenton was a scrawny jig with two gold teeth that had miraculously survived seven years inside. Agry watched him with a dull stirring of disgust, dull because Fenton was an irrelevant and insignificant piece of scum unworthy of his hate. Yet, today, hate him he did because Fenton was a jig, a nigger black and vile, and not a one of them deserved the breathing of even this foul and filthy air. Not a one except Claudine. His Claudine, for whom he would sacrifice all in the holocaust of his rage. He would give them fire and sword. There would be no quarter. Agry's intention was to burn the Valley of the Long Distance Runners into the ground and soak their nigger ashes with his piss.

At times, it seemed to him, his rage threatened to explode his body into atoms and with it the world itself. What energy he burnt in trying to contain it, what strength of will he needed to keep that fragile, leaking lid crammed shut, day by day, hour by hour. A lesser man, he knew, would long ago have cracked under the strain, but not Nev Agry. This was his pride. Yet Nev knew not where his anger came from; and vast though his portion was, it was no more than a shovelful flung upon the great unstable slag heap of anger, molten and dissolving at its core, that was Green River.

Fenton pulled off his tall chef's hat and used it to swab his face and blow his nose. As he put the hat back on he saw Agry bearing down on him and stiffened. Fenton's position permitted him to initiate a narrow spectrum of sycophantic banter and he was one of few jigs allowed to address Agry at all. Fenton flashed his gold teeth in a look-what-I-have-to-put-up-with type smile and jerked his head towards the Mexicans.

'Mr Agry. Jesus Christ. Most of these fuckers too ignorant to even speak English.'

Agry kept moving and Fenton trailed along behind him and to one side. Agry spoke without looking at him. 'Long as they know their place, Cookie. Know what I mean?'

'Yessir, Mr Agry.'

'You got somethin' nice for me today, Cookie?'

'Veal cutlet.'

'I'll take it in my cell. Fix me some of that Hollandy sauce shit you learned in New Orleans to go with it.'

Agry knew that when he was gone Fenton would curse him blind for the extra effort, maybe even blow his nose in the Hollandy sauce. For now Fenton smiled and bobbed his head. Again the dull stirring of disgust. Agry flicked his head and Fenton melted away amongst the ovens. Agry and Shockner cut through the back door of the kitchen and stopped at the top of a narrow staircase. The staircase was dimly illuminated by light filtering up from the room below. Along with the light came the rumble and hiss of machinery and a thin dribble of steam. Leaning against the wall, smoking, halfway down the stairs were two heavyweights, Atkins and Spriggs. They looked up and dropped their cigarettes and crushed them under their feet as Agry padded down the steps towards them. These were real cons – none too bright but armed robbers with dead cops to their credit – who had thrown in with Larry DuBois on cellblock A. Atkins and Spriggs both got a hard, dry handshake and a greeting by name.

'You seen Stokely Johnson yet?' said Agry.

'You mean the nigger Johnson?' said Spriggs, aghast. 'He's locked down ain't he?'

'Yeah. Perkins was meant to bring him.' Agry caught Shockner looking at him with veiled confusion. 'I guess he's already down there.'

'What's he here for?'

'With Wilson in seg it may be time to persuade Johnson to become king of the coons. Wilson's smart, but Johnson's just another dumb-ass jig we can get to grin and sing and dance for us, even if he don't know his self that's what he's doin'. Right?'

Spriggs had no choice but to nod in agreement. Agry squeezed Spriggs's arm. The triceps was rock solid. 'You come back to D later for some Old Grandad, okay?'

Agry moved on down. At the foot of the stairs he passed through a pair of heavy semi-transparent plastic doors and into the prison laundry.

The laundry was brightly lit and its damp heat was as punishing as the kitchen's. The rows of toiling machines, mangles and steam presses provided another despised work detail for the beaners and gooks. At the rear of the laundry was another passage which led to the linen store. Agry strolled towards it through the whorls of steam. In the passage were two hulking cons in soiled T-shirts. The more faded of the two T-shirts read: 'NUKE BAGHDAD'. The other read: 'EAT CUNT'. As Agry reached them the two men backed away to let him pass. Both men nodded without speaking. Agry walked through them without nodding back. Horace and Bubba Tolson. Enforcers for Hector Grauerholz. Muscles, tattoos, thick beards, three ear rings apiece. The Tolsons were Hell's Angels who'd raped a twelve-year-old girl whilst strung out on peyote buttons and Old Crow. After slaking themselves on the girl's body they'd driven their Harleys over her skull. When arrested Horace Tolson had been found picking her brains from the treads of his tyres with a matchstick. They were scum and Agry would not have had such in his crew. His guys were inside for killing men not children. But today he would use the Tolsons as required. In time of war you couldn't be too choosy about your allies. Agry went through the passage to the linen store. At the door he nodded to Shockner and went into the store alone.

The store was large and hot but well aerated. It was probably the sweetest smelling room in the joint. Banked high on either side of a centre aisle were stacks of fresh laundry piled on pallets and shelves. Five bare bulbs hung from the ceiling in a row. Only the farmost bulb was lit which gave the room the feeling of a sepulchre. Underneath the bulb, their eyes on Agry, were Hector Grauerholz, Dennis Terry and Larry

DuBois. Stokely Johnson wasn't there but then Agry hadn't been expecting him. That had been to set up Spriggs in case DuBois wouldn't play ball.

'I'm late,' said Agry. 'Forgive me.' He walked down the aisle towards them.

Dennis Terry stepped from the group and held out his hand. 'Nev,' he said.

Agry shook the hand. 'Dennis. How's it goin'?'

Terry, a grey man in his fifties, shrugged anxiously and returned Agry's smile. Unlike the others Terry wasn't a crew chief. He had spent twenty-eight years inside for strangling his fiancée – a schoolteacher in Wichita Falls who, Terry had convinced himself, had been fucking a Portuguese short order cook named Al. No concrete evidence of Al's existence was ever found, let alone of his having dicked the said fiancée, and so Terry was sent down for ninety-nine years by a judge who was a friend of the dead girl's family. These days, if he'd served any time at all, he would've been out on the street in four. It was a sad tale and Terry was a sad man. Thin and affable, he was uncomfortable around violent men. Agry knew that standing in the linen store with three psychopaths was hard on Terry's nerves. Yet despite his peaceable nature Terry was a key figure in Green River – and a wealthy man to boot – because he controlled Maintenance.

A building as big and old as this one required constant repair, rebuilding, rewiring, replumbing. Through hard work and shrewd politics Terry had kept his position – inherited in more civilised days when his predecessor succumbed to a stroke – for two decades. Here everything had to be bought and paid for – jobs, legal advice, toothpaste, a decent seat in the cinema, the right to pump iron in the yard – even the cell you bunked in. Maintenance included a lot of good skilled jobs, each of which had to be purchased. It also provided vast opportunities for smuggling contraband, blackmarket barter, luxury

improvements to accommodations and rapid repairs. Running
Maintenance was beneath the dignity of the Lifer crew chiefs
and they were happy to leave the work to Terry, guarantee
his safety and collect a healthy portion of his spoil. Terry, in
his turn, never had to raise his voice in anger and enjoyed
more home comforts than any of them. He lived as good a
life as it was possible to live in Green River. He would have
no stomach for what Agry had in mind but Agry hadn't invited
him out of etiquette. Terry was there to swallow nervously
and say yes to whatever he was told to do.

Now Hector Grauerholz shook Agry's hand and Agry stared
into a pair of bright button eyes that were empty of any
emotion he could recognise. Grauerholz was thin, small, cocky
and even by Agry's standards dangerously abnormal. He was
twenty-four years old and claimed the current prison record
for the highest substantiated number of murders: eighteen on
the outside and three on the inside. In solving a drug dispute
in Dallas he'd firebombed a jig crack factory and waited outside
with an Uzi, gunning down the inhabitants as they tried to
escape the flames. The factory was on the ground floor of a
tenement in Deep Elem and seven sleeping children and three
women were amongst the dead. Despite the fact that the
victims were black the trial judge had been so shocked by
Grauerholz's flagrant incapacity to experience anything
approaching remorse that he'd racked him up a prison sentence
totalling two thousand and twenty-five years, another record
that Grauerholz brandished with some pride.

Grauerholz had an open, innocent face and kept his hair
shaved down close to his skull. He looked, to Agry, like someone
in training for the priesthood. In the River he had gathered
together a mixed bag of backwoodsmen, red meat-eaters,
Angels, acid freaks and punks from the younger trash element
and built himself a small but serious drugs and muscle outfit.
Behind Grauerholz's choirboy looks was a core of virulent and

self-destructive nihilism which – if he hadn't been given room to breathe – would have exploded into wasteful bloodshed. Agry had given him that room, and enough respect and power to make him appreciate the pain it would cost him to lose it. Grauerholz was the child who would destroy the world just to see the sparks it made going up. But his help too was essential. Agry squeezed his hand for a second longer than necessary before letting go.

'I heah we gonna pitch some Wang Dang Doodle, Nev,' said Grauerholz.

'All night long,' replied Agry.

Grauerholz's face broke into a beatific grin.

Agry added, 'Long as your people got the balls for it.'

'You kiddin', man?'

Agry smiled. Grauerholz sucked on his cheeks, a tad pissed, and stepped back. But neither Grauerholz nor Terry was Agry's real concern. Larry Dubois was. Agry shook DuBois's soft, moist hand.

'Larry,' he said.

'You sure this is the right time to go, Nev?' asked DuBois.

Agry waited for some eye contact. He didn't get it. DuBois was seriously obese – like two-ninety-five obese – and had a habit of speaking to a point just above a listener's head, lowering his eyes to lock gazes only at the last moment.

'Wilson's in the hospital,' said Agry, 'and the jigs in B been on their knees sucking their own sweat for near on two weeks. We'll never get a better chance.' He paused. 'Why?'

DuBois shrugged his eyebrows. 'I just wanna be sure this isn't about', he finally brought his eyes down to meet Agry's, 'personalities.'

Agry felt a drench of ice water sluice through his gut. DuBois was oily, sensual and sly and kept two Puerto Rican wives in his cell on A block. It was whispered, but only whispered and never around DuBois, that he occasionally liked to take it in the ass from Cindy, the more lightly hung of his two wives, whilst Paula, the other, rubbed his cock and balls with stale chicken fat. This was treading close to faggotry – normally an unacceptable perversion – but Larry carried enough muscle to get away with it. In his day – before Agry came up – DuBois had been a much feared killer. Before that he'd struggled up from pimping to control millions of dollars' worth of vice and drug traffic between Juarez and El Paso. His battles with Agry were long past now, their peaceful co-existence being profitable to both parties, but Agry had often wondered if DuBois hadn't gotten soft under all that blubber. The meaning of the 'personalities' jibe was clear. It ignited a blue touchpaper in Agry's chest and he fought an urge to gut the fat fuck on the spot. He was obliged to confront the jibe and delicacy was required. Maybe at a later date he would have Cindy's bantamweight dick carved off and served to DuBois on a plate of fried chicken wings, but for now he needed him. With an effort Agry kept the rage inside and his voice amiable.

'You suggestin' I need help gettin' Claudine back?' said Agry.

DuBois looked away. 'I'm just thinking of the men, Nev. Some things are their business, some things aren't.'

Agry felt the pressure surge uncontrollably in his chest. The sulphate increased his sense of outrage. The fat scumbelly was saying – in front of Grauerholz and Terry – that he, Nev Agry, couldn't hold onto his own fucking wife. Agry glanced at Grauerholz, who was watching the exchange with glee in his eyes. Agry overcame the brain cells yelling for blood and tried again.

'We been through this before, Larry,' he said. 'The niggers are gettin' too proud. What are they now? Forty per cent the population? Fifty? We don't show them the iron fist, right now . . .' he paused dramatically, '. . . and in five years' time we'll be cleaning toilets and waxing floors with the beaners.'

'I have more dealings with them than you do,' said DuBois.

'They're good customers. Crystal, weed, crack, brown. You gotta understand their psychology. They never gonna get it together to run things. They never do. Look at D.C. Atlanta. Detroit. Bastards can't even run their own fucken cities. There was just ten white cons left in this joint, you know who'd be in charge?' DuBois tapped his chest with his thumb and shook his head. 'Not the coons, buddy. An' you know it.'

'We're prepared,' said Agry. 'We're ready.'

'Sorry, Neville.'

Agry's vision suddenly blurred. The only person ever allowed to use his full christian name was Claudine, and then only when preparing to go down on him. What's more DuBois had deliberately mispronounced it to rhyme with 'Lucille' as if it were some kind of a faggot name, as if he, Nev Agry, were some kind of a homosexualist. The rest of DuBois's words reached him as if from a great distance.

'Just can't see my way to backing you on this one,' said the fat man. 'It's not in my interests.'

Naked power play, then. No doubt planned for some time. The fat pimp was trying to make him look small, calculating that Agry wouldn't go for it without him. Something in Agry's face – something he wasn't aware of – made Grauerholz take one step backwards, and Dennis Terry two. DuBois held his ground, but a flicker appeared in his left eyelid. Agry leant towards him.

'You know your problem, Larry?' said Agry. He paused. 'Too much beaner jissom swillin' round your guts.'

'Careful, Nev,' said DuBois, but his face was suddenly a shade paler. He shifted his weight onto the balls of his feet.

Agry glanced at Grauerholz. 'Hec?'

The punk's face grew brighter than ever. He looked at DuBois then back to Agry. 'I say the niggers should go down. Where they belong.'

'Then fuck it,' said Agry, and he rammed his left-hand fingers into Larry DuBois's eyes.

Larry was quick but not as quick as he once had been in the brothels of Juarez. Agry's fingernails gouged through his eyelids. The move was meant to pop the eyeballs from their sockets but DuBois waltzed backwards with a dainty gait, knocking Agry's arm aside with his left hand while his right dipped under his shirt behind his back. Agry's razor was out and open. DuBois whipped out a snub-nosed revolver, scraped tears from his eyes, still moving away.

'Now, you fat cocksucker.'

With a lunge and slash of Shockner's razor Agry unzipped DuBois's belly from left hip to right.

Great sponges of yellow fat, bloody and obscene, bulged over DuBois's belt buckle. Buried deep beneath the fat the muscle layer held firm. DuBois roared and blundered sideways, trying to draw a bead with his gun while his left hand clutched the gaping blubber at his waist.

Agry stepped in to the fat man's left and kicked his legs from under him.

With a loud bleat of panic DuBois crashed onto his face, trapping his left arm beneath him. In the same split second Agry pinned Larry's gun arm to the floor with his left hand and dropped his knee full weight onto Larry's greasy skull. He reached over and sliced through the crook of DuBois's right elbow, severing the tendons that controlled the gun arm and piercing the brachial artery. DuBois bellowed and writhed, bucking his shoulder against the ground to free his head. Agry piled more weight through his knee. With a rooting, trowelling motion he shoved the razor into the shiny jowls under the angle of DuBois's jaw. Blood started to spray from DuBois's lips and nostrils with each shout and the bucking of his body became more frantic. His head started to skid on the blood. Agry dug the razor in deeper, almost up to the handle, searching for the carotid buried in that bloated neck. As DuBois's head slipped free and he started to roll away, Agry's blade finally found what it was looking for.

Agry stepped back out of the way.

Grauerholz gasped. 'Awesome.'

Dennis Terry vomited into a laundry trolley.

Agry grabbed an armload of towels and dumped them over the red cascade spilling out of DuBois's upper body. The fat fuck had had it coming a long time. Agry felt superbly calm, the internal pressure released. He wiped his hands and the razor on one of the towels. His shirt was drenched with blood. He started to unbutton it and walked to the shelves for a clean one. He stopped, bent down and picked up DuBois's gun. A Smith and Wesson .38 Special. Agry hefted the gun thoughtfully. They had to keep DuBois's death from the hacks until at least the next lock and count. He glanced at the diving watch on his wrist: two hours. He turned.

'Hec,' said Agry.

Grauerholz was buzzing, staring down at DuBois's monstrous, towel-covered corpse as if it were a piece of art. He looked up at Agry. Agry tossed him the revolver.

'Let's pitch some Wang Dang Doodle.'

Grauerholz caught the piece and stared down at the blue metal with astonishment. Santa Claus had never brought him anything so sweet. He clasped the gun to his chest and stared at Agry with such grateful adulation that Agry knew he was home. At that moment he could've asked Grauerholz to shoot off one of his own testicles and Grauerholz would've have asked him, Left or right?

'Whadda we do now, Mr Agry?' said Grauerholz.

Agry took a deep breath. The sense of power was intense, intoxicating. It was a moment to take his time with. He looked from Grauerholz to Terry. Terry was grey at the gills and his eyes were haunted with dread. Agry turned back to Grauerholz.

'We gotta lot of work to do before the third count. Your

guys're gonna take the mess hall from the builder's yard while Johnson and his half of B block are chowing down. We'll need a diversion.'

Grauerholz's eyes wobbled with excitement. 'Right,' he said. 'A diversion. You got it.'

'We got gasoline in the machine shop and the garage. My people will take care of that end.' Agry turned to Terry. 'Dennis, you and Tony Shockner are going to fix the watch command centre. I want it cut off from the main gate. You helped put that shit in. You can take it out again.'

Terry's complexion turned even paler. He tried to speak, failed, swallowed and tried again.

'So you're gonna . . . I mean this isn't just a . . .'

'That's right, Dennis,' said Agry. 'This is war. Rolling Thunder. Desert Storm. The Blitzkrieg. Call it what the fuck you want. The niggers are going down and so is anyone stands in our way.'

Terry couldn't hold his eyes for more than a second. Agry nodded towards DuBois's fat carcass and looked at Grauerholz.

'Get your boys to clean this up.'

'Sure thing, Mr Agry,' said Grauerholz.

Grauerholz started off down the aisle with a bouncing, skipping gait. Agry called after him.

'Then go get Ted Spriggs,' he said. 'Tell him the niggers've just killed Larry DuBois . . .'

Agry's lip curled with righteous outrage. He raised a clenched fist.

'. . . And that we are going to make those fuckers pay!'

SEVEN

BEHIND HER BACK the great twin iron-studded doors swung shut and Juliette Devlin was stranded in a no man's land between discipline and freedom. This no man's land she would carry with her, as she always did, into the teeming chaos of the prison. But for now, for a few moments, Devlin was alone.

The lights in the tunnel roof were bare fluorescence, harsh on her eyes. In front of her stood a blank steel door big enough when open to allow a fire truck through and heavy enough when closed to resist a rocket-propelled grenade. On the other side of the door she knew someone watched her on a closed circuit TV screen. The watcher would be a man and she knew that when she went inside she would be watched by many men more. No experience in her life had made her more acutely aware of her gender, her otherness. For she was a woman and this was a world of utter maleness. More than that, it contained individuals who endured and inflicted – and who had endured and had inflicted – suffering beyond measure. On one level at least that's what had brought her here. She had set herself the task of trying to measure some small portion of that suffering without measure and thereby understand the hearts of men.

As Devlin waited for the steel door to open she experienced a feeling somewhere between anxiety and excitement that she hadn't yet analysed to her satisfaction. The feeling was bound up with transgression, with doing something she wasn't meant to do in a place she wasn't meant to be. The excitement arose from the forbidden and therefore from guilt and dread. The Penitentiary was a monument to guilt and dread: it provoked those feelings in the same way that a gothic cathedral provoked a sense of the divine. But for Devlin there was more to it than that. There was always somewhere in her mind the phantom of her father, Michael Devlin; and in the prison itself there was Ray Klein.

Her father, retired now to a small ranch outside Santa Fe, had been governor of a federal prison in New Mexico and so Devlin had grown up in the emotional shadow of just such a place as this one. Her father had been a Johnson Democrat, a vigorous opponent of the death penalty, and a man ultimately exhausted by the failure of the Great Society to halt its own slide into polarisation and chaos. At the time of his retirement the Bureau had officially abandoned the concept of rehabilitation and his prison had boasted a recidivism rate of ninety-two per cent, a failure that Michael Devlin had taken for his own. As a parent he'd been officially liberal but actually selfish and demanding; no achievement by his children was ever quite great enough to earn his praise. Certainly if he was proud of Juliette, he had concealed it from her with some success. As an added bonus he was an Irish Catholic with a colossal appetite for Jameson's whiskey. But he never got mean drunk or raised his hand to any of them and so if he was a bastard, and sometimes a hypocrite, it didn't matter and she loved him anyway.

Devlin sometimes asked herself if that was all she was about: an attempt to vindicate her father. She rejected the idea. It was hard enough to vindicate her own life, and anyhow her father thought she was crazy. Perhaps, then, it was an attempt to punish him. Michael Devlin had never spoken to her about his prison and in her mind it had assumed the mystery and fascination of the dark forest in a fairy tale. Only there could certain truths be encountered and only then at tremendous risk. Her father thought she should be researching pre-menstrual tension, or depression in single parent mothers, or some other such namby-pamby bullshit. So did some of her PC friends. They didn't really understand why she should want to spend her time with killers and rapists. On some level maybe her work was a big Fuck You to all of them. Who were they to be disappointed in her? Whatever the reasons, Devlin was there: standing under the harsh fluorescence of the lights as she waited to enter the dark forest that was Green River State.

Devlin – she preferred 'Devlin' to 'Juliette' – had studied psychology and medicine at Tulane. Her IQ had been high enough to allow her to take enough drugs to fill the Superdome and fuck the brains out of a motley collection of longshoremen and Crescent City desperadoes without flunking any of her exams. It was also in New Orleans that she'd picked up a taste for gambling and found she was good at it. A psychiatry residency had cooled her down a little, but the sensible career path – into something warm and fuzzy and lucrative, like one of the psychotherapies – hadn't appealed to her. It irritated her that, just as in the movies, the guys got all the best parts – got to blow away the bad guys and drive a semi filled with nitro through a road block – whilst the girls had to hang around the edges of the action being nurturing and empathetic. When forensic psychiatry had presented itself as the toughest game in town Devlin had taken a seat at the table. The intellectual level of her colleagues, in her opinion, was generally feeble. Her research in Green River was unique in the literature and several noted figures in the field had told her it did not fall short of brilliance. Devlin felt she was about to make her mark.

In the tunnel there arose the grinding of gears and the creak of bearings and Devlin cleared her mind. In front of her the steel door jolted from its moorings and rolled open.

On the other side Devlin was glad to see Sergeant Victor Galindez waiting to take her in. Like the servants of any institution the guards at Green River regarded a privileged outsider like Devlin with fear and suspicion, but Galindez was more courteous than most. He greeted her and took her through to reception where she deposited her keys and pocketbook. She signed the visitor's book and a liability waiver. Galindez checked her briefcase then took her through the second studded gate and out into the yard.

Devlin wore a white cotton shirt, buttoned to the neck, faded black Levis and cowboy boots. Under the jeans, as was her habit, she wore a G string. Under the shirt she wore an athletic bra that she otherwise used only when working out. The bra stopped her tits jiggling about and her nipples from showing through the shirt. She wasn't afraid of provoking an assault but she did want to spare the prisoners who stared at her the pain of seeing too much flesh. Maybe they would've preferred to see more of her legs and tits, even if it was painful, but she didn't know. Anxiety about appearing vain had prevented her from asking Klein's opinion on this. She didn't even know if Klein himself would like to see more of her. Somehow he'd imposed a distance between them that she hadn't been able to bridge. Devlin didn't consider herself particularly attractive. She looked okay, she guessed, but nothing special. She was tall, five-ten, and slim but she felt that her hands and feet were too big and her face too boyish to be feminine. Her hair was thick and black and these days she wore it cut short at the back and sides. She used to wish that she had bigger tits and a smaller ass, but now that she'd become an official serious person she felt that she should leave such worries behind her, and by and large she had done. Yet she still wore her G string under her jeans to make her feel good and she occasionally wondered what Ray Klein would make of that if he were ever to put his hand on her ass. To date he had not done so and in a work situation she was sure he never would, but in the right time and place Devlin would've liked him to.

In fact she'd told her friend, Catrin, that she wanted to suck Klein's cock, and have him fuck her from behind on the deck of a shrimp boat on the Gulf during a thunder storm while she reached back between her legs and stroked his balls. Catrin's reaction had made Devlin wonder of herself if she really was as fucked up as she sometimes felt herself to be. Or maybe she just wasn't as sexually confused as most of her peers. Catrin, who had picked up too many of her opinions second hand from glossy magazines, had told her she demeaned herself with such fantasies and that she really needed a man who was in touch with his inner feminine. That is, someone who would lie in bed next to you with a hard-on and smile understandingly and go do some yoga or something when you told him you didn't want to fuck him tonight. Devlin hated all that bullshit. Speaking for herself, being a woman, there wasn't anything about her, much less in her, that was masculine. If she was occasionally ambitious and decisive it was her, not some inner man. If she was at other times vulnerable and needy that was her too. It was all her and she didn't see why it should be any different for a guy. She wanted someone who acted like a man and expressed himself like a man, who when he was compassionate and vulnerable did it in his own male way, as men always had done. And she wanted him to have a man's sensibilities and desires, like wanting to fuck her on a shrimp boat while she stroked his balls. Sounded good to her. Maybe too many guys had been reading the same magazines as Catrin. It was a painful thought but most decent men she knew of her own age preferred jerking off to the tedium of negotiating their sexual relations with women. Maybe she was just moving in the wrong circles. One circle she knew that wasn't wrong, even if it was a circle of Hell, was the hospital here at Green River, where she'd got to know Klein.

In some senses she knew Klein deeply from watching him work. In others she didn't know him at all. She knew little of his past except that he came from New Jersey and had trained in New York City. Before coming up he'd been an orthopaedic surgeon in a public hospital in Galveston. It was strange to know someone purely as you found them, without re-inventing them from a patchwork of dead facts about their life. In some ways it was scarey. She didn't know what crime Klein had committed to get himself sent up to Green River. She'd once asked Coley and Coley had looked at her darkly and said that wasn't a question folk put to each other in here. You could be told, but you didn't ask. She was pretty sure Klein would have told her if she had asked, but Devlin didn't want to be seen as some asshole outsider who didn't respect the rules of this dark world and so she hadn't. Alternatively she could've found out from Hobbes or one of the guards but that would've seemed like a betrayal of trust.

Galindez led her out from the gate of the reception centre which opened onto the yard. Beyond the yard and its mesh fences stood the main prison complex: six great cellblocks radiating from a domed central tower. The groping arms of the cellblocks were always quietly chilling and for a moment she imagined them reaching right across the surface of the globe until they met again on the other side of the planet in an identical domed plexus. Then all the prisoners of the earth could have roamed its walkways forever without ever knowing where they were. Perhaps, she thought, that was all any of them were doing anyway, herself included. She and Galindez turned left and walked along the concrete path that ran around beneath the sheer perimeter wall.

Each section of the hexagonal wall was a quarter of a mile long and topped with multiple banked coils of razor wire. Devlin felt the eyes of the riflemen watching them from their towers. The two sections of the wall that met at the main gate were of bare stones, unencumbered by any other buildings. Under the shadow of the other four wall sections crouched the workshops, the visiting hall, and the segregation block for punishments and special category prisoners. Nearest the main gate as they turned west was the infirmary. At this hour the exercise yards were empty. The noise of a band saw drifted from the carpentry shop. In the shade of the perimeter wall it was cool but Devlin could see the sun turning the roof of the prison into burnished plates of gold, welded together by the black iron girders. Under the glass it would not be so cool. She noticed Galindez looking at her and nodded towards the roof.

'Why did they build it with so much glass?' she said.

Galindez's cheeks were gaunt and badly scarred by childhood smallpox. He wore a heavy moustache. In repose his face was quiet, sombre, almost sad. Now he smiled.

'The warden says it's so that God can look down from his heaven upon the prisoners. Myself I don't think he bothers.'

He lapsed into silence and his face turned sombre again. Devlin was glad to reach the entrance to the infirmary. They stopped and Devlin turned to thank Galindez.

'This is a bad place for a woman to work,' said Galindez.

Devlin didn't answer. If she'd argued with this kind of shit every time it came up it would've been a full-time job. Galindez must have seen it in her face because he added, 'For a man too, I guess.'

'Then why are you here?' she said.

Galindez smiled and she suddenly felt naive.

'The pay's good. Very good for a Latino immigrant.'

'Where was your original home?'

'Salvador.'

'You still have family there?'

'Only in the graveyard,' said Galindez. 'I was in prison there too, on the wrong side of the wire.'

Devlin flushed with the embarrassment of the white liberal. She was irritated with herself. Galindez had been through what he'd been through. If he could deal with her questions she could deal with his answers. 'What for?'

He shrugged. 'For praying in the wrong church, reading the wrong newspaper, having the wrong friends. The usual reasons.'

Devlin wanted to look away but didn't.

He went on. 'At first it was hard in this country. Of course I would like to teach school again, but it's not possible. At least since I work here my wife doesn't have to scrub any more floors.'

Devlin nodded. She couldn't think of anything to say that wouldn't sound phoney and irrelevant. Galindez touched his cap.

'When you need an escort back to the gate, ring the reception and ask for me.'

'Thanks.'

Devlin watched him walk away for a moment, then she turned and went into the infirmary. Despite her years in hospitals the smell, as always, gave her a second of nausea: disinfectant with a strong undertow of poisoned human effluent and death. By the time she'd passed Sung and made her way to the sick bay office the smell had faded into the background of her awareness. She set her briefcase on the cluttered table. Frog Coley wasn't to be seen and she wasn't sorry. She had mixed feelings about Coley and as far as she could tell, he about her. He had a cruel tongue. Yet he also had a gravity, a moral power rooted in the pain he had embraced as his due portion. She would never possess such power. Her portion, in comparison, had been purchased cheap and she had some idea why someone like her might arouse the resentment of someone like Coley. Maybe he also felt threatened by the professional background she shared with Klein, though no more than she felt excluded by his closeness to Klein. The two men shared a strange kind of reciprocal mentor deal. Whatever, she felt that Coley had never given her her due. Maybe today she would get that due. In her bag she had the first fruits of their work together in the infirmary: a paper based on their research published in the *American Journal of Psychiatry*.

Devlin's research had evolved from a question that had haunted her for years: Is the tragedy of death, and therefore of life, an absolute right of all men and women? Or is the tragic a commodity doled out according to an unexamined set of social criteria? It was clear that in a worldly sense the latter was the case. If she herself were to die tomorrow in a car wreck the tragedy would ring clear: brilliant young psychiatrist cut down in the prime of her . . . et cetera, et cetera. But if Coley were to break his neck falling down the infirmary steps the world would little notice and would care even less. These values, it seemed to Devlin, were everywhere inscribed: in the law; in medicine; in the slaughter of war; in the indifference of governments; even in bumper stickers exhorting the salvation of the whales. Why not squid or hyenas? This arbitrary allocation of value galled her for in the end it trapped her along with the rest on a ladder without a top up which, as high as she was, she could continue to haul herself forever. Or at least until age and decay, white hair and sagging breasts, began to snap the rotten rungs beneath her feet.

Comforting then – no, exhilarating – was the utter indifference of the universe that contained this flyspecked world. In her mind were inscribed these words from Kant's *Critique of Judgement*:

Deceit, envy and violence will always be rife around him, though he himself is honest, peaceable and kind; and the other righteous men he meets in the world, no matter how deserving they may be of happiness, will be subjected by nature, which takes no heed of such deserts, to all the evils of want, disease and untimely death as are all the other animals of the earth. And so it will continue to be until one wide grave engulfs them all – just and unjust, there is no distinction in the grave – and hurls them back into the abyss of the aimless chaos from which they were taken – they that were able to believe themselves the final end of creation.

Devlin thought: we that are able to believe ourselves the final end of creation.

And this brought her back to the focus of her research: the individual locked in the cell of personality. Was the same value system inscribed within each of us and did we judge ourselves in front of ourselves by that same ruthless and arbitrary calibration? Devlin was attempting an answer.

Her idea had been to assess psychological function in two different populations of hospital in-patients diagnosed as having Aids. The first study group was in the University Medical Centre in Houston. The second was in the infirmary at Green River State. Devlin had chosen two standard questionnaires designed to evaluate mental health with a particular emphasis on depression. She had designed a third of her own, tentatively called the Existential Trauma Inventory. These were administered to both study groups. Patients suffering non-fatal illnesses in both hospitals provided control groups for comparison. Both groups of Aids sufferers were doomed to die. But who coped best? And how? And why?

The civilian cases of Aids at Houston received a high level of medical care and psychological support but were faced with losing a life that in conventional terms was 'good': free, affluent, full of hope and promise. By contrast the treatment the prisoners received was disgraceful; yet they appeared to have less to lose. The outer world placed a minimum value on their lives and cared only that they died as quietly and cheaply as possible. The key question was: was this so for the men themselves? Was losing a 'good' life more traumatic to the dying man than losing a life which was desperate and squalid? Which lives were more precious to their owners? Which deaths more tragic? Was it easier for the wretched of the earth to die in the River than it was for the free men in the high tech unit at Houston? Devlin wanted to take science to that boundary where it crossed over into philosophy. Was it possible to formulate, and answer, these questions in a way that was scientifically valid?

'One thing's for sure,' Klein had once said during one of their discussions.

'What's that?' she'd asked him.

Klein had walked to the door of the office and stared for a moment down the corridor to the ward. 'No one's stitching any quilts for these guys.'

Devlin had said, 'What about us, Klein?'

Klein had grunted, said, 'I'm just doin' my time the easiest way I can.'

She hadn't believed him. She believed that the work mattered as much to him as it did to her. More so. Much more. But Klein insisted on his cynical façade and the more she tried to penetrate it the more he insisted that that was all he was about.

Devlin's thoughts were interrupted by the door opening. Coley stuck his head in and regarded her with baleful yellow eyes.

'Hi, Coley,' said Devlin.

Coley gave her a ponderous nod. 'Doctah Devlin. We wasn't expecting you today.'

'I know. I wanted to surprise you.'

'Well, shit,' said Coley. 'I's all surprised to Hell.'

Devlin never knew whether she should be irritated or amused by the Uncle Tom act Coley put on for her, his Doctor this and Doctor that when he knew she wanted him to call her by her name. Now she wanted to smile. Instead she said, 'Fuck you, Coley.'

'Yessum, Doctah.'

'How are the men?' she asked.

'In status quo,' he said. 'That is, half of 'em are dying and the other half ain't.'

'And where's Klein?' she said.

'He over to see the warden,' said Coley. 'Dunno when he be back.'

'Why's he seeing Hobbes?'

'To find out if the board have approved his parole.'

'He had a parole hearing?'

Devlin tried to sound cool but inside, to her surprise, she was hurt that Klein hadn't told her. In fact she was furious. It was absurd. Coley watched her with the hooded yellow eyes that always made her feel like the alien she was. He nodded.

'Yeah. Last week.' He paused, studied her. He asked, 'You think you had a right to know 'bout it, huh?'

Devlin shrugged it off and turned away. 'It would've been nice to root for him, but it's not really any of my business.'

Coley shook his head. 'Didn't tell me either till after he'd seen 'em, and as well he didn't. I'd've known 'bout it I would've fucked him up for sure.'

Devlin turned back and stared at him. 'You'd have stopped him getting paroled?'

'I'd sure as Hell've tried.'

'I don't believe you.'

Coley held her gaze. 'You think I want to run this place on my lonesome? You think I can? Do you wanna come and help me when he's gone?'

'I don't believe you'd do that to him.'

'You still don't see the way of things in here, do you, Doctah Devlin? All your questionnaires and fancy bullshit. You don't see a goddamn thing. You think all this is real, realer than anything you know, hard core real. But you wrong. It's a game. Ain't no reality here at all. You live in the reality you die. You join the game you got a chance. And your man he's learned to play it good. You try to play it with him, he'll take you down. You claim to be a gamblin' lady. You should understand.'

'But I don't understand,' said Devlin.

'I seen the way you look at him,' said Coley.

Devlin squirmed inside. Suddenly her skull felt transparent, as if Coley could see all the secret pictures in her head. It was all she could do to hold Coley's gaze.

Coley said, 'In here the only duty a man has is to his self. Don't be looking for something that ain't his to give.'

Devlin nodded. She felt foolish, inarticulate. Coley was right. She swallowed. 'Will he get paroled?'

Coley blinked slowly, nodded. 'Pea Vine Special callin' all aboard. Like I say, he's a player.'

'Is that all?' said Devlin. 'I mean, what about all this?'

Coley looked at her, puzzled. 'All what, Doctah?'

'The work he's done for the men, with you.'

'You think Klein rather be workin' a drill press? Makin' belt buckles? This just another play in the game.'

'I don't believe that.' She felt a waver in her voice.

Coley shrugged. 'You believe what you have to, same as the rest of us.' He turned towards the door. 'You wanna wait here for him, he be back soon.'

'Coley?'

Coley stuck his head back inside the room.

'I've got something to show you later. It's important,' she said.

Coley arched one eyebrow. 'Call me when you need me. I ain't going nowhere.' He paused. 'I'll tell you somethin' though, case you don't already know.'

'What's that?'

'Your boy Klein look real pretty when he's shucked down.'

Devlin couldn't tell if she was blushing or not. 'What?'

'Without his shirt on,' said Coley. 'Big pecker, too, fo' a white boy. But he won't let Ole Frogman get close. Maybe you can offer a little somethin' extra I ain't got.'

This time she felt her face burning. Coley snorted with lewd laughter.

'Fuck you, Coley,' said Devlin.

Coley grinned. 'Don't pay me no nevermind, Doctah Devlin.'

Against her will Devlin found herself grinning back.

'Good luck in the game tonight,' said Coley.

Devlin had a bet riding on the Lakers to beat the Knicks by six points. As far as she could tell gambling was the only thing about her that Coley respected. 'Yeah,' she said. 'Thanks.'

Coley disappeared and the door closed behind him. Devlin sat down on the edge of the table. What Coley had told her sank in: Ray Klein might soon be released. Her guts tightened. Beneath the mountain of intellect and abstraction stuffed inside her head she knew her guts didn't lie. The possibility of Klein's freedom bore down on her, and with it all that Coley had said about the reality and the game. Klein free was a different reality. Wanting him – and the ache inside her told her she did – was a different game, and one at which Devlin felt less than expert. Devlin opened her briefcase and took out a pack of Winston Lights. She lit up, inhaled, and felt a little better as her nicotine levels rose. There was no sense in bullshitting herself. She didn't want Klein to vanish from her life. The question was: how to keep him there? She had one or two ideas about that one. But there was another question too: why the fuck would Klein be interested in someone like her? Devlin took another drag on her Winston. That was a question to which she didn't yet have an answer, but she was going to try to find out.

EIGHT

Ray Klein sat on a wooden bench on the ground floor of the admin tower and wondered if the big black patches of sweat on his denim shirt would piss off the warden. He'd sprinted the four hundred metres from the infirmary to get here on time and of course he'd been sitting now for twenty minutes with the sweat from the run fucking up his shirt. Maybe Hobbes would figure he was sweating from nervous tension. That would be bad. If Klein read Hobbes correctly the warden didn't like grovellers. Well, fuck him. It was out of Klein's hands anyway. A line from an old song ran unbidden through his head.

> When I was just a little boy,
> I asked my mother, 'What will I be?
> Will I be handsome? Will I be rich?'
> Here's what she said to me . . .

Klein found himself shaking inwardly with silent laughter. The voice in his head belonged to Doris Day. It was perfection. He was sitting in the asshole of creation listening to a thirty-year-old Doris Day record stored from God knew where inside his skull. Will I be handsome? Will I be rich? He heard

Doris take in a great breath and belt out: 'Que Sera Sera! Whatever will be will be!' For its day pretty subversive stuff, some kind of neo-stoicism maybe. Or even neo-Marxism. He wondered how many guys in their time had jerked off whilst thinking about Doris Day. Millions, probably. Klein considered trying it for himself sometime. His sexual fantasy life needed a new angle. Doris Day. Klein was mildly shocked to find himself developing a hard-on.

'What the fuck's so funny, Klein?'

With a jolt Klein straightened his face and looked up. Captain Cletus, lugubrious as ever, stood in the waiting-room doorway. At this late date Klein's self-esteem did not depend on his daring to piss off Cletus. Because Cletus was widely feared and hated he was an understandably, if excessively, paranoid character. He tended to interpret any laughter as being at his expense. Benson from A had once spent a week in seg for using the phrase '. . . as wide as the crack in Cletus's ass'. Klein could think of no better way of reassuring the Captain than to explain the true cause of his mirth. He stood up to attention.

'I was thinking about Doris Day, Captain sir,' said Klein.

Cletus walked over and stared at Klein from a distance of six inches for what seemed like a long time.

Finally, Cletus said, 'Doris Day?'

'Yes, sir,' said Klein.

Cletus continued his stare.

'I was thinking, "Whatever will be will be", sir,' said Klein. 'You know, que sera sera.'

'Que sera sera,' said Cletus.

'Yes, sir. Whatever will be will be, you know.'

'You are too smart a son of a bitch for your own good, aren't you, Klein?'

'I hope I am not, sir,' said Klein.

For the first time in three years Klein watched a smile appear on Cletus's face.

'You're waiting to see the Warden.'

'Yes, sir.'

Cletus stared at him for another lengthy moment.

'Come with me,' said Cletus.

Klein, sweating harder than ever, followed Cletus up the stairs of the tower. As he watched the Captain's huge ass mounting the steps ahead of him Klein cursed himself for letting his control slip and Doris Day for infiltrating her voice so stealthily into his unconscious. At the top of the fourth set of steps Cletus stopped at one end of a short wood-panelled corridor. At the other end was the door to Hobbes's office. Cletus turned to Klein.

'Sing,' said Cletus.

Klein looked from Cletus to the door of Hobbes's office and back again. He swallowed. 'Sir?'

'Que sera sera,' said Cletus. 'Sing it.'

'I don't remember the words,' said Klein.

'I don't know what the parole board has decided to do with your sorry ass,' said Cletus, 'but until you walk out them gates it's still mine. I put you on punishment, like, right now, the board will have to reconsider its decision.'

You cocksucker, thought Klein. He did not look at Cletus for fear of the thought showing in his eyes. He coughed.

'Listen,' said Klein, 'if I gave the impression of being a smart son of a bitch, it was not my intention to do so and I apologise to the Captain unreservedly and without let or hindrance.'

'Sing,' said Cletus.

This time Klein let him have the cocksucker stare. Again, Cletus smiled. Klein wondered if Cletus had smiled that way when he was working Wilson over in seg. He took a deep breath.

'Loud,' said Cletus. 'So I can hear you all the way to the bottom of the stairs.'

Klein let the breath out. 'I've got to admit,' he said, 'I didn't think you had the imagination.'

Cletus put his lips close to Klein's ear. 'When I was a kid I used to jerk off watching Doris Day movies.'

Klein looked at him. 'You're right,' said Klein. 'I'm too smart a son of a bitch for my own good.'

Cletus nodded. 'I still wanna hear that song.'

Then fuck you, thought Klein, and launched straight into it.

'When I was just a little boy,

'I asked my mother, What will I be?'

As Cletus disappeared, laughing, down the stairs, Klein continued singing.

'Will I be handsome? Will I be rich?

'Here's what she said to me . . .'

In the small corridor his voice echoed hugely. Damned, too, if it didn't sound half bad. Klein inhaled deeply and gave the chorus his best shot.

'*Que sera sera!*

'*Whatever will be will be . . .*'

As Klein took in another deep gulp of air the door of Hobbes's office erupted open. Klein's mouth snapped shut. Hobbes stared at him from the doorway: massive balding cranium, febrile eyes under heavy brows. If Klein had ever felt more of an asshole he couldn't remember when. An excruciating silence seemed like his only option.

'Klein?'

Klein's lungs were overfilled and he felt unable to blurt out all the air. His voice came out in a hoarse whisper. 'Yes, sir.' He held onto the rest of the air.

Hobbes considered him with mild astonishment, as if Klein's bizarre performance had just barely penetrated his consciousness and distracted him briefly from matters of more profound import. In his few dealings with him Klein had found the warden an enigma. Something in his bearing, his distance, his speech patterns, gave Hobbes a quality of not being of this world, as if he'd been catapulted into the present from some other time long past. Like the prison itself: designed for the nineteenth century, now floundering in the last days of the twentieth. In all modesty, or maybe in all stupidity, Klein rarely found himself in the presence of an intelligence he felt to be larger, deeper, more impenetrable than his own. Hobbes evoked such a sense; a sense of the unfathomable. If, now, Hobbes could not fathom Klein, it did not seem to perturb him overmuch.

Hobbes said, 'Get in here.' He disappeared from view.

Klein let out the breath that was threatening to pop the blood vessels in his face. He hauled his dignity back together and strode down the corridor into the office.

The office spanned the width of the tower on a north-south axis and was ascetically furnished: a bookcase, an old oak desk covered by a sheet of glass, three chairs. A fan with wooden blades turned in the ceiling above the desk. On the wall was a Ph.D. certificate from Cornell. Directly facing the door on a wooden plinth was a bronze bust of Jeremy Bentham. Juliette Devlin had told Klein that the bust was of Bentham, otherwise he would have taken him for a Confederate general or something. Except that Hobbes, like Klein, was a Yankee. Klein closed the door behind him and stood to attention, staring at the glazed bronze orbs of Bentham's eyes. At that moment he imagined that his own eyes looked somewhat similar.

Hobbes's voice boomed across the room: 'The last mind of any real stature to devote itself to the problem of incarceration.'

Klein felt a fleeting vertigo. What was Hobbes talking about? Surely not Doris Day. Klein looked at him and said, 'Excuse me, sir?'

Hobbes inclined his head towards the bronze bust. 'Bentham.'

'Yes, sir.' Klein's wits suddenly fell back into place. He performed a rapid calculation and added. 'Panopticism.'

Hobbes's thick brows rose half an inch. 'You surprise me. Come and sit down.'

Hobbes indicated the chair facing him and Klein walked over. Under the sheet of glass on the desk was an old architectural blueprint, in plan, of the prison and its walls. The south window at Hobbes's back threw his face into shadow. No doubt the effect was deliberate. As Klein sat down he saw a green cardboard folder on the desk with his own name and number printed on the front.

'So what does the concept of panopticism mean to you?' said Hobbes.

Klein looked up from the folder that contained his fate. He felt nineteen years old again, trying to remember the course of the phrenic nerve for the anatomy professor. 'Bentham was preoccupied with the idea that if you watched someone all the time, or at least got them to believe that they were being watched all the time, it would change their personality for the better. Force them to re-examine their souls. Something like that.'

'Something like that,' said Hobbes. 'What do you think of this theory?'

'I guess it depends who's doing the watching and who's being watched,' said Klein.

Hobbes nodded. 'How true.' He seemed pleased. 'Not all men are able to profit from the scrutiny of the panoptic machine. They cannot endure its light. Even less can they endure the light of self-knowledge.'

'Forcing people towards self-knowledge can be a dangerous business,' said Klein.

'How so?' asked Hobbes.

Klein didn't want to provoke Hobbes. Neither did he want to appear to be kissing his ass, if only because Hobbes wasn't the type to appreciate it, but what the hell. His fate was already decided. If Hobbes could tolerate Doris Day he wasn't going to be blown away by a little Plato.

'You remember the subterranean cavern in Plato's *Republic*? The dream of Socrates?'

Hobbes leaned forward. 'The Seventh Book,' said Hobbes. His brow was smoothed taut with excitement.

He seemed to be holding his breath. 'Make your point.'

Klein swallowed. 'In the cavern men are chained, buried far away from the light of the sun. Their heads are fixed to stop them from seeing anything but their own shadows cast upon the wall by the flames of a fire. When challenged the chained men violently defend their own dark ignorance. And Socrates asks: if they could seize hold of the man who tried to liberate them and lead them up into the light, would they not then kill him?'

Hobbes let out his breath, almost in a sigh. 'Would you kill him?' he said.

Klein looked at Hobbes for a long time. 'I don't know,' he said. 'You look at the sun for too long you go blind.'

'And yet no one saw farther than the blind seer Tiresias. There are some truths that can only be known in darkness.'

'Yes, sir. Maybe that's the problem with your panoptic machine.'

Hobbes raised an eyebrow. 'My machine?'

Klein didn't answer.

'You're a brave man, Klein.'

'I just want to get out of here and go back to watching the shadows on the wall.'

'A man like you must have learned something of himself in here.'

'A man like me?' said Klein. He shrugged. 'Maybe that's

why the shadows out there look so good. You can make believe they're something that they're not.'

Hobbes wasn't going to let him off so easily. 'And what would you make believe of yourself that you are not?' said Hobbes.

Fuck, thought Klein. 'I don't want to mislead you, sir. I'm just another convict waiting for the prison gates to open.'

'You're avoiding my question.'

'Even the bravest of us', said Klein, 'rarely has the courage for what he really knows.'

Hobbes's eyes wobbled in their sockets. For a second Klein thought he was going to walk around the desk and embrace him.

'*Virescit vulnere virtus*,' said Hobbes.

'My Latin isn't that good,' said Klein.

'I believe it translates as "Strength is restored by wounding",' said Hobbes.

Klein thought about his own wounds, the wounds of love, the false rape charge that had brought him to this office. Was he strengthened or merely more calloused, more cynical?

'Only if you're already strong enough,' said Klein.

Hobbes nodded gravely. 'Maybe so, maybe so. And yet the risk must be taken if the spirit is to grow.'

'I guess so,' said Klein. 'The question is, which risk, which wound?'

'Do you think we have a choice?' asked Hobbes.

In Hobbes's face was a yearning, a desperation that took Klein aback. He'd come here for five minutes' routine prison bullshit. Either another year inside to further rehabilitate himself or a paternal pat on the back and a firm handshake to send him on his way. Instead Hobbes's eyes were black pools swimming with a nameless inner horror that reminded Klein of madness.

'Again,' said Klein, 'only sometimes.'

'Even the man before the firing squad has a choice,' said Hobbes. 'He can fall whimpering to his knees or he can refuse the blindfold and sing.'

Hobbes sounded like just such a man. Klein felt powerfully drawn to explore Hobbes's state of mind, like a Marlow to his Kurtz. He cursed himself for going too far. There was something hypnotic about Hobbes. But Klein was here as a convict hoping for parole. The convict warned him to back off.

'Yes, sir,' said Klein, 'You're absolutely right.'

Hobbes sensed the retreat. He blinked twice and sat back in his chair. He seemed shaken. He put his hand in his pocket and clutched at something, Klein didn't know what. As if retracing his steps back to safety Hobbes nodded towards the bronze bust behind Klein and said, 'How do you know so much about Bentham?'

Klein considered pretending that he was a life-long student of Bentham's philosophy. Too dangerous. After all his decades in the system Hobbes could smell a liar from the other side of the yard.

'From Dr Devlin,' said Klein. 'As you know she's a forensic psychiatrist.'

'Most forensic psychiatrists don't know the difference between Jeremy Bentham and Jack Benny.'

Klein didn't smile. 'Dr Devlin does, sir.'

Hobbes nodded, calm again. 'An unusual woman. Your work together has been fruitful?'

'She's submitted a paper to the *American Journal of Psychiatry*.'

'Have they accepted?'

'Dr Devlin hasn't said so yet.'

Hobbes grunted. 'You know that when Bentham died he had his body stuffed and placed in a glass case. In London. I believe it's still there.'

'Yes sir,' said Klein. 'Now everyone can see him too. Forever.'

Hobbes's eyes widened again and the look returned, the look that dropped a slab of anxiety in Klein's gut. The look had a voice which said, 'Understand me. Be close to me. Don't leave me alone in here.' Klein recognised the voice for he had heard its call many times: from patients, women, fellow prisoners; the needy of every kind. From the ex-lover who'd condemned him to all this. 'Give me more than you've got to give,' they said. And inside his guts a voice of Klein's own called out to him too: 'Get me the fuck out of here, man.' Coley's motto came to comfort him: NOT MY FUCKING BUSINESS.

'Excellent,' said Hobbes. 'Excellent. The irony of Bentham the panopticist's bequest has never struck me before. I'm grateful for the insight.'

'Again I'm indebted to Dr Devlin for that.'

This wasn't true; it had sprung unbidden into Klein's mind. But as Cletus said, he was too smart a son of a bitch for his own good and he had to push Hobbes away. He had to escape these tentacles of connection reaching out towards him. He already had too many sucking on his blood, draining him. He always had. Patients, women, the needy of every kind. His ex-lover. And now Hobbes. Or was he, Ray Klein, also getting too paranoid? Hobbes suddenly pulled his hand out from his pocket and placed a pill bottle on the table in front of Klein.

'My own doctor tells me I should take these three times a day. I consider him a fool. What do you think?'

Klein picked up the bottle and read the label. Lithium carbonate 400mg. Klein suddenly felt empty of feeling. His mind registered without emotion the fact that Hobbes was taking a drug used almost exclusively for treating manic depression. The Arnold Schwarzenegger of mental disorders.

When swinging up into a manic phase of unhinged

grandiosity and visionary disinhibition, such patients often stopped taking their medication, which was what Hobbes appeared to be saying right now. 'Maniac' was a word much and inaccurately overused. The implication of the little brown bottle in Klein's hand was that Hobbes was at least a contender for the real thing. A maniac. Unlike most maniacs Hobbes wielded immense power over many lives. Klein looked up into Hobbes's eyes. Strangely, Klein felt calm for the first time since entering the office. It was simple now: instead of being everyday crazy, Hobbes was genuinely insane.

Hobbes nodded at the bottle in Klein's hand. 'You haven't answered my question.'

Klein put the bottle down on the glass topped desk. 'I advise you to go back to your own doctor and ask him.'

Hobbes frowned.

'But if I was you,' went on Klein, 'I'd do whatever I felt I had to.'

Hobbes's eyes swam with emotion. He nodded. 'Any man that doesn't do so isn't worth a damn.'

He grabbed the pill bottle and threw it into the aluminium waste bin under his desk. The bottle hit the sides of the bin with a dull clang. After the clang came a pause. Klein looked again at the green folder. Hobbes followed his gaze. He pulled the file towards him and opened it.

'The parole board was impressed by your performance,' he said.

Klein did not answer. Hobbes leafed through the file.

'As you know, they are morons to a man. A line memorised from the New Testament, preferably one that they'll recognise, is usually enough to get past them. Jesus always goes down well. That's why you failed last year. Wrong mental attitude.'

'Sir?' said Klein.

'Stubbornness,' said Hobbes.

'With respect, sir, I've been flexible enough to learn the rules in here.'

'Indeed. Your success, shall we say, has been remarkable. And yet every coin has two faces, is that not so?'

'Yes, sir.'

Hobbes glanced down at the file. 'For instance you are a healer, by all accounts a good one. Many inmates prefer to purchase their medical care from you rather than get it for free from Dr Bahr, not that I blame them. Yet contrast that with the case of Myron Pinkley's lobotomy.'

Klein kept what he hoped was a poker face.

'You get my meaning,' said Hobbes.

'If you mean am I aware of the duality of man's nature, yes, sir, I am.'

In a single beat of time Klein's mind was swamped with rage: a rage to know, a rage against Hobbes for fucking him around like this, a rage against himself for hoping, for standing there, for breathing, for being too smart a son of a bitch to lean across the table right now and tear Hobbes's fucking head off. The rage screamed: *Keep your fucking freedom, man, I don't fucking need it, it was never mine in the first place.* A counter voice replied: but that's why you do want it, you asshole: because it is theirs and because you need it, and because it was never yours in the first place. And because it isn't yours now, whether you get the parole or not.

The rage fell silent and as suddenly as it had been filled the space inside Klein's head was once again empty and cold. He shivered in the breeze from the ceiling fan. His shirt felt drenched. Across the desk Hobbes snapped shut the green folder.

'You're free, Klein,' he said.

Klein sat staring at him. He didn't answer.

'The board concurred with my recommendation. You will be handed over to your parole officer at noon tomorrow.'

Hobbes rose to his feet and held out his hand. Klein stood up and shook it.

'Thank you, sir.'

'It's alright to smile, Klein.'

'Yes, sir.'

But Klein didn't smile. The emptiness remained. He knew, somehow, that if he allowed it to fill up it would not be with joy but with a terrible sense of loss and he feared it. Hold onto it, he told himself, until you get somewhere safe. He let go of Hobbes's hand.

'Eighty-nine per cent of the men released from this institution return to prison again,' said Hobbes. 'Don't be one of them.'

'I won't.'

'Is there anything I can do for you?' asked Hobbes.

Klein hesitated. All he had to do – all he had to do – was walk out the door and keep his head down for twenty-four hours, and he could drive down to Galveston Bay for a swim. The thought of wading out into that water and of how much he wanted to feel it against his skin made him frightened even at this late date – especially at this late date – of rousing Hobbes to fury. He remembered what Cletus said about his ass still being theirs until he walked out of the gates.

'Don't be afraid to speak your mind,' said Hobbes.

Klein looked at him. 'The way things are, Coley can't keep the infirmary running on his own.'

'Dr Devlin has made that clear to me on a number of occasions. Things are going to change.'

Klein just couldn't help it. 'With respect, sir, that place is a disgrace to us all.'

Hobbes squared his shoulders. 'The prison infirmary is a disgrace to me, Dr Klein.' The madness in Hobbes's eyes was touched with fire. 'Your complaints, if not my own, have been noted. I assure you that events have been set in motion that will make the conditions in the infirmary an irrelevance.'

Klein wondered what the fuck that was supposed to mean. The thought must have shown on his face because Hobbes's expression suddenly became guarded. But his voice trembled with passion.

'You have my word that . . .' Hobbes searched for a word, '. . . improvements will shortly take place, not only in the hospital but across the whole of this correctional facility.'

Klein resisted the urge to take a step backwards. He nodded. 'I'm glad to hear that, sir.'

'Be glad then, that you won't be here to see it.'

With that Hobbes turned and walked across the room to the north window. He stood with his back to Klein and stared out over the yard at the brooding megalith of the cellblocks. His hands trembled and he clenched them on the window sill. His body seemed to be straining to contain some immeasurable force.

Klein, watching him, didn't know whether or not he had permission to leave. Suddenly he was scared for more than just himself. Whatever the real extent of Hobbes's sickness, this behaviour was the merest of hints, the leakage from the psychic Pandora's box whose lid Hobbes was struggling to keep shut. What 'events' had he already set in motion? Should Klein ask him? Should he walk over and put a hand on his shoulder? It was none of his fucking business. Despite himself he took a silent pace towards Hobbes.

'Good luck, Klein.'

Hobbes spoke without turning from the window. Klein stopped in his tracks.

'And, thank you for our conversation.'

In Hobbes's voice was a finality that somehow signalled more than just the end of the interview. Klein waited. If Hobbes turned to look at him maybe something would happen. But Hobbes did not turn.

'Good luck, Warden,' said Klein.

Hobbes, still staring through the window at his prison, nodded slowly, twice.

Ray Klein stepped silently to the door, opened it and left the warden's office without another word.

NINE

TONY SHOCKNER WAS lost. He'd known that beneath the enormous basement storage rooms of the prison there lay a jungle,
but Jesus. Now that he'd been turning this way and that for
twenty minutes its vastness and complexity blew him away.

Dennis Terry, the old Maintenance boss trudging in front
of Shockner with hunched shoulders, said that if you included
the sewers there was more space underground than there was
above. Down here in hidden, airless crannies was where some
of the cons distilled liquor from potatoes and brewed wine
from orange juice and bread, where others gathered in small
groups to share a sharpened eye dropper for injecting smack
and cocaine, where whores swopped blow jobs and ass-fucks
for cartons of Lucky Strikes and Hershey bars, and others
still dragged struggling – or pliant – victims to be gang banged.
Dennis Terry knew this jungle inside out. He was probably
the only con in the joint who did. For damn sure none of the
guards had a fucking clue. Shockner followed Terry doggedly
around the dank twists and turns, dragging behind him a pair
of gas cylinders – oxygen and acetylene – on a two-wheeled
trolley. Slung over his shoulder was a coiled length of piping
attached at one end to the cylinder heads and at the other to
a cutting torch. Terry, encumbered only by a flashlight, tool

belt and goggles round his neck, walked too fast and Shockner had to keep asking him to slow down. The torch and hose kept slipping from his shoulder. His clothes from head to toe clung to his skin in sweat-drenched folds.

'How much further?' asked Shockner. Terry didn't hear him above the din. Shockner shouted, 'Dennis! How much further?'

Terry called back over his shoulder. 'Another thirty yards, then we reach the steps.'

'Steps? Jesus, what steps?'

The old man didn't answer. Terry's subterranean kingdom was a dark, filthy, grease-and-rust-coated undergrowth of groaning ducts and hissing pipes. Shockner felt like he was in the movie *Aliens*. It sucked. Why couldn't Agry have sent some fuck else? Too paranoid. Agry didn't trust Terry; and he'd snorted too much speed. Shockner banged his elbow on the right-angled bend of a fat pipe rising from the ground. He swore out loud. The fat pipe meant that this shit went even deeper still. Christ. Shockner knew he wasn't a practical guy. Mechanics bored him. He hated changing the oil on his car and he sure as hell hated this shit. In some places the confusion of valves and pressure dials, boxed aluminium air-conditioning ducts and rusting flanges lowered the ceiling by feet. Even Terry had to duck his head to avoid cracking his skull and he was six inches shorter than Shockner. The noise was terrific, of heaving exhaust fans and their motors, of the gluey air being sucked back and forth through tarnished tin conduits. Plus half this shit was a hundred years old and rattled and flapped and shook like it was all about to fall apart. Agry had told him this was the safest part of the operation but it didn't feel that way. Claustrophobia City was what it felt like. Shockner would rather have been up top wielding a hand-spike and a jar of oven cleaner.

Terry stopped. 'Here,' he said.

At the end of a short passageway to the left was a heavy oak door. Terry picked a tool from his belt, walked up to the door and picked the lock. Beyond the door a narrow flight of stone steps led upwards. Unlike most of the steps in the prison the edges of these were sharp and clean. Few feet had ever trodden them.

'You'll have to give me a hand,' said Shockner.

'Sure,' said Terry, without enthusiasm.

Terry tucked his flashlight into his belt and took the cutting torch and the top end of the trolley. Shockner lifted the cylinders from the wheel end, taking most of the weight. Together they staggered up the steps, Shockner's hips and shoulders banging back and forth between the walls. At the top was a second door, this one plated with steel. The lock was modern and looked serious. Terry made no attempt to pick it.

'Right,' said Terry. His voice and bearing were weary.

Shockner set the trolley on one of the steps. Terry unhitched the torch from his shoulder and handed the flash to Shockner.

'Hold this,' he said.

Terry fiddled with the gauges on the cylinder heads. Gas started hissing from the nozzle of the torch. Terry took a Zippo from his pocket and ignited the gas. A loose, fluttering flame twelve inches long leapt out. As Terry adjusted the nozzle the flame became a jet and the flutter a roar. He pulled the goggles over his eyes.

'Best turn your head away,' said Terry.

'Can I smoke?' asked Shockner.

'Why not?' replied Terry.

Shockner sat on the steps in the dim light of the oxyacetylene flame and smoked a Winston. The acrid stench of burning steel swirled down the narrow stairway, drawn by the draught of the tunnel below. Shockner suddenly wondered how Nev Agry was able to get so many people to do something as crazy as this. Maybe not so many. Probably less than ten guys were in on this and only Agry himself had the whole picture in his head. The rest had only been told their parts. They were the blue touch paper. The other cons would explode in their hundreds when it was lit. And of the ten probably only Shockner and Terry had any reasonable claims to mental normality. And, shit, maybe it wasn't all that crazy after all. Out there in the world all it took was for some president or general to get a flea in his ear and suddenly you had a million guys from either end of the earth in a desert someplace trying to blow each other apart. At the top of the steps the sound of the torch cut out and then suddenly all Shockner could see was the tip of his cigarette.

'We're in,' said Terry.

Shockner dropped the butt and trod on it and climbed the steps again in the dark. Terry shouldered the door open and they entered a pitch black space. Terry took the flash from Shockner, found a switch on the wall and turned on a light. The room was maybe eight feet by ten and the floor was empty. On the walls were a series of large fuseboxes with cables running up into a steel box sticking down eight inches from the ceiling. To one side of the box was an ancient trap door.

'We're right under the basement of the watchtower,' said Terry.

Shockner nodded. Terry pointed to the steel box.

'That baby holds all the electrics, telephone lines, alarm junctions, video cables. That shit. It runs from here, down under the General Purpose wing, all the way to reception. I'll have to sit on your shoulders. You handle that?'

'Sure.'

Terry looked at his watch. 'We got thirty minutes. When we cut this open it'll trigger their smoke alarms, but by then that'll be all she wrote. Give me a smoke.'

Shockner gave him a Winston and Terry pulled off the filter. They stood smoking. Terry tapped the ash more often than was necessary.

'You think this is a bad idea, don't you,' said Shockner.

Terry laughed bitterly and just stared at the end of his cigarette.

'You can speak your mind,' said Shockner.

'Nev says it gotta be done.'

'That doesn't mean you can't have an opinion.'

Terry kept staring at the ash growing on his Winston. 'Bout nine years ago,' he said, 'I was up for parole. I thought about it a long time, 'bout what it would be like to be free. And I thought, yeah, out there, if I'm lucky, I'll maybe get to stack shelves at the mini-mart, or wear a paper hat in MacDonalds while some Porto Rican kid tells me how many pickles to put in a cheeseburger. And if I'm real lucky maybe I'll find me a woman, the kind that would be lonely enough to shack up with an old convict. Second-hand car. Cut the "save twenty-five cents" coupons out of the papers. Two rooms and an empty refrigerator on the Mexican side of Laredo.'

Terry looked up at Shockner and Shockner saw the pain and dread in his eyes.

'In here I got two hundred men working for me. The warden asks my advice.' Terry flicked his head at the steel box above them. 'I told him where he'd have to put this shit. I eat good. I live good. I can call Agry and DuBois "Nev" and "Larry" to their faces. They ask me for favours.' He paused and some of the anger sagged out of his voice. 'I told the parole board to fuck themselves.'

Terry dragged the Winston down until the coal was touching the tips of his finger and thumb then dropped it on the floor. He watched his foot grinding it out.

'Nev talks about five years' time,' he said. 'Ain't going to be no five years' time after this. He's gonna take this place down and us with it. I love this shithole. You understand?'

Terry's face filled with stark despair.

'I can't start again elsewhere, Tony. This is the end of the line. I am this fucking place. They transfer me to Huntsville I'll spend the rest of my days swabbing floors and bumming Winstons from guys like you.'

'You're looking on the down side, Dennis,' said Shockner. He knew it was bullshit the minute he said it and Terry ignored it.

'This is your first tour, right?'

Shockner nodded. Terry nodded too, grimly. For the first time Shockner felt a glimmer of fear. Terry looked at his watch again.

'We can sit this out you know, you and me.'

There was a plea in the old man's eyes that Shockner couldn't bear to look at.

He turned away. 'The niggers killed DuBois. Nev says we can't let that stand. He's never been wrong before.'

'Who gives a fuck who killed DuBois? We can stay down here for days,' pleaded Terry. 'I got places, stashes. Food, videos, drugs, whatever the hell you want. Nev's headed for Huntsville, seg for life, death row. We can come back up when it's all over, when that mad fuck is either dead or gone.'

Shockner's guts were in turmoil. Suddenly Agry's voice rang in his head. Semper fucking fi, Tony. Agry had treated him right and not many had. If Shockner had ever had a father, it was Nev Agry. More than a father. A friend. Semper fucking fi. He looked at Terry. Whatever Terry saw in his face, it turned him white.

Shockner said, 'Enough's enough, Dennis.'

He turned and walked towards the door. 'Call me when it's time.'

Shockner climbed down the staircase and sat on the steps. He lit another Winston. Up behind him, above the noise of the fans and ducts, he thought he could hear Terry weeping.

TEN

KLEIN STRODE PAST Correctional Officer Sung and into the grim magnolia precincts of the infirmary with his head buzzing. He was out of here tomorrow. Out. What Coley called 'The Pea Vine Special' had finally pulled into the station and Klein had a ticket to ride. But whatever joy his impending freedom might have brought him was buried beneath a dense pall of foreboding. As he'd left the administration tower Captain Cletus had called after him, 'Walk softly, Klein. You still got plenty time to fuck up.'

Cletus was the kind of guy who couldn't wish his grandmother a happy ninetieth birthday without warning her that she still had time to fuck up. Yet Klein's guts were alive with the sense that turds of epic dimensions were about to hit a giant fan and that he was centrally situated in the spray zone. He ran through the evidence to justify his sudden paranoia. There was none. Henry Abbott had detected a vibe and told him to stay clear of Nev Agry. Well, okay, but Abbott wasn't the US weather satellite. And then Hobbes had revealed the fact that he was a bona fide maniac and had made some vague noises about 'improvements'. And that was it. Zero. Absolute zero. He was crazier than Hobbes and Abbott were. Only the bravest of us. Jesus. Where had he found the gall to pull out that one? Still, it had worked. Now he had other things to think about. Get it together, Klein. His intellect kicked in. The truth was simple: he was shit scared of going back out into the world and he was transferring his anxiety onto the ravings of madmen. Fear of freedom was undignified so he was looking to protect his pride. He was scared of facing the future, not of Cletus or Hobbes.

And then there was Devlin, too. She was out there in the world, where he would shortly be. What was he going to do about her? Could he do anything? Did he want to? Did she? Was his dick big enough? Would it still work? Did she like oral sex? He didn't even know if she had a boyfriend. He'd never asked. For all he knew she was a radical lesbian. On the other hand she was a sports freak, the only woman he'd ever met who had a bookie and talked about point spreads. As far as he knew a weakness for gambling on golf, basketball and boxing were not noted lesbian characteristics. Sports were not Klein's strong point either. He'd never made it onto any of his high school teams and his most enduring memory of junior high was of stumbling in circles round the playing-field whilst a beer-gutted coach shrieked, 'Those Viet Cong are gonna be *on your ass!*' His failure to distinguish himself in these endeavours, indeed the innumerable humiliations they'd brought him, had, he reckoned, fuelled his otherwise eccentric devotion to karate. But karate was not a sport. All those high school football heroes, he knew, now had beer guts and squalling children and wives they didn't want to fuck any more. Bastards. He, the mighty Klein, the shotokan warrior, had gone on to greater things. And was now a despised convict.

What the fuck, he asked himself, would Devlin see in a fool like him? A seedy loser and convicted rapist? It was humiliating alright but nevertheless true: he was scared of being free. For the first time since he'd kicked the habit Klein felt an overwhelming desire to smoke a cigarette.

The corridor ahead of him filled with the bulk of Earl Coley heading for the stairs with an armload of sheets and pillow cases. Coley looked at him sourly.

'Devlin's waiting for you in the office,' said Coley.

'I didn't think she was due in today,' said Klein.

'It's a surprise. Says she got somethin' special to show you. Pro'bly her pussy. I reckon that bitch is in heat.'

Coley's words cut him. The days Devlin came to the infirmary Coley was always more brutal than usual. Klein had never challenged him about it. Maybe he should have but he knew that Devlin was a reminder to Coley of who Klein was and what he represented: a white man with a future. Today that future had arrived, and Coley could read it on Klein's face.

When Klein first started work on the wards Coley had told him never to make any friends in the River. Friendship was a luxury and luxury meant pain: sooner or later they always took it away. The pain was there now in Coley's yellowed eyes. Coley walked past Klein and started up the stair.

'Frog?' said Klein.

Coley stopped but didn't turn. Klein hesitated. He felt like he was running a knife into the broad, stooped back that loomed above him. He swallowed.

'They're letting me go,' he said. 'Tomorrow at noon.'

Still Coley did not turn. His massive shoulders heaved and bunched. Then dropped. 'Don't expect me to congratulate you,' he said.

'I don't,' said Klein.

There was a pause, then Coley looked down at him over his shoulder. His voice trembled.

'Guys used to pay me to work in this place. I was on easy street. These days costs me two tens of valium just to get the fucking floors swabbed.'

Klein said, 'I paid you, Frog.'

Coley blinked. He shook his head. 'Maybe you paid me too much.'

Klein's chest ached. He wanted to tell him, straight out, the things he'd thought but never said. You're a great physician, man. I worship the ground you fucking walk on. You are a great man. A great healer. A great friend. I'm sorry you can't come with me but I can't change that. And I'm sorry you're my fucking friend too but I can't change that either. And even if I could I wouldn't. I wouldn't even if you would. Do you hear me you fat fuck? The words, so loud in his head, stuck high behind his chest. He felt stupid.

'I'll be along in ten minutes,' said Klein.

Coley grunted and disappeared around the turn in the stairs.

Klein hammered the butt of his hand into the wall. Fuck this place. And all of us in it. He pushed himself away from the wall and walked towards the office. Fuck it. He was out of here and anger was easier than hurt. Use it. Why not? Twenty-four hours and it was just a bad memory. They would all of them, Coley included, be just another stupid bunch of regrets. His mind swilled over with bitterness and guilt. He shoved open the door to the office and saw Juliette Devlin.

Klein took a mental step backwards.

Devlin was standing over the desk with her back towards him, leaning on her elbows with her hips in the air as she scanned a neurology journal. A Winston Light smouldered between her fingers. It reminded Klein that he admired women who smoked. It was a blemish on their God-given perfection that made him feel slightly more relaxed about his own failings, which were monstrous and many. In respect of Devlin this flaw was essential for he found her very perfect indeed. She was tall as hell with legs that went on forever, an attribute Klein admired even more than her smoking Winstons. She also had small, tight-looking breasts, or at least he hoped so for he had never seen them in the flesh. Best of all she possessed a full, muscular ass with a one-and-a-half-inch gap between the top of her thighs, a vision whose radiance now scorched his retinas and evoked in his guts a primal yearning to be swallowed up by the earth. Devlin also had a brain the size of a planet. This too Klein appreciated, though it in no way mitigated the primal torment. She turned her head to look at him: long neck, angular features, brown eyes that didn't waver when they met his. The short hair that gave her the air of a cocky punk kid was the final six-inch nail hammered into the hands and feet of Klein's unrequited, renegade desire.

This power surge of sensory input fused Klein's nerve-endings in a single instant. In the next instant – a reflex conditioned by Klein's arduous survival programme – the renegade desire was beaten down and dragged away, bellowing defiance, to a padded cell in the depths of his unconscious.

When Devlin saw his face she stood up straight and turned to face him. 'What's wrong?' she said.

Klein immediately felt compelled to censor his thoughts. It was another aspect of the problem he had with women. He feared that if they had any idea of what took place in his mind they'd run screaming for the cops. For him this wasn't a joke. He was aware that in Devlin's case at least this was somewhat absurd since she gave a convincing impression of being a hard ass and had seen the worst that the world had to offer. But old habits died hard.

'Coley's having a bad day,' he said.

Devlin said, 'He'll survive.'

Her answer irritated him. Maybe it had been heard down in the padded cell.

'Survive?' said Klein. 'We all survive, until we don't. You've got to have something to survive *for*.'

Devlin looked at him. 'What are you surviving for?' she said.

'I don't know,' replied Klein. 'Maybe that's why I'm having a bad day too.'

A look of dread came over Devlin's face. 'The board refused your parole then?'

Klein hadn't known she knew about his review. Coley must have told her.

'No,' he said. 'I can leave tomorrow. At noon.'

Devlin broke into a smile. 'But that's great. Isn't it?'

Klein felt angry with himself that her joy seemed greater than his. It didn't make sense.

'Yeah, it is,' he said.

'Why didn't you tell me you were going up for a hearing?'

Klein shrugged. 'I didn't think it was any of your business.'

Devlin's cheekbones flushed with colour.

Klein added, 'What I mean is, it was something I needed to keep to myself.'

'But why?'

Klein hadn't really thought about it but now he knew.

'Because if you'd been wishing me luck and hoping for me and shit, and then they'd turned me down, I would have had to pretend that it mattered to me less than it did.'

There was a pause while she took in what he'd said.

'That's bullshit,' said Devlin.

'Maybe.'

Devlin held out her hand, palm upward, the cigarette still smoking between her fingers. 'I could've written to the board. I could have helped.'

'I know,' he said.

This was exactly the sort of scene he had avoided by keeping his parole hearing to himself.

'I didn't want your help.'

Again the colour flared on Devlin's cheekbones. She gave him a long, hard stare and dragged on her cigarette. To his surprise the combination of high cheekbones, sucking lips and hard stare gave Klein an immediate hard-on over which he had no control. Devlin blew out a billow of smoke.

'You know Klein,' she said, 'there are times when I think you are a half-decent guy.'

So he'd pissed her off. Well, at least he could stop worrying about seeing her in the world when he got out. He needed time alone and anyway she would probably have broken his balls within a week. Then he thought about how nice it would be to have his balls broken by the likes of Devlin. Devlin, very cool, stabbed the cigarette out in the ashtray and continued.

'You're intelligent, you're committed, and sometimes you make me laugh, which in here is an achievement.'

'Gee, thanks Miss Devlin,' said Klein.

Devlin, without smiling, walked across the room towards him. Klein, with effort, held his ground.

Devlin said, 'There have even been times when I've thought about sucking your cock.'

Klein experienced a transient blurring of vision. He blinked and begged his legs not to give out on him. He heaved the quivering musculature of his face into what he hoped was the expression of a man who took it for granted that beautiful women thought about sucking his cock. Devlin stopped toe to toe in front of him.

'But most of the time,' she said, 'I think you're just an asshole.'

She made a circle of her finger and thumb and held it in front of his face.

'A big asshole.'

Klein waited for a witty riposte to spring to his lips. There had to be one in there somewhere. But he was hypnotised by her eyes, stranded, speechless. Hi, I'm Ray Klein and I'm just an asshole. A big asshole. Thank you for listening. His mouth felt as if it contained an inflated condom. For Chrissakes, man, speak.

He said, 'I need a smoke.'

Devlin was only an inch – two inches – shorter than he was. Her gaze was almost level with his own. The muscles round her eyes crinkled a little. Was it amusement? Or the contempt he so richly deserved?

She said, 'I thought you'd stopped.'

'I did,' said Klein. 'But now I know for sure I'm an asshole I feel entitled to start again.'

He watched her unfasten the top button of her shirt, and then the next. Her eyes flicked down to his mouth. 'Then start,' she said.

Klein resisted the urge to lick his lips. Instead he looked at hers. Like her cheekbones they were flushed with blood. Down below in the sweat-stained confinement of his prison denims the hard-on of his life, now a sovereign power independent of his will, bellowed for satisfaction. Klein's Nietzschean psychological survival strategy had enabled him to resist making a pass at Devlin for over twelve months. He'd even resisted fantasising about her, about the size and colour of her nipples, the density of her pubic hair and the no doubt sublime beauty of the cleft between her buttocks. Instead he had relied on the copies of *Hustler* magazine that he occasionally accepted in his subterranean private clinic as payment for medical consultations. Certainly if Devlin had emitted any signals that she was attracted to him Klein had not dared register them. But now he was almost free. Free to smoke, free to fantasise, free, by God, to be just as big an asshole as he pleased. The hard-on roared with approval, urging him on: free to shuck these goddamned pants and let her taste his seed as she so clearly longed to do.

Instead of shucking his goddamned pants Klein stood paralysed, staring at Devlin's tumescent lips.

Devlin slid her hand into his hair and round the back of his head. He felt her fingers clench into a fist, pulling him towards her. She opened her mouth and kissed him.

Klein closed his eyes and his nervous system turned into what felt like a sea of molten copper. His arms hung, heavy, by his sides and his entrails, heavy too, sank inside him. He leaned into her, onto her, through her. He felt himself dissolving, vanishing. Even the hard-on of his life, now pressing against her belly, lost its separateness and was swallowed up into the meltdown of his sensorium. He didn't even know whether or not his tongue was down her throat or hers down his. A groan that fell just short of a whimper escaped from his throat. He would realise later that this was the one and only moment of pure and untrammelled bliss that he had ever experienced. But for the moment he was incapable of thought.

Devlin pulled his head away.

Klein, swaying on his feet, slowly opened his eyes. He found her staring at him. She looked as if she was shocked by what she'd done. Maybe she wasn't quite as cool as he'd thought. Cool enough, though. A sudden thought sent a bolt of fear straight through him. She had changed her mind. The kiss that had shown him the meaning of bliss had been for her a horrible error. He was after all a stinking convict, unworthy of her attention. The mighty sovereign hard-on shouldered him contemptuously aside and seized control of his limbs. With both hands Klein grabbed Devlin by the waist and pulled her crotch against his. Now Klein felt a moment of shock. She looked up at him for a beat. He waited for her to knee him in the balls. Devlin's mouth drooped open. Her tongue invited him. They kissed again.

Klein squeezed her waist, the lower edges of his hands digging into the hard bony blades of her hips. Through the cotton of her shirt he felt her flank muscles tense. He pulled the tails of the shirt from out the back of her jeans. He paused with the white cotton bunched in his fists. He slid his mouth from her lips and pressed his cheek against hers. He felt her breath against his ear. It wasn't simple. It should've been but it wasn't. Suddenly all the needs that he had so ruthlessly welded into the various cages of his psyche started rattling their bars and yelling to be heard. Sex, grief, sorrow, joy, loneliness, hope, excitement, anger, and more sorrow and yet more and then more sorrow still. Sorrow for the autumn leaves and the winter sunsets over the Bay that he'd yearned for and missed whilst trapped in stir. For the friends he'd lost and for those he might have made and never had. For the men who'd died in front of him and for those like Vinnie Lopez who now would die without him. For Earl Coley and Henry Abbott and all the others who would never see the seasons change inside these stony walls. For the pain and rage that had doomed him to this awful place and the pain and rage he'd known whilst stuck inside it. For the man he might have been and the man he merely was. And Klein knew that for all he'd fought and struggled he had, in the end, failed to keep his own ghosts, and the ghosts of this prison, from entering his inmost heart.

He felt Devlin's breasts against his chest and his cock rubbing her belly and the lonely fire burning in his own. And he found the sorrow there too. The only flesh Klein had touched in three long years had belonged to sick male convicts. Now his fingers were about to touch the skin of a woman, and not just any woman but the woman he felt to be the most beautiful in history. His hands trembled. He lifted her shirt and put his hands inside. As his fingertips brushed the hollow of her back and his skin touched hers a wave of nameless emotion swept through his body and his clenched eyes filled with tears and his anguish tore itself free from its moorings and soared, howling, through the deep and infinite spaces of his chest. In that moment all sorrows and all desires, and all pasts and all futures, were together gathered into this one present. And in this present Klein loved her. Utterly and forever. And he knew that he would love her utterly and forever until he and all his sorrows were turned back into dirt.

'Klein?' said Devlin.

Her voice was soft in his ear and filled with concern. Klein realised that she could feel his tears running down her neck. He had never in adulthood cried in front of a woman. Never. An overwhelming sense of shame suddenly extinguished all other feelings within him. He kept his head pressed to hers so she couldn't look at his face.

'Are you okay?'

'I'm fine,' said Klein, in a flat, hard voice. 'Just don't say anything.'

The shame was of that unique form which a man only ever feels in front of a woman, never in front of another man and never in front of himself: the shame of showing her your weakness and pain. Klein was all too well aware of the acreage of literature devoted to the benefits of this sort of display, all of it heavily fertilised with bullshit. He did not believe a word of it. Since it was not within the power of woman to understand or comfort the pain their only gain in being witness to it was that of emotional advantage, which in his experience they invariably seized on with clawed hands. Maybe it was sad that Klein would be happier to kneel weeping in front of Nev Agry than in front of a woman he loved, but it was true nevertheless. The contempt of a man, if that be his response, could be dealt with. That of a woman – and who amongst them did not harbour it in their heart? – felt like a sickness worse than death. Devlin would have thought him crazy to hear any of this and maybe he was. But Klein had heard enough men weeping, and seen enough of them with their wives and girls and enough boy children with their mothers, to think otherwise. Klein lowered his lips to Devlin's neck and licked away the tears and with them his shame. He willed his heart to match the hardness of his cock. Then he kissed her again on the mouth.

This time bliss and the angst of shame took a back seat to raw sexual convulsion. No more censorship. No more sorrow. He bit her lips, her face; he scraped his fingertips down the long white curve of her throat; he grabbed the flesh of her back in handfuls as if he would tear it away from her ribs and spine and consume it. From Klein's larynx came bursts of hoarse, amorphous sound, a primal stridor punctuated by the suck and smack of saliva and tongue, the howl and lament of a deprivation so brutal and a need so deep that it chanted its wordless song from the very marrow of who he was. He held her grappled tight against his chest and lifted her half off her feet and reeled backwards, manhandling her across the room, all the while his teeth gnawing at the angle of her jaw, her neck, the thin stretched skin over her collar bone. He felt his back thud into the wall by the door and rolled, still holding her, so that she was pinned against the yellow-painted bricks. Klein paused and leaned back to look at her.

Devlin's chest heaved in shallow gasps. Her eyes were huge, with awe and the shadow of fear. She tilted her head and shoulders back against the wall, arching her belly into his cock, her mouth, red and wet, lifting towards him. Klein held back, poring over her features, the sight of her filling him with an ache more terrible than any he had known in the darkness of confinement. Devlin turned her face to one side and looked down at the floor. Her eyelids drowsed half-shut. She took hold of her shirt and pulled it up over her breasts. She wore a white lycra bra that held her tits tight against her chest. The dark, hard stumps of her nipples stuck out towards him and Klein's soul went into free fall, tumbling towards oblivion. Her abdomen, stretched taut from her heaving rib cage, undulated in and out with the beat of her breath. Still looking away from him Devlin reached up with her left hand and pulled one cup of the bra down, releasing her tit. The muscles in Klein's cock and balls clenched and he felt a thin trickle of pre-ejaculate flow out. He lifted his hand to her jaw and turned her to face him. She opened her eyes, now black and turbulent as the sea. Klein held her gaze for an endless pulse of time. Still looking at her, he put his hand on her cunt and lifted her onto her toes.

Devlin's breath shuddered out, a deep guttural exhalation, and her eyes never blinked, never wavered from his own. She pushed down into his fingers and he felt the denim of her jeans give just a little as the lips of her cunt parted. The spots of colour on her cheeks were now a fierce red. Klein felt her hand on his cock, a strong, full-blooded grip. She tugged upwards. He trembled as he felt the slickness of his own moisture on his glans. They kissed, sucking, her teeth banging hard into his. Klein grabbed her hips and turned her, her mouth still clinging to his, to face the wall. He pushed his cock against her jeans, into the cleft of her ass, and felt her push back against him, her forearms braced to the wall, her head sagging down between them. He slid his hands under her armpits and pulled her tits free. She squirmed as he pulled hard on her nipples. He closed his eyes and bit the skin over her vertebrae where they curved down into the nape of her drooping neck. He felt the gathering momentum of ejaculation swell up through his pelvis. It was too soon. He stopped his thrusting and hung onto her back, his sweat drenching her shirt and skin. The moment of his coming receded and Klein immediately wanted it back. He heard the brassy clink of a belt buckle falling open and groaned. Devlin was popping the buttons on her flies, shoving and wriggling her jeans down over her hips with one hand. Klein saw the black of a G string disappearing into the cleft of her ass.

As the lava of impending orgasm again surged through his cock he realised that he hadn't jerked off in a week and that at this instant there was no way he'd be able to fuck her for more than a dozen strokes before he came. A whiff of panic smoked through his guts. He wanted to give her the fucking of her life but it had been too long. Three years. He wasn't ready. He had to be ready. He was the Nietzschean. The shotokan warrior. By force of will he would override his autonomic nerves and fuck her until she could no longer stand. The smoke of panic became acrid and dense. The Nietzschean coughed and spluttered. An alarm bell started ringing.

It took several seconds, and Devlin twisting towards him with an urgent expression on her face, before Klein realised that the ringing came not from within his head but from the bell bolted to the far wall of the office. Klein turned, dazed. Beneath the bell a red light bulb flashed on a board next to the words 'Travis Ward'. Devlin hauled her jeans up.

'Cardiac arrest, Klein,' she said. 'Klein?'

'Fuck,' said Klein.

He slid both his hands up across the sweat slicking his face and ran them through his hair.

'Stay here,' he said.

He checked the red bulb again and bolted for the door.

'You want help?' called Devlin.

'No.'

Klein hit the corridor at a sprint. Travis ward. Second floor. He took the stairs three at a time. At the top of the first flight his foot slipped and he crashed his shin into the edge of the step. He swore vilely and sprinted on, shards of pain shooting up through his knee. An image of ultimate horror sprang into his mind: Frog Coley slumped in a great heap on the floor with Gimp Cotton going through his pockets for the keys to the dispensary. No: only Frog would have had the sense to set the alarm off. As Klein shouldered through the door at the top of the stairs he heard the roar of Coley's voice.

'One of you fuckers give me a hand! Wilson!'

Klein hit the ward running, between the rows of beds. The gate dividing the ward in two was open. At the far end Coley stood over Greg Garvey, both palms on his sternum pumping his chest. Klein passed through the gate and reached the bedside. He pulled Garvey's head back, pinched his nose closed and put his mouth over Garvey's lips. The lips were dark blue. He blew into Garvey's lungs, let the chest deflate, blew again. As he did so he reached down into Garvey's groin and felt for the femoral pulse. It was there but only faintly and only in time to Coley's pumping.

'Stop a minute,' Klein said.

Coley stopped and wiped his brow on his forearm. Under Klein's fingertips the pulsations stopped and didn't come back. Klein lifted Garvey's right eyelid. The pupil was dilated and did not react to the light. The left pupil was the same. Coley started pumping again.

'Did you see him go?' said Klein.

Coley shook his head. Sweat fell from his nose onto Garvey's chest. 'I was changing a bed at the other end. Found him like this on my way back from the sluice.'

'He's gone, Frog,' said Klein. 'There's nothing we can do.'

He put his hand on top of Coley's. Coley stopped pumping. After a moment he pulled his hands away. He stared at Klein's sweat soaked shirt. 'Where were you?'

Klein's jaw clenched. 'I was in the office. You know that.'

Coley just looked at him.

'Greg was terminal. We did our best for him,' said Klein.

'We?' said Coley. His voice was fierce with suppressed loss. 'You gone, motherfucker. Ain't got no "we" round here any more. Why would you give a shit?'

'Frog,' said Klein, softly.

Coley had seen hundreds of men leave the infirmary wrapped in plastic and headed for Potter's Field. Klein knew this wasn't about Garvey's dying. So did Coley. Coley heaved in a big breath and let it out through flared nostrils.

'Sorry, man,' he said.

'Forget it,' said Klein.

Coley drew the sheet up over Garvey's face. Then he stood upright and stared across the aisle at Gimp Cotton with a blank expression that prickled the hairs on the back of Klein's neck. Cotton cringed back into his mattress. Klein noticed a large black haematoma covering the left half of his face.

'I didn't do nothin'!'

Cotton's voice was a squeal of terror. Coley moved towards him. Klein stepped round the bed and stood in his way.

'Frog,' he said.

Coley's eyes stayed on Cotton for a another full ten seconds. The Gimp squirmed, twisting the sheets between his hands.

'I didn't do nothin'! Tell 'em, Wilson.'

Coley looked at Klein. He spoke loud enough for Cotton to hear him.

'I was gonna send the Gimp back to the population this afternoon.' He turned deadly eyes back on the cowering figure. 'Think I'll keep him here for a while after all.'

Coley pushed past Klein and walked off down the ward. As Klein watched him go Reuben Wilson caught his eye. Wilson was one of the few well-balanced minds in the joint. At that moment Klein didn't feel that his own mind qualified as one of them. A word with Wilson might do him some good. He walked over to his bed.

'Garvey looked like he was sleepin', Doc. Nothin' I could do.'

'Garvey's number was up,' said Klein. 'Don't worry. How's your belly?'

Wilson shrugged stiffly. 'Fine, I guess.'

'Let me see,' said Klein.

He sat on the edge of the mattress. Two weeks before Wilson had almost died in the segregation block. A blow of considerable force, the exact nature and circumstances of which would never be officially established, had been delivered to Wilson's left ninth and tenth ribs from the rear and ruptured his spleen.

Wilson had leaked two litres of blood into his peritoneal cavity while he lay on the floor of his cell calling for help. Captain Cletus, who despite being a professional motherfucker knew a dying man when he saw one, had been on night watch and had roused Klein from his cell. Klein, finding no blood pressure and a pulse over a hundred and sixty, had shoved a line into Wilson's subclavian vein and squeezed in two bags of saline whilst waiting for the ambulance to take him to the general hospital. Three days after receiving twelve units of blood and emergency surgery to remove his spleen, Wilson had been transferred back to Green River.

Wilson lifted his T-shirt for Klein. A fresh scar ran from Wilson's sternum almost as far as his pubic bone. Inside his abdomen the muscle layer was held together by number two nylon sutures. The skin wound had healed well. Klein ran a hand over Wilson's belly.

'Looks good,' said Klein.

'No kidding,' said Wilson. 'It's the biggest fucking scar I ever seen, and I seen my share.'

'The surgeons needed space to work and they didn't have time to worry about what the ladies sucking your dick would think.'

'I guess that's one problem I don't need to worry about,' said Wilson. 'Least for a while.'

'I guess not,' said Klein.

A cold hand squeezed his heart. Wilson was serving ninety-nine to life for a murder that even Cletus had difficulty believing he'd committed. Wilson had been a contender for the middleweight world title, upset some big promoter with Mafia connections and had woken up in a Dallas motel room to six armed cops telling each other that this was one loud nigger was going all the way to the chair. In the room next door was a dead whore, strangled, her mouth stuffed with a pair of Wilson's monogrammed Versace underpants. No drugs or alcohol were found in Wilson's bloodstream nor any other evidence linking him to the dead woman. Just the underpants and a few of Wilson's pubic hairs. It seemed unlikely that a stone cold sober Wilson would strangle a stranger and then bed down for some Z's in the adjoining room. But this was Texas, Wilson was a nigger who wore expensive foreign underwear, and the woman was white. A number of pop stars and Hollywood actors had mounted a campaign on Wilson's behalf and he had become a *cause célèbre*, but once the brief flare of publicity had died down the stars had lost interest. When he finally got back to court two years later no one remembered who Wilson was any more, especially in Hollywood, and the judge had rejected his appeal. He would be free to apply for parole in twenty-four years' time.

Wilson pulled a pack of Camel filters from under his pillow. He tapped one loose and offered it to Klein. Klein sighed and shook his head. Wilson stuck the butt in his mouth.

'I heard what Coley said back there. That mean you got your parole through?'

Klein nodded. Wilson smiled and held out his hand. They shook.

'Well done, man. Don't pay Coley no mind. He's just crazy about you,' said Wilson.

'You can do me a favour before I go,' said Klein.

'Name it,' said Wilson.

'I want to see Claude Toussaint, say goodbye,' said Klein.

Wilson nodded. 'Sure, why not?'

'I don't think Stokely Johnson will let me through without your word.'

'Give me some paper,' said Wilson.

Klein pulled a soggy notebook and a ballpoint pen from his shirt pocket and handed them over. Wilson scribbled briefly in the notebook, tore out the page, folded it and handed it back.

'Obliged,' said Klein.

'You like Claude,' said Wilson.

'When I first came down,' said Klein, 'Claude was good to me, got me in like Flynn with Agry. He invited me to coffee mornings and cocktail parties in their cell.'

'When he was a lady Claude like to play at that society hostess shit,' said Wilson.

'You blame him?' said Klein.

'Some do. Not me. Man's got to survive best he can. Claude had a good deal going over on D. Why'd he move back into B?'

'The word on D is that he had no choice. They say Hobbes transferred him back on your request.'

'Shit,' said Wilson. 'He told us he requested it himself, got sick of being Agry's bitch.'

'Maybe that's so and he put that story around to protect himself,' said Klein. 'If Agry thought Claude had left him he'd have him impaled on a wooden stake by second count.'

'Agry is one mad motherfucker,' said Wilson.

'Agry's just plain crazy. Hobbes is insane. I mean thorazine and straitjackets insane, or at least on his way.'

Wilson's expression darkened with concern. 'The lockdown is insane, right enough. I can't see any sense to it, less he just wants to show the population who's really boss. How is it on B?'

'Hot,' said Klein.

Wilson shrugged. 'Well it ain't your problem. None of it is any more. Like Coley said, you gone, motherfucker.'

Wilson smiled. Klein smiled back. He glanced at his watch. 'I got to go inform Cletus about Garvey's death.'

'Drop by again before you leave,' said Wilson.

Klein nodded and walked down the ward and out of the door. At the top of the stairs Coley was waiting for him. He glanced at Klein's eyes, then looked away down the stairs.

'This ain't personal,' said Coley, 'but I don't want the woman around no more. I want her gone. Now. I ain't bein' spiteful, I just . . .'

Coley struggled for words, failed, turned to look at Klein. 'You understand?'

Klein nodded. 'Sure, Frog. I'll take care of it.'

Klein put his hand on Coley's shoulder. Coley shook his head and averted his face. Klein squeezed Coley's shoulder.

'I'll be back after third lock and count,' said Klein.

Coley nodded without speaking. Klein let go and headed down the stairs for the sick bay office.

Now all he had to do was kick his new lover out of the building and report a death to the Doris Day fan club. He felt depleted. He looked at his watch. If he had time after filling in forms for Cletus he had to brave Stokely Johnson and his long distance runners in the canteen. To say goodbye to Claude Toussaint. It wasn't something that he had to do, but he wanted to. With a sinking in his gut he turned into the corridor to the office – and Devlin. He hoped she'd understand. He didn't want a scene. His last day in prison was already more complicated than he'd hoped. Cletus's warning nagged at him. Still, he'd resisted the smoke Wilson had offered him. And things weren't likely to get any worse. He shoved open the office door and went inside.

ELEVEN

HECTOR GRAUERHOLZ WAS high. Fizzing. Crackling. Wired. Not with drugs, mind. Hec rarely took them, and then only downers to quell the natural excess of wayward chemicals produced by his brain. At eight a.m. on the average morning Grauerholz behaved like a man hopped up with methedrine. Now he was really soaring. He felt as he imagined an eagle must feel cruising the thermals with a small animal in its sights way down below. A rabbit maybe. Or a pigeon. Yeah. A sudden doubt bothered him. He didn't know for sure if eagles preyed on pigeons: maybe you didn't see too many up there in the mountains. They were too busy shitting on statues and living in coops and stuff. Maybe it was the other way round then: he was an eagle trapped in a coop. Fuck, yeah. That was it. A coop big enough to fly in. Electric currents buzzed through his bones. Nitrous oxide pumped through his chest. Sheet lightning danced behind his eyes. Man, this was it, man. Primitive chords jangled in his ears, like cavemen playing guitars in a stainless steel dungeon. Wang Dang Doodle. All night long.

Grauerholz was in the builder's shop in the lee of the north wall, right opposite the rear gate and loading doors to the mess hall and kitchens. The shop was kind of a big open hangar, with a corrugated perspex roof and folding aluminium doors. It was jumbled with pallets stacked with brick and breeze block, lumps of pre-cast concrete; bags of cement, steel mesh, iron girders coded with white numbers and coated dull red with weather-proof paint. Lounging on a stool by the folded back doors, reading the sports section, was a black screw called Wilbur. Agry had said to go easy on the guards. Grauerholz didn't quite get that one but he was game to try. Larry DuBois's gun, tucked against his belly under his shirt, felt like a hard-on. He reminded himself to save ammo, not to go wild. That would be tough too. Some guys liked a blade, liked the feeling, the personal contact. He remembered Agry rooting around in old Larry's jowls with the razor, the look on Agry's face. Grauerholz could dig all that sure enough, but he preferred guns, no question. He was still full of wonder that they worked the way they did. Pop, pop, pop and man that was all she wrote. Awesome. Too fucking amazing for words. Horace Tolson lumbered past him with a sack of cement balanced on his shoulder. One side of his beard was grey with dust.

'Get Bubba to fetch Sonny Weir,' said Grauerholz. 'Then tell the guys it's time to run old ninety-nine.'

As Horace changed course across the yard towards his brother, Grauerholz walked over to Wilbur. As Wilbur saw him coming he stood up, folded his paper away and shoved it in his back pocket. Folk were always edgy around Grauerholz, ever since he could remember. He'd never understood it until one day he'd asked Klein what he thought their beef might be. Klein had told him it was because Grauerholz was the purest example of a psychopath he'd ever even heard of. As he approached Wilbur Grauerholz put on the choirboy smile that he imagined people liked. Wilbur looked more nervous than ever.

'Permission to use the saw, Boss Wilbur,' said Grauerholz.

Wilbur relaxed a little. 'Sure, Grauerholz. And cut out that smartass "Boss" shit. It's "Mr" and "Sir", you know that.'

'Yessir, Mr Wilbur. Thank you.'

Grauerholz walked to the rear of the shop. On his way, arms held out for balance, he trotted along the top of an iron girder that lay on the ground waiting to replace a corroded vault rafter in the roof of C block. The prison was so fucking old there was always something needed replacing. Both ends of the girder were bevelled, like wedges, where they would be bolted to the ridgepiece and wall plate. It was thirty feet long and had the number '99' painted in white on its side. Threaded through the bolt holes at three points on either side were loops of thick nylon rope for ease of carrying. Grauerholz jumped off the end and skipped towards the heavy iron bench at the rear of the shop.

The breeze block saw was bolted to the back of the bench. It was currently sheltered from Wilbur's view by a large sheet of steel leaning against the front end. Grauerholz switched on the power at the wall and hit the red button on the saw unit. The dark grey circular blade started spinning with a nerve-grinding whine that was amplified by the sheet of steel.

Holy shit. Suddenly Grauerholz remembered the feeling he'd had whilst raping a woman in her Fort Worth apartment, one of those bitches who wore a suit and pulled down sixty G's a year. As he'd fucked her without coming he'd listened to Howlin Wolf at top volume singing 'Wang Dang Doodle' on his walkman and had carved his initials – H G – on her tits with a linoleum knife. It had given him the same light-headed feeling he was getting now. Man. He hadn't killed the woman. Instead he'd left her with the scars and hundred thousand dollars' worth of psychotherapy to pay for. If he'd thought about getting caught – and he hadn't been – maybe he would've killed her, but the thought had never crossed his mind.

That was because, as Klein had carefully explained, Grauerholz was one of those individuals – rare even in Green River – for whom there was no gap between thought and

action, and for whom any consideration of future, of consequence, was quite alien. Some folk talked of taking each day
as it came. Grauerholz took each minute. The only time he
thought about the future was when he reminded himself that
win, lose or draw he would one day end up exactly like his
gentle law-abiding Pa: fat, forty and totally fucked. In other
words worse than dead. So why the fuck worry? He liked
prison life. Free bed and board with a constant vibe of
impending action, a game played day and night for heavy
stakes. He'd missed the pussy at first, of course, but after a
while you just forgot about that shit. Most guys only jerked
off or purchased blow jobs – or got freebies from certain of
the screws – to reassure themselves that their equipment still
worked. They sure as hell didn't get much pleasure from it.
At least Grauerholz hadn't. The best part had always been
hearing those bitches weep when he punished them and now
that they weren't around to provoke him any more he'd more
or less forgotten all about them, and sex too.

The point Klein had tried to make was that it was the
absence of any gap between impulse and action that made all
these assholes fear him. He wasn't big and he wasn't strong
and he wasn't particularly bright; but he was crazier than a
snake humping a goat, a sheep-killing dog who needed
chaining up and shooting, and that's what people shied away
from. He didn't know if it had been Klein's intention or not,
but he'd left Grauerholz feeling pretty good about himself.

Grauerholz's reverie ended as Bubba Tolson brought Sonny
Weir stumbling over, poking him in the back with a thick
finger. Sonny's face was a pale green colour and his lips trembled and writhed like a box of live fish bait.

'Hey, Sonny, where y'at?' said Grauerholz with his choirboy
smile. He had to speak loud over the screech of the saw blade.
Weir managed a simpering smile in return.

'I got diarrhoea,' he said.

Grauerholz tutted and shook his head. 'Shoulda called in sick,' he said. 'Don't take care of your own health ain't nobody else gonna.'

'I don't like goin' to that goddamn sick bay in th'infirmary. All them faggots, you know?'

Grauerholz nodded to Bubba who towered over Weir's scrawny form.

'Fraid I might catch something worse, you know,' continued Weir. 'Hey, Jesus!'

Bubba seized Weir from behind with both arms, one encircling his thin body, the other clamping a thick dusty hand over his mouth and nostrils. Weir struggled and kicked his legs. Bubba lifted him off the ground and carried him behind the steel sheet concealing the breeze block saw. Grauerholz looked over to the far corner near the doors, where Horace Tolson was hefting a sack of cement onto the top of a pile. Horace stopped to look at him. Grauerholz gave him a thumb-up sign, then clenched the thumb into his fist as if pressing a detonator.

Horace picked up a brick, strolled over to Boss Wilbur, and coshed him to the ground with a single blow.

As Horace dragged Wilbur's body inside, out of sight of the gun tower on the west wall, Grauerholz stepped behind the steel sheet and smiled at Weir. The screeching whine of the breeze block saw increased in shrillness and intensity. Behind Bubba's immovable hand Weir's face was all puffed up and purpled red, his eyes rolling and bulging above his cheeks.

'Okay, Stoolie,' shouted Grauerholz above the noise. 'Which one of them arms you wanna hang on to?'

TWELVE

WITH A MIXTURE of infuriation and bewilderment Devlin watched Klein walk away across the yard towards the main prison and third lock and count. Her liberal mental health professional instincts called upon her to understand why he'd bundled her out of the infirmary and dumped her at reception, why he'd been so cool and inaccessible so soon after the sexual fury she had unleashed in him in the sick bay office. Greg Garvey had died in difficult circumstances. There was a bad feeling on the ward. Coley was down about it. It was better she wasn't around that day. Blah, blah, blah. The liberal instincts nodded empathetically and told her it was natural for the death to affect Klein and Coley and the others. Her gut told her: bullshit. Prisoners had died before while she was there. They dropped like flies, usually to the accompaniment of tough-guy ribaldry and displays of defensive machismo. It had to be bound up with the sex, and Devlin wondered if somehow she'd fucked up.

Thinking back now, as she sat enduring the usual interminable wait to be cleared through reception, she was shaken, and disturbed, by how much she'd wanted Klein to fuck her, standing there bent over against the wall. And not just fuck her but fuck her savagely and recklessly in that humid, squalid room surrounded by hurt and dying. Guys had been hot for her before, plenty, but nothing she'd experienced came close to Klein's weeping, sweating, rageful carnality, at once tender and frightening, animalistic and lovely. She'd had her own moments of lust too, but nothing like the delirium she'd felt in that room. No condoms. No precautions. My God, she must have been out of her mind. Or maybe, for once, she'd just been out of her mind and in herself. Something in her rebelled against the chiding voice of sense. She wished he had fucked her and come, dangerously, inside her. She wished he'd returned from seeing Garvey die and finished the job. The voice of sense, the liberal instincts, reeled with horror. What was she saying? Her gut answered: I'm saying fuck you all. I want his cock inside me, I want his hands on me, I want to hear him moaning in my ear. I don't care what he's done or where he's been or where he's going. I know him. I want him. For a few minutes I knew him better than I've ever known anyone. And he knew me. I love him.

I love him.

The competing thoughts were wiped away. For a moment Devlin sat within a powerful inner silence. Unlike her conscious mind the ancient core of herself, a wise crone ten thousand years old, was not surprised or shaken or horrified. The crone knew that Devlin had watched Klein for a year. Watched the crinkles of concentration round his eyes when he sutured a wound, watched the muscles moving under the thick-veined skin of his forearms, watched his hair grow long and his habit of slicking it back with the sweat that forever poured down his rawboned face. And she'd listened to the rise and fall of his voice and of his laughter, and to his use of profanity and to his easy way with the men, who leaned on him more than he could ever bear to let himself know. And she'd smelled his prison-food breath and his useless prison-store deodorant, and the smells of the infirmary clinging to his hands and clothes, and the smell of him that leaked out from his pores. And all this time she'd been falling in love. And the wise crone had known it and she, Devlin, had not. And now she did.

Devlin stopped herself thinking about what Klein felt in return for her. She knew there were a hundred and one interpretations she could put on his actions, some that she wanted to be so and others that she feared. She wasn't going to play he loves me, he loves me not. She would wait and see and the silence inside would see her through the wait. Klein would be free of this place tomorrow and they would meet again in a different world. That scared her too. If it scared her, she reasoned, then it must be scaring Klein a hell of a lot more. Klein had convinced himself he was a look-out-for-number-one, not-my-fucking-business, get-out-of-my-face-or-I'll-fracture-your-fucking-skull, hard ass. In fact his failure to actually be so at times verged on the comical, at least to Devlin. He thought he was too cool and too shrewd to get involved – with the Aids guys, with Coley, with any of the other convicts. She didn't blame him for defending himself that way, she just didn't think his armour was as tough as he thought it was.

Perhaps in her way she herself was not so different. She'd invented herself in much the same way, justifying her toughness as a necessity if she was to compete in a tough game. Sometimes she'd wondered if she'd overdone it. Her mother still asked Devlin when she was going to give her some grandchildren. Typically she never asked her sons, Devlin's two brothers. Two guys had asked Devlin to marry them. She'd refused and broken off with them. She had too much to do, though sometimes she wasn't sure exactly what that too much was. The more achievements she accumulated the farther away whatever it was she was looking for seemed to go. She'd had a hunch that she'd find it here in Green River State Penitentiary. After all, she'd told herself, it was just unlikely enough a location for her to be right. And for a moment back there with Klein she had found it. It had flowed through her, startling and clear, and through the strong fingers melting into her flesh. Now, sitting here feeling rejected and confused, she wasn't so sure. How could something so immutable change so quickly to doubt? Klein had twenty-four hours to go and she would be waiting for him at the gate. Then she would find out. A phrase appeared in her mind: *Give me to drink mandragora, That I might sleep out the great gap of time My Antony is away*. She blushed in front of herself. Christ, Devlin what's going on with you?

An officer called her to the window of the reception office and she collected her belongings and signed out. As she put her pocketbook back into her briefcase she noticed the green journal. Fuck. She'd forgotten the only reason she'd had for coming here today: the first publication of their research work in the infirmary.

Aids and Depressive Illness in a Closed Institution:
a Pilot Study at Green River State Penitentiary.
by
Juliette Devlin Ray Klein Earl Coley

She'd sat on the news of the paper's acceptance by the journal for weeks without telling Klein or Coley, so that she could surprise them. But Klein was leaving tomorrow and she couldn't be here before noon at the earliest. She was chairing a case conference in Houston. The three of them would never be together again to celebrate their achievement. An image of Earl Coley lumbering down the ward alone came into her mind and tears sprang to her eyes. It was for Coley most of all that she was proud of the publication. She wanted to see his face when he saw his name next to hers. She wanted to see how much it would mean to him. Her own first publication had thrilled her and that had been routine, expected, her job. She hoped that for Coley it would be some small tribute to the vast but invisible contribution he'd made to the sick men flowing through his hands. She had to get the journal into his hands today. Sergeant Victor Galindez walked past her and stopped.

'Something wrong, Doctor Devlin?'

Devlin turned. She let the tears stay in her eyes. She didn't often exploit her gender, at least not as far as she was aware, but nothing was more important than that she get the journal to Klein and Coley. If the tears of a woman were what it took then so be it. She walked urgently towards Galindez. She added some medical authority to the tears.

'Sergeant, I need to go back to the infirmary,' she said. 'I've forgotten something of great importance.'

Galindez glanced at the window behind her. 'You've checked out I see.'

'Yes.'

'That's too bad. What is it that's so important?'

A number of invented excuses flashed through her mind. Most guards couldn't have cared less about Coley and Klein and their research. They wouldn't consider it important at all. Galindez wasn't like the rest. Devlin didn't want to lie to him. She looked into Galindez's face and made her choice. She took out the journal, opened it at the title page of their paper and held it out to Galindez to see.

Galindez took the journal. He absorbed the heading, then read the introduction and abstract without speaking. He lowered the journal and looked up at her.

'Congratulations,' he said.

'Klein and Coley haven't seen it yet. There was a death on the ward and I left without showing them.'

'It's no problem. I'll deliver it for you,' said Galindez.

Devlin's guts sank. It wasn't enough. She wanted to be there to see their faces. To see Klein.

'Klein's leaving tomorrow,' she blurted.

Galindez raised an eyebrow. Perhaps her face revealed too much. She calmed her voice.

'It's a year's work, unique work. I just wanted to show them together, so we could celebrate the achievement . . .'

Galindez held up his hand. 'I understand,' he said.

He glanced down again at the journal. Prison work demanded of its practitioner – correctional officer, screw, guard, hack – that in the service of society he abandon most of his gentler human impulses. Some found that sacrifice easier than others. Devlin could see Galindez struggling between the letter of the law – each visit to be scheduled, processed and cleared at least a day in advance – and the temptation to be generous. Such opportunities didn't often arise. She could see that Galindez knew how much the journal would mean to Coley and Klein. Perhaps it stirred some memory of his own imprisonment in Salvador. As he handed the journal back he looked at her and she willed her eyes to melt his heart.

'Let's go,' he said.

Devlin beamed at him. 'I won't forget this,' she said. 'Do I check in again?'

Galindez glanced at his watch and shook his head. 'I have to be on D block for third lock and count. I'll fake the paper-work later, as long as you don't tell anyone. Come along.'

Galindez took her arm and led her back out into the yard. They started down the path under the main wall towards the infirmary. Galindez set a brisk pace.

'You don't have to accompany me,' said Devlin.

'Yes I do,' said Galindez. 'Now you've signed out you're not officially in here. I'll hand you over to Officer Sung. When you've finished get him to call me and I'll walk you to the gate again.'

'I really appreciate this,' said Devlin.

Galindez nodded and they walked on. Galindez asked her several questions about her research with an insight that surprised her. She wondered what subject he had taught in Salvador. As they approached the infirmary Galindez, without altering his pace, suddenly glanced over his shoulder towards the prison blocks. His eyes narrowed and he frowned. He lifted his hand and rubbed the back of his neck. Devlin followed his gaze. There were a few guys pumping iron behind the high wire fences, a few others trailing back from the workshops towards the General Purposes Wing. Directly opposite the infirmary doors the giant granite spoke of B block pointed towards them, the steel door of its rear gate sally closed. She could not see or hear anything unusual but the tension in Galindez's face made her anxious. Galindez glanced up at the nearest gun tower. The guard within stood mute, apparently unperturbed. Galindez looked ahead to the infirmary. They had fifty metres to go. The main gate was now over four hundred metres behind them.

'What's wrong?' asked Devlin.

Galindez shrugged. 'I thought I heard something. Did you?'

She shook her head. They walked on in a tense silence, Galindez preoccupied, alert. A few seconds later Galindez stopped and strained his ears in concentration. Devlin listened too. Nothing. Then, very faintly, she became aware of a shuffling, rumbling sound. The machine shop, she thought. But no, Galindez was right: it was coming from the prison itself. It reminded her of something but she didn't know what. She glanced at Galindez. His complexion was several shades paler. He looked back towards reception and the main gates. All seemed quiet. Galindez turned to her.

'Don't be alarmed,' he said calmly, 'but I think we should go back.'

Suddenly Devlin felt frightened. 'Whatever you say.'

From the north wall on the far side of the prison, a half a mile distant, came a stuttering flurry of crackles and pops. Galindez snapped his radio from his belt.

Devlin realised that the crackles were rifle fire.

And then she remembered what the noise from the prison reminded her of: a football crowd urging a running back towards the end zone – the sound of a roar arising from many throats.

Two hundred metres across the yard the rear gate of B block started to roll open on its electric motor and the human roar became abruptly louder and no longer like that of a football crowd: these throats were clamouring with raw terror. Hundreds of men were screaming for their lives. Devlin tried to make out what was going on inside.

As the steel door crashed open a huge black and orange fireball exploded from the entrance and sent an oily cloud of flame billowing across the tarmac towards them.

Galindez uttered something in Spanish that Devlin could not make out. Suddenly the fenced-in walkway leading from the General Purposes Wing was alive with khaki-clad figures sprinting for the main gate. More rifle fire. Khaki-clad. Officers.

The guards were fleeing the prison.

Devlin stood numbed. Behind the fleeing guards appeared men in denim, running in all directions with wild shouts and shaking fists and crazy dancing jumps. The radio in Galindez's hand squawked with static and a babble of fuzzy competing voices she couldn't understand.

The oily cloud issuing from the rear of B block cleared. Amidst the coils of smoke – reeling, staggering, screaming, his upper body wreathed in flame – was a man on fire. Beneath the flames Devlin saw that he wore regulation khaki pants.

Galindez grabbed her arms and squeezed, he spoke urgently but calmly, his eyes boring into her.

'You mustn't be seen. The infirmary is safe. Go inside and stay there until we come and get you.'

He turned her and shoved her towards the infirmary doors, twenty metres away.

'Run!' he said. 'Get inside and stay there. Run!'

Galindez started running towards the burning man.

Devlin jammed her briefcase under her arm and sprinted towards the infirmary.

THIRTEEN

CLAUDE TOUSSAINT SAT quietly at one end of the formica-topped mess-hall table eating lima beans, creamed carrots and breaded fish sticks. Around the table sat four other guys listening to Stokely Johnson running down some heavy lines on the current hot topic: how to get a protest petition about the lockdown past Hobbes to the State Governor. Since returning to B block Claude had adopted a policy of not speaking unless spoken to. This had spared him a certain amount of humiliation, but not much. Whenever D block, the whites, or 'that Agry faggot' cropped up in conversation, dark looks were cast in Claude's direction. Claude kept his eyes down on his plate.

'Fuck the state gov'nor man,' said Stokely. 'That cocksucker spends half his day signing death warrants on any brother that hasn't paid his parking tickets on time. Even if he do get a petition from us he just use it to wipe his fat white ass. Motherfucka, you know what happened to those pig-cocksuckers tried to kill King in LA. Almost gave them medals. You think they give you a better hearin'?'

'Then what we s'posed to do, Stoke? Send smoke signals to Mr Farrakhan? The Reverend Jackson? Go to church ever Sunday and pray?' Myers was a weary three-time loser from

Brownsville. Armed robbery and assault. He rolled his thick shoulders and shovelled carrot mush into his mouth.

'We should burn those fuckers down, that's what we should do,' said Stokely. 'Show them who the fuck we are.'

'Stoke is right. Shit, we outnumber the screws fifty to one.' Reed was one of Stokely's radicals.

'Bullshit,' said Myers. 'They send in the National Guard, shoot ten or twenty of you yardbirds down and we all crawl back to our cells on our chickenshit knees.'

'You not talkin' to no chickenshit.' Stokely's voice was quiet with threat.

Myers had seen too much to care. 'So what? So we not chickenshits. So we burn them down and some of us die on our feet 'stead of on our knees. Like Wilson says it just give them th' excuse to kick us back down and tell the world we just the kind of animals they already think we are. I agree with him.'

'Wilson ain't here. He ain't sweatin' it on the block like we are.'

They all looked at him silently for a moment. Then Myers said, 'They hurt him pretty bad, Stoke.'

Stokely lowered his head and blew out a long breath. He blinked hard twice. He said, 'I just wanna send 'em a message they won't forget.'

Myers spoke softly, the bitterness contained in his eyes. 'Niggers On The Rampage. That's th' only message they'd get. Only one they'd print. No one gives a shit, Stoke. Not really.'

Stokely banged his fists on the table. 'I give a shit,' he said. He closed his eyes. The muscles in his neck were corded. He opened his eyes and stared without seeing at his plate, at the soggy beans and fish sticks. After a moment Myers reached out, put his hand on top of Stokely's clenched fist.

'Man, we know you do. That's why we need you in one

piece, to hold the centre fo'us, not shot full of fucken holes or rottin' down in seg.'

The men at the table fell silent. No one was much interested in the slop in front of them. Claude put his plastic fork down in solidarity. He couldn't afford to look at things the way they did. Maybe he should've had more soul, but all that mattered now was getting out of here, and Hobbes, motherfucker or not, had given him a chance. A chance to sit in Alfonso's and sip One Hundred Pipers through a straw. Claude remained profoundly confused by the racial hatred that permeated the prison. It was like the heat they all learned to live with: a background tension so constant and pervasive that you took it for granted and almost forgot about it until some violent incident threw the divisions into grim relief. Claude was more confused than most because he'd lived on both sides of the divide. He wasn't interested in politics. By definition there were a lot of bad eggs in the River but most of them were just guys. Sure you didn't hear much Waylon Jennings on B block or much rap on D but most times shooting the shit over lunch was the same whoever you were with: basketball, women, backache, legal appeals, news from home, tales of sex and violence lavishly embellished by the imagination of time. Claude couldn't see much difference until on those days you stepped out into the yard and found Mexicans on one side and Bloods on the other and suddenly there was only one place you could stand.

According to Ray Klein, by whose friendship Claude, as Claudine, had been immensely flattered, it was a tribal deal. Klein said it was primitive and mysterious but deep. It was, like, an animal thing, a survival mechanism or something. Men were tribal animals by nature and instinct. When everyone was comfortable and civilised and safe it was easy enough to sing that 'We Are The World' shit. But when the shit hit the fan your guts told you to go stand with your own kind or risk getting your balls cut off or worse. It wasn't even necessarily a race thing, Klein had pointed out, or a religious thing. Look at the Middle East, Moslem against Moslem, or South Africa, black against black. Look at the American Civil War for Chrissakes. Tribes. Old tribes and new tribes; in theory whatever was most likely to keep you alive. Except that it caused a hell of a lot of death.

Claude glanced at his fellow diners and didn't feel especially tribal or safe at all. Half-black, half-white, half-woman, half-man, no wonder he was fucked up. They were sitting six tables down from the canteen entrance and the hall was half empty. Since the lockdown started the screws had been feeding the cons from B in two shifts, one side of the block at a time. The hacks were afraid of the pressure building up in men like Johnson. Most of the screws hated the lockdown too. More pain in the ass work, more resentment, more chance of trouble. Claude reckoned that as far as your average screw was concerned the best prison to work in would be one that was totally fucking empty. Or maybe with just a few rich junkies to sell drugs to. A con from ground tier called Green came up to Stokely and handed him a scrap of paper. Stokely read it slowly. Straining his eyes sideways without turning his head Claude glanced over Stokely's shoulder and made out the words.

> Stoke,
> The Doc's a right guy.
> Give him what he wants.
> Wilson.

Stokely caught Claude reading it and crammed the paper into the breast pocket of his shirt. He looked to the front of the mess hall. Klein was standing there, empty-handed, waiting. Stokely turned to Green.

'What's he want?'

'Says he wants to talk to Claude,' said Green.

Stokely turned to Claude, his lip curling. 'What is this shit?'

Claude spread his hands, palm up. 'I don't know.'

He felt exposed. He wanted to see Klein but not here in front of the guys. But with the lockdown maybe this was the best he could expect. And shit, he had the right to talk to whoever he wanted didn't he? When he couldn't bring himself to say so out loud he knew that he didn't have the right after all.

'I heard Klein saved Wilson's life in seg,' said Myers.

'I believe that when I hear it from Wilson his self,' said Stokely. He shrugged and turned to Green. 'He got the balls to ask, I guess he can come on through.'

Green went and told Klein, and Klein walked over. He looked wary but not scared and Claude envied him. Respectful of the formalities, Klein spoke to Johnson before anyone else.

'Johnson,' said Klein.

'Klein,' said Stokely. 'What can I do you?'

'I'd like a minute with Claude,' said Klein. 'That's okay with you.'

Stokely, respect satisfied, nodded to the next table a yard away. 'Take a seat.'

The plastic seats were bolted to the floor so Klein couldn't pull one over. He sat on the edge of the chair nearest Claude. Claude stood up and moved to the other table and sat down opposite Klein. As he did so he realised Stokely didn't like it. Claude felt pleased. It was just about the first move he'd made without Stokely's say so since moving back to B. Klein smiled at him with genuine pleasure.

'How's it going, Claude?'

'Good,' said Claude. He was aware that Stokely, picking at his food while the others argued about tonight's game between the Lakers and the Knicks, was listening in. 'I mean real good. The lockdown's a bitch but, you know. Back on the block it's good for me. You know, back with the brothers. Like, where I belong.'

'I'm glad,' said Klein.

Claude was suddenly afraid that Klein would take all this back to Agry. Agry would have his lips cut off. He calmed himself. Klein wasn't that kind of guy. He was cool. Claude wanted to say, 'If Agry asks 'bout me . . .' but he couldn't afford to, not with Stokely in earshot. He felt like he was walking a tightrope between two tanks, one filled with sharks, the other with piranha. No one knew the whole truth except him and Hobbes. He wanted to tell Klein. About how Grierson had waylaid him on the way to group therapy and taken him down to the lumber room to see Hobbes in secret. And how Hobbes had told him he was coming up for a parole hearing and if he cut out this transvestite shit and moved back to B he'd have a chance. A good chance. A chance to make it to Alfonso's and get his cock sucked. Claude wanted to hear Klein say yeah, go for it, man, and maybe give him some advice on how to deal with the board and shit. But Stokely was listening.

Klein said, 'Hobbes is really putting it to you guys.'

Stokely butted in. 'We can take everything that cocksucker's got to give and then some.'

Klein turned to look at him. 'I don't doubt it. But I think Hobbes is up to something weird, I don't know what. He's sick. In the head.'

Claude suddenly felt queasy. Stokely snorted.

'Shit, Klein, we don't need no doctor to tell us that. Hobbes just need wastin'.'

'Maybe,' said Klein.

Claude sensed a fight and the talk about Hobbes was making him nervous. He said, 'Like Stoke says, we gettin' by. How 'bout you anyway?'

'My parole came through,' said Klein. 'I'm out of here tomorrow.'

For a second Claude felt sick with fear. Abandoned. Klein was the only guy in the place he could talk to when he was down, when the pressure of pretending to be a woman and the strain of living under the hammer of Agry's unpredictable rages got too much for him. Often, as Claudine, he'd wept in the sanctuary of Klein's cell. Agry had not objected. If anything it had helped root Claudine's femininity more deeply in his mind. Bitching and crying at the doctor's was the kind of thing Agry imagined women did all the time. To a similar effect Claude had regularly made the effort to nag Agry about keeping his cell tidy, though in reality he didn't give a shit. Even living on B block, knowing Klein was around had made him feel that bit safer. Now he was leaving. Claude swallowed his disappointment but not before Klein saw it in his face.

'I'll write you,' said Klein. 'Soon as I get settled.'

'Be the first letter I ever got in here,' said Claude. He mustered a big smile. 'Shit man, that's great. Great news. It's right too. It's right.'

He wanted to tell Klein about his own upcoming shot at parole but he did not dare. Stokely would see how he was using them and would find some way to fuck him up. Claude reached across the table and pumped Klein's hand.

'It's right,' he said again.

'I just wanted to pay my respects before I left.'

Claude's heart squeezed. Pay his respects. No one paid their respects to Claude Toussaint. People had kissed his ass when he was Agry's wife because they knew he – or she – could have them worked over by Agry's men. And sometimes she had done so just because she could do it. But they hadn't respected him. They'd feared Agry.

'Thanks, Klein, I,' he was lost for words. 'I mean, good luck, man. Take care of yourself out there.'

'I'll try,' said Klein. 'I'd best get back for third count. Don't want to collect a penalty on my last day.'

'Sure,' said Claude. He fought with a lump in his throat. Klein stood up. 'When you get out, you look me up.'

Claude clambered to his feet. 'Jesus, man, you better believe it.'

'Well.' Klein stuck out his hand. Claude shook it again. Klein smiled at him.

Then, from the rear gate sally of the mess hall, came a scream. A wet, blubbering scream that pierced Claude's bowels as it peaked and then shuddered to a halt in a breathless sob.

Klein turned his head. The smile on his face dissolved into an expression of pure dread. Claude turned in the direction of Klein's stare.

'Wounded man coming through!'

Stumbling down the centre aisle, half-dragged, half-carried by a man on either side, was Sonny Weir of A block, a small time thief and supposed stool pigeon. Cradled in his right hand was the stump of his left arm, cut clean through six inches below the elbow. He was covered in blood and his face was crazed with pain and terror. His mouth twisted into grotesque shapes, sucking for more air to scream with.

'Wounded man coming through!' hollered Bubba Tolson again.

Bubba, his beard powdered with grey cement dust, had one massive tattooed arm wrapped round Weir's waist. On the other side was the psycho's psycho, little Hector Grauerholz.

Up and down the canteen there was a commotion, a clamour of gasps and obscenities, as the men of B block stood up in their seats. The bloody huddle veered towards Claude's table. Klein started forward, Claude guessed to help the bleeding man. Stokely was on his toes, watching, tensed and suspicious. All attention was on the gruesome spectacle of the wounded man.

Claude turned away, nauseated.

From the corner of his eye he saw a bulky figure emerge

from behind the serving hatches and glide, fast and silent, towards Stokely Johnson.

It was Nev Agry.

Claude's bowels turned to slime water. He opened his mouth but his throat was paralysed.

To his left Grauerholz and Tolson suddenly heaved Weir's body through the air towards Klein. Weir toppled forward in a shower of blood and fell, smashing his face on the back of a plastic chair before Klein could catch him.

Nev Agry was five paces from Stokely's back, his eyes glittering. Stokely, fists clenched and cocked, was focused on Bubba Tolson, who bore down on him screaming something about niggers.

The dull whomp of an explosion and a gust of flame erupted from the back of the mess hall. Then another.

Yells of panic crowded Claude's head.

Inmates began to clatter from their tables, spilling trays of food, falling over each other to escape the fire.

Stokely kicked Bubba Tolson in the belly and stepped back to regain his balance. Agry closed in, his face shining with malice. His hand came up from his side. A razor winked as it rose to strike at Stokely's neck. Stokely still hadn't seen him in the confusion. Claude's voice tore free of his throat.

'Stoke!'

As Stokely turned to face Agry, Hector Grauerholz raised a pistol and shot Stokely Johnson through the side of the face. Blood splashed Claude's cheeks as Stokely spun and went down.

Klein fell on Grauerholz, wrestling for the gun in his hand.

Myers reeled away screaming as Bubba Tolson dashed a jar of oven cleaner into his eyes and ran on past.

Shattering glass, more explosions – one, two – more flames. Molotov cocktails. Panic-stricken men scrambled down the hall, stampeding for the door in a mob. Noise and smoke swirled past Claude as he stood rooted to the spot, staring at his worst nightmare: Nev Agry.

And Claude suddenly knew that all this – all *this* – was for him. And he felt sick to his gut. All for him: Nev Agry had come to take his woman back.

After that something seemed to switch itself off in Claude's brain. He watched without emotion as Agry raised his foot and stomped mindlessly on Stokely's bloody head. As if in a slow motion underwater dream Claude felt himself dragged through space, felt a hand hook under his left armpit and clamp the back of his head in a half-nelson. He did not resist. His limbs were putty. He felt Agry's blade against his neck, heard Agry's voice bellow in his ear.

'Klein!'

Klein had Grauerholz's neck locked in the crook of his left elbow, the psycho's gun wrist gripped in his right hand. He froze and looked up from Grauerholz's purpling face.

'Let the kid go,' said Agry. 'I need him.'

Klein glanced at Claude and tightened his arm round Grauerholz's throat.

'I need you as well, you stupid fuck,' said Agry. Claude felt Agry shake him like a doll. 'And this bitch too. But I can do without you all, I have to.'

'I hate to say this, Agry,' said Klein. His teeth were gritted with the effort of controlling his anger. 'But you just made it to the top of my shit list.'

Klein let go of Grauerholz's neck and with a fast move of both hands twisted the revolver from the psycho's grip. Grauerholz fell coughing to his hands and knees. Klein cocked the pistol and held it down by his thigh. He stared at Agry. Claude felt the blade disappear. A hand shoved him in the back and he staggered forwards towards Klein. Klein, surprisingly light on the balls of his feet, moved over to give himself space.

'Take her back to D block, Klein,' said Agry.

Klein didn't move. Agry grinned at him.

'Understand right now, Doc, before you fuck yourself up. This is total war. Us against the rest. And there's only one side of the line you can stand on.'

Klein looked at him and understood that Agry was right. His face became cold, expressionless. He walked over and took Claude by the arm. Claude still felt numbed by the chaos of which he was the centre. Klein spoke into his ear with quiet urgency. 'Let's go.'

A raw cough came from the floor. 'I want...' Another cough. Grauerholz pushed himself backwards onto his knees. 'I want my fucking gun back, Nev.'

Agry sneered at him. 'You just lost it, asshole. Johnson was mine, I told you. Mine. Now get the fuck up and get to work.'

Grauerholz stumbled to his feet. He stared at Klein with molten hatred. Klein, aiming from the hip, pointed the gun at Grauerholz's chest.

'There's something you should understand too, Agry, before Hector here fucks up.'

Klein was white in the lips and trembling with rage. Claude had never seen him anything like this way before. Even Agry took a pace backwards. Klein, the gun rock steady on Hector Grauerholz, stared Agry in the eye.

'If I have to I will kill this little fuck. And if I have to I will kill you too. And I will kill as many more assholes as get themselves in my way. Because I will tell you something: you guys have really rained on my parade.'

For a second Claude thought Klein was going to shoot Grauerholz where he knelt. Agry held out a pacifying hand.

'Hey, Klein, take it easy,' said Agry. 'What's in a bunch of niggers?'

'I was set to go home tomorrow,' said Klein.

He swung the gun as if he might shoot Agry instead. He looked that close to losing it.

Agry, the master of losing it, recognised the condition when he saw it. 'How the fuck was I to know 'bout your fucking parole?' he said.

'I only just found out myself, you cocksucker.'

If Claude had ever watched a more unlikely conversation – Nev Agry explaining himself to Klein and being told he was a cocksucker and Klein getting away with it – he couldn't remember it. But amidst the smoke and blood of his dreamy state it all seemed natural enough.

'Shit, Klein, we all have our bad days,' said Agry.

Klein glanced down at the gun in his hand. His shoulders relaxed. He took a deep breath.

'Just stay out my fucken way,' he said.

The hall was filling with oily smoke and alarms were going off. Four fires were burning in scattered pools. The stampede of the fleeing black convicts into the central atrium had left them alone. From the back of the hall came a new commotion.

Agry glanced towards the noise and said to Klein, 'Might be easier if you stayed out of ours.'

Through the rear gate of the hall burst six of the biggest white convicts in the joint, led by Horace Tolson, Bubba's equally bearded and monstrous twin. They charged in unison down the length of the near deserted hall, voices raised in battle. They were preceded by the first ten feet of a red thirty-foot iron girder that they carried between them. Claude watched vacantly as the bevelled tip of the girder sped towards him. His arm jerked painfully in its socket as Klein dragged him out of the way. As Tolson and the girder thundered past Claude read the number '99' written on its side. He looked at Klein. The sight of the girder seemed to sober him.

'Goddamn you,' Klein said, quietly, to Agry.

Agry shrugged, smiled, back in control again. 'Just do us both a favour, Doc, and we'll forget what's been said.'

Klein, accepting the inevitable, said, 'What do you want?'

'Walk the little lady back home for me. To D.'

Claude slowly realised that 'the little lady' meant him. That is, her.

Claudine.

Shit, he thought. Not Claudine again. A woman's fucking work was never done.

Her arm jerked in her socket again and Claudine stumbled down the aisle of the canteen as Klein hauled her along behind him. From up ahead came a shattering crash of destruction as the girder found its mark in the central watchtower. Claudine didn't care. She was dwelling on how unfair it was. She'd only just got used to being Claude again. And now it was back to her. Claudine. Oh well. She sighed and started thinking about what dress and which lingerie to wear. Something sexy, she supposed. A nice surprise.

For when Nev got back home from work.

FOURTEEN

KLEIN FLINCHED FROM the rending crash as the bellowing of Horace Tolson's ramming squad climaxed in the destruction of the central watchtower window.

The reinforced plexiglass cracked without shattering but the bolts fixing it to the frame were torn free. The red girder penetrated six feet into the command and control room and its rear end clanged to the flagstones as the squad let go of their ropes. Keeping close to the wall as he led Claude around the atrium, Klein watched as Bubba Tolson ran up to the hole in the tower's side with a flaming Molotov cocktail and pitched it inside. There was a blast of flame and smoke. Seconds later the door of the tower swung open and two scorched guards staggered out, carrying old man Burroughs between them. One of them dropped Burroughs's legs and sprinted for the exit. The other hitched Burroughs over his shoulder and staggered after the first.

The smoking atrium was July 4th in a precinct of hell by way of Hieronymus Bosch. Whilst some men fled, guards and inmates alike, the guards ripping off their hats and shirts as they ran, others wheeled pointlessly back and forth emitting a pandemoniac whooping and screaming obscenities. A number of black inmates lay insensible on the ground, rolling with the random, frenzied kicks delivered to them by the revellers. From the stairway to the laundry came a stream of white guys, mainly from the Agry and DuBois cliques. They carried weapons from the garage, the machine shop, carpentry, the kitchen. Hammers, saws, wrenches; screwdrivers and crowbars; stumps of wood and steel; tyre irons, trowels, a blow torch, grease guns; cans of paint thinner and lumber preservative. Anything that might bludgeon, cut or penetrate. Anything that might blind, corrode or burn. They were all of them intoxicated, though not with alcohol or drugs. Not yet. The vast store of jailhouse wine and potato liquor, buried by the gallon in a thousand crannies, and of PCP and crack and weed and smack, stored by the ounce and the sixteenth of an ounce in hollowed out bricks and the seams of clothes and the soles of Reeboks, all this would be consumed later in a desperate search for oblivion. Now, welded into a single feverish consciousness, they were drunk with anarchy and parched by the thirst for annihilation.

There wasn't a screw left in sight. As Klein dragged a glassy-eyed Claude towards the gate of cellblock D he kept an eye peeled for Grauerholz. No one, including the shave-headed psychopath, came at them. From the gate of cellblock C came a cacophony of wailing voices and rattling bars. Caught in the middle of their third lock and count the Blacks and Latinos on C were sealed in their cells. The men from A block had finished their count and were out and the riot had broken before Klein's own block, D, had started theirs. Klein glanced over his shoulder as he heard a rattle of wheels behind him.

From the mess hall came a large three-sided laundry trolley covered by a dirty tarpaulin, pushed by four Agry crewmen. Agry was with them, sweating with the exertion of power, egging them on with abuse, yelling at stragglers to drag them niggers out of their fucken way. The trolley trundled past the scorched watchtower and came to rest outside the arched gateway to cellblock B. Agry ripped the tarpaulin aside. On the bed of the trolley stood an oil drum and two crates of bottles with scraps of cloth stuck in their necks. Agry directed the men as they manoeuvred the open side of the trolley into the cellblock entrance. At his command they tipped the oil drum so that it crashed over the raised step of the doorway and emptied out its contents in a splashing torrent.

As the smell suddenly hit his nostrils Klein said, 'Jesus.'

The stink was of gasoline. Gallons of inflammable liquid flooded down the main ground floor walkway of cellblock B. Agry's men dragged the trolley away and Klein's guts clenched with nausea as hysterical sounds – of desperate men trying to batter their way out of their locked cells – erupted from inside the block.

One whole half of the cellblock, three crammed tiers, was still full with those who'd been waiting their turn in the mess hall. Now they were staring through the bars with the stink of impending incineration scorching their lungs.

With a flourish Agry pulled a book of matches from his shirt pocket.

Klein squeezed the revolver in his fist and shut his eyes.

He could shoot the cocksucker now, and maybe it would make a difference. He could blow Agry's mad brains out and maybe it would save the bastards inside from incineration. Maybe without Agry to lead it the whole riot would burn out in a single pop, before things escalated into total war.

Yeah. And maybe Agry's guys would tear Klein limb from limb, when all he had to do was go back to his cell and shut the door. And wait for this shit to finish.

Not my fucking business.

In his time Klein had heard a lot of people in terrible pain. He remembered children mangled in car wrecks; the sobbing of a man who'd accidentally severed the arm of his eight-year-old son with a chainsaw when it bounced off a nail in the wood. Klein had steeled himself to those sounds and done his job. He tried to steel himself now. Not my fucking business. But here he had no job to wrap around him for protection. It wasn't his job to kill Nev Agry. It wasn't his obligation. His only obligation was to himself. To survive and go free.

Yet despite all the suffering he had witnessed in the emergency room he was not prepared for this: the screams of the trapped men echoing and keening from the valley of the long distance runners was the most terrible sound he had ever heard.

No. The men in B block weren't his business.

In the frame of the arched doorway Agry lit the book of matches and held it flaring above his head. He looked across the atrium towards them and Klein realised he was staring at Claude. He felt Claude's fingers digging into his arm.

'Semper fi!' screamed Agry.

Agry pitched the flaming matchbook through the archway and bolted for cover.

Klein turned his face to the wall.

A second later a blast-wave of heat rolled over his back, the sound drowning out the frenzy of the condemned men. When he turned back Claude was on his knees, sobbing wildly and biting his hands, tears pouring down his face.

'Jesus God,' sobbed Claude. 'Jesus God.'

Agry stood with his men dancing and cheering around him, waving their lumps of wood and steel in the air. Klein fought down a bolus of puke. Acid leaked from the membranes of his gut. He could have blown Agry away. He hadn't.

Live with it.

He steeled himself. Against himself. Against that weakness within, against the pity which would destroy him.

Live with it.

Klein steeled himself.

'Jesus God,' chanted Claude.

Klein hauled him savagely to his feet. He shouted in Claude's face.

'We gotta look out for ourselves!'

Self-loathing foamed up into his gullet.

He steeled himself.

'Ourselves!'

'Jesus God.'

With an effort Klein steadied his own heaving chest. Then he bent down and hooked his arm round Claude's waist and dragged him through the gateway into cellblock D.

FIFTEEN

Victor Galindez flung himself on top of the burning guard in the yard and tried to smother the flames.

Burning cloth and skin and hair filled his nose and mouth with acrid fumes. The guard writhed and screamed underneath him. Each time Galindez beat out a patch of flame the gas-soaked shirt reignited. Galindez tore the cloth apart, wrenching it in handfuls from the guard's chest. Strips of skin came away with it. The guard was still screaming. Galindez suddenly recognised him: it was Perkins.

'Galindez!'

Galindez turned. Sung stood beside him aiming a fire extinguisher. Galindez rolled aside and Sung hosed Perkins down with a white cloud of carbon dioxide foam. A few seconds later the fire was out. Galindez, on his hands and knees, stared at the injured man. Perkins's scalp was a scorched, crinkled cap of burnt hair and blistered skin. His eyelids glistened with fluid exuding from the delicate, damaged skin. Galindez had never seen a man burned before. A visceral horror lurched through his anus and balls. Perkins opened his mouth and Galindez bent forward to hear him.

'The men,' croaked Perkins.

He paused, took a wheezing breath, spoke again.

'They're still in there.'

Galindez found tears springing to his eyes. Terribly mutilated as he was Perkins still thought of the men in his charge. Galindez looked up at Sung.

'You got to get him out of here.'

Rifle shots crackled from the North Wall. Galindez grabbed Perkins by one arm. Sung dropped the fire extinguisher and grabbed the other arm. They hauled Perkins to his feet.

'You got to walk, man, you understand?' Galindez shouted into Perkins's shrivelled ear. 'You got to walk.'

Perkins nodded feebly. The radios on their hips squawked and crackled frantically.

'This is Bill Cletus. All officers report to the main gates. Get out of there. Repeat. Get the fuck out. All of you out. Now.'

The message continued, Cletus carefully restating the single command: get out. Now. Galindez looked towards B block, then at Sung.

'Get going,' said Galindez. 'Go!'

Sung draped Perkins's arm over his shoulders and wrapped an arm round his waist. The Korean was tough. He would get Perkins clear. Sung nodded to him. Galindez nodded back.

Sung and Perkins began to stagger away across the yard.

Galindez realised that he had picked up the fire extinguisher, that its weight, like the weight of some dread obligation, was pulling on his arm.

Perkins's last thought had been for the men.

Galindez clapped his free hand to his eyes. Mother of God. His mind swam with faces. His wife, Elisa. His children. The long journey from Salvador to Panama City. The longer one from Panama to Laredo. The struggle and the pain they had gone through to get what they had. And to accept all that they had left behind them. All that they had lost. All these things scorched his mind in one compressed and terrible flame of awareness. It had cost them so much. Only God knew how much and how much it was worth. And only God knew what he had to do now to keep his immortal soul.

The radio still squawked at his hip but Galindez couldn't hear it. Nor the rifles high up on the walls.

Perkins's last thought had been for the men.

Two hundred of them.

Galindez dragged his hand away from his face. The choice was no longer his.

Victor Galindez sprinted towards the rear gate and sally-port of cellblock B.

Perkins had opened the rear gate in order to escape and had unwittingly caused the fireball that had engulfed him. Galindez, the extinguisher bashing into his leg, staggered into the doorway and stopped. Before his appalled gaze the interior of the cellblock was hell. Galindez thought he had known hell, in the interrogation cells in Salvador, but now for the first time the word was real. This was the hell the Jesuits had imprinted on his growing childhood mind. The central walkway was a river of fire, fiercest at the far end and petering out about halfway down the block in the scorched trail of the fireball that ended at his feet. Dense black fumes filled the glass vault, blocking out the sun and turning the whole block into a death house.

The tiers to his right were empty; those to his left full, squirming with terrified inmates. A few yards away men reached through the bars and screamed for help as they saw him. Further down the block the steel grilles were silent as the prisoners took what shelter they could in the rear of their cells. The cell doors couldn't be opened from the small guard's station at this the rear gate, only from the cellblock office at the inner gate. Galindez ran into the guard station pulling out his keys. He opened a steel locker in one corner. It was crammed with clothes, bottles of suntan lotion, porn mags, soda bottles, odd items of sports gear. Perkins was a slob.

Galindez hauled the rubbish out until he found what he wanted: a regulation mask for use in tear gas situations. As he ran back out something caught his eye. Leaning against the wall was a pair of mops and buckets left by the cons who'd swabbed the walkway that morning. He dashed over. One of the buckets was still full of murky water. Galindez set the extinguisher down, removed his cap, took the bucket and drenched himself the best he could. He jammed the cap back down over his hair. Hoarse shouts came from the tiers as the men understood what Galindez was about to attempt.

'Muthafucka! Muthafucka!'

'Fuck! *Fuck!*'

'Go *for* it, man!'

'Go you sucka, *go!*'

'Fuck you, man! *Fuck you!*'

Galindez ran forward hauling the extinguisher in his left hand. As the movement tore sheets of skin from his palm he realised he'd burned his hands ripping off Perkins's shirt. He squeezed tighter, attacking the pain. As he got to within a few yards of the river of fire and he felt its heat on his face he stopped and set the extinguisher down. There would be no oxygen in there. He took half a dozen breaths, heaving in and out as deeply as he could. The shouts of the convicts, more frenzied than ever, were muted by the crackle of flames. Galindez pulled on the gas mask. Through the thick glass lenses the flames were distorted. He aimed the long black cone-shaped nozzle of the fire extinguisher at the ground just ahead of his feet, muttered a last prayer and switched on the white spray.

Victor Galindez took a deep breath, held it, and waded forward into the flames.

Crouching low, moving the white cloud from the funnel in a short repetitive arc in front of his feet, Galindez strode forward in a fire-free pocket of airless space. Too fast and he ran into the flames; too slow and he'd never make it to the other end of the walkway. After each step the flames closed in again behind him. His back began to burn. He felt the damp hair at the edges of his cap hiss and shrivel against his scalp. Steady. Steady. One step, then another. Inside the mask sweat streamed into his eyes and steamed over the lenses. Don't breathe. No oxygen out there. The roar of the funnel and the fire filled his ears. Now walking blind. Steady. Steady. Planting one foot down ahead of the other, hoping he was moving in a straight line, hoping, doubting, praying, expecting each moment to find himself blundering into the bars of one of the cages. If he did that he'd be finished. He wanted to turn back. He didn't dare. He wanted to run. He didn't dare. He wanted to breathe. He didn't dare. Don't turn. Don't run. Don't breathe. He had lost track of distance and time. Seconds were hours. Yet he had to be close. He had to be close. His shoulder rammed into something hard. He turned his back into the hardness. They weren't bars. Smooth and hard but not dense. Glass. Glass. He was past the cages. The heat was intense. He swept the foam in a semi-circle around his feet and slid sideways with the hard smoothness against his spine. His head was exploding with heat and claustrophobia and the effort of holding his breath. Suddenly the hardness behind him disappeared and he stumbled.

His back had been against the glass shell of the inner gate office and he'd stumbled half-through the sliding door which was ajar. He wrenched the door open. He was inside. He slammed the door shut. The extinguisher fell from his hand. The stale air erupted from his chest and he clung to the wall, heaving. Smoke. Smoke. More smoke than oxygen but the mask protected his lungs. He was still almost blind. He reeled across the room from memory, fumbling in his pocket, pulled out his keys. His hands found the control unit for the tiered cell doors. By touch he jammed his pass key into the panel and twisted. The keyboard awaited the appropriate code number. 101757. He prayed he'd remembered it correctly and pulled off the mask to see. Smoke assailed his throat and eyes. He glanced at the keyboard and hammered in the numbers. There was a pause that stretched out into eternity. Mother of Jesus.

A slow rising rumble and a crash of steel on stone thundered above the noise of the fire. The tier doors were open. Dimly he heard desperate shouts of relief. Galindez sagged against the control panel. Each breath was a wire brush soaked with Clorox scouring out his lungs. He dragged the mask back on, shoved himself away, grabbed the fire extinguisher. He slid back the glass door and paused on the threshold. Through foggy lenses he saw a man wrapped in a wet sheet stagger past, plunging towards the atrium. The yard was better, thought Galindez. The yard was safer. At least he could reach the infirmary from there. More men crowded past the doorway, heading into the interior of the prison. The yard was safer. But he couldn't face the fire a second time. He followed the fleeing men.

Five metres later he burst free of the blaze and into the light from the great central dome. He dropped the extinguisher and fell to his knees, tearing the mask from his face. Running legs passed before his eyes. Sounds of violence and chaos.

As Galindez raised his head to take his bearings, something hard and heavy smashed into the back of his head.

And the violent chaos turned black.

SIXTEEN

IN CELLBLOCK D the frenzy of destruction had already begun. The great majority of the men could have had no forewarning of Agry's blitzkrieg and yet to a man, as if acting on some preprogrammed instinctive impulse, they fell to their work of dismantling the prison within moments of the opportunity presenting itself. They attacked the ageing masonry, the woodwork, the light fittings, the furniture in their cells, even the stone flags of the walkway, with any implement they could find, anything they could rip away and grab onto and swing. Water poured from dozens of cells, from smashed faucets and blocked toilets deliberately flushed, and fell in glittering cascades from the upper tiers. Torn sheets and the stuffing from disembowelled mattresses floated through the air. And noise, noise. Of mindless damage and massive rage stored too long and finally released.

Klein walked through this Armageddon stony-faced.

Behind him Claude Toussaint stumbled along in a blank-eyed daze. Klein pulled Claude along ground tier. Convicts leered at Claude as he passed. None of them tried to harm him despite the colour of his skin. Klein stopped outside Agry's cell and jerked his head for Claude to go inside.

Claude stared at him. 'Take me with you,' he said.

'Wait for Agry,' said Klein. 'You'll be safe enough here.'

'I'm scared,' said Claude.

Klein looked at his face. A pleading child stared back at him. Klein thought of Vinnie Lopez. Same age. Twenty-two. Klein forced himself to harden his heart. He needed the steelworks and ice more than ever. He shook his head.

'You're on your own, Claude. If you cling to me Agry will come down hard on both of us.' He put his hand on the nape of Claude's neck and squeezed it gently. 'Look, I don't believe Agry wants to kill you. If you can endure what he does to you, you can *survive this thing. We both can. You understand? Endure.*'

After a moment Claude nodded.

'I'd best get dressed,' said Claude.

Klein suddenly realised exactly what 'endure' involved for Claude. He took his hand from Claude's neck. Klein swallowed. Claude turned and walked through the muslin sheet into Agry's cell without looking back.

Klein strode back to the spiral staircase without catching anyone's eyes and climbed up to second tier. He shoved two men out of the way as they clattered down the steps past him. He waded through the wreckage accumulating on the catwalk. Some men sat quietly in their cells, hoping to be ignored, praying that there were no outstanding grudges held against them. When Klein reached his own billet he took his shaving mirror from the wall and propped it on the floor between the bars, facing the stairs he'd just climbed so that he had a view of anyone approaching along the catwalk. He reached in his pocket and pulled out the pistol he'd taken from Grauerholz. He swung out the cylinder: five rounds. Jesus Christ. Klein lowered the hammer of the gun on the live cartridge next to the spent shell. He'd have four shots in sequence then the blank to remind him he had only one round left. Maybe he'd want it for himself. He put the gun away. He clenched his teeth. This was as far as he was going. Anyone coming through that door was dead. Anyone who fell bleeding and weeping for help on his threshold could lie there until they died. He wasn't moving from his hole until this riot burned itself out and he was free. Not for anyone. From the floor by the door the piece of tape on his mirror caught his eye.

NOT MY FUCKING BUSINESS

Ray Klein slid his cell door shut and lay down on his bunk to wait.

SEVENTEEN

WARDEN HOBBES STOOD at the north window of his office and stared out at his prison. In the midday sun its fabulous geometry seemed roofed in burnished gold.

Smoke drifted from the rear gate of cellblock B.

The occasional rifle still cracked from the towers.

In the yard no one moved and it was empty save for the bodies of several wounded men. All the bodies were clothed in blue denim.

Hobbes knew not what was going on inside the prison, though he could guess.

Behind him the telephone on his desk started ringing.

Hobbes ignored it.

For the first time in an infinity of time his mind was empty of thoughts, of words, of notions. Time past and time future were finally forged together in this most momentous of times present.

Hobbes looked at his watch.

By the testimony of the guard in the West Wall watchtower it was just twenty-three minutes since Sonny Weir had been dragged, screaming and bleeding, from the builder's yard. That was all the time it had taken for absolute order to succumb to absolute anarchy.

The telephone rang on and Hobbes ignored it.

This wasn't a moment to be contaminated with triviality. It was a moment of history. More than that: a historic moment. It deserved, from him at least, a few seconds of sombre contemplation.

The phone rang on; and Hobbes ignored it.

After all, for the first time in one hundred and four years, Green River State Penitentiary had been placed, and placed entire, in the hands of its inmates – that they themselves might use it as they pleased.

PART II

THE RIVER

EIGHTEEN

NEV AGRY KNEW he couldn't trust Claudine any further than he could shove his dick up her ass and in every sense that wasn't quite as far as he would've liked.

On the other hand where was the sense in having a woman you could trust all the way? Jesus, none at all and Agry could testify to that from his own experience. The single worst year of his life, including all the hard time he'd done in the River, had been with a woman he'd been stupid enough to marry, shit, nearly twenty years ago now. She'd spent all the dough he'd earned at the packing plant, nagged him halfway crazy and had doled out tenth rate strictly flat-on-her-back sex like she was opening the gates of fucking paradise. She'd been as devoted and faithful as the day was long, something she never tired of reminding him of and for which he was meant to be eternally grateful. The day she'd told him she was pregnant Agry had silently packed his green kitbag in front of her blotchy tear-stained, bleating face and pulled out of town on an east-bound freight. Despite all the crazy stunts he'd pulled since then, including burning down B block to get Claudine back, nothing in the history of his life mystified him so much as the fact that he'd married Marsha.

Since then he'd preferred his women to have a wide streak

of bitch in them. At least they were only after what was in your wallet – and if you were lucky your pants – and not in ripping off the next forty years of your fucking life. And it kept a man on his toes. Plus the sex was better and what the fuck else did a man need a woman for? He couldn't think of a single thing. And even having said that the best sex Agry had ever had was in prison. And the best sex he'd ever had in prison was with Claudine. While his men took the penitentiary apart Agry drank bonded bourbon and fucked Claudine for fifty-five minutes straight, struggling with the sulphate that delayed his frantic need to come, before finally ejaculating in a violent spasm that almost wrenched his guts from their moorings.

For a few moments afterwards his throat had been swollen and he'd almost felt like crying without knowing why. Now he realised that he felt full. For the first time in his life he felt full. He kissed Claudine on the nape of the neck – her high yellow skin beaded with his sweat beside him, luminous in the candlelight, and Claudine murmured. And the fullness felt good.

Nev Agry hadn't drifted into professional crime; he'd chosen it. He'd decided on that freight train that marriage was the last time he'd ever drift anywhere. He'd hitched up with a couple of hard cases he'd met in the brig during his military punishment and had robbed a bank in Starkville, Mississippi. A combination of intelligence, will and belligerence had made him the natural leader of their small band and Nev had liked it. For eight years he'd lived high off the hog on the proceeds of a series of small-town bank jobs: Montana, Florida, Michigan, never the same state twice. During that time he'd killed five men: one civilian, two bank guards, a deputy sheriff and one of his partners who'd objected too strongly to the size of Nev's cut. The first and last time he'd hit a bank in Texas, in Sulphur Springs, he'd left one cop paralysed from the waist down and another with a titanium plate in his skull. Thirty-five years to life.

On the street Agry had lived outside the society on which he'd preyed and had paid little heed to its mechanisms. Once inside, thrust into a densely structured society he couldn't escape, he had seen that there were only two mechanisms that counted: domination and submission; and two kinds of inmate: the leaders and the led. The vast majority were more than content to be the latter. He'd also seen that, at the right moment, submission was a path to domination. You couldn't go against the hierarchy. He'd learned that the hard way as a teenage Marine when he'd broken a drill sergeant's jaw. It was the hierarchy that contained the power, not the individuals who filled it. A weak man high in the hierarchy was vastly more powerful than a strong man outside it.

Nev was strong and at the time he'd come up to the River the barn boss on D, Jack 'Hammer' Cutler, was just recovering from his second heart attack. Jack still moved the wheels but his time in the infirmary had taken all the piss out of him and his crew was on the wane, losing influence and muscle. Agry had allied himself to this, the weakest crew. He'd also befriended Dennis Terry in Maintenance. He'd also courted Bill Cletus, then just a sergeant. Using Terry's contacts with outside suppliers and his own still-fresh contacts in the world, he'd organised a new smuggling network, strengthened Cutler's crew and become Cutler's right arm. One night he'd arranged with Cletus to have his own and Jack's cell doors left open. In the wee hours he'd straddled Cutler's chest with his knees and clamped an immovable hand over his mouth and nostrils. Next morning Cutler was found dead from his third and final heart attack.

The internal economy of the River was as complex as that of Manhattan. You had two and a half thousand guys who worked and lived in a shithole. They wanted things: home comforts, sex, drugs, magazines, tobacco, candy bars, pictures of girls, any crumbs of pleasure and relief they could get their hands on. The turnover of faces was pretty fast. There was a hard core of men with long sentences but Agry reckoned over a two-year cycle eighty per cent of the faces changed. These men had visitors – girlfriends and wives, brothers, mothers – and visitors brought gifts: cash and drugs. A mother tearfully kissing her son goodbye at the end of her monthly visit would slip him a couple of twenties, maybe even a couple of C's. A girlfriend might have a condom wrapped round a gram or two of coke stashed in her cheek or up her cunt. Postal gifts too, radios and training shoes with a little something extra stowed inside. Plus the men earned prison scrip for their jobs. Easily a million bucks a year – maybe double that – in hard cash money flowed in every year, was translated into goods and comforts, and then made its way out again in the pockets of truck drivers, delivery men and guards. To an inmate the cash itself was toilet paper. Agry turned it into something you wanted: something to ease the pain, something to remind the homesick souls of all they'd left behind.

Agry sometimes reflected that he'd made more of himself in here than he ever would've done outside. He ran a business, an organisation, in the toughest market there was. Some of his guys didn't know shit from toothpaste but if he asked them to they'd ram their heads through the bars of their cell door. Others, like Tony Shockner, had more brains than he did and took care of a lot of fine detail for him. Violent punishment, when necessary, was always swift and extreme. His men usually handled that. Periodically, when he heard a whisper that some new hardcase not long up thought him soft, he would unleash a spasm of his own personal brutality.

Agry's crew supplied drugs and liquor on D but left the rest of the prison to DuBois and Grauerholz. Drugs gave a good return on the dollar but, ubiquitous as they were, there wasn't the turnover. Agry reckoned he'd made more on electrical goods and porn than Larry ever did out of cocaine and Mexican brown. He'd built something extraordinary: that was the word Klein had once used in Agry's cell, eating coffee cake and sipping tea with Claudine. Agry had never quite warmed to Klein. He was too self-contained. An outsider with power and therefore unusual. Maybe unique. And maybe Agry was jealous, just a little, of the peals of laughter Claudine gave out when Klein said something funny that Agry would never have thought of. But Klein wasn't a threat and he was good for Claudine. Plus he'd sure as hell given Agry better treatment for these goddamned chest infections than that cocksucker Bahr had ever done. And Agry appreciated that word too: extraordinary. No one had ever said that about him before. Now that extraordinary was being torn apart all around him.

And yet Agry, sweating in the candlelight, felt full.

Agry's bedroom was dense with humidity and the body heat of sex. Perspiration clung to his scalp and made the pale hairs on his chest and belly look dark. In her red lipstick and underwear Claudine looked like a million dollars. Agry smiled to himself. She was costing the state of Texas at least that much and probably a lot more, now that the joint was being trashed on her behalf. If it was costing him too he would have paid anything to get what he had right now: this scrawny high-yeller bitch lying by his side.

Agry owned two double cells on ground tier, one knocked through into the other, at the cost of a huge bribe to Bill Cletus. In the room was a double bed with an orthopaedic mattress and peach-coloured sheets. The light was almost gone now and candles burned on the table throwing flickering shadows onto the raw granite blocks of the cell. Agry thought it was kind of romantic. He hoped Claudine thought so too, though she hadn't said as much as yet. There was something hanging between them, something he had to clear up.

'Why did you leave me?' he said.

Claudine started to turn her head towards him. Agry put his hand on the back of her neck so she couldn't turn any further. His fingers dug into the side of her throat until he could feel her pulse throbbing. It was steady, and not more than eighty despite the speed she'd snorted. Claudine was a cooler customer than most people gave her credit for. Agry had lived with her for four years. He knew. She'd dropped straight from the hole between her mama's legs into a federal housing project in New Orleans and had been living on her wits against the odds ever since.

'I di'nt leave you, honey,' she said. 'They took me. You remember it.'

Agry did indeed remember it. It had been like having blunt nails hammered through his hands. And the end of his dick. Cletus, whose pockets had bulged with Agry's money more than a time or two, had turned up with half-a-dozen of his men dressed in padded vests and football helmets and violated the sanctuary of his suite in broad daylight. They'd dragged Claudine out of her cell and marched her off to B block. As she'd tottered off down the tier on the high heels Agry had paid a fortune for, with Cletus poking her in the back with his nightstick, the other six screws had held Agry pinned to the floor of his cell while he'd foamed at the mouth and threatened their families with extermination.

The humiliation had been without parallel. They'd even denied him a period in seg which would at least have afforded him a dignity of sorts. Agry had made a dozen written applications to Hobbes for a meeting, an explanation. They'd all been refused with Hobbes, so high and fucking mighty, telling him no prison official, and the warden in particular, was required to explain their actions to 'the likes of him'. The likes of him. Hobbes had had the gall to finish his letter with some kind of fucking quotation: 'He who has no rule over his

own spirit is like a city that is broken down and without walls.'
Whatever the fuck that was supposed to mean.

The only word he'd been able to get from the guards was
that Hobbes had moved Claudine to appease the niggers, and
in particular that blackest of vile nigger cocksuckers Reuben
Wilson, who'd felt that Claudine's 'captivity' in D block was
degrading to the black population as a whole. As if any level
of degradation existed that they hadn't already plumbed on
the day they were fucking born. Well, Agry had found another
level for them: he'd burned the fuckers down in their own
cells, he'd settled their shit good. And as for Hobbes, kissing
the ass of Reuben Wilson, the only broken city he had to
think on was the wreck of his own fucking prison, his baby.
Agry allowed himself a moment of gloating. There was still
work to do. Good work. If they hadn't all been against him
before – Hobbes and Wilson – they were now. Agry snorted
with contempt. He who has no rule over his own spirit. Agry
had such rule. He'd shown them good. Finally there was
Claudine and her betrayal. Her parole. An anonymous note,
typed, had arrived in his mail three days before: Toussaint is
coming up for parole. Would she confess? He leaned on the
nape of her neck.

'Whose idea was it to take you to B?' he said.

The pressure pushed Claudine's lips and face into the mattress,
distorting her voice. 'I don't know. It sure warn't mine.'

'Was it Wilson?'

Claudine didn't answer. Agry's hand went into spasm.

'Wilson! Wilson!'

Claudine's neck was as close to breaking as it would ever
be. She wheezed and struggled, unable to speak. Agry released
the pressure. Claudine squealed into the pillow.

'Yeah, Wilson. Was Wilson asked fo' it. I dunno why. I dunno.'

'Who told you?'

'Stokely Johnson.'

'What did Johnson say?' growled Agry.

'He din'n know why either. Just said I's a disgrace t' the brothers and it was up t' him he'd of had me killed.'

'That's all? That's it?'

'That's all.'

'You lying yellow bitch.'

'They treated me bad, Nev. Real bad. You don't know how bad.'

For a second Agry felt in his throat the pleasure it would give him to kill her right now. The words sprang to his lips to confront her with her lies, her parole hearing. He swallowed them back. Whilst he knew and she didn't he had control. There would be a better moment to spring it on her. He let go her neck.

Claudine broke into a spasm of thin coughs and suddenly Agry, watching her squirm, was choked with pity and understanding. She was only human after all. Why shouldn't she want to get out of this fucking place? She needed time, sympathy, tenderness, all that good shit he'd read in *GQ* magazine about what the ladies wanted. On the table next to the candles was a bottle of Johnson's baby oil. He leaned across Claudine's back, took the bottle and poured some into the palm of his hand. He ran his hand over her back, spreading a sheen of oil.

'How's that feel, baby?' he said.

Claudine replied without opening her eyes. 'Good.'

Agry leaned on his left elbow and worked the oil into her skin a square inch at a time. This was something else he'd picked up from *GQ*. The babes loved it. They didn't want just non-stop fucking. For himself he had never tired of the beauty of Claudine's skin, its tone, its smoothness, the way it caught the light of the candles. The beauty flowed in through the tips of his fingers and his rage subsided and he felt a resurgence of the sense of fullness. It was the fullness of the king. The King. He was a king in the fullness of his power, glutted with conquest and victory. King of the world. His men now roamed the streets of that world, burning, raping and looting as was the privilege of an army of conquest. They had defeated superior numbers by sheer ruthlessness of purpose. He, Nev Agry, had imposed his will on the densest concentration of human disobedience, human anarchy, scowling, psychopathic, runaway human desperation to be found anywhere on the continent. He had evicted the false authorities from the precincts of his palace. He had driven the barbarians from the gate. He had taken back his stolen Queen with swift and merciless retribution. His word was justice. His word was law and the taste of it on his tongue was sweet.

Everything that had gone before and everything that was to come was worth this moment. Let the Devil demand whatever due he would. Most men grovelled their lives away, kissing the ass of fear day in and day out, sweating their yellow guts out for whoever cracked the whip above their heads. And the whip was always there, no matter how rich you were or how poor, because the whip sounded inside your own fucking head and it was the fear of dying, so you let the nearest cocksucker bossman piss in your mouth when he felt like it, or you delivered your balls into the cold, grasping hands of a greedy woman and let her twist them off, and all because you were afraid of dying. Well, Nev Agry wasn't afraid. He was one in a million. He was extraordinary. He was a king in the fullness of his power. And he wasn't afraid of God nor of man.

Claudine flinched and cried out and Agry returned from his reverie to the task in hand, rubbing oil on Claudine's back.

'Sorry babe,' he said. 'I press too hard?'

'A little,' she said.

Agry pressed again on the same spot – her left lower ribs – and again she flinched. A darkness rose in Agry's chest.

There was a bruise on her cheek too, which she'd told him she got coming back from the kitchen.

'That's a bruise,' he said.

Claudine didn't answer. Agry grabbed her shoulder and rolled her over on to her back. She looked at him for a second and he saw the fear in her eyes. He didn't want her to feel fear. Not for him. And whoever else she felt fear for would have to die: She closed her eyes.

'What did Johnson do to you?' he said.

Claudine covered her eyes with her forearm. She clenched her jaw to stop her lips trembling. Agry felt his heart melting. He grappled in his memory to recall the gist of that goddamn article in *GQ*.

'Babe,' he said, He stroked her hair. 'You don't have to keep it to yourself. It don't do no good to bottle up that shit.' A word sprang to his lips. 'It's traumatic.'

Claudine abruptly burst into tears. Goddamn, this stuff really worked. Agry felt a flutter of pride at his own sensitivity. The words tumbled from Claudine's mouth. 'Johnson raped me.'

Agry grabbed Claudine and pulled her to him. The darkness in his chest swelled enormously and became a fathomless blackness that reached his eyes and made him dizzy. He squeezed. The blackness was a vast pit screaming to be filled with human pain. Nothing else would do. Not freedom, not wealth, not love. Pain. There was a cracking sound and Claudine grunted. Agry concentrated and managed to loosen his arms. An image of Johnson's face swam into his mind and the blackness was swept away by the urge to vomit. He fought the urge down and grabbed the bottle of Maker's Mark from the table. His worst fantasies were confirmed. He stuck the neck of the bottle into his mouth and poured. He lowered the bottle without gasping. No, not his worst; only second worst. She hadn't wanted Johnson. The black nigger shitdog had had to rape her. Agry fought the urge of his

fingers to close round Claudine's throat. He stroked her hair
in silence. Claudine took her arm away from her eyes and
looked at Agry with her big, dewy brown eyes.

'I'm sorry,' she said.

'It's okay,' said Agry, without conviction.

'You know what he threatened to do to me?'

'I said it's okay for Chrissakes. He's dead. I wish the fucker
were still alive but he ain't.'

'If it makes you feel any better,' said Claudine, 'he always
wore a rubber.'

'Jesus,' gasped Agry.

No trace of the recent sense of fullness remained. He
suddenly felt intensely conscious of his own body. He wasn't
as strong as he'd used to be but he kept in shape. He could
still bench one-seventy-five for six reps. But he didn't have
the type of physique where it showed to good advantage. He
was naturally thick in the body and hips, short in the arms.
Plus he was fifteen, twenty years older than Johnson. It galled
him. Then the question arose from the depths of his bowels.
He felt his cock shrivel and go numb as his mind, against his
will, asked the question again, nagging, taunting, insistent.
He felt a constricting band of anxiety tighten around his chest.
He blurted the words out.

'What was he like?' he said. He couldn't bring himself to
look at her.

'What do you mean?' said Claudine.

Agry turned on her savagely. 'I mean exactly what you think
I fucking mean.'

Claudine cowered and for a second Agry was gratified to
see the fear in her face. Let the bitch fuck with him and he'd
make what Stokely Johnson threatened to do to her look like
plastic surgery. He paused. He calmed himself. Jesus Christ.
Johnson was just another dead nigger. Agry was king of the
world. He was glad that only Claudine was around to see this.

He swiped a handful of sweat from his face and flicked it against the wall.

'Well?' he said. 'And the truth. No bullshit to make me feel better.'

'He was longer than you,' said Claudine.

The band round Agry's chest wound in by another three or four notches. He kept his expression neutral. He was too cool a guy to let this kind of shit get to him. He had no worries. Size didn't matter anyway, everyone knew that, if they'd read the right magazines.

'But only by about an inch,' continued Claudine.

Agry felt his face turning purple. Only an inch. Fucking hell, man. Who wouldn't have killed his own mother or betrayed his best friend for an extra inch? The band of terror was strangling him. He couldn't breathe.

'But you're thicker, honey. That's what counts most,' said Claudine.

Agry searched her face. Was she fucking with him or what? He couldn't tell. He couldn't fucking tell. She had her butter-wouldn't-melt face on.

'Thicker?' wheezed Agry.

Claudine smiled at him the way only she could. Those full lips set in a permanent pout. Cheekbones any real woman would've killed for. And the eyebrows. Shit. Claudine put her hand on his cock and Agry felt his throat vibrating with need. He got a hard-on that hurt. Suddenly he knew why he'd blown this scum barrel apart.

'Thicker all the way,' said Claudine. 'From one end to th'other.'

She bent over his belly and started to blow him. Fuck. He had things to do. Without losing his hard-on he bellowed through the muslin sheet.

'*Tony!*'

Claudine was pumping him ruthlessly. Agry's eyelids fluttered with a weirdness he couldn't exactly call pleasure. Tony Shockner coughed behind the muslin.

'Tony?'

'Boss,' said Shockner, discreetly.

'Get Hector Grauerholz up here. Ten minutes.' Agry panted for air. 'All his boys too. I got something special for 'em.'

He broke off in a strangled groan as Claudine started in with her teeth.

'Do it,' said Agry.

Shockner's footsteps walked away. Agry pulled Claudine off him and dumped her over on her belly. He grabbed the baby oil and squirted a blast between the cheeks of her ass. From one end to the other she'd said. Goddamn. This time, he resolved, he'd even try to remember to give her a reach around.

NINETEEN

THOUGHTS TUMBLED THROUGH the gravitational field of Hobbes's awareness like fragments of falling masonry. Before he could get out of each one's path it fell onto him and through him and was suddenly gone, replaced by another thought, another fragment, another emotion of awesome weight and power.

His heart swelled with a pity so deep and all-embracing it bordered on love. The prisoners locked so ruthlessly in the glass and granite boilerhouse were, after all, his men. Their care, their nurture, remained in his hands. That some of them had to be sacrificed in order to pierce the screen of hypocrisy and criminality that prevented a true and utilitarian reformation of the penal system caused Hobbes no satisfaction. Indeed, it caused him an exquisite pain.

Hobbes had devoted his life – his *life* – to these most wretched of men. He had ransacked the literature of penology, psychopathology, sociology; of education, psychology and philosophy; he had ransacked his own brain whose intellectual capacity was, at the least, considerable; he had mounted a ceaseless surveillance of his own heart and soul to detect those whispers of hope that kept his back bent to the task. He had endured spasms of melancholia, the devastating depressions that brought him to his knees, weeping to a God he did not believe in for the solace of death. He had not sought the higher office that a man of his abilities might readily have achieved. Instead he had left a modern federal prison in Illinois to re-open Green River and turn it into something extraordinary.

So far was he now from the visions of reform and social re-engineering that had inspired him, so poisoned was he by the bitter gall of failure, that he could not at this moment scrape from the bilges of his memory a single one of the noble ideas that had so electrified his imagination a quarter of a century before. Something to do, he dimly recalled, with returning men to society scorched clean by the purifying fires of discipline; a fantasy of restoring the dignity of citizenship to lost and mutilated souls. Would he have invested in this fantastic enterprise the accumulated energies of a lifetime if he had known that by its end he would turn out to be nothing more than a glorified turn-key laying slop on the plate of a cringing felon? The bitter gall rose once more into his throat. He could have been anything he wanted. A physician, like Klein. A judge. An academic. Doctor Campbell Hobbes. Professor Campbell Hobbes. Instead he had entered a bureaucracy as foetid and labyrinthine as the sewers beneath Green River and had fought for these, the wretched of the earth.

As Hobbes stared out of the north window at the twilight redness of the western horizon his shoulders shook with a furious mixture of rage and grief. He was the son of the sun, yet the sun would take aeons to die whilst his own life had passed in a twinkling. There was no justice. The machine had thwarted him at every turn. Not only did no one care for justice, no one knew what the word meant. Sentencing and parole practices were straws blown hither and thither in the flatus issuing from the anuses of politicians. His budgets were slashed, repeatedly; his programmes underfunded; his cells barbarically overcrowded. The naked corruption of prison

guards, of suppliers and contractors, of parole board trustees –
all was officially sanctioned at the highest level. Anything that
kept the wheels turning was acceptable to them. Anything
that kept costs down and prisoners docile. And if the inmate
population was permanently tranquillised with narcotics, paid
for out of their own pockets, then so much the better. As for
the Aids crisis, the official reaction was again one of indifference. After all these years the State Governor of Prisons still
regarded Hobbes as an East Coast intellectual soft on crime
and homosexuality. If the population was reduced by Aids
deaths then no one was weeping. To the argument, vehe-
mently advanced by Hobbes, that the inmates represented a
hothouse of infection from which the disease would spread
into the civilian population, he had been told that they were
only niggers and Mexicans and other welfare-seeking trash, and
that no one would miss them or their families either. Beyond
that, any white person that fucked a nigger, especially without
a condom, deserved to die; and even more especially so if that
white person were a woman or a faggot.

To Hobbes they had long ago abandoned the moral
authority required to exercise the law. And yet in recent weeks,
as the possibility of radical change had offered itself and he
had wrestled with his conscience, Hobbes had come to understand that he too had been a slave to his own miserable vanity
and grandiosity. The fantasy that he could make a difference
alone was nothing more than a flight from true redemption,
a wretched craving for the empty plaudits of those he most
despised. He would no longer chain himself to the principle
of personal identity. He would throw away everything he had
in a delirium of liberation. He would turn away from the
lethargic suicide upon which he had long ago embarked.
Instead he would embrace his destiny, and the destiny of all
men, in the glory of irredeemable loss.

Hobbes stared at the pall of oily smoke that still lingered

in the humid air over the rear gate of cellblock B. To control the sense of horror he'd felt during those first moments – when he'd realised just how far Agry had gone – had taken all the will he could summon. But summon it he had. He'd cancelled the alarm to the local fire department. Yes. He'd forbidden any rescue attempt. He had pulled his guards out and prohibited all communication with the prison. If there was any lesson to be learnt from history it was that change could only be achieved by sacrifice and blood, the more senseless and arbitrary the better. What Hobbes had concluded from history was that man could only be shunted forward by violent cataclysms. The historian's retrospective search for causes and explanations was a vain futility, thick-fingered apes probing a dunghill for grubs. Cause was irrelevant. All that mattered was the spasm itself, endlessly returning to mock the vanity of the humanists and their pitiful institutions. Strength could only be restored by wounding. *Virescit vulnere virtus*. Perhaps here, on this filthy little piece of Texas swampland earth, a new start could be made, here where Hobbes himself had released from its cage the primitive craving that sought to abolish and thereby recreate reality. Yes. In a stroke of terrifying boldness, John Campbell Hobbes had forsaken reason, motive, or outcome and had tapped directly into the radical unmodified energy of history itself.

There came a knock on his door. Hobbes turned.

'Come in,' he said.

The door opened and Captain Bill Cletus came in and closed the door behind him. His bulky figure was dressed in a black jumpsuit festooned with equipment: radio, Mace, nightstick, handcuffs, a Browning automatic pistol. Cletus saluted.

'Sir,' said Cletus.

Hobbes nodded and walked over to his glass-topped desk. He motioned to the chair.

'Sit down, Captain.'

Hobbes took his own seat behind the desk. There were no lights on in the room and what dim illumination was available from the sinking sun fell through the south window onto Hobbes's back. Cletus was a heavy-featured man in his forties, a veteran now of over twenty years' daily contact with the worst that society had to offer. The Captain's face was tanned by the sun and burnished by the steady caress of callousness. Whenever a visit to a dying relative was refused to a grieving prisoner, whenever a man was dragged off to the hole, whenever a mutilated body was scraped from the flagstones and carted off to the morgue, Bill Cletus was there. After all this time Hobbes knew no more of what lay behind that face than he had on first meeting the young guard, then fresh out of an infantry battalion in the aftermath of Vietnam. No complaint, and there had been many, had ever been upheld against Cletus or his men. It was part of the contract and Hobbes had always kept it. Would Cletus now uphold his end? Hobbes opened the drawer to his desk and took out a glass ashtray. He set the ashtray on top of the desk.

'Feel free to smoke,' said Hobbes.

'Thank you, sir,' said Cletus.

'How are the men?' asked Hobbes.

'Solid,' said Cletus. 'They know what's required.'

'And the inmates?'

Cletus shrugged. 'We believe that C block are still locked in their cells from the midday count. Mostly Mexicans and blacks so I reckon Agry's keeping them cooped up. The rest are running wild. The power lines to the main building have been cut but not those to the infirmary or workshops. As you ordered we're enforcing a complete communications blackout and we won't be plugging into the emergency power generator until it suits us. Basically we're leaving them to it and tonight's gonna to be hot, dark and bloody. By morning most of 'em will be begging to turn themselves in.'

'We can't accept a piecemeal surrender,' said Hobbes. 'They all come out together or not at all.'

'I agree. There's a herd instinct in there. At the moment it's for blood, but when it turns, we want it working against the die-hards. I don't want my men trapped in there with thirty or forty hard core crazies, otherwise this could go on for a week.'

'You've confirmed the final count on the hostages?'

'Yes, sir. There's thirteen men trapped inside the main building.'

'And the injured who got out?'

'Mainly cuts and bruises, but Officer Perkins is in the burns unit in Beaumont. If he survives the night he'll have a chance. Sung, who got him out of there, got hit with a piece of flagstone. They removed a clot from inside his skull this afternoon and he's going to be okay. As far as we know there are no hostages inside the workshops.' Cletus took out a pack of unfiltered Camels. 'All things considered the evacuation procedure went pretty well.' He tapped a cigarette loose and put it in his mouth.

'What about the infirmary?' asked Hobbes.

'No personnel in there. Just Coley and the other inmates.'

'Were any other officers caught in the fire that might still be inside?'

'Not as far as we know. Sergeant Galindez broke procedure by re-entering B block after the evacuation was ordered.'

'He went into the fire?' said Hobbes.

'He opened the cell doors to let out the inmates. He's one of the missing thirteen. Kracowicz saw him clubbed down, couldn't get to him. How badly hurt he is we don't know.'

'He must have saved many lives,' said Hobbes.

'He broke procedure,' said Cletus flatly. 'And he left Perkins and Sung when they needed him.'

'Surely he acted with valour,' said Hobbes.

'If he survives,' said Cletus, 'I'll be putting him on a charge.'

Hobbes decided not to argue. He knew that to Cletus the whole population, all two-and-a-half thousand of them, wasn't worth the life of a single guard. The riot procedures had been developed in the light of experiences at Attica, New Mexico and Atlanta. When a disturbance reached a point at which it was considered uncontainable the guards abandoned the prison. The ultimate restoration of order was not in doubt; only the number of casualties.

'How are the men responding to the hostage problem?'

Cletus lit his cigarette. 'They want them out, naturally, but they trust me to tell them when and how. They don't want any of that Waco shit. As for the guys in there, well, they're as well prepared as they could be.'

This last was stated with some pride. Cletus had sent his men on regular seminars in psychological preparation for being taken hostage. It was a fact that guards were rarely killed in these circumstances. Rioting inmates vented themselves on each other, usually along racial lines. Even in the midst of chaos the power of the state, embodied in the khaki uniform, made itself felt and the prisoners still feared it. The trapped officers were going through hell but they were unlikely to die, unless the more vicious inmates were provoked or panicked by an untimely rescue attempt.

'What's the Governor's position?' asked Cletus.

Hobbes looked Cletus in the eye.

'He supports us one hundred per cent. He's put the National Guard on alert but he agrees with me that there's no sense in deploying them at this stage. He is particularly keen to maintain a media blackout for as long as possible, as am I.'

Apart from this last statement Hobbes was lying. He had not contacted the state governor at all, nor did he intend to until the last possible minute. This was not their affair.

'I want the media blackout to be very clearly understood, Captain,' said Hobbes. 'I don't want TV cameras in helicopters hovering over our heads.'

'Me neither,' said Cletus.

'I won't have Green River turned into a menagerie. This is not the streets of Los Angeles. This is the panoptic machine. Our duty is to discipline and punish, not to provide a circus for the debilitated intellects of our citizenry. By their choice this is a place of obscurity and pain wherein the citizen's eye has forsaken the right to count its victims.' Hobbes paused and wiped a fleck of spittle from his lips. 'This is not their business.'

'I agree, sir,' said Cletus.

He took a puff on his Camel and hid behind the smoke. Hobbes experienced a spasm of doubt. Was the Captain humouring him? Did he think him a fool? Would he make coarse jokes at his expense when he got back downstairs? Hobbes felt dwarfed by the task, by the impossibility of communicating even a fraction of a per cent of his vast insight, an insight as monumental and punishing as the stones of the prison itself. He suddenly wished that Klein were back in the room. There, he felt, was a man who might understand, who might just catch a glimpse of the beacon that flickered in an immense darkness. Klein was trapped too. But for Agry's impatience Klein might have been free tomorrow. But there was no point dwelling on the merciless humour of fate. And anyway in every crisis dwelt the secret of power.

'Do you know what the word "crisis" means?' asked Hobbes.

Cletus frowned. 'I think I do, yes, sir.'

'The Greek root means "to decide",' said Hobbes. 'But the Chinese is better, a combination of two characters: one meaning "danger"; the other "opportunity". Are you following me?'

'I'm not sure,' said Cletus from behind his smoke.

'In order to discover the opportunity, in order to make the decision, one must plunge into the whirlpool of danger and surrender to its pull.'

Cletus looked at him for a long beat. 'You sound like you think this riot is just what the doctor ordered,' he said.

Hobbes paused. In the dim light it was difficult to make out Cletus's eyes. Did he have the capacity to understand? Probably not. Was the attempt worth it?

'In the city of justice,' said Hobbes, 'we are the sewer, the darkest region, where the power to punish no longer dares make itself known to the people it serves. We no longer treat the sewage and we lack the nerve to flush it away. Nor are we physicians, examining the faeces of the sickening body in order to identify the disease. Neither toilet cleaners nor diagnosticians, we have become hoarders of turds. Is that fit work for men such as we, Cletus? Collecting shit?'

'It ain't perfect. I know that as well as anyone. But somebody's got to do it,' said Cletus.

Hobbes reeled inwardly as a wave of despair verging on nausea swelled through his entrails. He closed his eyes as he spoke.

'There was a time when the problem of incarceration exercised the greatest minds of the enlightenment. De Tocqueville. Bentham. Servan. We've given up, Cletus. This is the end of an era and reason has lost.'

'You okay, sir?'

How foolish he had been to imagine that this brute would be capable of grasping his vision. Hobbes opened his eyes.

'When justice abandons those moral and rational principles that gave it its original authority the time has come to give the prison back to its inmates. Let them generate a new morality more fitting to our times.'

'I just want my men back safe,' said Cletus. 'I wouldn't know about the rest.'

'Your wife's born again isn't she, Bill?'

Cletus shrugged and indicated the Camel burning between his fingers. 'Won't let me smoke at home if that's what you mean.'

'Then you should know that there is no safety here on earth. Or maybe in heaven either. After all, even the brightest of God's angels fell. The only place of safety is hell, where there's nothing left to lose.'

'I may not be much for Jesus,' said Cletus, 'but I do believe that God put the kind of animals we got in this prison on earth to test us. Like they say, we got a short time for to be here and a long time to be gone. I reckon sooner or later we're all called on to do what we think is right.'

Hobbes nodded gravely. 'Few of us are privileged to meet the immensity of fate head on. Most men avoid it, even in the moment of their own dying.'

'I guess that's what I mean,' said Cletus.

The last glimmerings of light were fading and they were talking in near darkness. The end of Cletus's cigarette glowed close to the tips of his finger and thumb. He took one last drag and crushed the butt out in the glass ashtray and stood up.

'Best get back, if that's alright with you, sir.'

Hobbes stood up too. 'If I could exchange places with your men, I would.'

Cletus looked at him steadily. 'I know you would.'

'We understand each other then,' said Hobbes.

He held out his hand and Cletus shook it. Hobbes watched him walk to the door, open it and leave. As the lock clicked shut Hobbes felt a great isolation fall like a shroud and it seemed to him as if the now dark chamber of his office were the universe itself and he its only occupant. He tried to recall what Klein had said this morning. 'Even the bravest . . .' Hobbes couldn't remember the rest. It was frustrating. Instead, a tune of almost unspeakable banality intruded into his isolation and wouldn't go away.

'When I was just a little boy,
I asked my mother, What will I be . . .'

Hobbes sat in the centre of the universe and listened to the loathsome song grind round the interior of his skull.

TWENTY

LIKE A TROPICAL wind the ancient violence of men swept in random gusts and sudden squalls throughout the interior of the Green River Penitentiary. It sucked men from their cells and pitilessly exposed them to fire and blade. It revealed without mercy the ugliness, the virulence, the heavy stench of man in his uninhibited purity of being. As it howled up and down the stacked cages of cellblock D Ray Klein lay on his bunk and waited, with all the resolve he could muster, for the less than desirable circumstances in which he found himself to improve.

His cell door was closed but wasn't locked down. If he'd had the equipment he would have welded the steel shut. Instead he'd tied a tin cup to the bars and placed it on his locker. In the unlikely event he fell asleep and someone slid the door open the cup would fall to the floor and wake him. Paranoia suggested an alternative: the intruder could cut the string first. Klein scratched sleeping off his list. In an attempt to relax he closed his eyes and constructed fantasies of being free: reading the *New York Times* and drinking fresh orange juice in a diner; going to bed at three a.m. and waking up at ten; driving Devlin along I 90 to New Orleans where she'd fuck him in a cheap hotel where the ceiling fans were too slow to stop them slathering in each other's sweat. He wondered what Devlin was doing now. Maybe soaking in a tub, or eating goat cheese salad in an air conditioned café. No, she'd be settling down to watch the Lakers game. He wondered if the Knicks would keep them to a six-point spread.

It wasn't working.

None of the fantasies were powerful enough to divert his mind from the maelstrom of noise and suffering beyond the bars of his cell.

The rioters had devoted their first hours of command to the business of blind destruction. Anything that could be smashed, bent, dismantled or spilled had been thus smashed and spilled. Anything that could be advanced from a state of order into one of chaos had been thus advanced. And as men shat and pissed themselves in fear, the ambient smell became viler and more pervasive than usual. It put Klein in mind of Ludwig von Boltzmann and his theory of entropy. Maybe he should have laid that one on Hobbes: Disorder always increases in a closed system. Hobbes probably knew that already. From Nev Agry's ghetto blaster on ground tier came a sound to bewilder even Boltzmann: drifting surreally through the bedlam was the genteel sound of Bob Wills and his Texas Playboys.

> The moon in all your splendour,
> Know only my heart,
> Call back my Rose, My Rose of San Antone.
> Lips so sweet and tender,
> Like petals falling apart,
> Speak once again of my love, my own . . .

As the Playboys crooned in the twilight and the sun started on its way down, the electric lights failed to come on. All power to the blocks had been cut off. It was typical that Agry would be the only man to have a fat supply of Duracells, so he could bombard them with his fucking music. He'd had the same song going on a loop all afternoon. Deep within my heart lies a melody. Shit. It was enough to make Klein get out on the tier and sing 'Que Sera Sera' again. Somewhere in the distance, at times even drowning out Bob Wills, the same man had been screaming – in a thin, keening, slavvering shriek – for something over an hour.

Klein discovered that he felt no pity for the screamer. In fact he found himself wishing that the guy would just shut the fuck up and die. The screaming was an indulgence. If the guy was hurt that bad he wouldn't have been able to keep the noise up for that long. He was a goddamned fake. Someone ought to cut his throat. Or at least stomp him out. Then again maybe he was being gang fucked, in which case maybe the screams were an extravagant expression of pleasure, the freedom of total submission. It had been known. Klein called a halt to the sick drift of his thoughts. His turn might be next. A melancholy light, the last that the day was prepared to donate, filtered through the glass square into the rear of his cell. Soon it would be dark and there was no sign that power would be restored.

While the light held up, masked execution squads roamed the walkways looking for victims and drugs. As D was Agry's block most of the action was elsewhere. Klein was thankful he wasn't on A, or on the run in the labyrinth down below. There were old scores to settle. Justice had to be seen to be done. Petty humiliations nursed for years on end now emerged as savage vendettas. Debts small and large were collected in blood and pain. Spurned sexual advances were now made good. Retribution on a biblical scale. And every act of terror was fuelled, stoked, blasted by the prison itself. The years of confinement, the lock and counts, the flaccid cocks, the yearning of visiting-time, the wives who sought divorces and went off to fuck someone else, the hourly rituals of helplessness and degradation, the ammoniac stench of piss, the pious faces of the parole board, the crumbs of pleasure gleaned from stale cookies, from liquor brewed with a sockful of bread and a can of peaches, from a cum-stained picture of a wet-beavered woman, from a furtive blow job purchased from some sorry junkie who needed the cash. And the fear. The fear. The fear of day and the fear of night. The fear of minute to minute and the fear of hour by hour. Day by day. Year after year. The malignancy that consumed the arteries and nerves, the kidneys, the adrenals, the heart. The have-I-taken-the-wrong-seat-in-the-cinema fear. The fear of being alone and the fear of being not-alone. The am-I-too-young-and-pretty fear of having half a dozen ungreased cocks shoved up your ass one after the other in the block latrines or pinned to a bench in the chapel. The fear of waking up to each day's dawning. The fear of life and the fear of death. The screams that now echoed round the vault sang the battle hymn of fear's republic. Base, unqualified Fear as it staggered, blinking, naked, big with vengeance, from a thousand bitter hearts and bellowed for its own fair share of itself.

Klein contained his own fear in a hard tight ball up high behind his sternum. He contained it with reason. Superior, Platonic intelligence, rational calculation, ice cold knowledge. These weapons would see him through, as they had seen him through the last three years. If fifty men died in the riot it would be the worst in US prison history. That gave odds of fifty to one in favour of survival. If he stayed in his cell instead of wandering around amongst the crazies the odds were better still. Two days, three days, the cons would lose interest, start to get hungry and hot and bored. The riot would fizzle out into abject surrender as all riots ultimately did. All Klein had to do was stay clear.

The screams continued. Maybe it was a guy got burned in B block, coming out of shock and into intolerable pangs. Klein steeled himself. He would not ask himself what he might do to help. He would not feel pity or compassion. Let them whimper prayers to God. Let them pump themselves with booze and smack. Klein steeled himself. He would not listen to their need. He forced himself to listen instead to the trickling water and the drunken shouts. In his head he sang along to the endless circle of Agry's goddamned tape.

It was there I found, beside the Alamo,
Enchantment strange as the blue up above . . .

Klein sat up and swung his feet from the bunk as he heard the sound of heavy feet sloshing through the water on the tier. He glanced down at the shaving mirror: a pair of boots came trudging towards his cell. Klein stood up. He pulled the .38 from his pocket. Because he wasn't too familiar with guns he checked the cylinder again: the blank round still lay under the hammer. Klein held the revolver down by his thigh. A huge figure loomed in the doorway, blocking out what little light was coming from the roof. The man lowered his head so that his long flat face could peer through the bars.

'Doctor,' said Henry Abbott.

'Henry,' said Klein.

The relief he felt was a shocking measure of his anxiety. He turned slightly to conceal the gun.

'Come on in.'

Abbott slid the door open. The tin cup clattered to the floor. Abbott paused to look at it.

'It's okay,' said Klein.

As Abbott lumbered into the cell Klein slipped the revolver back into his pocket. Klein nodded towards the bunk.

'Sit down.'

'I see you followed my advice,' said Abbott.

Klein's memory reeled back across the day trying to remember amongst all the chaos what Abbott had advised. Breakfast was the last time he'd seen Abbott. A long time ago. Klein sat down on a stool opposite the bunk. Yeah. Henry had told him to avoid all contact.

'Avoid all contact,' said Klein.

A flicker of concern passed across Abbott's face. He started to rise. 'If you want me to, I'll leave,' he said.

Klein raised a hand to stop him. 'I'm glad to have your company.' There was a deacon-like poise to Abbott that Klein found reassuring. 'Makes me feel safer,' he said.

'Why?' said Abbott.

For a moment Klein was stuck for an answer. Like a child, Abbott had a habit of springing incredibly concrete, on first impression almost stupid, questions that on reflection proved to be piercing.

'I guess I mean we can protect each other if there's trouble.'

Abbott thought about that, then nodded solemnly. 'I see.'

Abbott's face was constructed of simple, slab-like elements conceived by his creator on a large scale. There were no wrinkles on his forehead and his mouth was never fully closed. The anti-psychotic medication he was given and which in Klein's opinion he needed contributed to the overall effect of a flat, unreflecting surface upon which observers could inscribe whatever fantasies they chose. Abbott was as brutal, stupid, dangerous, cute or beast-like as you cared to make him. Henry himself was rarely in a position to prove himself otherwise because he didn't get the chance: no one ever asked his side of things and, in general, people avoided his fathomless eyes.

Henry had very pure eyes: when you looked into them his eyes were all you got. Because his face was so motionless there were few crinkles, squints or brow movements, no play of muscles to set the eyes in any sort of context. Just grey irises circumscribed with brown; muddy sclera; deep sockets. Klein coughed and looked away at the drips of water falling past his door from the tier above. He was sharing his cell with a psychotic mass murderer seven inches taller and eighty pounds heavier than he was. And yet he did feel safer.

'This trouble must be harder on you than it is on me,' said Abbott.

Klein wondered if Abbott had somehow heard about his parole. 'Why, Henry?' he said.

'Because you're a doctor.'

Abbott's thoughts were often oblique. He made odd connections between things. Klein said, 'I don't understand.'

Abbott inclined his head towards the din outside. 'There are wounded men out there. I've seen them. A doctor has a duty to tend them but you are following my order to avoid contact. So you can't. I came here to release you from the obligation I placed on you.'

Klein stared at him. The sweat rolling down his flanks felt like lice crawling on his skin.

'That's thoughtful of you, Henry,' said Klein. 'But the main reason I'm staying here is because I don't want to get killed.'

Klein paused. Abbott blinked slowly once.

'Your advice was good. Your vibe was correct. I know there are wounded men out there but I owe them nothing. Do you understand?'

This time Abbott didn't blink. Neither did he nod. Klein steeled himself.

'This isn't my war. These aren't my people. My knowledge doesn't oblige me to risk my life. At other times and other places maybe it would, but not now and not here.'

Klein waited. There was a long silence. Abbott's attention seemed temporarily elsewhere and Klein guessed that he was listening to the hallucinated voice that Abbott called The Word. In previous conversations over a long period Klein had learned that The Word controlled Abbott pretty much the way a parent controls a child. A jealous and unpredictable parent. A high percentage of The Word's commands and vibes made good sense, and maybe more so in prison, where paranoia was wisdom, than on the outside. The Word told him which crews to avoid, which hacks to say 'sir' to, how fast to do his work, when to get back for lock and count, and when and when not to eat his oatmeal.

But if The Word was generally Abbott's guide and protector it was also, at darker moments, his cruellest persecutor and most implacable foe. It was The Word that had reduced him to the trembling, filth-encrusted animal that Klein had first found squatting in the corner of its cell. It was The Word that had instructed him to wipe out his own family with a ball-peen hammer. Within the cosmology of Abbott's mind The Word was God and Devil both. No power on earth, and certainly none in the River, could ultimately compete with The Word. When The Word spoke, Abbott could do no other than carry out its command and no bully's threat, no officer's club, no warden's sanction could sway him from his purpose. Thus had Myron Pinkley lost the use of his hand. Abbott – the Abbott that thought of himself as 'Abbott', the Abbott that Klein was so fond of, the two hundred and sixty pound, six foot seven inch frame of muscle and bone and feeling – all this was the tool of The Word, to be sacrificed without question if so commanded.

Klein knew that even the most powerful drugs had failed to silence The Word's voice. They helped suppress the persecutory, self-punishing, contemptuous side of its tongue, the side that periodically scourged Abbott into a state of suicidal self-neglect, but the voice never completely disappeared. Probably, thought Klein, it even spoke to Abbott in his dreams.

But if this lonely, withdrawn, expressionless man, this shell that at times seemed almost an automaton, was indeed all that was left of Abbott, who then was The Word? In his friendship with Abbott Klein had become fascinated with The Word. He longed to meet him, to converse with him, but Abbott was capable only of a garbled translation of The Word's words and then only when he was feeling particularly secure. Klein's belief was this: that The Word was not the voice of God. The Word *was* God.

Abbott had once towered over his English students and moved their hearts with the music of poets long dead. Now he could at best string together a simple sentence denuded of metaphor or hidden meaning. It was all gone. He was all gone. Almost. What little of Abbott remained to himself was God's humble servant and the elaborate hellhole in which Abbott's body was imprisoned was merely a new Garden of Eden. In Klein's mind a moment came when you had to put aside the kind of knowledge Devlin had such command of – the genetics and biochemistry and the psychodynamics and emotional expressivity and the dopamine levels and the 5-hydroxy tryptamine receptors – and just stand in the shoes of the madman and take a look for yourself. Maybe that was impossible. But there had been vertiginous moments in Abbott's company when Klein had come close, when he'd felt the imprint of a total power, when the prison had become the merest backdrop to the primal drama of God – The Word – and man. Not the God of Christ or Abraham or Mohammed but a prereligious God. The God who ruled before make-believe or metaphor or imagination were invented, before choice, before will, before Good and Evil, perhaps even before language. Abbott's ego, his self, him, was a very small remnant; an eroded stump of 'I'; a few fragments glued together with fear and maybe – Klein hoped so – the bit of human recognition that Klein gave him. Ruling the empyrean above this wretched figure was The Word, a being, a force, a limitless authority contained entirely within the limitless space of Abbott's mind and yet separate from him, from Abbott, alien to him, and utterly and frighteningly so. Abbott's ego had given up all claim to rule his own vast internal universe and clung instead to a squalid island of consciousness at the edge of an infinity.

So while Abbott endured oatmeal with glass, the foul labour in the sewers, imprisonment, forced medication, and all the other insults and injuries of which his life was composed, The Word enjoyed – The Word was – unimaginable freedom and power. Who knew what force had cleaved the two – God and Man – asunder? Klein, for sure, did not know. But in these quiet moments when he sat alone with Abbott and listened to the soft breathing of The Word who might at any moment order his death, Klein often wondered what would happen if the two were to be joined together again. What would become of the shuffling, retarded giant if he were suddenly filled again with the God that was himself? What fire would blaze in those flat blank eyes? What sound would echo like the crack of doom from within that massive chest?

And again, at such moments, Klein would wonder what had happened to the God within his own self. Klein was appallingly sane. He saw himself sometimes as Abbott's mirror image. Where Abbott's self was a broken slave cowering at the feet of a dark God that was himself but didn't know it, Klein's God was a thin shadow of a deity, virtually extinguished by the glaring floodlights of knowledge, science, insight and rationality. Free will, choice, understanding, imagination, the ability to calculate consequence and outcome – these were the foemen of God, the chains that confined him to a narrow cell in the bowels of that same infinity over which Abbott's Word enjoyed total dominion. In this sense Klein knew he was as fragmented as Abbott: where Abbott sifted through the broken pieces of self and came up with a derelict shell of humanity that lived, literally, in the sewer of the sewer of the world, Klein had sifted the fragments of God in a search for some purpose beyond mere survival and had ended up in cell-block D telling his companion: 'I know there are wounded men out there but I owe them nothing.'

Klein suddenly remembered where they were and what was going on around them. He had been lost in the blank discs of Abbott's eyes. The sepulchral silence that the eyes had thrown over him vanished like smoke. Again came the keening of the wounded man. With the smoky silence went God. Klein was once again a convict with parole in his pocket and a riot to survive.

'You are right,' said Abbott.

'What?' said Klein.

'This isn't the time or place to die,' said Abbott.

'I'm glad you agree,' said Klein. 'We stay here for a day, two days, we'll be fine. We can take it in turns to sleep.'

'We can look after each other,' said Abbott.

'That's right,' said Klein. 'No one else is going to.'

As he finished speaking, looking into Abbott's big open face, Klein felt a sudden self-disgust. They could look after each other. Yeah. Until that triple set of gates under Hobbes's tower opened in front of him one by one, and then it would be fare thee well, Polly my dear, but I must be on my way, and Klein would be gone. And after that Abbott could go back to his sewer and take care of himself. The shackles round Klein's God's ankles cut deeper into his divine flesh. Perhaps it was shameful but Klein the man just wanted to get outside and drink that orange juice and take that shower and lie on damp sheets with Juliette Devlin. He'd had enough of pain and fear, his own and everyone else's. Even after thirty-four months in this shitsack he wasn't hard enough. His nerve-ends, dulled as they were, needed to be dulled further. Yet if he could get through those gates the dulling wouldn't be necessary any more. He could even let the nerve-ends grow again.

For Abbott and the others it was different, wasn't it? They were on a different set of tracks to him; always had been. Klein thought of the research Devlin had designed to answer her great question: is it harder to die if you are a guy with a future than if you are a poor illiterate scumbag with nothing to look forward to but six feet of stony ground in Potter's Field? The chaos boiling up in Klein's guts shouted 'You bet your fucking life it's harder.' He searched for the hard tight ball high up in his chest where he'd packed away all his fear. It had gone: dissolved, broken apart and flooded down into his colon, his rectum, his balls, turning his muscles to lard and his blood to milk and water. His eyes flickered back and forth from the dripping water at the door to Abbott's slab-like face, and then to the john where any minute now he knew he would have to shit out what felt like his life. His heart kicked him ten to the dozen in his chest. A monstrous wave of panic gathered within him and rose towering, hovering, above him, ready to wash him away.

A simple thought, that hadn't occurred to him before, thumped into his mind: for the next few hours the dirty little patch of land contained within these prison walls was probably the most lawless piece of turf on the entire surface of the planet. Not only that, but it was swarming with some of the most violent men in history.

The wave above him trembled unsteadily. Maybe staying put in the cell was crazy. With the gun he could make it. It was possible. He could sneak through the block, down by General Purposes, out across the yard. Now, while there was still light to travel by. Once it got dark anything could happen. He could see the main gate in front of him. He could see Bill Cletus ordering it open, feel the cool, comforting pressure of the handcuffs as they accepted his surrender, his innocence, as they bundled him away to spend his last few hours of confinement in the safety of a small town jail in another county, miles from Green River, miles from Coley and Agry and Abbott and Grauerholz, miles from the stink and the screams and the blood. Now's the time, man. Once night fell it would be suicide to move around out there. Now's your chance.

Klein lurched to his feet from the stool. His legs trembled. He grabbed the bars of the cell door. The wave was still there, looming far above his head. Suddenly he knew that he had to let it come. If he tried to run in front of it the wave would catch him and take him down, would smash him apart on the rocks of panic, impale him on the shank of some drunken killer who smelled his fear. The wave began to move and Klein threw himself upon its mercy.

Deep breaths. His knuckles turned white as he clung to the bars. Take deep breaths you fucker. The panic wave swept over him, pinning him to the door. His eyes stung with sweat. A noise he couldn't decipher escaped from his mouth. Deep breaths. His thighs and belly pressed into the steel as his knees buckled beneath him. Deep. Breaths. Burning spasms wracked his anus, his bladder, his glans. He wondered if he were shitting and pissing himself, he couldn't tell, and even at this extremity a voice of shame in his head wished that Abbott weren't here to smell his excrement. Deep breaths. At last he heaved in a ragged breath, held it for a second, let it go. Count it. Count and breathe. One to ten. He counted one to ten. Put that hard tight ball back together. One to ten.

The wave rode over him and receded into the twilight. Slowly, slowly, Klein put the ball back together and pulled himself up into it. The different parts of his body reconnected with each other. His shirt was drenched with sweat and clung to his skin. Suddenly he shivered. His legs promised to hold him up. He let go of the bars. His clenched and trembling sphincter assured him he hadn't shat his load; yet; but if he didn't get to the john he soon would.

With an effort Klein turned round. Abbott stared at him. 'You look white,' said Abbott.

Klein realised that the panic attack which had seemed like half a lifetime in fact hadn't lasted more than a few seconds. He nodded to Abbott.

'Watch the door for me,' said Klein.

He walked with careful, clenched steps to the toilet and drew the blanket curtain aside. He unbuckled his belt. As he dropped his pants and sat down Klein emptied himself in a great foaming rush. Parole board, Hobbes, Nietzsche, God, riot, and several yards of shit – the whole stinking mess just poured out and Klein was filled with an astonishing sense of peace. He heard angels singing. He let out a beatific groan of gratitude. From beyond the curtain came Abbott's voice.

'Are you alright, Doctor?'

And Klein laughed. He laughed a great raw, belly shaking laugh and inhaled deeply of his own deflatus. God was it foul. He laughed again.

'I'm great,' he called back to Abbott. And it was true. If he'd ever felt better than he did now, squatting on the john behind the blanket, then he couldn't remember when. Klein recalled that Martin Luther had conceived the Protestant Reformation in a similarly transcendent bowel motion, and now he understood why. He took a wad of toilet tissue and wiped the sweat from his brow. Marvellous. He took another and wiped his ass. He paused, listened. The guy who'd been screaming had stopped. Klein stood up and buttoned his pants and as he flushed it all away he raised his hand in a salute. He felt ready for anything.

Perhaps that was just as well for Abbott called out, 'Someone is coming.'

Klein whipped the curtain aside and stepped back into the

cell. In front of the half-closed cell door Claude Toussaint appeared in the garb of Claudine Agry.

Klein grinned. 'It's the Rose of San Antone.'

Claudine was wearing a tight red silk dress and high heels and she looked like she'd dressed in a hurry because her genitals made an unsightly bulge in the front of the skirt. Her face had been lavishly made up, but was now smudged with sweat and tears. She looked at Klein with wide, haunted eyes. Klein's grin faded.

'Klein?'

Klein stepped towards her. The elation of a moment before was already a fast fading memory. Claudine tottered into the cell and threw her arms around his neck.

'What's wrong?' said Klein. He took hold of Claudine's arms and held her back so he could see her face.

Claudine turned her head into her shoulder. She looked distraught. 'It's all my fault.'

'Keep calm,' said Klein, 'and tell me what's wrong.'

Claudine bit her lips, then said, 'Nev's sent Grauerholz to the infirmary. I think he wants them all killed.'

For a second the information didn't register.

'All who?' said Klein.

'All of them all!' sobbed Claudine. 'Coley, Wilson. The Aids guys.'

In a dungeon in a cavern in a mine ten thousand miles deep inside him Klein heard the clinking of cosmic shackles suddenly wrenched against divine flesh.

'Why?' Klein's voice was cold.

Claudine squirmed against his grip. 'You're hurting me.'

Klein's hands clenched tighter on her arms. He shook her.

'Why, goddamn it? Look at me.'

Claudine looked at him. 'I don't know,' she said.

Claudine fell against his chest sobbing. Klein let go of her arms and held her. He stared over her head at Abbott and

Abbott stared back, his great empty eyes seeing all the way into him. The vertiginous feeling returned. The shoes of the madman. Klein pulled Claudine's chin up.

'Okay,' Klein said. 'Better take me to see Nev Agry.'

TWENTY-ONE

JULIETTE DEVLIN, SITTING on the table of the sick bay office, unstrapped her watch from her wrist and made a deliberate effort not to look at the time. She had checked it so often since the Korean CO – she couldn't remember his name – had shoved her inside the office and told her to stay put that time had slowed to a crawl. The evident seriousness of the situation – the fireball, the gunshots, the men spilling out into the yard – had clicked her mind into what she thought of as sensible-little-lost-girl mode. Stay put and keep calm until Mommy came to find you or a friendly policeman asked you where you lived. Neither the Korean nor Galindez had returned to take her home. She had concluded that both of them had to be killed or captured. The rapid gunshots from the walls had died down several hours ago. Since then she had heard only four rifle shots, randomly spaced. The telephone on the table was dead and she had given up expecting it to ring. The last time she'd looked at her watch she had finally remembered a fact so obvious that she must have been blocking her recollection of it: she'd signed the visitors' book declaring that she had left the prison.

No one knew she was in there.

Devlin dropped the wristwatch on the floor and stamped

on it twice with the heel of her boot. The glass case cracked. When she stamped on it a third time the glass shattered to dust and the hands were shaved off the face. For a moment she felt better. Time immediately speeded up a little. It may not have been a sensible thing to do but that mode was past its sell-by date. The little lost girl would soon start blubbering. Staying in this room was driving her crazy. Devlin thought of the two and a half thousand men trapped with her behind Green River's granite walls. They hadn't had sex with a woman for, what? Say an average of five years each. A cumulative total of over ten thousand years. That was a long time to go without a fuck, and a lot of these guys had an extra Y chromosome. Devlin reached for the crumpled pack of Winstons and rummaged inside.

There was only one cigarette left.

A sense of panic hit her, immediately replaced by one of relief. It was perfect. If there was one situation more serious than being trapped alone in a prison riot it was being trapped just about anywhere without any cigarettes. It gave her the excuse she needed to abandon sensible little lost girl and get out of this yellow room. Devlin stuck the Winston in her mouth and defiantly lit it.

There were two doors out of the office. One led into the corridor to the main exit and Crockett Ward. The other door led into a small shower room and beyond that to the dispensary. Devlin walked over to the second door, took a drag on her cigarette and went through.

The shower room was tiny and tiled in pale green, a colour which heightened the slight smell of mould. There was a wash basin in one wall below a discoloured patch where a mirror had once been fixed. Opposite the basin were two shower stalls in shallow porcelain tubs. One of the stalls still boasted a tattered plastic curtain. Klein had once told her that one of the main attractions of working in the infirmary was being able to take a shower in private. Devlin's shirt was damp with the steady trickle of her sweat but she wasn't tempted. She walked out of the opposite door into the dispensary.

The lights were on. The dispensary contained a long wooden lab bench with two built-in sinks. The walls were lined with shelves stacked with basic medical supplies: drip feeds, cartons of specimen bottles, syringes, needles; plastic bags of saline and dextrosaline; dressings, swabs, adhesive tape. One section of shelves was stacked with drugs: mainly anti-biotics and tranquillisers. At the other end of the dispensary a pair of swing doors led onto the corridor. Standing bent over the table, his weight braced on the palms of his hands, was Earl Coley. Devlin recognised him by his bulk for his head was covered by a white towel. From beneath the towel came the sound of a deep inhalation followed by a series of shallow, stuttering grunts.

'God-damn,' sighed Coley from under the towel.

Coley's body sagged and he shifted his weight from his hands to his elbows. He showed no sign of having heard her enter the room. Devlin wondered if he were sick. She walked towards him.

'Coley? You okay?' she said.

Coley jumped back from the table, startled, dragging the towel from his head.

'Muthafucka!' gasped Coley.

His eyes wobbled in his skull. He focused on Devlin, recognised her.

'Jesus Christ.'

He relaxed and leaned back against the wall. He closed his eyes and clutched a hand to his chest and took some deep breaths. He staggered over to one of the sinks, turned the tap on full blast and ducked his head underneath it. As the cold water cascaded over his head and neck he muttered a long stream of obscenities, amongst which Devlin heard the word 'bitch' occur several times. Coley straightened up and rubbed his face with the towel. On the lab bench where he'd been standing was a half-gallon bottle made of dark brown glass. Coley lowered the towel and looked at her. Devlin shuffled.

'Hi,' she said.

Coley didn't answer. Devlin raised her cigarette to her lips.

'Shit, man.' Coley sprang forward and clamped his hand over the mouth of the brown bottle. He grabbed a plastic top from the table and screwed it onto the neck of the bottle.

'This stuff's flammable as hell. You wanna blow us all away?'

Devlin immediately understood. She walked to the sink and stuck the cigarette into the still running water. She turned the tap off and threw the damp butt into a waste bin.

'Ether?' she said.

Coley nodded sullenly. He picked up the brown bottle and took it to a cupboard. He put the bottle inside, shut the cupboard and slotted a small padlock through the hasp. He turned back to Devlin.

'Time to time it helps me wind down,' said Coley. 'I ain't no addict.'

'I didn't think you were,' said Devlin.

'I don't take no valium, smack, weed, nothin'.' He stared at her defensively. 'Shit I don't even smoke.'

'Coley, it's okay,' said Devlin. 'In the old days half the anaesthesiologists in the country would take a hit of ether from time to time.'

Coley relaxed. 'Just din't want you to think it interfered with my job.'

Coley went over to a cardboard box half-full of paper towels. He tipped the towels out onto the floor and carried the box over to the bench.

'What the hell you doin' here anyway?'

'I was looking for some more cigarettes,' said Devlin.

'No shit,' said Coley. 'What's wrong with 7–11? I thought I tol' Klein to get rid of you.'

'He did,' said Devlin. 'I came back.'

'What the fuck fo'?'

'I told you this morning, I've got something to show you and Klein.'

'Well you surely picked the right day for it.'

Coley walked over to the drug shelf and grabbed two plastic tubs. He checked the labels and took them over to the card-board box. He twisted the lids off and poured a stream of white tablets into the box.

'Do you know what's going on?' asked Devlin.

Coley shrugged. 'Guys stabbin' each other, robbin' each other, gettin' drunk and stoned. Usual riot stuff.'

'It's happened before?'

'Last race riot was 'bout four year since but that was just a bunch of Mexicans and niggers fucked each other up in the machine shop. This different. Ain't had nothin' near this big before. Guys in here'll tell you 'bout Atlanta, New Mexico, though. Cons take over the whole joint, blacks kill the whites, whites kill the Mexicans, Mexicans kill each other and maybe a few Chinks and Indians too. That's what we lookin' at now.'

'What will happen?'

Coley went to the shelves and took down some more plastic tubs. He spoke over his shoulder.

'When they get tired of the killin' and the cuttin' the warden 'll send in the guard and maybe they'll kill a few mo'. We all on punishment, no privileges, maybe lockdown, fo' a few weeks, then I guess we all get ready fo' the next one.'

He saw something in her face and smiled gently. 'Don't worry, Doctah Devlin. We safe enough in here.' He showed her the tubs of pills. 'Specially we get rid of this shit.'

He emptied the tubs into the box.

Devlin walked over and took an empty tub from Coley's

hand. The label read: Tab Thorazine 50mg. She looked at Coley.

'Only thing we got that they'll want is drugs. Anything'll make 'em high. Or low. Pref'rably stone cold unconscious. They'll be comin' for 'em sooner or later. But that's okay with us, right?'

'If you say so,' said Devlin.

'Better they on thorazine and benzos than coke and speed and booze.' He smiled again. 'You wanna give me a hand?'

Devlin smiled. 'Sure.'

They went through the bottles and tubs on the shelves and pulled down anything that might have some psychotropic activity. Valium, quinalbarbitone, temazepam, haldol, fluphenazine, stelazine. Tablets, capsules, ampoules. The bottom of the box became a kaleidoscope of multicoloured chemicals. Devlin was no longer surprised by the quantity of major tranquillisers stocked by what was nominally a small general hospital unit, though on first arrival she had been. She saw Coley reach for a large container of Amitriptyline.

'That's pretty toxic if you take too many,' she said.

Coley cackled. 'I don't know 'bout you, Doctah, but I all for that toxic shit. One less cracker take a razor to my throat is one mo' cracker to the good.'

He threw the tablets into the box. For Devlin dumping a load of neuroleptic drugs on people ignorant of their effects went against the grain of her training. But she remembered the screams of the burning guard.

'I guess we can worry about the lawsuits later,' she said.

Her hand fell on a carton of powerful laxatives. She showed the box to Coley.

He grinned. 'That's th' idea.'

After that Devlin found herself adding some diuretics, anti-hypertensives and a sprinkling of digoxin. When the box was half-full Coley gave the massed pharmaceuticals a stir and topped it up with a few handfuls of syringes and needles.

'Anything to keep 'em busy,' he said. 'Let's go.'

Devlin held the swing doors open and Coley carried the box out into the corridor. She followed him past the entrance to the ward. The ward was quiet. They walked through a stout wooden door held open with a wedge and past the TV room and bathrooms. They stopped at the first of two heavy duty doors that blocked the corridor. This one was made of plate steel and had a peep slot at head height. Coley held the drug box under one arm while he took out his keys and unlocked the door. Beyond was the guard's room, the doctor's office used by Bahr which contained old medical records and which Klein and Coley rarely used, and a small shabby room for visitors – lawyers and relatives. They came to the second door – this one a steel-barred gate – and Coley unlocked that too. At the end of the corridor they turned a corner and passed through into a porched hallway where two studded wooden doors opened onto the yard.

The doors were pushed ajar but not locked. Only the duty CO had the keys to this, the only entrance to the infirmary. It was usually only locked down at night and Sung had left it open. Sung – she'd remembered his name. She wasn't a racist after all.

'What happened to Sung?' she asked.

'Last I saw he was carrying a guy with smoke comin' off him towards the main gate.'

'Was Galindez with him?'

'Just Sung.' Coley handed her the drug box. 'Stay outta sight,' he said. 'Anyone sees a woman in here they really have a reason to kick the door down.'

Devlin felt a sudden panic. She squashed it down with a joke.

'Ten thousand years without a fuck,' she said.

Coley looked at her. 'What's that?'

Devlin said, 'I worked out that if you added together all the time all the inmates had gone without a woman it'd come to about ten thousand years.'

'Believe it,' said Coley. 'Lotsa blue balls out there. Lotsa sour testosterone. Like sweet milk gone to the bad.'

Devlin found Coley's analogy rather vile. She stood back behind the doors as Coley pulled one of them open. She peered through the crack between the hinges. The sky above the east wall was black. From above the main gates a pair of searchlight beams prowled the yard. The cellblocks appeared to be in total darkness. Coley clicked a switch on the wall and a light came on above the doors on the outside wall. The proximity of the light made the yard and cellblocks even less visible.

'Give me the goodie box,' said Coley.

She handed him the box of drugs and Coley disappeared outside. Devlin went back to the crack in the door. At the foot of the steps to the infirmary Coley came into view and set the box down.

'Hey, Coley!'

The voice rang out from the darkness beyond the porch light. Devlin couldn't see who the voice belonged to. Coley straightened up from the box and squinted into the yard. Without haste he started to walk backwards up the infirmary steps.

'Hey, Coley, where y'at, man? Hang about!'

Coley didn't stop but still didn't hurry, didn't show panic or fear. He pointed at the box.

'They's some real good shit fo' y'all yonder,' shouted Coley into the dark. 'Benzos, barbs, codeine. All I got. You boys go enjoy yourselves.'

He turned to mount the last two steps.

A figure erupted from the penumbra.

Devlin yelled, 'Coley!'

The figure sprang up the steps holding a monkey wrench twelve inches long. Coley swivelled, as cool as he was huge, and lashed his foot into the man's throat. As the man flipped backwards down the steps the wrench span from his fist at the apex of the arc swinging for Coley's head. Coley ducked the flying steel which hit the studded door and clattered to the stone flags of the porch. Coley paused for balance and skipped up the last step. A second man emerged from Coley's blind side and threw his arms round Coley's legs. Coley, struggling to stay upright, wrapped one hand round the assailant's neck and dug his other into his pocket. He ripped out his key ring and threw a desperate glance at Devlin. As he toppled over like a massive, stunted oak he flung the keys inside the hallway.

'*Lock the doors!*' he bellowed. '*Get inside!*'

Devlin found herself moving, without any concrete decisions to guide her actions, through a whirlwind of intensely sharp perceptions. Shouts and a stampede of running feet. A loud grunt as Coley crashed into the right-hand door and tumbled onto the flagstones. The dazzle of the porch light. Spectral figures milling in the gloom beyond. Gleaming on the floor: the bunch of keys. Beyond them: the bright steel of the wrench. Devlin stepped over the keys and grabbed the wrench with both hands. She heard someone scream.

'*Leave him alone, you cocksuckers.*'

The man's head swam into sight at her feet, his eyes glazed with fear as he stared at something rising above her head. Her legs were well spaced, slightly bent, rooted. Like splitting winter logs on her father's ranch. Another loud grunt, this time from her own chest. A violent shock wave ran up her wrists, her arms, and jolted her spine. Beyond the shock wave: a distant sense of fragmentation, a brittle, muted crumbling. Not at all like the crisp snap of a splitting log.

She heard someone say, 'Jesus.'

Other shouts echoed that she didn't register. A meaty arm encircled her waist and dragged her through the doors, flung her into the hallway. She turned, panting. Coley was heaving the big doors shut. A face appeared in the narrowing gap. Coley's left fist shot through the gap and socked the face out of sight. As the face disappeared Devlin saw two huge men, giants, bearded, tattooed, monstrous, lumbering towards them up the steps. She hurled her weight against the door with Coley. The doors closed. A simple, fragile latch, a century old and not even a lock, rattled into place.

'The bolt!' wheezed Coley.

The doors juddered as the weight of the giants ran into them. The screws holding the latch in place squealed from the wood, the iron buckled. The doors bulged inwards for a second. Coley braced his weight against them. The doors settled shut again. A pause.

'The bolt!'

A long flat oblong bolt sat on the right-hand door at chest height. Devlin grabbed the iron knob fixed to the bolt and pulled. The bolt didn't budge. Unused, maybe for decades, it was rusted into its moorings. Devlin's eyes flashed to the two iron hasps fixed to the inner edge of each door. From outside she heard the bellow of the two charging giants. Coley leapt away from the door and snatched the keys from the floor.

'*Come on!*' he screamed.

Instead of following him Devlin found herself stepping forward. Her hands threaded the handle of the monkey wrench through the two iron hasps. As she stepped back there was a crash as over five hundred pounds of psychopathic flesh and bone smashed into the far side. The doors bulged mightily. The wrench screeched against the ancient iron hasps, and trembled for an endless, motionless instant, as it took the kinetic energy into itself and dumped it in the entropy pool.

The instant passed and the doors groaned back into place. Coley ran past Devlin and battered at the knob of the sliding bolt with the heel of his hand.

'Move, you fucka.'

The bolt creaked forward a quarter inch. The iron was marked with gritty orange rust. Coley hammered again. As the rusted sections jerked apart the bolt moved easily on clean iron.

Through the door they heard a thin voice scream:

'Break that fucker down now!'

Coley nodded towards the wrench. Devlin understood and grabbed the head of the wrench.

'You pull and I'll push,' said Coley.

An approaching bellow, two voices, from outside.

'Now!'

As Devlin slid the wrench free Coley shot home the bolt. The flat iron bar was longer than the wrench and seated itself in four widely spaced hasps, two to each door. When the giants rammed them a third time the doors barely bulged at all.

Loud blasphemies, muffled by the thick wood, filtered through from the porch.

Coley rested his hands on his thighs and bent forward, breathing heavily. He looked up at Devlin with his bulging, hooded eyes.

'Thought I tol' you to lock yourself inside,' he said.

The bolting of the door had opened the floodgates in Devlin's neuroendocrine system. She felt like shitting, vomiting, fainting and laughing all at the same time. A spasm of trembling shook her from head to toe. She shook the spasm off.

'Fuck you, Coley.'

Coley straightened up. 'You'd left me outside I'd be nice and dead. Now I got to worry 'bout takin' care of you and all these goddamn sick muthas.'

'Get me a pack of cigarettes and I'll take care of myself,' she said.

Coley glanced at the wrench in her hand. 'You know somethin', Doctah?'

Devlin shook her head.

'You are a bad muthafucka.'

Devlin's pelvic floor muscles clenched in a feeling that bordered on the sexual and she blushed deeply. To her intellect the thought seemed ridiculous: but her guts told her that she'd just received the greatest compliment of her life.

She looked down at the wrench. Its jaws were clotted with hair and blood. Not like splitting a log at all.

'Best hang onto that,' said Coley. 'You pretty handy with it.'

'Hey Coley!' There was a tapping on the doors. 'Frogman!'

'Stand back there,' said Coley.

Coley threw a switch and the hallway and corridor became black as night. Devlin stepped across the hall and stood back behind the corner of the corridor to the CO's office. Coley slid open a panel in the door and stood to one side, his back to the door. Illuminated by the light above the porch a face Devlin didn't recognise appeared, peering blindly into the dark within. For a moment Devlin was taken aback: the face was that of a boy, literally a scrawny boy with an eighth of an inch of stubble covering his shaved skull. He looked like he should be wearing orange robes and banging cymbals.

'You hear me, Frog?' said the boy.

Coley didn't answer.

'You got you a lady in there with you?'

'No,' said Coley. 'I got me a pretty white boy from A lets me go down on him.'

'You lyin' to me, Frog? That ain't nice.'

'He got a bigger dick than you have.'

'Listen, Frog, we ain't got nothin' 'gainst you personal. We just want the faggots.'

'Only faggots round here is you and me. You want me to show you a good time you jest come back tomorrow.'

'You know who I mean, Frog. The Aids fuckers. They gotta go, man. I promised Nev Agry. Shit, we doin' 'em a favour, you know that.'

'Kiss my ass.'

'Listen, you can go. You got my word. Your boy too. We just want the Aids guys.'

The voice, the face, were so innocent, so angelic, that Devlin could almost believe him. An angel asking permission to execute the sick. She shivered and squeezed hard on the steel handle of the wrench.

'Kiss my ass,' repeated Coley.

The face in the peephole twisted into a grimace of frustrated rage. 'You know we comin' in there, one way or th'other. Warden don't give a shit, man. Screws all gone. We took the whole fucken joint down in twenty fucken minutes. You think you can keep us out of this little shithole?'

There was a silence. Devlin could hear Coley breathing in the dark. The angel suddenly grinned. She wondered if he could hear her heartbeat. She knew he couldn't see her, yet he seemed to be looking straight into her eyes.

'I'm talkin' to you now, Missy.'

Devlin turned away from the eyes that couldn't see her.

'Doctor Devlin, right?'

The sound of her own name echoing in the dark sent a glut of fear through her stomach.

'Ain't never fucked me no doctor before. My boys neither, but they'll be linin' up behind me.'

Devlin put one hand on the wall for support. The bright eyes still seemed locked onto hers.

'I'm gonna make you all a promise though, cause I know you and me already got somethin' special goin'. See, I'm gonna fuck you in the ass. But my boys, I'm only gonna let them fuck you in the mouth or the pussy. You got mah word of honour. You see, Doctor Devlin, I want you all t' stay nice an' tight, just for me.'

Coley slammed the peephole shut. For a moment there was a murmuring outside, then a shuffle of feet, then silence.

Devlin felt numb. She leaned her forehead against the wall. Everything she'd heard had registered and then vanished into some sealed neural tract where it wouldn't bother her. The only thought she had was to tell Coley to open the slot in the door again so she could ask the angel how Klein was. She suddenly felt an overwhelming anxiety on his behalf. He'd only had twenty-four hours to go and he was trapped in the main prison. She felt Coley's hand on her shoulder.

'He hasn't got any enemies, has he?' she said.

Coley looked puzzled. 'Who?'

'Klein.'

For a moment Coley's eyes crinkled at the edges as he looked at her face and saw whatever was written there. Then he smiled gently.

'Ever'one likes Klein,' he said. 'Nobody got no reason to come down on him. Nobody at all. He'll be safe, you hear me?'

Devlin nodded. Coley reached in his pocket and handed her a paper towel. She realised that her face was wet with tears.

'I'm sorry,' she said. She wiped her face with the towel. 'I was just worried about him.'

'Me too,' said Coley.

Devlin looked at him. 'Thanks,' she said.

'What fo'?'

'For not making me feel like an asshole.'

'Man, you too bad to be an asshole,' he said.

Devlin smiled.

'Grauerholz'll be back,' said Coley. 'We'd best get ready.'

Coley squeezed her shoulder and lumbered away down the corridor. Devlin blew her nose on the paper towel and shoved it in her pocket. Then she followed him back through the steel-barred gateway that had never looked so fragile before.

TWENTY-TWO

RAY KLEIN DRAGGED Claudine along the second tier walkway of D block and down the spiral staircase. Klein inhaled quick, sharp breaths through flared nostrils, as if the atmosphere were thinned of oxygen. His muscles trembled, yet his mind was very cool, his movements cleanly driven by he knew not what. A word offered itself. Outrage. Total outrage. He realised he had never known what it meant before. Not really. Not even when the detectives had come to the hospital and told him he was being charged with rape.

Agry was going to kill the Aids guys where they lay, helpless in their beds.

Again: outrage. Klein felt no anger that he was aware of. He was beyond it, taken out of rage by the simple extremity of Agry's plan. Klein thought he had known this place. Thought he had known its bestiality, its baseness. He had even felt himself a part of that baseness, had listened to the screams of the wounded man and wished him dead just to spare himself the inconvenience of hearing the noise. But the infirmary was a sacred space. They could kill each other, they could torture the paedophiles, white could slaughter black and black could slaughter Latino and Latino could slaughter white until Klein was the last man left alive in the cellblocks but the infirmary was holy ground. Without the infirmary there was nothing. Without the infirmary even the flickering shadows cast upon the subterranean wall of the cavern disappeared.

They reached ground tier. Behind him Claudine was still crying. Klein stopped and turned on her.

'I need to know what the fuck this is about, Claude,' he said.

Claude cowered behind Claudine's tears. She shook her head.

'I don't know.'

Klein shoved her backwards into the wall. He lifted his arm and she raised her hands to her face in fear. Klein knocked the hands down. He held her face still and scrubbed his shirt sleeve across her mouth, wiping away her red lipstick. She looked at him.

'I'm talking to you, Claude,' said Klein. 'I know Claudine's kept you alive but this isn't the time to shit me. I won't say anything to Nev that could hurt you, but I need to know what the fuck is going on.'

Claude blinked away the tears in his eyes and, for a while at least, Claudine too. He swallowed and nodded.

'Okay,' said Klein. 'Nev must know he can't win this. The whole thing is suicide. He'll spend the rest of his fucking life in seg.'

'It's my fault,' said Claude.

'Fuck your guilt,' said Klein.

He sighed, reined himself in. Claude was shrewd but he wasn't a rocket scientist. As he blinked his big brown eyes at him Klein realised that Claude, trapped at the centre of a mad war, was more bewildered than any of them. More gently Klein said, 'Just tell me what you know.'

'Nev wanted me back. I'd known he was that crazy about me I wouldn've agreed to go back to B.'

'Agreed to who?'

Claude looked away without answering. Klein shook him.

'Agry thinks you were moved by force on Hobbes's orders, at Wilson's request.'

'I know.'

'Wilson thinks you asked Hobbes to do it. Who's right?'

'I'm just another po' muthafucka wants to get back on the street, Ray. I didn' ask fo' nobody treat me special.'

'What happened?'

'It was the warden.'

'Did Wilson ask him?' said Klein.

Claude shook his head. 'Hobbes as't me. He told me if I left Nev, stopped livin' like a woman, he'd get me parole. If I didn' he said the board would turn me down agin and I'd have to serve out my time.'

'You got six years left, right?'

Claude nodded. Klein couldn't find it in his heart to blame him. To avoid another six years in here Klein would've let the whole block line up and butt fuck him.

'You must have known Agry couldn't take the loss of face,' said Klein.

'I thought he'd have me killed. That's what I tol' Hobbes but he promised he'd protect me.'

'How?'

'The lockdown.' Claude cringed with shame. 'He locked the brothers down so's Nev couldn't get to me. Shit I didn' know this would happen.'

'Hobbes did,' said Klein.

Claude's eyes widened. 'That muthafucka?'

Klein nodded. Hobbes, with his talk of events and improvements, and his mad-pills that he wasn't taking and his panoptic fantasies of dragging them all from darkness into light. Hobbes had known that this riot was going to happen. It was Hobbes's riot, not Nev Agry's. Yet there had to be more. Killing Claude should have been enough for Agry. Even with the lockdown

Claude's death could have been purchased for the right price and Agry's pockets were deep. With Claude gone there were other boys in the River pretty enough to satisfy Agry's sexual vanity. There was a piece missing. Several pieces. Klein just couldn't see what Agry's end was in all this. The riot would lose him everything, Claude included. After this they wouldn't let Agry out of solitary confinement until he had Alzheimer's disease and two artificial hips. Unlike the case of Hobbes, Klein just didn't believe Agry was that insane.

'Did Hobbes say anything about Agry, or vice versa?' asked Klein.

Claude shook his head. Before Klein could press him any further Agry's voice cut in from behind them.

'You botherin' my woman, Doc?'

Klein turned and peered through the near darkness. Agry stood with Tony Shockner and two other crewmen just inside the gateway to the central atrium. Agry had a shit-eating grin on his face.

Behind his wire-rimmed spectacles Shockner looked drawn. The four of them walked towards him. Klein gathered himself. The weight of the gun in his pocket was no longer much of a reassurance. He felt like the captain of the high school chess team facing up to the local chapter of the Hell's Angels. His sense of outrage withered. Then he pictured Horace Tolson smashing Vinnie Lopez across the skull with a crowbar.

'Where's Grauerholz?' said Klein.

The grin faded from Agry's face. He cast a glance at Claude, saw her tear-stained make-up and smudged lips. 'You go fix yourself.' Claude pushed himself away from the wall and walked off without looking at Klein and Klein felt that bit more alone. Agry looked at him.

'What'd you say, Doc?'

'I said where's Grauerholz?'

'He's gone to kill himself some faggots,' said Agry.

'Why?' said Klein.

Agry's lip curled grotesquely. 'Whaddya mean, "why?"' His eyes shone with hatred. 'Because they're there. That's why.'

'You could stop it if you wanted to,' said Klein.

'If I wanted to?' He glanced at his confederates and grinned. 'It's my fucken idea. Those cornhole fuckers are dead. I mean, what is this, Klein? You tryin' to tell me something?'

Klein found himself breathing heavily again. He felt split between wanting to smash Agry's face in and fall to his knees begging for mercy.

'It just seems unnecessary,' he said.

'You know something, Doc?' Agry's face was squirming with malevolence. 'You're right. It's totally fucking unnecessary. What the fuck has necessary got to do with it? You think any of this is necessary?'

One part of Klein's mind calculated that he was faster than Agry and in better shape. He could take out Agry's knee for sure, probably hammer his throat to mush or put an elbow through his temple. Then threaten Shockner with the gun, get him to call off Grauerholz. Another part of his mind pointed out that his limbs were almost paralysed with the adrenaline overload of fear. The debate ended as Agry flung a pointing finger out at Klein's chest.

'You think you're necessary, Short Time?' said Agry.

Klein didn't answer. The hatred in Agry's eyes was beyond rational appeal. Agry jabbed himself in the chest with the finger.

'Even I'm not necessary.' Agry grinned. 'Not any more. What's done is done. The ball's rollin', Doc. Ain't nobody gonna stop it now. Nobody at all.'

Klein glanced at Shockner. Shockner, his face more gaunt than ever, was staring at Agry as if he realised for the first time exactly where Agry had led them.

'You paid your dues, Doc,' said Agry, 'and you been good

to Claudine. That's the only reason you gonna be able to dandle your grandkids on your knee and tell 'em you once pointed a piece at Nev Agry.' He turned to grin at his men again, then back to Klein. 'But I got a great idea: you feel so bad about it, you go tell Grauerholz yo'self to leave them faggots be. I give you permission, you hear that, Tony?' He glanced at Shockner. 'The Doc here wants to go parley with Hector, you let him. After all,' he turned back to Klein with a sneer, 'the faggots gave him a good deal. Swannin' round th'infirmary like he was still in the world, whisperin' sweet nothin's to that lady of his. Better than makin' belt buckles in the machine shop. Ain't that right, Doc?'

Klein said nothing. Most people thought he was some kind of hero for working in the infirmary. Agry understood that the deal was stacked heavily in Klein's favour. He owed them more than they owed him.

Agry nodded. 'Yeah,' he said. 'He knows.'

He held Klein's eyes for a long beat, then turned away with contempt. As he walked past Agry pushed him with a bulky shoulder. Klein stumbled back a step into the bars of a cell. Shockner and the others followed Agry down the walkway. Klein felt shrivelled. There was a sour taste in his throat. He wanted a cigarette.

'Hey, Doc!'

Klein turned. Agry called down the darkened walkway.

'I need some ointment rubbed on my haemorrhoids, I'll let you know, okay?'

There was a cackle of coarse laughter from the two crewmen. Agry laughed too. Then, still laughing, he swivelled on his heel and strolled back towards his cell.

Klein stood in the dark. A million words went through his mind without him hearing them, so many words that all he was aware of was a hum as empty as silence. Time passed. He didn't know how much. The hum became comforting. Perhaps, if he listened to it for long enough, the riot would be over. One word he didn't want to hear somehow intruded.

'Doctor.'

Klein ignored it. He felt a hand the size of a baseball glove on his shoulder.

'Doctor?'

Klein's vision focused in from a vanishing-point in the darkness. Henry Abbott's face swam into view. Klein smiled at him blankly.

'Henry,' he said.

'There's danger down here,' said Abbott.

'Yes,' said Klein. 'You'd better go back to your cell.'

Klein felt his legs move him towards the main gate sally.

'Where are you going?' asked Abbott.

Klein stopped. 'I have to go to the infirmary,' he said.

There was a pause. Then Abbott's voice echoed in the dark with that flat, lumpen tone which denoted a simple and irrefragable truth.

'Of course,' said Henry Abbott. 'They need you.'

TWENTY-THREE

THE RED IRON girder with the number '99' painted on its side still poked out from the scorched and shattered windows of the central watchtower. In the dark the white figures '99' were faintly luminous and if Klein hadn't seen them he might have blundered into the girder itself. Maybe then he would have dislocated a kneecap, or ripped a ligament, and been forced to drag himself back up to the safety of his cell but it was clear to Klein by now that it wasn't the kind of day where he'd be lucky enough to break a leg. He stepped over the girder.

The fire in B had burned itself out and inside the block Agry's men, and those he had inherited from DuBois, were busy looting the abandoned cells. Klein circled the tower and headed down the General Purposes wing. The low-ceilinged corridor was pitch dark and he couldn't see more than a few yards ahead. He passed shadowy figures slumped against the walls and sprawled on the floor. Some of them were silent and unmoving. Others made dull noises, whether from intoxication or injury he could not tell. He made no effort to find out. There was a spill of books and torn and charred pages from the entrance to the library, and from the chapel as he passed came sounds of splintering wood and guffaws of drunken laughter. Klein did not turn his head. Whatever was going on in there he didn't want to know. Three white convicts drifted aimlessly towards him coming down the centre of the corridor. One of them carried a plastic bucket, the other two, lengths of wood. Klein altered course to one side to avoid walking through them. They stopped as he approached them and stared at him sullenly. The one with the bucket raised it to his mouth and slurped a mouthful of brew. Klein avoided their eyes and hoped like hell they'd ignore him. As he drew level the con with the bucket called out.

'You wanna drink, Doc?'

Klein kept walking. 'Thanks, pal, but not now. Maybe later.'

He kept going, he was past them. He wanted to look over his shoulder but didn't. He strained his ears for approaching footsteps but none came. He felt his shoulders hunched tight around his ears. Relax, he told himself. If you're tense you can't move so quickly. He was past them, now he was passing the gym. He heard the sound of a basketball thudding into the wooden floor, a chorus of shouts. He kept walking but he couldn't help glancing in. Fires were burning in empty drums of kitchen oil with holes punched through their sides. The home-made braziers threw a surreal, darkling light on the players as they jostled for possession of the ball. On one side of the gym a naked man, half-kneeling, his black skin shining in the flames, hung by his wrists from the wooden exercise bars, face to the wall, while a grimacing white con, pants around his ankles, fucked him with frenzied, grunting shunts. Nearby another con stood watching, flies open, jerking himself off.

Klein turned away.

Whatever he felt was no good to him. Or anyone else. He shut it down. He hadn't seen anything. He walked on past. The exit into the yard loomed. Beyond its archway he could see the concrete path to the main gate, searchlight beams weaving lethargically back and forth, glittering on the tall steel mesh fences. It did not surprise Klein that Hobbes and Cletus had closed shop and decided to wait them out. He'd heard enough about riots elsewhere and the disasters that usually accompanied gung ho rescue attempts. But if he could just speak to Cletus he was sure the Captain would protect the infirmary. Cletus was corrupt and a brute, but he wouldn't stand by while sick men were butchered. Klein saw two figures sitting by the wall just inside the gate. They were both bloody and one of them was slumped forward with his head on his chest.

As Klein steeled himself to walk past them one said, 'That you, Klein?'

Klein walked past. Easier this time. He could feel the fresh air on his face from the yard.

'They'll cut you down, man. Don't try it.'

Klein stopped and turned. The man was Hank Crawford, a middle-class Joe from Fort Worth Klein had played chess with a time or two. He'd been an oil company accountant and was serving two years for fraud. To end up doing time for that must have required the services of the worst defence attorney in Texas legal history, but here he was. Klein crouched down beside him. Crawford's right pants leg was saturated with blood from the knee down. Above the wound was knotted a canvas belt. The other man was shot through the groin and as the searchlight passed by Klein saw from the waxy pallor of his skin and the blue of his lips that he was in bad shape. Klein turned back to Crawford.

'We tried to give ourselves up,' said Crawford. 'Hundred yards from the gate a megaphone told us to get back. We kept going. One warning shot, then pow, Bialmann took one in the leg. I turned to help him and they shot me from behind. I think maybe there's two more guys still out there. You'll never make it.'

Klein took the information in without speaking. He looked

out across the yard. From here the view to the infirmary was blocked by the tip of the long arm of B block.

'I'm trying to get to the infirmary,' said Klein.

'You'll never make it there either.'

'Why not?'

'Grauerholz and a whole buncha guys gone over, reckon they're gonna wipe out the whole damned place.' Crawford looked away from what he saw in Klein's face. 'Damnedest thing I ever heard.'

'Did they come this way?' asked Klein.

Crawford shook his head. 'I believe they went through B, that's nearest. But I'm tellin' you man, there's nothin' you can do. Those psychos are blood crazy. It was when I saw their faces I decided to surrender. I don't even want to be in the same State.'

'How long since they went?'

'Shit I can't tell day from night at the moment.' He weakly lifted his arm and looked at his watch. 'Maybe a half-hour? Less.'

Klein started to stand up. Crawford pawed at his arm. 'Anything you can do for me, Doc?'

Klein blinked. He wanted to leave Crawford where he lay. He didn't have time. He had to get to the infirmary. Or at least find out what was going on. He didn't have time, goddamnit.

With a grunt Klein stuck his fingers in the hole in Crawford's pants and ripped it open. Crawford inhaled sharply through gritted teeth. Blood leaked in retarded dribbles from a bullet wound in the rear of the knee. Klein could see that the politeal artery had been severed and the distal femur shattered. The guards used M16s. The tourniquet was badly applied. If anything it was making the bleeding worse.

'I ain't a bad guy, Doc,' panted Crawford, 'you know that. I only been up three months. I'm just tryin' to serve my time.'

His face was almost as waxy as Bialmann's and was covered by a thin sheen of sweat. Klein put a thumb to his femoral pulse. A hundred and thirty. Klein wondered how much blood he'd lost. However much it was he couldn't afford to lose much more.

'Yeah.' Klein sighed. 'Me too.'

He untied the belt round Crawford's leg. Crawford stiffened and clenched his teeth. The bleeding didn't get any worse, but what clotting there was was fragile. The leg needed immobilising or a movement could dislodge the clot and exsanguinate him. Klein leaned over to Bialmann, felt his carotid pulse. After ten seconds he started to rip the man's shirt off.

'How's Bialmann?' said Crawford.

'He's dead,' said Klein.

Crawford started crying quietly.

Klein wadded the shirt into a pressure dressing and belted it in place over Crawford's wound. He stood up. This was everything he hadn't meant to do. It was fucking stupid. He was fucking stupid. And Crawford too. Stupid. Klein knew that if Crawford lay here all night without even water to replenish his plasma volume, maybe crawling around with the raging thirst he would develop from the blood loss, he'd either be dead by morning or well into acute renal failure. It was *knowing* that was the problem. If Klein had been just anyone, if he hadn't known, he could've tied the belt, shaken Crawford's hand and inadvertently left him to die with a clear conscience. But Klein did know. The obligation stood before him, immovable and absolute.

'Give me your hands,' said Klein.

Crawford did so and Klein grabbed them.

'Now get your good leg under you. You're gonna stand up and it's gonna hurt like all fuck.'

Crawford bent his good knee and placed his foot square on the floor. He sobbed with terror. 'I can't.'

'Fuck you,' said Klein. 'Get up.'

Klein stepped back and hauled on Crawford's arms. Crawford had no choice but to thrust himself upright on his good leg. He shrieked with pain. As he reached his full height his eyes rolled upwards and he started to pass out. Klein dropped to one knee and came up under him, folding him over his right shoulder in a fireman's lift. He stood up and staggered with the weight. He leaned one hand against the wall. As he got his balance and turned back into the dark maw of the General Wing he saw Henry Abbott standing there watching him. Klein took a deep breath.

'Henry,' he said heavily. 'What the fuck are you doing?'

'I thought that you might need help,' said Abbott.

Klein squeezed his eyes shut and took some more deep breaths. Crawford was bleeding to death and was twenty pounds overweight. Abbott was insane and had the intellect of a Brahma bull. He, Klein, was fucked in the head. It was simple really. He opened his eyes.

'Let's go,' said Klein.

Before Abbott could say anything else Klein started back down the wing at a crouching, shuffling run. This was the sort of shit that Robert Mitchum pulled off on Omaha beach whilst lighting his cigar with a Zippo and taking out a Nazi machine gun nest with a grenade. After ten paces Klein was wheezing for air and wondering exactly which of his lumbar discs was going to pop out first. You're in good shape, he told himself. William James has prepared you for this. Yeah. And Crawford is a fatassed cunt. He staggered past the gym. Basketball and gang rape by firelight. He hurdled a body on the floor. Infuckingsane. He knew if he stopped he'd never get moving again. He kept going. Then from the chapel up ahead his old buddy Myron Pinkley emerged with blood caked on his clothes and hands. He held his arms in the air and yelled in a reedy voice.

'For behold the days are coming in which they shall say, Blessed are the barren, and the wombs that never bore, and the paps which never gave suck!'

This prospect seemed to please Pinkley for he started shaking with laughter. Klein could think of other inmates he would rather have seen at that particular moment. Pinkley caught sight of Klein blundering towards the watchtower and trotted along beside him. He bent over and screamed in Klein's face.

'The fetters of the law have been removed. On the wings of the righteous shall the spirit of Jesus soar amongst us. The foul and iniquitous shall be plunged into the pit of everlasting fire.'

Whether Pinkley saw Klein soaring on the wings of the righteous or embarked on the long plunge to Hell, Klein never found out. A look of stark terror wiped the fervour from Pinkley's face as he looked over his shoulder in time to see his very own favourite-right-hand-in-all-the-world clamp around his throat and lift him off the floor. With a squeal of panic Pinkley vanished abruptly from Klein's vision and Klein staggered on. His right arm was about to part company with his shoulder. His thighs were wobbling beneath him. He reeled across the central atrium and sagged, heaving, against the ruined watchtower.

After the claustrophobia of the corridor the forty-foot dome curving high overhead was a marvel, a thing of beauty. He caught his breath. Abbott emerged from the darker darkness of General Purposes.

'Where's Pinkley?' asked Klein.

'I put him back in the chapel,' said Abbott.

'Thanks, Henry,' said Klein.

Abbott pointed at the body on Klein's shoulder. 'You should have let me carry him,' he said. 'He's heavy.'

Klein smiled stiffly. A ludicrous macho pride prevented him

from handing Crawford over. He could no longer feel his arm anyway.

'You're a good man to know, Henry.' He nodded across the atrium. 'We're going into B. Stick by me, in case you run into any more trouble.'

Abbott nodded solemnly. Klein hefted Crawford and lurched the last fifty metres across the the floor of the atrium. As he went he told Henry to grab two pieces of wood from the wreckage on the ground. As Klein hobbled through the main sallyport of B block the stink of burnt gasoline filled his lungs and made his ragged breathing more painful than it already was. His feet slid in a greasy residue clinging to the walkway. Here and there flashlights wove about amongst the empty tiers and men called out to each other as they ransacked the cells for drugs, booze, cigarettes and cash. Klein leaned against the glass window of the guards' office. His machismo was reaching its limit, as sooner or later it always did. In another sixty seconds he would have to let Crawford fall to the floor.

'Go in the office, Henry,' said Klein, 'see if you can't find us a flashlight.'

'I already have one,' said Abbott.

'What?' said Klein.

Abbott reached into his pants and pulled out a four-battery heavy duty flash encased in black rubber.

'I always carry one,' he said.

Of course, Abbott worked the sewers. He was used to wandering in the dark. 'Find me an empty cell,' said Klein.

Abbott walked ahead shining the flash into the cells of ground tier. The first two contained dead bodies, men incinerated by the initial, fiercest, blast of the fire. As they reached the third there was a movement within. The light beam fell on khaki clothing. Then a bruised face, blinking, a hand raised to shield the eyes. Two faces. A third. Three guards. The guards were huddled at the back of the cell.

Klein said, 'Open the door, Henry.'

Abbott slid back the steel door. Klein shuffled sideways into the cell. Almost weeping with relief he bent forward and dumped Crawford onto the bunk. Crawford opened his eyes and screamed. As the blood returned to Klein's shoulder, and with it a mass of agonising sensation, he felt like joining him.

'Fucks goin' on, man?'

The voice came from the walkway outside and Klein turned. One of Agry's crew, a white trash musclehead with tattoos named Colt Greely, stood peering through the bars. In his hand was a sharpened screwdriver. As far as Klein knew Greely had never killed anyone. Klein massaged his aching shoulder. His right hand scintillated with pins and needles. He couldn't move the fingers. Greely glanced nervously at Abbott, towering silently beside him. Klein reasoned that anyone calling himself 'Colt' had to be an asshole, and a gullible one at that.

'Henry!' snapped Klein. 'Keep cool now!'

While Abbott didn't move a muscle, and indeed had shown no signs of doing so, Colt Greely leapt a yard to one side, his eyes glued to Abbott. He called to Klein.

'What the fuck, man? Don't do that!'

'Sorry, Colt,' said Klein. 'Abbott just killed four guys in the chapel with his bare hands. Once he flips I can't stop him.'

'Jesus.'

Greely gaped in horror at the flat, impassive face staring down at him. The shiv in his hand trembled unconvincingly. Greely looked at the shiv as if the hand holding it didn't belong to him. He hastily shoved the weapon into his belt.

'Abbott's taken a shine to Crawford here. He made me carry the fat bastard halfway across the fucking joint.' Klein nodded towards the khaki shirts cowering in the toilet. They too were staring at Abbott with naked terror. 'He wants these jokers to take care of him.'

'Shit,' said Greely. 'Why not?' He smiled nervously at Abbott.

Abbott just kept staring at him. 'Hell, Crawford's one of us ain't he?'

'Go get him some smack,' said Klein.

'Smack?' said Greely stupidly.

'Heroin,' said Klein. 'You know? Not coke. The best you can get, brown if possible. Right, Henry?'

Abbott stared at Greely without responding.

Greely bobbed his head gratefully. 'You got it, Doc.' He disappeared.

Klein turned to the guards. Burroughs, Sandoval, Grierson.

'Grierson,' said Klein.

While Klein made Crawford comfortable on the bunk and reapplied the pressure dressing to the wound Grierson stepped forward and watched. Klein took the two broken planks from Abbott and placed them front and back of Crawford's leg. The movement caused Crawford to shudder with pain.

'What I want you to do,' said Klein, 'is tear a sheet up and bind this splint in place, like this. Let him drink what water he wants. When Greely brings the smack let him snort a little at a time, for the pain.'

'I got it,' said Grierson.

'It won't harm your chances any with the crew.'

'I guess.' Grierson stole a glance over Klein's shoulder at Abbott. 'He really kill those guys?'

Klein didn't see any harm in stoking Abbott's reputation. Henry didn't seem to mind.

'Gruesome,' said Klein. 'Be glad you didn't see it. What's Grauerholz up to?'

'He came through about thirty minutes since with sixteen or twenty other guys, coked and ripped to Jesus from what I could see. We thought our number was up but they went on past.' Grierson paused. 'Greely said Agry sent 'em to kill all the faggots in the infirmary.' He glanced nervously at Abbott. 'I mean the Aids guys.'

'What's happened to the blacks?'

'They took a beating. If Vic Galindez hadn't opened the cages most of 'em'd be dead. Agry's men are still huntin' in armed gangs, full of piss and vinegar. I guess the niggers are hiding out down below, what's left of 'em, every man for himself. Lot of 'em still locked down in C with the Mexicans.'

Like the white cons the guards used 'Mexican' as a deliberately inaccurate and therefore insulting term for the Latinos, the vast majority of whom had been born here in Texas.

'What's Hobbes gonna do?' asked Klein.

'Unless they start killin' hostages he'll wait until the booze and the drugs run out and they start cryin' for their mamas. I reckon maybe three days.'

'Or maybe ten,' growled Burroughs sourly.

'Will he stop Grauerholz assaulting the infirmary?'

Grierson frowned. 'I wouldn't count on it, but Hobbes is kind of an unpredictable guy.'

'What about Cletus?'

'I can predict him. He wouldn't let one of our guys twist a fucken ankle to save that bunch of losers.' He glanced at Abbott again. 'I mean . . .'

'Yeah,' said Klein. He began to wonder why he hadn't hired Abbott to walk around behind him for the whole three years he'd been here. 'Mind this leg till we get back.'

He stood up and walked to the door. He flexed his right-hand fingers. Abbott handed him the flashlight.

'I live in the dark,' said Abbott. 'You can't see as good as I can.'

For a second Klein thought he heard something in Abbott's voice he hadn't heard before but he wasn't sure what. Emotion, maybe. He looked up at him. The eyes were as pure and empty as ever. He took the flash. *I live in the dark*. The voice still echoed in the back of Klein's mind. He shook it off.

'Let's go.'

'Klein?'

Klein turned back to Grierson.

''Bout five minutes before you showed up the Tolsons and some other guys came through here. They was carrying that damned iron girder thing they used to smash into the watchtower.' Grierson saw the look on Klein's face. 'I thought you oughta know.'

Klein pushed past Henry Abbott and started jogging down the walkway. The light of the flash wobbled across the floor in front of him. He caught a glimpse of a face, a moustache, pressed between the bars of a door.

'Klein!'

Klein ignored the voice. The face was too vague to register. He heard it call again, behind him. Too many fuckers wanted his attention. And Grauerholz had the battering ram, upon which Klein wished more sorely than ever he had honourably broken a leg. When Earl Coley and all his patients were dead, Klein wondered, how would he feel? Coley would've told him to walk away and forget it. Would Coley do the same for himself? The hospital building was old and Coley had spent nearly twenty years inside its walls. If there was any place in there a man could hide Coley would know it. Yeah. Coley would know it and he would survive. He would let Grauerholz and his bunch kill whoever they wanted because he knew he couldn't stop them, and he would remember all the advice he'd given Klein and save himself because it wasn't his fucking business. Then he and Klein could mourn the dead together, and tell each other they'd done the only thing they could do by turning their backs. As Klein jogged towards the rear sallyport of B block its looming arch revealed more and more of the yard beyond. A thick, fast-congealing dread arose in his throat and coated his tongue with the taste of shame. He stopped running and walked the last few yards to the sallyport. He heard a distant noise: raucous voices raised in unison punctuated by a regular percussive thud. Between the upper edge of the gateway arch and the granite horizon of the great encircling perimeter wall he could see a band of clear night sky flecked with stars. He stuck the flashlight in his pants and walked down the ramp to stand in the doorway.

Across the yard a group of men were clustered about the foot of the infirmary steps. On the steps themselves were six men. Between them they held the red iron girder and swung it in short heavy arcs against the double doors of the infirmary. The thirty-foot length of the girder and the angle of the steps made the work awkward but Klein didn't doubt they would get there. The crowd were chanting something guttural and short in time with the regular thuds of the battering ram. Some of the men on the edge of the crowd staggered drunkenly in small aimless circles. One of them fell to his hands and knees and threw up. When he'd finished he crawled forward through the vomit. Someone pointed at him and yelled. The crawler, oblivious, moved into the path of the battering ram. The bevelled rear end of the girder hit the crawler in the side of the head with a crunch that Klein imagined but couldn't hear. The crawler fell face down and didn't move. The ramming squad did not break their rhythm. None of the mob bothered to check the crawler out. Some doubled over with laughter.

The lights were on in the hospital and at the barred second-floor windows Klein could see the silhouettes of people within watching down on the girder and its grim work. The shame inside him dissipated into an appalling sadness that was somehow even worse. There really was, after all, nothing he could do. If there was no reasoning with Agry, Grauerholz and his mob were beyond any communication at all short of napalm. Grauerholz made Nev Agry look like Oscar Wilde. And Klein had humiliated him in the mess hall by taking his gun. Listening to their primitive chanting Klein realised that you could have offered them the world, and all that was in it, and they would still have preferred to carry on with what they were doing right now, battering down a door in pursuit of blood.

A sudden and terminal exhaustion wiped his legs from under him and Klein sank to his knees and sat back on his heels. A knowledge he had never felt before, icy and silent of all emotion, filled him: if he could have killed these people right now, he would've done it. He would have killed them all. He would've gassed them and burned them and shelled them. He would've buried them alive in a single unmarked grave. He would've slaughtered them en masse, denying any one of them the dignity of an individual death, and he would've expunged from the face of the earth all records of their existence. He would've accorded them no rights, no due process, no court of appeal. He would've prescribed their extinction as readily as he would an antibiotic to extinguish bacteria. Many of these men he had spoken to, some he had laughed with, others he had treated. He had recognised them as fellow men. Fellow men. Some of those they were now bent on murdering had been their cell mates a few weeks before, had shat in the same latrine, masturbated over the same porn mags, swopped and read each other's letters from home. Now they planned to kill them in their beds.

Klein's mind reeled with incomprehension. It was a phenomenon, something to be observed without true understanding, a virus, a cancer, an exploding star, for there was no understanding, and there was no forgiveness. There could be no forgiveness nor even punishment, for punishment implied understanding and justice and reparation and none of these things could be for these creatures who once were fellow men. There could only be eradication, cold and without vengeance, for a phenomenon such as this could not meaningfully require vengeance any more than an earthquake required an act of vengeance upon the earth. They were no longer men. He would not recognise them as such. They were not evil men or mad men or misunderstood men. They were not greedy men or angry men or violent men. They had forsaken that which made them men of any stripe to become instead biological particles in a bizarre natural phenomenon. And Klein wanted to eradicate them and knew that he could not. He felt huge hands grip his shoulder and lift him to his feet. He heard the breath of the giant in his ear.

'They must be stopped,' said Henry Abbott.

Again some subtle change in Abbott's voice called out from the fringes of the delirium fogging Klein's mind. He ignored it.

'They must be eradicated,' said Klein.

'Not necessarily,' said Abbott. 'Stopping them would be enough. There's a difference.'

Klein turned, shrugging off the hands. For once Abbott's pedantic, plodding thought processes irritated him. 'What difference is that, Henry?'

'It's the stopping them that counts. Not the killing. It's a question of logical and moral priority.'

'Jesus Christ, it must be time for your next injection.'

As soon as the words left his mouth a high-voltage current of raw shame blew the circuits in Klein's gut. He was reduced to the cruelty of taunting a friend for a terrible affliction. He had turned himself into scum. He grabbed the front of Abbott's shirt and looked up into the long gaunt face.

'Henry, forgive me for that. I'm sorry. I'm a piece of shit. I . . .'

Anything else was bullshit. His throat dried up. He rested his forehead against Abbott's broad chest. He wished Abbott would wrap his massive arms around him and crush him to death.

'Fellow men,' said Abbott.

For a moment Klein thought he'd mis-heard him. He felt eerie. He swallowed. Without raising his head he said, 'What was that?'

'Fellow men,' repeated Abbott.

Klein looked up at him. In the flat eyes there was a glimmer of light. A tiny glimmer, as of the most distant stars that you can only see if you don't look directly at them. Klein had never seen it before. Then he realised that he had: on that very first night when he had entered Abbott's filthy cell.

Abbott said, 'I think we should go in there.'

Klein glanced over his shoulder and realised that Abbott meant the infirmary.

'I'll take you,' said Abbott. 'Through The Green River.'

A chill ran down Klein's spine and he didn't know why. Through The Green River. That voice change. As if, for once, Abbott knew. Klein stepped back and looked at him. The glimmer had gone. He couldn't see it. Klein's heart swelled and he felt tears in his eyes. Fuck, man, he told himself, you'd better get your shit together, because if you ask him to this big guy will go the very last bloodstained fucking yard. He'll wade through Grauerholz's mob and he'll take them out in handfuls. But they will kill him. And you have a duty.

A duty. If he couldn't help the guys in the hospital he could at least stop Henry getting himself killed, for Henry was a crazy man talking crazy talk. And Klein wasn't. Klein was just an asshole losing his cool. That was the difference. Klein wiped his face on his sleeve. He smiled.

'No, Henry. If I thought we had even a thousand to one shot I'd take it, but we don't. There's too many of them.'

'They are many and we are few,' said Abbott.

'That's right.'

'But only one amongst us knows the River.'

More crazy talk. He had to get Abbott away from there

before the big man lost control and got himself slaughtered for nothing.

'We all know the River, Henry, and if we don't get out of here it's gonna drown us. Come on.'

He took Abbott's arm. Behind them a cheer arose as a splintering and rending of wood and metal announced the last hurrah of the hospital doors. The tears swam back into Klein's eyes, blurring his vision. He didn't want to see it. He wouldn't. He didn't turn back to watch. There were two more serious obstacles for Grauerholz to get through, the steel gate and the steel door in the corridor. Without anyone to resist them it was just a matter of time.

'Let's go,' said Klein. 'Let's go!'

He pulled Abbott back through the sallyport and into the black and gasoline-stinking hell of the block, only now, as he reeled down the walkway without using the flash, Klein could hear and see another hell, where the screams of the damned rent his ears and the voices were of his people dying on their blood and piss-soaked mattresses. A roll call of names: Vinnie Lopez. Reuben Wilson. Dale Reiner. Earl Coley. The Frogman. The Frog. Stumbling blindly onward Klein felt stinging liquid tumble from his eyes. The Frogman. Klein realised that in some childlike portion of his heart he did not believe that the Frogman could die. The Frogman would live forever. Klein heard his own name shouted out – 'Klein!' – but it did not belong on the roll call. Images swam into his mind, of the Frog penetrated with knives and dying. 'Klein!' And Klein couldn't help him. Or the others either. 'Klein!' He couldn't be there for any of them. He fended off their ghosts. Klein can't be there, guys. He would be but he can't. He can't, fuck you. Let him be.

'. . . Devlin!'

Klein froze. Devlin didn't belong on the roll call either. She was drinking a cold beer and watching the Lakers thrash the Knicks, counting the cartons of Winstons she would take from Klein. He realised that the voice wasn't in his head. Latino accent. Angry. He turned.

'Whatsa matter, Klein, you fucken deaf, man?'

A pale, moustached face shouted at him through the bars. Victor Galindez. Sergeant. Klein collected himself and walked over to the cell door.

'Galindez?' said Klein.

'You heard about Grauerholz?' asked Galindez.

'They just broke the infirmary door down,' said Klein.

He saw Galindez noting the stains on his face. Klein, embarrassed, scrubbed a shirtsleeve across his eyes. 'Smoke,' he said, by way of excuse. 'Nothing I can do for them.'

'I was trying to tell you,' said Galindez. 'Doctor Devlin is there too.'

Klein's mind went blank. 'She's at home watching the Lakers,' he said, blandly.

'She came back,' said Galindez. 'I took her back. She had something she wanted to show you and Coley.'

This time Klein took it in. And suddenly he felt cool. Everything that had happened in the last few hours dropped away from him. The craziness and the fear, the shame, the guilt, the grief. All of it. His mind was clear.

'Devlin's in the infirmary,' he said.

'That's right.'

Klein switched the flash on and shone it on Galindez. Galindez blinked and turned away. His uniform was scorched and filthy. His face was badly bruised, his eyes bloodshot. Klein wanted to think him a liar but Galindez had risked his life to save men who would have laughed while they cut his throat. He was telling the truth.

'They say you opened these cages. In the fire.'

Galindez did not reply. Klein's light beam fell on something sitting on the stool in Galindez's cell. Klein thought he knew what it was, but he didn't believe it.

'What's that?' he asked.

And then he believed it. Before Galindez could answer, Klein believed what he saw. And in the instant of his believing he heard inside his skull the strangely sonorous voice of Henry Abbott saying: 'Through The Green River.' And Klein at last understood. Through The Green River.

'It's a head,' replied Galindez without looking at the stool. 'Special company just for me.'

'Come on out of there,' said Klein, quietly. He slid the door of the cell open.

Galindez hesitated. 'They'll kill me.'

'You released the blacks. You'll be the first screw to die anyway.'

Klein stepped into the cell. The head on the stool had been crudely severed from a black inmate that Klein could not recognise. He pulled a blanket from the bed. 'How long've you been in here with this thing?' Klein draped the blanket over the head.

'I don't know, maybe eight hours.'

Klein rummaged around in the rear of the cell. He pulled out a damp, crumpled set of prison blues, shirt and pants. He held them out to Galindez.

'Time you got changed,' said Klein.

Galindez took the clothes. His eyes narrowed. 'We're going somewhere?'

'Yeah,' said Klein. 'We're taking a walk through the Green River.'

Galindez looked bewildered. 'What?'

Klein turned and looked at Henry Abbott, standing mute in the gloom on the other side of the bars. This time, in Abbott's eyes, Klein could see the glimmer again.

Of distant stars.

'They are many and we are few,' said Klein.

Without speaking Abbott nodded, once, and as he held that

infinite gaze Klein's spine tingled and he felt something tighten in his throat. Something awesome and fierce. For a moment he couldn't go on. He swallowed.

'Klein?' said Galindez. 'What do you mean?'

Klein said: 'There's only one amongst us knows the River.'

TWENTY-FOUR

JULIETTE DEVLIN FOLLOWED Earl Coley in silence as he trudged up the steps to the second floor. She expected him to go into Travis Ward but instead he pulled out his ring of keys and unlocked a door set back in an alcove at one end of the corridor. The door was stiff and Coley used his shoulder to shove it open. It clearly hadn't been used in a long time. Coley switched on a light. Leading upwards was a cobwebbed staircase.

'Come on,' said Coley.

She climbed up the stairs behind him, wondering what he had in mind. At the top Coley switched on a second set of lights. Beyond a grilled iron door was a disused ward built under the eaves of the roof. Two rows of five cast iron bedsteads faced each other under the bare lightbulbs. Coley unlocked the gate and stepped through.

'I've never been up here before,' said Devlin. There were no windows in the ward and it had an eerie atmosphere that brought gooseflesh out on her forearms.

'Ain't been used since World War Two,' said Coley. 'Me and Klein were thinking of opening it up again, things got any worse downstairs, the crowdin' I mean. But they's bad vibes here.'

'I can feel them. What was it used for?'

'This where they used to keep the boobies. I mean them that went insane, guys with syphilis of the brain, all that shit.'

'God,' said Devlin.

Coley walked towards a door at the far end. Devlin followed him. By nature and training she didn't suffer from squeamishness, but this place definitely retained some bad spirits. She saw that some of the beds were equipped with mouldering leather straps.

'I's told they did exper'ments here too. Lobotomies. Injected guys with insulin and malaria and snakeroot and Jesus knows what. They just sto'ies passed on down or that true?'

'It's true. In their time they were all reasonable ideas.'

'I guess. We still got a coupla straitjackets back here somewheres.'

She followed him through the door into a drab office containing a scarred table, a broken chair and a set of green metal filing cabinets. From a row of hooks on one wall hung two yellowed straitjackets. Devlin pulled one of the filing drawers open. It was crammed with cardboard folders, many lightly coated with green mould. On another day she would have been fascinated to find them. They had to contain enough material for a paper or two. But she couldn't see anything in the room that was any use to them now, unless Coley hoped to persuade Grauerholz into a straitjacket.

'Why have you brought me here?' asked Devlin.

Coley closed the filing drawer, grabbed the cabinet in both arms and levered it away from the wall. Behind it was a small door without any lock or handle. A thin steel cable ran from a hole in the back of the cabinet through another hole drilled in the door. Coley stuck the tip of a key into the crack at the edge of the door and pulled the door open. A black void gaped inside. On the inside of the door were two heavy bolts. He looked up at Devlin.

'This my secret. One time sixty year back the boobies went ape and killed a doctor and two trusties right where we standin'. Took 'em limb from limb. That's when they realise they put this office at the wrong end of the ward.'

'Shit,' said Devlin. 'I thought I was going to be the first doctor in history to die in here.'

'They cut this do' so they could hide, it evah happen again. You can bolt it from th' inside.'

Devlin laughed. 'You don't expect me to go in there?'

'This deal ain't no joke, Doctah Devlin. Grau'holz be back, an' he will get in.'

Devlin had thought about Hector Grauerholz on the way up. She had never met him but she had read his file. She knew what he had done, what he was capable of. He'd interested her as a case because the psychiatric and social court reports were unanimous in finding his personal background to be strikingly normal, completely free of the usual indicators of sociopathology. He came from a stable, affectionate, blue-collar family of modest means without a felony conviction between them. There was no suggestion of childhood abuse. No evidence of organic brain damage or mental disorder. Hector should've married the girl next door. Instead he'd started killing people. His florid criminality had just appeared, full blown and without any antecedents. In this sense he was an affront to science as well as to the law. Damnit, he had no right to be that bad. Devlin had once asked permission to interview him, and Hobbes had agreed, but Grauerholz had refused to meet her. Perhaps now she would have her chance.

'You be safe in here,' went on Coley. 'Look.'

He reached through the door and switched on a light. Inside were roof trusses and beams, a mattress, a number of cardboard boxes. In the boxes light glinted from the tops of canned foods.

'I fix this up myself,' said Coley, ''bout fifteen year since.

Word went round that they was gonna close this ole shithole down and move us all to a new facility. I reckoned me to hole up in here say three, fo' week till ever'one gone, ever'one, then come out and sneak ovah the wall.'

'You think it would've worked?'

Coley stared through the door at his secret. 'Doctah, I ain't seen the sun come over the horizon in twenty-three year. Was a time I saw it ever'day, winter and summer, rain or shine. Now that sixty-foot wall always in my way. I ain't seen a tree or a field of cotton or a blade of grass since them doors closed behind me.'

He turned to look at her. Her heart squeezed inside her chest.

'You dream 'bout bein' free, you believe anythin' 'll work.'

'I won't go in there,' said Devlin.

'Listen, Doctah, you a woman. You know what that mean? They rape yo' ass for forty-eight hours straight then pass you on to they buddies. They stick they dicks into blood and mush and think it's Christmas. Maybe you dead by then, don't matter, they keep on fuckin' anyway. 'Cause you a woman.'

Devlin's insides squirmed and she couldn't help flinching. Graphic pictures flashed through her mind.

'Sorry, Doctah Devlin, but that's the way it is.'

Devlin forced the pictures away. She glanced into Coley's den.

'There's only two people in this building can walk properly. That's you and me,' she said. 'And you and me are going to keep those bastards out.'

Coley stared at her without speaking.

'Okay, Coley.' Devlin held out her hand. 'Give me the keys.'

Coley relaxed visibly. He unhooked two keys from his ring and put them in her hand.

'If they get through the third door downstairs I'll come up here and hide. Until then I'm with you. Deal?'

Coley read the resolution in her face. He nodded.

'And there's something else,' she said. 'I want you to drop this "Doctah Devlin" shit. Makes me feel like Scarlett O'fucking Hara. It's "Devlin", okay?'

Coley grinned. 'Klein don't know it yet, but you gonna break his balls, Devlin.'

'Fuck you, Coley.'

From the ward outside came a voice.

'Frog? You in there?'

Coley stood up. The door opened and Reuben Wilson leaned against the jamb. His voice was deep, rich, and he had watchful eyes that took in Devlin's body with a glance and held her with a frank gaze. He was slim with wide shoulders and a hard-looking jaw that was just a little too big for his face. Devlin had never spoken to him. Sweat ran down his throat and into the shallow cleft between his pecs at the neck of his shirt. As soon as she realised she found him attractive Devlin blushed and had to look away. Wilson glanced from Devlin to Coley to the hole in the wall.

'What's goin' on?' asked Wilson.

Coley bent down and switched off the light in the hidden den.

'You just mind yo' business, nigger,' said Coley. 'What you doin' up here?'

'Buncha crackers outside smashing the doors down.'

'Grauerholz,' said Coley. 'We already told him to kiss our dirty black ass.' He looked at Devlin. 'Our white ass too.'

Devlin blushed again, this time with pride.

'Way I see it,' said Wilson, 'Agry sent 'em for me.' He glanced at Devlin as if he were embarrassed for her to hear this. 'You open the doors I'll turn myself over. Reckon Agry wants me alive, for a while anyways. No sense you all gettin' hurt.'

'I tol' you you a pussy, Wilson,' said Coley. 'Now I know

you an asshole too, and a high and mighty asshole at that. The crackers're here to kill the Aids guys.'

Wilson's face remained impassive but in his eyes was a brief struggle to comprehend. 'Why?'

'Shit, you the politician,' said Coley. 'All 'at matters is they come to harm my people. They just gotta come through me first.' He paused. 'They know Devlin here's with us too.'

Wilson looked at her. His mouth twisted sourly. She felt stupid.

'That's bad,' said Wilson.

'Wasn't fo' her they'd already be cuttin' yo' pecker off to take back to Agry,' said Coley. 'Saved my old ass too. She's a muthafucka, man.'

Wilson smiled at her and Devlin went weird inside.

'Always pleased to meet a motherfucker,' said Wilson.

He held out his hand and Devlin walked over and shook it.

'Reuben Wilson,' he said.

'Juliette Devlin.' She paused, uncertain, then said, 'I saw you take out Chester Burnett in five at the Superdome.'

Wilson blinked in astonishment. 'New Orleans?'

'Must be ten years ago. I had twenty bucks on Burnett to go the distance.'

Wilson smiled with pleasure. 'I apologise.'

'That's okay. The time you lost the split decision to Pentangeli I had money on him too.'

From behind her back came a chortle of wheezy laughter from Coley. Wilson pretended not to hear it and drew his shoulders back.

'I had a broken bone in my hand hadn't healed proper,' he said.

'The fourth metacarpal,' said Devlin. 'That's why I bet Pentangeli.'

'Goddamn,' murmured Wilson.

Coley walked over and stopped by Wilson in the doorway.

'See what I mean? Tonight she bettin' you can't get your pussy ass into gear to he'p us keep out the crackers. Trouble is she can't find no one to back you.'

Coley strode off down the ward. Wilson caught Devlin looking at him, supporting himself against the jamb. He stood upright and coughed. Devlin realised she was about half an inch taller than him. For some reason it made her feel awkward.

'You like to bet outsiders then,' said Wilson.

'A sure thing's no fun,' replied Devlin. 'That's why I never backed you.'

Wilson put a hand on his stomach. Devlin knew from Klein what had happened to him in solitary. 'Well I sure ain't a sure thing no more.'

Devlin walked past him and through the door.

'I'd better go call my bookie then.'

Devlin left the doors to the old mental ward unlocked in case she did have to make her way back up there. She checked that she still had the keys to lock them in her pocket. As she and Wilson went downstairs a sound started, getting progressively louder, of a great hollow thud that echoed dully through the heavy air. They found Coley downstairs in the dispensary. On the bench were two wide rolls of adhesive tape.

'Strap him up,' said Coley. 'If I do it I'll have to listen to him fussin' and cryin'.' Coley put on a mocking, high-pitched whimper: 'Careful there, Frog, I'm a-hurtin'.'

'Hey, Coley,' said Wilson darkly.

Coley winked at her. 'Maybe for you he act like a man.'

Coley busied himself unlocking a cupboard. Devlin looked at Wilson and hesitated. There was a brief moment of embarrassment between them, then Devlin slipped into doctor mode.

'Take your shirt off,' she said.

The thick scar bisecting Wilson's abdomen was ugly, maybe all the more so because the rest of him looked terrific. She had him lift his arms above his head and took the rolls of tape and bound them round his torso from just below his nipples to just above his hips. She wasn't sure just how much physical support the strapping would really give to Wilson's healing muscles, but psychologically it would make him feel a lot more secure. As she wrapped the last loop of tape round his waist her belly bumped into his cock. Wilson had a burgeoning erection.

'Excuse me,' he said.

She looked up at him. He wasn't making a big deal of it or trying to hit on her. He was just being coolly respectful.

'No problem,' she said.

Devlin felt momentarily turned on. She thought about Klein and how he'd pushed her against the wall and the thought turned her on some more. Two first-class hard-ons in one day was more luck than she'd had in a long time. Without her making a big deal of it either she let Wilson's cock rest against her while she completed the taping. A vague ethical doubt flitted across her mind, but Wilson wasn't her patient and anyhow it wasn't like she had his cock in her mouth. She wondered, as she'd wondered before, if she would ever have enjoyed sin quite as much as she did if her mother and father had not been such devout Catholics. When she finished the roll of tape she stepped back.

Wilson lowered his arms. 'Thanks.' He rolled his shoulders and twisted his hips from side to side. 'Feels good.'

'See what I mean?' said Coley. 'Different man.'

On the bench he'd laid out a collection of scissors and scalpels. He unwrapped a sterile blade from its sealed foil envelope and slotted it into place on the handle of one of the scalpels.

'These're here fo' when you need 'em. They sharper than any shank but they no good fo' stabbin', Just slashin'. It comes to it you gotta stay outa their way, keep cuttin' and movin'.'

His hand suddenly darted out towards Wilson's throat.

Without apparent haste Wilson took a step forward and out. The blade missed his neck by half an inch. Coley suddenly found Wilson to his blind side, fist cocked ready to smash the side of his head in. He nodded.

'Maybe you do after all,' said Coley. He indicated the scalpel to Devlin. 'You okay 'bout this?'

They looked at her, big tough guys, and Devlin felt the weight of her gender pressing down on her. She shrugged. 'My anatomy's pretty good. I mean I guess I know the best place to cut someone's throat. But I've never killed anyone,' she said.

Wilson grinned. 'Shit, neither have we.'

'I've butchered hogs,' said Coley, 'and killin' crackers ain't no different, 'cept maybe they make more squealin'.' He put the scalpel back on the bench. 'Let's go see what's goin' down.'

They went through into Crockett ward. As they entered the murmur of the patients changed to a battery of questions shouted at Coley. Coley waved his hand at them to shut up. At the windows two of the more mobile patients were peering outside. The sound of the thudding from the front doors was louder in here. Each crashing blow was accompanied by a shout, drunken voices raised with the jubilation of hate.

'*Fuck!*' A pause.

'*Fuck!*' A pause.

'*Fuck!*' A pause.

Wilson glanced at Devlin to gauge her reaction. Devlin said, 'Nice to know they haven't got much imagination.'

Coley went to the window and peered through the bars beyond the reinforced glass. Devlin looked over his shoulder. In the light from the porch she could see a mob of twenty, maybe thirty men gathered around the foot of the steps. Some of them were rummaging in the cardboard box of drugs. Others had sampled them and were already staggering. On the steps themselves six brutes, led by the two bearded giants, held a long iron girder which they battered with a regular beat into the double doors.

'*Fuck!*'

'*Fuck!*'

Coley said, 'Least they won't get that thing round the bend in the hallway. It's too long.'

'Coley, whatsa score, man?' Vinnie Lopez had pulled himself up to a sitting position. Coley sneered at him with brutal humour.

'You gonna get yo' little Mex balls cut off.'

'My balls from Cuba, muthafucka.'

Devlin watched Wilson's face. He was staring at Lopez's emaciated frame as if he didn't recognise him.

'Vinnie?' said Wilson.

Lopez read Wilson's expression. 'Where the fuck you been, Wilson? Why you don't come training with me no more?'

Wilson's eyes flickered away, like he didn't know whether or not it was okay to look at the bones sticking through Vinnie's skin.

'Been busy, Vinnie.'

'Fuck, man, you look like shit. You nearly fat as Coley. I gotta get you back down the gym.'

'That's what I need,' said Wilson. He smiled uncertainly.

Coley pushed Wilson out of his way. 'You fuckers gonna get all the trainin' you can use. Wilson, you stay here.' He jerked his head at Devlin. She followed him down the ward. Coley stopped at the desk at the nursing station and took a tube from a drawer. They went out through the barred gate of the ward and into the corridor. Standing between them and the porch hallway were three doors. The first was a simple wooden door, no bars, no bolts, just a mortice lock. It was usually left jammed open. They walked through past the empty TV room, two bathrooms, the linen closet, two storerooms. The next door was heavy, of solid steel plate with a peep slot.

Coley unlocked it and pushed it open. Ahead of them, beyond Sung's office and Bahr's room was the last of the inner barriers: a gate of inch-and-a-half steel bars. The crunch of the battering ram against the outer doors became deafening. Coley gave her the tube.

'Glue,' he said. 'Some kind of epoxy resin shit. Go squirt it into the lock there case one of 'em got th'intelligence to pick it. I'll be back in a minute.'

Devlin took the tube and walked towards the steel barred gate. As she approached it the brute crash from the porch resolved into smaller details: the splintering of wood, the rattling of the oblong bolt as it mounted a heroic resistance to the assault, the tortured creaking of the old hasps and hinges. She unscrewed the cap of the glue tube and inserted the applicator into the lock and squeezed. When the glue started dribbling out around the nozzle she pulled it out. From the darkness of the hallway came an ear-splitting clatter, a final bursting of rent timber and wrought iron. Suddenly a swell of voices rose, a whoop of triumph, the sound of scuffling, then a single voice raised above the others. She couldn't make out any words. The whooping died down into a deathly quiet. Devlin stood rooted to the spot, transfixed by the silence. The silence lengthened. The sound of her own breathing became very loud to her ears.

A figure rounded the corner from the porch and stood alone on the other side of the gate. The angelic, shave-headed boy. Hector Grauerholz. He smiled at her beatifically.

'Doctor Devlin? I b'lieve you wanted to talk to me.'

A massive charge of adrenaline flooded Devlin's nervous system and drained her muscles of the power to move. She could neither blink nor swallow. She did not feel frightened. She felt filled from head to toe with a neutral shimmering liquid. At a physiological extreme of fight or flight was a pain-less, anaesthetic acceptance of death. This was how a rabbit felt staring into the headlights of a truck. Or the bright button eyes shining from the other side of the bars. Grauerholz stepped right up to the door.

'What was it you wanted to say?' said Grauerholz.

There was no threat in his tone, but rather a bizarre innocence, a child asking his grade school teacher permission to go take a pee. Devlin's body trembled and the scientist in her head told her that was good because it meant she was at least capable of some movement. Now concentrate on your larynx, the scientist said, and scream.

Silence.

Grauerholz pressed his face between the bars. Devlin didn't move. His sour breath drifted into her nostrils.

'We got Ray Klein, you know.'

Devlin swallowed. Her mouth was dry. 'I don't believe you,' she said. Funny, she could talk on Klein's behalf but not her own. The neutral liquid began to contract inside her skin.

'You don't let us in we gonna hafta bring him down here and peel the skin off his pecker while you watch.'

The liquid had drained towards her torso from her arms and legs and head. She realised she could move again if she wanted to. Something Coley had said earlier on popped into her mind and out of her mouth.

'Kiss my ass.'

'I'd love to,' said Grauerholz.

He shot his hand between the bars and grabbed her left wrist. He yanked her against the door. His other hand slipped through the bars and groped for her cunt.

'Gonna eat your pussy too,' he panted. His mouth gaped in a childish giggle, leering through the bars at her face.

Devlin, mastering her revulsion, crammed the nozzle of the tube of glue into his left eye and squeezed.

'Eat this instead,' she said.

With a strangled 'Fuck' Grauerholz reeled back from the

bars and doubled over, clutching his face, scraping at his eye, a skein of semi-transparent goo entangling his eyelid and fingers.

'Bubba!' he wailed.

Suddenly there was a rush of feet and a crowd of bulky figures came charging round the corner from the hallway. Devlin started to walk slowly backwards. The half-blinded figure of Grauerholz disappeared as sweating hulks crowded against bars, their arms straining towards her as they shouted obscene threats, told her to get them panties off, pleaded with her to suck their cocks and show them her tee-tees. Their eyes were bestial, their mouths gaping, wet with drool. The liquid that had filled her was now concentrated in a swollen balloon in her stomach and she realised that it was her fear. She had been so utterly terrified that she had felt nothing. Now, for the first time since Galindez had pushed her towards the infirmary all those hours ago, she felt really scared. One of the beasts on the other side of the cage took out his penis and started to masturbate.

In her growing up, Catholicism had imbued Devlin with the concept of evil – a numenous force, an unknowable thing-in-itself, a must-be, a kind of prime mover that was not itself phenomenal, for it could not be observed or explained, but which had to be posited if certain phenomena were to occur. Like, say, the mindless mass murder of the helpless. Her scientific education, on the other hand, denied evil. If the sequence of causal dominoes, one falling into the next, of a person's life could be reconstituted in sufficiently intricate detail then mass murder inevitably popped out at the other end. That process of reconstitution was the matrix of her profession. If an event made no sense it was because of insufficient information, not because of evil. Billions of words of psychological discourse denied its existence, scorned the very idea. Now, as Devlin stared into the writhing mass of matted beards and scarred faces and tattooed arms she knew the thing-in-itself of evil. It was not that she felt it, saw it, smelt it. She felt her fear, she saw their twisting faces, she smelt their bodies. Evil did not make itself available for perception. Evil never survived to stand on trial. But it was there, in them, in the foul air, in the steel bars they rattled with their fists, in the granite blocks that enclosed them.

'Devlin!'

She turned. Earl Coley was dragging a fire hose through the solid steel door. She ran back up the corridor to help him. A torrent of vocal fury swept after her.

'*Niggercocksuckerbitchfuckencuntfuck.*'

As she reached Coley he shouted over his shoulder.

'*Hit it!*'

The ancient yellow canvas hose buckled and writhed in Coley's fists. A jet of water erupted past her and Coley braced himself against the force. His eyes widened as Devlin seized hold of the hose and tore it violently from his grip. She felt herself scream something, she didn't know what, through clenched teeth, then the power of the water pitched itself against her and she fought back, wrestled the squirming tube down against her hip, felt its energy feed into her savagery. The water jet hurtled down the corridor ahead of her and blasted through the bars of the gate into the fat bellies and bristling beards, the grotesque faces bloated with hate. She strode back down the corridor towards them, the hose unravelling behind her, ignoring a shout from Coley. Her lips were working, her voice scraped harshly in her throat, and again she heard not what she said above the cataclysm of battering water and the war music echoing to a rage of drums inside her skull. One by one she scraped them off the bars of the cage and blew them down the hallway. The masturbator and his seed, the furious giants, all the tattooed cocksucker scum and the filth and pain they would inflict upon her people. She was six feet from the cage and the hose would stretch no further and only one person was left gripping the bars. A psychotic angel, his one-eyed face contorted by a violence without measure, his scrawny hands seized upon the steel with the strength of the insane. Devlin dropped the hose to twist and twitch at her feet and hauled the monkey wrench from her belt. She heard Grauerholz screaming at her in breathless blurts of incoherence.

'Bitch. Die. Bitch. Die. Fuck. Cunt. Niggers. Niggers. Die. Cunt. Bitch.'

She chopped the wrench into his right-hand knuckles and he whimpered and snatched his fingers away. She raised the wrench again and stared into his single, glaring bloodshot eye. Grauerholz wouldn't let go. Devlin smashed his left hand from the bar. He staggered back, dangling his bloody knuckles before him. He sobbed with frustration. One of the sodden giants loomed behind him and took him by the shoulders. Grauerholz let himself be led slowly backwards, away. As he went his sobs evoluted into giggles, one eye rolling, the other congealed and distorted by the resin.

'We be back, niggerfucker. We be back. We be back.'

Devlin watched them disappear around the corner.

'We be back niggerbitch.'

The corridor before her was suddenly very empty and in the emptiness the hiss of the hose expending itself against the wall seemed like silence. In a spasm that came from nowhere Devlin jackknifed forward and vomited a thin stream of bile into the water swirling at her feet. She held onto the barred door with one hand. She trembled from head to foot and then became very still. After a moment she felt Coley's hand on her back.

'You okay?'

Devlin spat sour liquid. She leaned forward and scooped a little water into her mouth, spat again. She scooped more water across her face. She straightened up and looked at Coley and nodded. Coley pulled a paper towel from his pocket and handed it to her. She took it and wiped her face and blew her nose.

'Thanks.'

Her voice surprised her by coming out steady. Down the corridor behind Coley, Reuben Wilson stood in the steel doorway watching her. He nodded. Devlin nodded back then turned to Coley. Coley seemed stuck for anything to say. Then the thing she'd been looking forward to all day popped back into her mind and she momentarily forgot all she'd just seen and done. She smiled at Coley.

'I just remembered,' she said. 'I've got something to show you.'

TWENTY-FIVE

'WHERE THE FUCK you goin' with the beaner, man? Nev's real pissed off with him for lettin' the jigs loose.'

Colt Greely, his arms covered with tattoos from wrist to shoulder, stood by the B gate office, blocking Klein's passage through the sallyport into the atrium. He pointed at Galindez.

'What's he doin' in them duds?'

'He's coming with us,' said Klein.

'I like you personal, Doc, so I'm givin' you a free warnin'. Don't fuck with us.' Greely cast a worried glance over Klein's shoulder at Abbott. 'An' if we need to we got guys take care of the boobie there in ten fucken seconds.'

Klein shone the flashlight in his face and Greely screwed his eyes up. 'Whose idea was the head, Colt?' said Klein.

'What fucken head?'

'The one someone left on a stool in his cell.'

Greely put his hand on the hilt of the shiv in his belt. 'I think you better come talk to Mr Agry.'

'Did you do the cutting or just help hold him down?' said Klein.

'Nigger was already dead. Doc. But between you an' me, we enjoyed it jus' the same.'

Greely took a half step backwards and Klein decided that

Greely had to go down. He decided coldly and without anger. From now on that had to be the way if he was to get through to Devlin. He switched off the flashlight and stuck it in the back of his pants. He smiled. 'Say, Colt, any of the guys tuning in to the Lakers game?'

Greely was taken off guard. 'Yeah,' he said warily. 'Last I heard the Knicks were five points ahead, second quarter. Why?'

'I got a lot riding on the result,' said Klein.

Klein skipped forward and stomped a hundred and eighty pounds of lean weight through the inside of Greely's right knee. He had practised the move for years but this was the first time he'd tried it for real. When it worked as smoothly as it did he was surprised. Greely's lateral and anterior cruciate ligaments snapped in one with a dull pop and the knee joint came apart. As Greely's mouth opened to scream Klein chopped his left hand into his throat and swung the full rotational power of his right hip into mowashi empi, a roundhouse elbow strike to Greely's left temple. Greely dropped like a sack of shit and lay twitching and wheezing on the walkway. The combination had taken less than two seconds. Klein looked around the dark cellblock, at the scattered, roving light beams. No one seemed to have noticed. He looked down. Coldly, and without pleasure, he stamped his heel on Greely's head and the twitching stopped. It reminded him of the painful procedures one had to inflict on patients in medicine: you didn't enjoy causing hurt, but it was for the best. Greely had been excised like an infected boil. Klein took the shiv from Greely's belt. He stood up. Galindez was looking at him.

'Hide him in there,' said Klein.

Galindez paused then nodded and dragged Greely into the end cell with the charred bodies. Klein turned to Abbott.

'You're in the catbird seat, Henry. Where to now?'

Abbott bent down and from the walkway at his feet picked up a heavy ball-peen hammer. The neck and head were crusted with clots of blood. Klein felt a momentary chill as he remembered the crime for which Abbott had been sentenced. Henry raised his arm and pointed with the hammer through the sallyport.

'The mess hall,' said Abbott.

Galindez emerged from the cell, saw the pointing hammer, glanced at Klein. Klein handed him Greely's sharpened screwdriver.

'Let's go.'

They walked through the atrium where the forty-foot glass dome now offered no light at all. Through the gates of cell block D Klein saw a faint yellow glow, maybe from candles or fires or home-made oil lamps. An occasional flash beam carved through the darkness. He decided to use his own flash as little as possible so as not to draw attention. It made the going slower but it seemed better than attracting a cloud of psychopathic moths carrying knives. They passed the entrance to C block. Inside was a terrified, murmuring quietude. Six hundred mainly black, Latino and Native American inmates were still sealed helplessly in their cells from third lock and count. They knew what had happened on B and had been listening to the sounds of terror for eight hours. Galindez shrank into the shadows from an approaching flash beam as a bunch of men emerged swaggering and laughing from C block. Redneck accents. Klein felt glad to be white. The beam shone in his face and he froze. A voice he couldn't place growled from the dark.

'Klein?'

Klein showed them he was unarmed. He wondered if they'd seen Galindez. 'It's okay boys.' He indicated the bloodstains Crawford had left down the front of his clothes. 'Nev sent me to check out a couple guys got shot by the screws.'

A grunt, then the flash beam left his face and fell on Henry Abbott and his bloodstained hammer.

'Jesus Christ.'

The flash backed off a pace. With the light out of his eyes Klein now recognised Ted Spriggs. Spriggs was a tanned, crew-cut professional criminal who was an enforcer for Larry DuBois. Klein knew him well enough to exchange nods in the muscle yard. Behind him were half a dozen others. Some of them carried bulging plastic garbage bags. They were all looking apprehensively at Abbott. It was to Klein's advantage that none of them had ever spoken to the mad giant but that all of them remembered the sight of half a dozen screws trying to subdue him.

'Abbott's been watching my back,' explained Klein. 'Killed three jigs tried to jump us in the yard. One blow each with that hammer and man that was all she wrote.'

Abbott listened to the further amplification of his homicidal reputation with a laconic blink. Klein dearly hoped Abbott would not be called on to defend it. Spriggs nodded. He kept his eyes and the beam on Abbott.

'I got some guys hurt bad on A, you got the time.'

'Sure,' said Klein. 'I'm just going down below to my office, grab some first aid stuff.'

'Place is crawlin' with niggers down there, Doc,' said Spriggs. 'Come daylight we gonna flush 'em out but tonight you oughta stay close to our people.'

'Without my gear I can't do much good,' said Klein. 'It's not far to go.'

'You want some of my guys with you?'

'Thanks, Ted, but Henry's all I need. And it's easier for two of us to move without getting noticed.'

'I guess, but be careful, the coons're mean as snakes. Was that crazy black fuck Johnson started this whole mess, killed Larry DuBois at a parley.'

'I didn't know that,' said Klein. He wondered how many knew the truth about Agry. Shockner? Grauerholz? Grauerholz wouldn't care.

'You know niggers,' said Spriggs. 'Prob'ly doin' our job for us right now, killin' each other. Lucky we got a bunch of 'em still locked down in C.' He rattled a bunch of keys. 'We just got finished shakin' 'em down, one cell at a time. Wouldn't reckon on niggers havin' so much cash. Drugs and shit, yeah, that's how they live with themselves, but cash? We reckon their bitches smuggle it in on visits, you know how niggers treat their women. Stay at home on welfare and let them bring in the bacon.' He grinned. 'Maybe we got somethin' to learn from 'em there. White gals it's th' other way round.'

'Tell me,' said Klein.

He refrained from asking Spriggs how they planned to spend the cash they'd taken. Spriggs was normally a reasonably intelligent guy but he was caught up in the insanity with the rest of them. Then Klein thought about the blacks in the labyrinth below his feet and pondered the intelligence he himself had displayed in abandoning the safety of his cell.

'I'd best get on,' he said.

Spriggs nodded. 'You take care of him, big guy,' he said to Abbott.

Abbott didn't react.

Spriggs smiled at Klein. 'You got the balls to hang out with this guy, the jigs're a Sunday-school social. See you round.'

Spriggs moved off with his men, giving Abbott a wide berth. When the light of Spriggs's torch had faded Galindez re-emerged from the dark and joined them.

'Can we open the cells in C block?' said Klein.

'Not with the power down,' said Galindez. 'Even if we had a set of keys there's a hundred and eighty doors. We'd never make it.'

At three doors a minute that was sixty minutes' work. Agry's crew would kill them in five. Klein scrubbed sweat from his eyes.

'Why?' asked Galindez.

'Something Spriggs said. If we could release six hundred men against Agry, maybe he'd have to pull Grauerholz back from the infirmary.'

Galindez thought about it. 'The doors are opened by electric motors on each tier, powered by the main supply.' He frowned. 'There's a secondary power supply on a separate circuit. Has its own generator in case of emergencies. Last time they used it was when a hurricane took the lines down outside.'

'Can we switch it on?'

Galindez shook his head. 'Has to be done from the admin block. The Warden wouldn't have any reason to do that. He wants these guys in the dark, getting scared.'

'Where is this generator?'

Galindez shrugged, 'It's out in the yard, by the east wall.'

'Can we plug into it?'

'I wouldn't know how.'

Klein thought: Dennis Terry. The old master of Maintenance would know where the generator was and, if it was possible, how to trip the circuit. Klein started walking as fast as was safe in the darkness, across the atrium and into the mess hall.

The mess hall floor was slick with garbage and swill. As they trod across the slippery tiles and between the serving counters into the kitchen they saw the results of the first burst of orgiastic destruction. The cooking vats had been tipped over, big cans of oil had been ruptured and spilled, sacks of wheat flour and lima beans slashed and scattered, drums of powdered eggs emptied around. At one end of the kitchens a stairway led to the laundry, at the other another led down to a series of storage rooms. As Klein led the way towards the door to the second stair he heard a groan and stopped. Galindez and Abbott pulled up silently behind him. Off to his left Klein could hear ragged, whistling breathing. He pulled the flash from his belt and snapped it on. At first he saw nothing, dazzled by the light which bounced back from the stainless steel cupboard doors of the serving counter. Then the beam picked out a figure on its hands and knees, caked with kitchen oil and flour. His head hung between his arms and his shoulders trembled with the effort of supporting himself. Klein took two steps towards him and the man raised his head as if a vast weight were strapped to the back of his skull. The side of his face and neck was matted with congealed blood and he wheezed in painful gasps through his gaping mouth. With agonised slowness he turned towards the light. In his eyes was the expectation of death. It was Stokely Johnson, Wilson's lieutenant. Klein went over. Johnson sagged forward onto his elbows. Galindez helped Klein manhandle Stokely into a sitting position against the stainless steel door. Klein squatted down.

'Johnson,' said Klein. 'It's Klein. You hear me?'

Stokely looked at him and blinked in recognition. Klein examined his face. Stokely's nostrils were blocked with clotted blood. The bullet Grauerholz had fired into him had entered two inches below his right temple and left a small, well-circumscribed wound. There was no exit hole. Unlike Crawford's M16 wound this was of low velocity with minimal shock wave and tissue cavitation. The bullet had probably penetrated the maxillary sinus and shattered several bones in the middle third of the facial skeleton but there were no vital structures in the path the slug had taken. Klein recalled that Agry had stomped on Stokely's head, in retrospect a more dangerous assault than the gunshot. He checked Stokely's pupils and found no evidence of intracranial bleeding. He did find intense fear. Reasonably enough, Stokely probably thought himself at death's door.

'Don't bother speaking,' said Klein, 'but listen. You will not die from the bullet that's in your face.'

Stokely's eyes fluttered shut and his shoulders slumped with relief.

'It looks bad and feels bad,' went on Klein, 'but there's no way it's going to kill you.'

Stokely opened his eyes. With relief Klein saw that he believed him.

'There's no reason you can't stand up and play a game of basketball if you want to. You don't have to crawl around like a fucking whipped dog.'

'You muthafucka,' breathed Johnson and raised his fist. Klein grabbed his wrist. For a moment Johnson strained against him.

'See?' said Klein.

Stokely realised where Klein was coming from. He relaxed and Klein let go.

'Your long distance runners are scattered in the tunnels down below. Agry kicked seven shades of shit out of them. They need you to pull them together and fight back. You understand?'

'Why should you care . . .' Despite the pain each word cost him Stokely took in the extra breath and added, '. . . muthafucka?'

'Because Agry's sent your pal Grauerholz to wipe out my people in the infirmary. That includes Coley and Wilson. If you can squeeze Agry's balls hard enough he'll need Grauerholz back here.'

Stokely regarded him for a long beat then, painful as it was, he smiled. 'That's just where I want him.'

Klein stood up and held out his hand. Stokely took it and hauled himself to his feet. He glanced at Galindez and Abbott. He shuffled for a moment as if embarrassed.

'I, uh, I . . .'

Klein said, 'You thought you were dying, you panicked, now you feel like a yellow asshole. You're not, forget it, let's go.'

Stokely looked at him. 'Wilson was right 'bout you.'

Klein snapped the light off as a shout echoed from somewhere in the mess hall.

'Niggers, man! I saw 'em!'

A light beam wafted towards them. Klein ducked low and headed for the staircase door. There were more shouts. Someone slipped and cursed and metal crashed loudly as a body hit the ground. Klein snapped the torch on just long enough to see the door and its handle then switched it off.

'There! Cocksuckers goin' down b'low!'

Klein grabbed the handle blind and slid the door open. The others piled in after him. Galindez hauled the door shut behind them, cutting off the shouts from the kitchen. Klein shone the light down a short, wide flight of stone steps. At the bottom a corridor led off into darkness with doors visible to either side. They ran down the stairs and down the corridor. Behind them Klein heard the door slam open on its runners and the redneck voices shouting excitedly, like shitfaced weekend hunters in pursuit of easy game. The corridor was jumbled with ransacked cardboard boxes hauled from the storage rooms and their feet crunched on plastic forks and spoons, styrofoam cups, toilet rolls.

'What the fuck we runnin' for?' panted Stokely Johnson.

Klein ignored him and kept going. The corridor ended in a T junction and Klein turned left. Twenty yards on he stopped at a doorway leading down a narrow set of stairs. He waited for the others. Abbott came last at a long-legged loping walk. Klein saw the flash beam of their pursuers hit the wall of the T junction. He illuminated the stairs for Galindez.

'Down.'

He pushed Abbott after him. Stokely coughed a scatter of

fresh blood droplets on to Klein's shirt. He hawked and spat red phlegm.

'I say we turn 'em here,' he said.

'When I have to fight I will. I think we can lose these clowns below,' replied Klein. He followed Galindez and Abbott down the steps and heard Johnson behind him. The staircase was only wide enough for one man at a time. At the foot of the steps he switched the flash off and felt Stokely's hand on his shoulder.

'Trust me, man.'

Klein nodded reluctantly. They were standing in a tunnel beneath a tangle of pipes and ducting. Normally there was a lot of noise down here, of tepid air being pumped through the ageing air-conditioning system. Now it was quiet. Voices drifted down from the corridor above. A light beam passed the entrance and disappeared.

'I tell ya the jigaboo's got the big looney with him. Hey!'

The torch beam returned and swung straight down the stairs. Stokely Johnson stood in full view, the light glittering from the sweat on his bloody face.

'We got him!' The flashlight started to descend.

'Come on down muthafuckas! I wanna rip yo' muthafucken dicks off!'

Klein's rectum contracted violently and he took an involuntary step backwards. The sound booming through the narrow space from Stokely's chest was the most evil A Number One baddest-nigger-in-town voice he'd ever heard. It made Ice T sound like Daffy Duck. There was a yelp from the stairs as a pair of legs lost their footing and slid down the steps towards them. A terrified face appeared briefly, then a pair of arms from behind dragging him back up.

'Fuck this shit, man!'

Bodies clattered back up to the corridor. A voice, thin and reedy after Stokely's tour de force, dribbled down the staircase.

'We'll be back, you black turd.'

Stokely did not dignify them with a reply. Footsteps disappeared.

Klein said, into the blackness, 'Only thunderbolts are to be preferred to cannon.'

'What's that?' said Stokely.

'Napoleon,' said Klein. 'Pity you weren't with him at Waterloo.'

Klein put the light on. The beam was swallowed up in the tunnel ahead. Anywhere else underground and Klein would never have found his way back up again but he'd been through here a hundred times, to pay his rent to Dennis Terry. He led them through the dark and got the next two turns right first time. They came to an ancient boiler and a tangle of pipes. On the other side, where you'd never find it less you knew it was there, was a door. The door was locked.

'Give me that shiv,' said Stokely.

Galindez handed over the screwdriver. In two fierce jerks Stokely had the door open. A dim flickering light drifted down a short flight of wooden steps. Klein called up.

'Terry? Dennis Terry? It's Ray Klein.'

No answer. Klein climbed the steps. At the top was a small room, immaculately decorated to look like the set of the Dean Martin show: grey carpet, a bearskin rug, a bar along one wall with two high stools, an old-style stereogram, a TV in a walnut cabinet, a sofa to match the carpet. A third high stool stood behind the sofa. The room was illuminated by a burning candelabra standing on the bar. Next to it was an empty glass and a bottle of gin with an inch of liquor left in the bottom. In two separate heaps by the stereogram were a stack of album covers and a heap of long-playing records, each one snapped in half. Klein took a step forward. The top album cover was of Sinatra's 'September Of My Years'. Terry had used his wealth to recreate a fantasy of the world he left behind thirty-five years before, when Dino was even cooler than Sinatra and Eisenhower was in the White House. On the bar was a silver-framed photo of a pretty twenty-year-old girl, the fiancée Terry had strangled for teaching English to the wrong Portuguese short-order cook. The illusion of Fifties hep was broken by the ceiling, across which ran a series of three-inch cast iron pipes carrying electric cables. One of the pipes had been wrenched from its mooring and cracked in two at a joint. A handful of wires were dragged down in V shape by the end of a leather belt that had originally been looped around the pipe.

Klein found Terry sprawled behind the sofa by the stool with the other end of the belt around his neck.

He was still breathing. As Klein unwrapped the belt from his neck Terry's eyes flickered open. He mumbled something unintelligible in a slurred voice. Klein hauled him unceremoniously to his feet. Terry staggered. Klein took his arm and walked him round to the sofa. Terry collapsed onto it with a groan and sat with his head between his knees, massaging the back of his neck.

'Water,' said Klein.

Galindez went to the bar and brought Klein a glass of water. Terry held out his hand for it.

'Thanks,' he croaked, weakly.

Klein dashed the water in his face. Terry reeled back, spluttering. Klein handed the glass back to Galindez.

'What the hell, Klein?' said Terry. He blinked through the water in his eyes at Stokely and Abbott. 'Christ.'

Klein sat down next to him. 'Listen Terry, you fucking old lush, you wanna commit suicide you're gonna do it like a man and go out there and get your throat cut with the rest of us. Okay?'

There was a silence. They all seemed taken aback by Klein's violent technique. Galindez brought a second glass of water and handed it to Terry. Terry looked at the Salvadorean for the first time.

'Jesus,' said Terry, glancing at the others and back to Klein. 'Where's Yul Brynner and Steve McQueen?'

Klein felt in the breast pocket of Terry's shirt and pulled out a squashed pack of Pall Malls. He pulled one out and stuck it in Terry's mouth. He lit it with a gas lighter from the same pocket. Terry inhaled, coughed violently, and inhaled again.

'Thanks, Klein.' He looked up over his shoulder at the pipes hanging down from the roof. 'Listen, I . . .'

'Haven't got time, Dennis,' interrupted Klein. 'We've all got our reasons. You still want to die later we can fix it for you. Right now we need you more than Yul and Steve.'

'Go on.' Terry's eyes brightened.

'Galindez says there's an emergency electric generator in here somewheres.'

Terry nodded. 'Runs on fuel oil. It's out by the south-east wall, in that redbrick outhouse between the machine shop and the garage. Why?'

'We want you to splice in the power supply and open the cages in C block.'

'C's still locked down?'

Klein nodded. 'You cut the power lines during their third count.'

Terry dragged on his Pall Mall, squinting thoughtfully into space. 'That would put a shovelful of red hot chilli peppers up Nev Agry's ass, wouldn't it?' he said.

'It's possible then,' said Galindez.

'Oh, sure,' said Terry, sardonically. 'I just gotta get over there, break in, disconnect the control circuits from the admin block, and fire up the turbines from a cold start. Then I got to get all the way back to the gate office on C with the fucken lights on and break into the circuit board to fix up a bypass loop to spring the cages. Easy as fallin' off a log.'

'You fucked up fallin' off that stool right enough,' said Stokely, bitingly.

'What the hell's he doin' here?' said Terry.

'Why not fix the loop on C first,' said Galindez. 'Then they're sprung as soon as the power comes on line.'

'That's not bad for a Mexican,' said Terry.

'How long will it take?' asked Klein.

Terry grimaced and pulled on his cigarette, relishing both the difficulty of the task and the attention it was getting him. 'Both jobs are a goddamned son of a bitch. Gotta dismantle a lot of casings both ends before I can even start on the fine stuff.'

'Nobody else can do it,' said Klein.

'I know nobody else can fucking do it,' said Terry, affronted. 'Not counting travelling time, and everything going smooth, maybe three, four hours.'

Klein nodded. It was a long time but they had nothing to lose.

'What do you say, Dennis?'

Terry shrugged, 'Guess I ain't got nothin' better to do.' He smiled to himself. 'Be the last job Maintenance ever do inside the River.' He dropped the cigarette butt onto the immaculate grey carpet and trod it out with his heel. 'How'm I gonna get past all them niggers?'

'If you're polite, Stokely here will fix you up with some guys, right?'

Stokely nodded sullenly. Klein stood up.

'Agry's got people believing Stokely killed Larry DuBois, started this whole thing.'

'Lyin' faggot muthafucka!' said Stokely.

'Agry killed DuBois,' said Terry. 'I saw it. He's crazy.'

'I don't know,' said Klein. 'Takes more than being crazy to run D block. I can't make sense of it. Agry's got more to lose from this riot than anyone else. He's totally fucked himself.'

Terry's face twisted bitterly. 'Yeah. He's fucked me too.'

'Any idea why?'

'He's crazy about that nigger bitch, ever'one knows that.'

'It's not enough,' said Klein. 'It's enough to kill Claudine, sure, but not enough to commit suicide.'

At the word 'suicide' Terry's face went red. 'Ask him yourself,' he said. 'An' speakin' of suicide what the fuck you doin' here anyway?'

'I'm going over to the infirmary.'

'Ain't that takin' that Hippocratic oath shit too far?'

'Grauerholz is trying to break in there. Agry sent him to wipe out the Aids guys.'

Terry didn't get it. 'And?'

'Henry here managed to convince me we could stop them.'

Terry pushed himself up to his feet. He looked at Abbott, still standing silently by the door, then again at the results of his own botched suicide hanging from the ceiling, then back to Klein.

'You're right,' he said, 'I'm gonna kill myself I may as well join the fucken professionals.'

Klein shook Terry's hand. 'Should never have smashed those Dean Martin records, Dennis. You'll never get 'em all on CD.'

'Yeah, well. Maybe it's time I had a change.'

Klein held Terry's rheumy eyes for a moment and nodded. Then he let go his hand and walked over to the door. Stokely Johnson held out his hand too. Klein took it.

'You tell Wilson I want his ass back over here by mornin',' said Stokely.

Klein nodded and started down the steps.

'Good luck, Klein,' said Stokely Johnson.

Klein nodded without turning around and climbed back down into the dark with Abbott and Galindez behind him. At the bottom of the steps he turned to Abbott and said, 'Up to you now, Henry.'

There was a pause and Klein suddenly told himself he was out of his mind. Henry was strong in heart but his mind was . . .

Abbott said, in his new, resonant voice, 'Follow me.'

They followed Abbott into the tunnels through utter blackness. Every few yards Klein blinked the light on to make sure Abbott was still in front of them. On two occasions, when negotiating an intersection in the maze of tunnels, they heard indistinct human sounds off in the dark. Abbott took them down another flight of steps. As they descended the air got more stifling and foul. A layer of mossy slime clung to the walls. Halfway down Klein trod on something soft. He stopped and shone the flash: it was a black baseball cap. He picked it up. It was clean and dry, couldn't have been there more than a couple of hours. Embossed on the front was a white Spike Lee 'X'.

'Henry,' whispered Klein. The giant stopped. Klein showed him the cap and said, 'There's someone down here.' He found himself wishing he could impersonate Stokely Johnson.

Abbott took the cap from Klein's hand. He seemed unperturbed. His new voice was more sonorous than ever. 'There's only one way to the River. And this is it.'

They continued down the steep, slippery steps. At the bottom the stench became overpoweringly noxious. The food served by the prison mess generated a repellent and universal halitosis so tenacious that even the infinite ingenuity of the inmates had failed to find a cure. Here that same food celebrated its final transubstantiation into a faecal miasma as tangible as it was vile. Klein, gagging, snorted deep breaths through his nostrils to try to acclimatise himself as quickly as possible. It didn't work. He felt a thick scum coating his throat.

'Jesus,' he gasped.

Klein switched the flash on. They were standing on a kind

of concrete jetty that opened out to their right into a work area, an underground yard scattered with pallets of bricks, dredging gear, bundles of canes tipped with brass threads that screwed into each other to form long unblocking rods. At the rear of the yard Klein's torch picked out a crude wooden shed. To their left the jetty ended in three steps that disappeared into the dark. Abbott took the flash from Klein's hand and pointed. The beam struck out over a glittering, scum-flecked stream of black, infected water. The stream flowed slowly away down a perfectly cylindrical brick tunnel about eight feet in diameter. Klein's stomach lurched at the thought of wading through the waist-deep sewage.

Abbott said, 'Green River.'

Klein stood in silence for a moment, contemplating Abbott's Green River. If he could have separated the sight of the sparkling water and the smooth tunnel walls from the stench he might have found it mysterious and beautiful.

'The starry floor, the watery shore, is given thee till the break of day,' said Abbott.

Galindez too was finding the atmosphere difficult to breathe. 'You can get us to the infirmary through there?' he said to Henry.

Abbott crammed the Malcolm X cap onto his head. Klein thought it made him look oddly distinguished.

'This is the way,' said Abbott.

Galindez stared at Abbott and Klein could hear him thinking: there must be two fucking miles of tunnel down here and this guy is a retard, insane, and a mass killer to boot. He glanced at Klein and raised one eyebrow.

'If Henry says he can take us, he can take us,' said Klein.

'I have some masks in the cabin, if you want them.'

'We want them,' said Galindez.

They were halfway across the yard before they saw them: young Black cons armed with knives, Bloods, lupine and hungry for prey, emerging from the foul and stinking darkness and silently bearing down on them from two different sides at once. This was it then.

Their voyage down the River had begun.

TWENTY-SIX

DEVLIN DREAMED. SHE dreamed of playing a bizarre video game, the rules of which she did not understand with a man she did not recognise. She dreamed of being locked in a room for a group therapy marathon facilitated by her old psychotherapy supervisor with a bunch of people that included a number of ex-lovers she didn't particularly want to see again. She dreamed of escaping the room and wandering through an adobe-walled village whose streets she was convinced she knew by heart, and yet where each turning she made took her into a strange street she did not recognise. She sat down by a stone water trough to rethink her bearings. And then she woke up.

For a moment, with her eyes half-closed and her head pillowed on her arms on the desk, she was able to recall these fragments of the dreams and she thought about them but could make no interpretations that made any sense. She opened her eyes and raised her head. She was in the sick bay office and Reuben Wilson was standing on the other side of the table holding a cup of coffee.

'I didn't mean to wake you,' he said.

'It's okay,' said Devlin. She felt embarrassed to have been caught sleeping, as if it were a sign of feminine weakness.

'That's pretty cool,' said Wilson, 'bein' able to catch some Z's at a time like this.'

'You're mistaking cool for exhaustion,' she said. She looked at the coffee. 'Is that for me?'

Wilson nodded and handed her the cup. She sipped it. Wilson hadn't put his shirt back on since she'd taped him up. Her eyes flickered briefly across the wide, flat plates of pectoral muscle above the tape. She looked back down at her coffee. Wilson pulled a pack of Camel filters from his pocket and shook one into his mouth.

'May I?' said Devlin.

'Sure.' Wilson handed her the pack. 'I didn't think doctors smoked.'

She drew on the flame from his lighter and inhaled deeply. 'I didn't think boxers smoked either,' she replied.

'That was a long time ago,' he said.

As the nicotine and tar flooded her grateful nervous system Devlin felt a fleeting dizziness and Wilson's words reached her as if from a distance. Her limbs tingled. The rush vanished as quickly as it had come and left her with a deep sense of relaxation. It was terrible, but she couldn't think of a single thing on earth that at that moment would have made her feel better than the cigarette between her lips. She slumped back in the chair and took another drag.

'How did you know about that fourth metacarpal bone?' said Wilson. 'That was top secret.'

'I was a med student at the time doing orthopaedics,' she said. 'The surgeon advising you showed us your X rays. I read your name on the film.'

'I'll be damned.'

'What it's worth I thought you should've got the decision in that bout. But it's not often the judges get to let an Italian beat a black fighter.'

Wilson smiled and nodded.

'Why did they set you up for murder?' asked Devlin.

Wilson sat down gingerly on the edge of the desk.

'Most fighters get ripped off, I mean like eighty per cent of the purse ripped off, by their managers. You want the big fights there's only a few guys can get them for you, then they take most of your dough in what they call "expenses". I was bringin' a law suit against my manager and he was managed by some wise guys owned hotels in Vegas. A dead whore didn't cost much and it sent out a message that every other fighter in the game heard loud and clear.' He shrugged. 'That's the way it is.'

'You don't sound bitter,' she said.

'Bitter?' He looked off into space. 'I came down here I didn't sleep for two months. I'd lost everthin' I could lose. Shit, I still owe my lawyers money. Lyin' awake waitin' for the first count I tortured those guys to death a million different ways, killed their fam'lies in front of 'em, had their wives fucked to death by wild dogs . . .'

He paused and looked at her. He blinked twice and the rage in his eyes snuffed out.

'Excuse me,' he said.

'It's okay,' said Devlin softly.

Wilson took a hit from his Camel. 'Anyhow when I found myself holding a Zippo under an aluminum foil of heroin with a cardboard tube in my mouth, just to get some rest, I realised "bitter" was just another knife they had in my guts, and I was twistin' it for 'em. I'd already started on these,' he raised the cigarette, 'but I flushed the smack down the toilet and went to sleep.'

'I'm glad,' said Devlin.

Wilson smiled. Devlin felt the awkwardness again. Wilson's suffering, the injustice he'd endured, was so atrocious she felt shrivelled. She didn't consider herself a white liberal guilt tripper, she'd seen enough of misery to appreciate the random ferocity of fate, but with Wilson standing in front of her she was at a loss for something to say that wouldn't sound trite. She'd smoked the Camel down to the filter. She stubbed it out and picked up the pack from the desk.

'I take another?'

'Sure.'

She lit it with a match from her own pocket. 'So you took up politics instead,' she said.

Wilson snorted. 'Politics?' He shook his head. 'Politics turns you to shit, don't care who you are or where. That's just how people see what I do. It's their conception not mine.'

'So what is it that you do?'

'I give advice. Mainly I try to get the younger guys ready to return to the street. Way I see it, if you can learn to live right in here, back out in the world you walkin' in high cotton.'

'How? I mean how do you learn?'

'The Man expects us to live like animals, in here, out there, the same. I guess you read Malcolm.'

She nodded.

'Same thing. I ain't a believer but I respect religion. I respect myself, I respect you. That's it. That's all it takes. Most of the young bloods done wrong to get here. Even if they're proud of their crimes, and I understand that, they still know how hard their mamas tried. I don't want them to use me as an excuse to give up hope. It would be easy for 'em to point at me and say, "See! Don't make no fucken difference! Live right and the Man will fuck you anyways!"'

Devlin shivered at the sudden change in Wilson's voice. If the words were someone else's, the shattering pain and anger were his own.

Wilson nodded. 'They know I know, see. They know I been there. And I tell 'em one thing, an' I tell 'em till they sick of list'nin' me tell it, an' sometimes I beat 'em till they hear me, cause it's real simple. But it's real hard too.'

He paused. The fire drained from his voice and became concentrated in his dark eyes, and he spoke quietly and with great intensity.

'I tell them: in spite of all they've done to you – in spite of *all that* – you still can be the man you are, instead of the animal they want you to be.'

Devlin felt tears prickling her eyes. She blinked them away. Wilson stubbed out his smoke. He smiled, relaxed.

'Lot of 'em can't be reached. That's your bitterness again, workin' for the Man. But some can. Smaller proportion of my people on smack and crack than any of the other blocks. Maybe of all the young guys come through here just ten or twenty don't come back again that would've done, it's enough. Maybe a few more stay out on the street a coupla years 'stead of a coupla months, or maybe don't pick up a smack habit in here to take on home with 'em, it's enough. It's enough for me.'

Devlin wanted to tell him how extraordinary she thought that was but again all the words she could think of sounded trite. She said, 'Then why does Hobbes have it in for you?'

'I've been thinking about that ever since I went to seg and I didn't know the answer till today. Hobbes always treated me straight. He's got eyes and he knows what this shit is all about. And he never called us niggers before. The lockdown was bull-shit. I couldn't figure it out, but when this came down today I knew: Hobbes wanted this riot to happen. This is his baby.'

'But why?' said Devlin.

'I don't know. It's funny, but this mornin' Klein told me that Hobbes was insane, not crazy insane, he said, thorazine and straitjackets insane.'

'What did he mean?'

'Don't know that either, but it looks like he was right.'

Devlin asked the next question as matter-of-factly as possible. 'Do you think we'll get out of here alive?'

Wilson considered her frankly. 'Coley says the guards don't know you're in here.'

She nodded.

'Then they ain't gonna do shit to help us. We hold out long enough maybe some of my guys come for me, but I reckon they must be in bad shape.'

'You're saying we're not going to make it, then.'

'The authorities aren't too keen on breaking sieges by force any more. You remember Waco an' all that shit. Unless they start killin' hostages, an' Agry's too smart for that, this could go on for a week, maybe more. And Grauerholz will be back. He got all the time he needs.'

'Why should they want to kill all the patients?'

Wilson shrugged. 'You watch CNN, you tell me. You're the shrink. Same all over ain't it? Bosnia, Lebanon, South Africa. Race, religion, family, tribe. Folks killin' their brothers all the time. You think they don't hate the Aids guys in here? Sure they do. Got more reason to hate them than most the other folk they hate.'

The door opened and Coley walked in.

'What's up, Coley?' said Wilson.

'Things quiet out there, they waitin' on something. Lopez is keepin' watch. Muthafucka hasn't looked so well in weeks.' He looked at Devlin. 'Grauerholz set fire to our box of drugs.' He smiled, 'But we got half a dozen crackers out cold out there, an' maybe half a dozen more pukin' their yellow guts up.'

'So what's next?' said Devlin.

Coley shrugged. 'They got two choices: the windows on Crockett and the doors. Windows're high up an' they'd have to climb through one at a time. I reckin they'll try to get the gate open again.'

'Maybe they could spread the bars with a car jack,' said Wilson.

Coley shook his head. 'Then they one at a time again. No, they waitin' on somethin' else. We just gotta wait too.'

Coley padded towards the door to the shower room and dispensary. 'I'm gonna take me a snort, no one objects. Might be my last.'

Devlin caught sight of her briefcase leaning against the desk on the floor. 'Coley,' she said. 'Come here.'

Coley exchanged glances with Wilson. He came over. Devlin stood up.

'Sit down.'

Coley dumped his bulk on the chair. 'You muthas up to somethin'?'

'Not me,' said Wilson.

Devlin opened her briefcase and pulled out the green journal.

'What's that?' asked Wilson.

Devlin glanced at Coley. 'The American Journal of Psychiatry. It's the shrinks' equivalent of Sports Illustrated.'

'No shit.'

Devlin opened the journal and spread it out in front of Coley.

'This is what I came back for,' she said.

Coley looked down at the page for a moment in silence. Then he looked up at Devlin.

The muscles round his eyes were trembling.

Devlin's heart swelled up into her throat. She swallowed. Still looking at her, Coley pulled a pair of wirerimmed spectacles from his shirt pocket and put them on. Then he looked again at the journal. He raised a hand to his head and his fingertips dug into his cropped iron-grey hair.

Aids and Depressive Illness in a Closed Institution: a Pilot Study at Green River State Penitentiary.

by

Juliette Devlin Ray Klein Earl Coley

Coley looked at the page without speaking for a long time. Then his big shoulders started to shake with emotion. Suddenly he snatched his glasses off and shielded his eyes with his hand. He shouted at them.

'Don't you muthafuckas know when a man needs some peace an' quiet to read in?'

Wilson was staring at Coley in bewilderment. He started to speak but Devlin shook her head and motioned towards the door. Coley kept his face hidden as they walked away. Wilson went out into the corridor. As Devlin followed him she glanced backwards. Coley was still hiding behind his left hand. His right repeatedly stroked the page in front of him, as if it were a thing of great beauty. He lowered his hand and looked up at her. His cheeks were wet. They held the moment between them, without word or gesture. Then Devlin stepped outside and closed the door behind her.

'What was that?' said Wilson.

Devlin walked him down the corridor. When she was sure she could speak steadily she said, 'It's a research paper we wrote together with Klein.'

'Coley's name's in there?'

'He's a co-author, yes.'

Wilson glanced back over his shoulder. 'I only ever got my name in the sports pages. You done good.'

'Thanks,' said Devlin.

Once again she mounted a titanic effort to hold it all in. She felt like she'd been through ten years' emotion in a day, emotions she'd never felt before, emotions she'd never imagined. But she had to hold them back or fall apart. She turned away against the wall of the corridor. And she found the strength from God knew where and she held them back.

She felt Wilson hover uncertainly behind her. After a moment he said, 'He didn't mean nothin' with that muthafucka stuff, shoutin' at us, he just . . .'

Devlin started laughing. 'I know what he meant. I'm sorry.' She tried to stop laughing, then feared that if she did she'd start crying. 'I'm just happy he got to see his name. Before . . .' Her laughter dried up. 'Before it was too late.'

She fell against Wilson and put her face into the angle of his neck. Wilson stood rigid and awkward. She put her hands on his shoulders and pulled him against her.

'Hold me.'

Tentatively, Wilson put one arm around her. She felt his cock grow into her belly and in amongst all the crazy emotions it felt right. She lifted her head to look at him.

'I don't mean any disrespect,' he said. 'I just can't stop it.'

'It's okay,' she said. Then, 'I'm glad.'

Wilson swallowed. His eyes flickered briefly to her lips.

'Come on,' she said.

Devlin took him upstairs to Coley's secret hiding-place and opened the door in the wall the way Coley had showed her. She switched the light on inside. Wilson looked at the mattress inside. He hesitated.

'You sure about this?' he said.

'If we're all going to be dead by morning, who's going to care?'

'Klein?'

Devlin stared up at the mildewed ceiling of the office waiting for the words she wanted, then looked into Wilson's eyes. 'Klein's the best man I've ever known.'

Wilson blinked and looked away.

'He doesn't know it but I'm in love with him, and I pray to whatever God there might be that he's locked up safe in his cell until this is over. But Klein isn't here.'

Wilson looked back at her face.

'And if he knew about this I know he would understand and I know he would want it to be this way.' She stopped and took a deep breath, startled at the power of her own feelings, the heat in her cheeks, the ferocity in her voice. 'Because that's the kind of man Klein is.'

She saw Wilson's eyes veil over with jealousy and suspicion and she almost put her hand to his lips to stop his mouth. But she knew that he had to say it just like she knew she had to hear it.

'What's this 'bout then?' he said. 'You want to fuck you a nigger before you die?'

She flinched, because it was worse than she'd expected and she saw for the first time the cruelty that Wilson, of necessity, had had to possess somewhere within him in order to chop down thirty-three men in the ring. And although his sudden cruelty was needless, she forgave him, because she knew enough about him not to judge him on that alone, and because what she had to say herself was true.

'No. I've fucked niggers, as you put it, before.'

Wilson's lip curled and he turned to walk away.

'I love Ray Klein and I don't love you and none of this will change that,' she said. 'I brought you up here because you're as good a man as he is.'

Wilson stopped. Devlin watched his back. After a moment his shoulders sagged and he breathed deeply.

'I'm sorry,' he said. He took another breath and swung round to face her. 'I'm sorry. I disrespected you, I disrespected me, I disrespected my people. That's it.'

He turned away and walked to the door.

'All the people we're ever going to be is right here and now, in this building. Isn't that what Coley means when he says "my people"? You don't have to qualify. You don't even have to be sick.'

Wilson leaned against the doorway and doubled forward, stifling a groan. Devlin rushed over and took his arm.

'You okay?'

'Yeah,' gasped Wilson. 'Just a cramp. Going now.' He slowly

straightened up. 'Maybe Coley's right about me bein' a pussy too.'

Devlin took his hand. 'I don't think so.'

She pulled on his hand. 'Come with me.'

She took him into Coley's room and stripped off his clothes and he lay down on the mouldy mattress. Then Devlin took her clothes off while he watched. She'd never known anything like this. She didn't feel vain or ashamed or coy. She didn't feel hot, like she had with Klein that morning, but sexual in some other way, as if about to perform an ancient rite. Watching Wilson's face watching her she felt desired but also honoured, treasured, a sense that she represented more than just herself. She knelt straddling his thighs and took his cock in her hand and squeezed it. It was hard. Wilson groaned and closed his eyes and pulled away as if it were too much. A pearl of semen appeared at the tip of his glans and she realised that he would probably come very easily after so long without a woman. She knew this wasn't safe, but safe seemed absurd and she badly wanted to make this gift to him. With her free hand she parted the lips of her cunt and gently, because of his wound, lowered herself onto him. The first inch slid in and Wilson gasped and dug his fingers into the mattress.

'Easy, easy,' he said.

She paused, feeling him, feeling herself get wetter. She rose back up a little, holding him in place with her hand, then sank down slow and steady. Wilson cried out and pushed himself in all the way. He grabbed her waist with both hands and pulled her onto him, straining up inside her, and she squeezed him and suddenly he jerked half-upright and she felt him come, and come. She put her arms round his head and pulled him against her breasts. A wave of tenderness moved through her as she squeezed him and felt his spasms and thought he would go on coming forever. Then he went limp and slowly lay back, his eyes closed tight, on the mattress.

Devlin climbed off him and lay beside him with her head on his chest. She wondered what was going through his mind, if he was disappointed with her, or ashamed at coming so quickly. She felt his arm wrap across her shoulders and press her against him. The pressure increased and his fingers dug into her and for a moment she felt scared. Then she realised, though she couldn't see his face, that Reuben Wilson was crying very quietly, and didn't want her to know.

Devlin kept her face to his chest. She didn't say anything, she didn't look at his face. She just lay there while he held her and pretended not to notice. And she wondered at the mystery of it all and at the same time deeply understood it, understood what it was that she meant to them, these men Wilson, Coley, Klein, these tortured minds and bodies who endured extremes of pain and fear without showing it to each other, and who now broke down because she was near. The sense of representing more than just herself became intense. She was more than Devlin, more even than a woman. She was all that they'd yearned for and had missed, all that they yearned for and could not have. She was that which they needed to make them fully men, not just to fuck, even when they couldn't fully fuck her, but also to protect, even when they couldn't fully protect her, to be strong for, even when they were weak, to be proud for, even when they were ashamed, to love, even when they lived with so much hate. Perhaps then – amongst hate – more than at any time else. Thinking of hatred she thought of Grauerholz and knew that even he – even Grauerholz – in the dark mirror, the photographic negative, of his evil, needed her in all the same ways. In an instant she no longer hated Grauerholz for wanting to kill the men – for that was between him and them – and she no longer feared what he would do to her, for she was what he would do to her, and she now accepted that terrible portion of her identity as she now accepted the good. She would kill him if she could, for herself and the men, but she would not hate or fear him. In a moment of revelation Devlin suddenly felt that she understood something of men for the first time, something that could not be evaluated scientifically, as she had tried to do, nor even conceived in words nor written down. It was something to do with them being them and her being her and the one seeing the other for all that they were and that being enough. Enough to close the gap between them, just for a while. She'd found, at last, the answer to Galindez's question, to her own and others' endless enquiries, about why she had chosen this work at Green River State Penitentiary. She'd found what she had come for: this moment that she would never be able to explain to anyone else.

'You okay?' said Wilson.

'Yes,' she replied. 'I'm fine.'

'Guess we'd better get back.'

They dressed hastily without looking at each other. Devlin realised that she hadn't kissed Wilson at any time. She decided not to let it bother her. As they stepped over the joists to the hole in the wall Devlin caught Wilson's eye and grinned at him. Wilson shook his head. He grinned back.

'Coley said you were a muthafucka. I didn't believe him.'

'He also said you were an asshole,' said Devlin.

'Guess that makes Coley one smart dude. Thanks, Devlin.'

'Thank you.'

Wilson looked at her until he saw that she meant it. He nodded and turned and clambered through the hole. 'Why the hell Coley build this place anyhow?'

On the way back downstairs Devlin explained the escape plan Coley had never got the chance to test out and Wilson reckoned it just might have worked. As they reached the ground floor corridor Deano Baines, one of the Aids patients, came hobbling from the entrance to Crockett ward.

'Vinnie Lopez says they bringing cutting gear up the front steps.'

Devlin opened the door to the sick bay office. Coley still sat at the desk in his spectacles, poring over the journal in front of him. He didn't look up.

'Coley,' she said.

Coley put the tip of his right index finger on the sentence he'd got up to and raised his head.

'They's two – *two* – spellin' mistakes on the third page! What the fuck kind of standard is that? Don't these high and mighty cocksuckers realise what they got here?'

'Grauerholz is back,' said Devlin. 'Lopez says they've got cutting equipment.'

Coley reverently closed the journal and put it into the drawer of the desk. He stood up.

'We'll see 'bout that,' he said. 'Ain't no goddamn crackers comin' in here till I finished my readin'.'

His gaze fell on Devlin's crotch then flicked up to her eyes. She found herself blushing uncontrollably. Coley looked at Wilson, darkly. He put his spectacles away and stood up. Devlin reached down and discovered three buttons of her flies gaping open. As she did them up Coley lumbered past without looking at her and went down the corridor. She felt numb. She exchanged glances with Wilson and they followed Coley. They passed through the inner wooden door, stepped over the coiled fire hose and stopped at the solid steel door. Coley opened the sliding peep hole and bent forward to peer through.

'Fuck,' he said and straightened up.

Devlin bent down to look through the hole. At the other end of the corridor, beyond the steel gate, Grauerholz was watching a pair of his men dragging a trolley loaded with two gas cylinders up to the bars. A third man carried a cutting torch connected to a length of double hosepipe. The pipes fed into the cylinder heads. Grauerholz squinted down the corridor at Devlin. His left eye was still glued shut.

'That you, Coley?' called Grauerholz. He grinned. 'We

gonna cut through this here gate, then we gonna cut your fat black balls off.'

Devlin closed the slot. Coley was unlocking the steel door. Wilson was standing by the faucet supplying the fire hose.

'Crackers want dousin' down agin,' said Coley. 'You ready?'

Devlin picked up the hose, avoiding his eyes. There was a steel handle on the nozzle to control the jet. She pulled the hose snug against her hip. She was more preoccupied with what Coley thought of her than she was with Grauerholz.

'Hey,' said Coley.

She looked at him as best she could.

'Don't pay me no nevermind,' he said. 'I just old-fashioned.'

'Okay,' she said.

'Okay.'

Coley swung the door open and stepped through. At the far end one of Grauerholz's men held out a burning lighter whilst a second dipped the nozzle of the cutting torch towards it. A yellow flame billowed out. The cutter brought the flame to a roaring blue cone three inches long. He pulled a set of goggles over his eyes and crouched down by the lock. Grauerholz looked at the fire hose in Devlin's hand. He put his face between the bars and grinned at them. Devlin felt uneasy.

'Hit it,' she called to Wilson.

Wilson turned the faucet on. There was a pause. A slight bulge rippled lethargically along the length of the fire hose, no sign of the whipping serpent of several hours before. As the ripple reached Devlin she opened the nozzle. A weak jet of water spurted in a six foot arc and splashed harmlessly onto the flagstones a yard short of the gate.

'Surprise, cornhole fuckers!' Grauerholz was jiggling against the bars with excitement.

'Damn,' said Coley.

'It's wide open!' called Wilson. 'That's it.'

The spurt from the hose degenerated into a trickle that made a shallow pool at her feet. She glanced at Coley.

'Musta cut the water off from the mains supply outside.'

The corridor was filling with the stench of burning steel.

'Get back,' said Coley.

Devlin dragged the hose back through the solid steel door. Coley followed her, slammed it shut and locked it.

'We're fucked,' he said. 'They be through the gate in ten minutes, through this door in twenty-five.'

'We'd better start a barricade,' said Wilson. 'Other side here.' He jerked his thumb towards the wooden door behind him.

'No,' said Devlin. 'I've got a better idea.'

Coley looked at Wilson.

'When this lady says she's got an idea,' said Coley, 'I tell you, you'd better listen.'

'Frog,' said Wilson, 'you ain't tellin' me nothin' I don't already know.'

They both looked at her.

'How many cylinders of oxygen do we have?' asked Devlin.

Frogman Coley raised one eyebrow and nodded thoughtfully. 'Goddamn,' he said. 'We got just as many as you need.'

TWENTY-SEVEN

THE BLOODS SWARMED from behind the workshed and across the underground yard from an ambuscado silent as disease. They came in two bunches of five or six guys each, dark huddles, shadows amongst shadows, mobile, dense and impenetrable against the shifting gloom. At fifteen feet Galindez snatched a brick from a pallet and hurled it overarm amongst the heads of the nearest group. There was a thud and a groan and a shape staggered away and fell to his knees. Klein flashed the beam from one group to the other catching black angry faces, men who had been stomped down and burned down without mercy and who now thirsted for payback on anything with pale skin and a pulse. A sense of confusion, of impending panic, blurred Klein's mind. He pulled the revolver from his pocket and held it out in the light.

'*No one has to die!*' he shouted. The echoes made his voice bigger and more threatening than it really was.

'He's got a piece!'

The groups slowed and split up but kept on coming. Klein had to shoot up or put up and he didn't want to shoot. Five little bullets and ten big men. There'd be no quarter then, no chance of a stand-off. The die would be cast and only the bloody victors would leave the jetty alive. As his finger closed on the trigger a hand enveloped his shoulder.

'Take the River,' said Abbott.

The hand dragged Klein backwards, turned him and gave him a shove towards the steps at the edge of the jetty. Klein walked sideways, looking back. Abbott propelled Galindez after him. Where before Abbott had been hidden behind the glare of the flashlight he was now silhouetted in all his towering magnificence, the cap perched eccentrically on his massive skull making him look like some monstrous king of the beggars in a medieval debauch. The Bloods saw him for the first time and stopped in a hesitant semi-circle.

'Jesus Christ.'

'Fuck.'

Abbott stooped and grabbed a brick hammer from the pallet. He held both hands aloft, a hammer in each.

'*Be forewarned: The River is mine.*'

His voice pealed back and forth from the enslimed, glistening walls of the tunnel like the rage of a pagan deity.

The Bloods wavered, unsure whether to plunge forward or retreat. As Klein descended the steps he kept the beam in their faces. Tepid water sloshed about his ankles. He felt down for the next step, then another, then found the floor of the sewer. He waded out into the channel, stinking water up to his knees. Galindez was halfway down the steps. Klein heard a mumbled exchange amongst the blacks. One of them darted forward, crouching low. A blade glittered. Abbott's arm carved a blurred, whiplash arc and a splintering crack reverberated through the gloom. The man piled forward into the stone without a murmur.

'*The River is mine.*'

The hairs on Klein's neck tingled at the resounding thunder from Abbott's lungs. The semi-circle of assailants backed off a pace, hovering, muttering. Galindez waded past Klein and into the mouth of the tunnel. Klein backed towards him. He held out the gun again, hoping the Bloods could see it.

'Henry!'

Abbott slowly lowered his arms. He seemed to stare at his opponents for a long beat. Suddenly, or so it seemed because the semi-circle took a collective jump backwards, Abbott walked over to the jumble of building materials. He stopped and shoved the handles of the hammers into his belt. None of the blacks moved. They seemed as mystified as Klein.

'Henry!'

Abbott stooped and grabbed a bag of cement and folded it over his left shoulder as easily as he might have put his cap on. Klein was convinced: Abbott's mind had finally gone.

'Henry, move your ass!'

Without haste Abbott turned his back on the gang and clomped towards the jetty with the bag balanced easily on his shoulder. No one followed him. He trod down the steps and into the water. His face betrayed not a trace of fear and in his eyes, it seemed to Klein, was a supernatural light.

'Follow me,' said Abbott.

Abbott strode into the tunnel, the water but a trivial resistance to his shins. Klein looked back at the yard. The Bloods were crowding towards the edge of the jetty.

'We gonna fuck yo' ofay ass, muthafucka!'

The brilliant disc of a flashlight, incredibly bright after the minutes of gloom, blazed into Klein's eyes and blinded him. A brick hit him full square in the chest and he grunted and staggered. He slipped on the slimy bricks below. He felt his legs vanishing from beneath him, teetered, said goodbye to the point of no return. He had just enough time to mutter 'Balls' before foul water engulfed him and swilled over his face. A series of frantic thoughts shrieked through his mind. Keep your fucking mouth closed. Don't breathe. Don't swallow. He rolled over, his feet and knees scrabbling for purchase on the treacherous bed of the channel. Just keep your mouth closed. Don't breathe. Hands seized his arms and hauled him to his feet, dragged him through the water. As he felt air against his face he threw up, saliva and scalding gastric juice, dry retching. Light glittered on the turbulent water beneath him, moving, he was being carried forward. He scrabbled his feet underneath him, started walking, still leaning into the hands on either side. He shook water from his eyes. He imagined a vile potpourri of malignant micro-organisms feasting on his conjuctivae. His hair was plastered in foul strands clotted with faeculence across his face. He heaved for breath.

'I'm okay,' he gasped.

He shook the supporting hands away and staggered forward under his own power. The flash was still in his left hand, the gun still in the other. He hadn't breathed or swallowed the turd-infested water, a fear vastly more intense than that of death. He stopped and turned. They were twenty feet into the tunnel. Abbott and Galindez were watching him, Galindez concerned, Abbott with what looked like serenity. What the fuck was wrong with the guy? Klein suddenly felt like an asshole, but at least that was an approximation of normality. Klein shoved the gun back into his pocket and scraped the hair from his face. His breathing steadied. He drew himself up to his full height with what he hoped was a semblance of dignity.

'Follow me,' said Klein.

They ploughed forward through the sewer. Here and there they passed blind alcoves with dead wire-grilled bulbs. The bulbs put Klein in mind of Dennis Terry and he hoped the old man was making better progress in his mission to C block than they were in theirs. Behind him Abbott, the cement bag still folded over his shoulder, started to hum in sepulchral tones. The tune had a sacred character, vaguely familiar. A hymn. Klein recognised the melody but couldn't place it. A line offered itself: 'And did those feet in ancient time . . .' It fitted with the melody but Klein could remember no more. He wondered how far the sound would carry down these tunnels but he didn't ask Abbott to stop. As he sloshed on Klein pondered on the change in Abbott over the past few hours. People with schizophrenia often relapsed into acute psychosis when under severe pressure. Abbott's speech patterns had changed, become more fluent, in their own way perhaps even more coherent. He couldn't judge what passed for logic in Abbott's alternative universe. Where The Word held sway. It occurred to Klein that The Word was taking over and a chill ran down his back. He glanced over his shoulder. Abbott hummed on, the hammers swinging by his sides. Klein remembered uneasily that Abbott had been found singing a hymn while he watched the bodies of his family burn. Klein did not doubt the affection and esteem in which Abbott held him and he valued it. But so, he imagined, had his family too. When they reached an intersection in the tunnel Klein was glad to give Abbott the opportunity to go in front.

Above their heads were two cylindrical intersecting cross vaults. The channel they were standing in emptied into a new conduit that flowed across them at right angles. The new conduit was of greater diameter by two feet or so and flowed more quickly. On the other side of the intersection the continuation of their own tunnel also emptied into the bigger channel which flowed from left to right. Klein hoped they wouldn't have to wade against the current.

'Which way?' he said.

'West,' replied Abbott.

'I left my compass behind,' said Klein. 'I only know up from down.'

'Down,' said Abbott.

'Listen,' said Galindez.

Klein listened. From the tunnel behind them came the distant sound of voices and splashing feet. Klein wasn't surprised. The guys they'd rumbled were young Bloods, veterans of the street gang wars in Deep Elem and San Antonio where the violent theorem of a life for a life was obeyed with the remorselessness of mathematical law. They weren't going to let three ofays get away with humiliating them.

'After you,' said Klein.

Abbott stepped down into the new channel. The water came halfway up his thighs and Klein grimaced at the depth. He held onto the wall of the intersection for balance and jumped. He landed up to his waist but his feet didn't slip. Galindez followed. A dark object floated towards him and Klein sucked his belly in to let it pass. He reprimanded himself for his squeamishness. He was a goddamn doctor, it shouldn't matter to him. He pushed from his mind the thought of the microbes bathing his genitals.

'We got a three to one chance they'll miss us,' said Galindez.

'No,' said Abbott. 'They will follow the River, as they must.'

Klein knew he was right. Going with the flow was the natural choice. Abbott waded out in front of them.

This tunnel had a six-inch platform running down one side just above the water level. Here and there rats scurried along it. Unlike the bugs he couldn't see but could imagine, the rats didn't give Klein a problem and he was cheered. He was a tough guy after all. This sewer was longer than the last, and Klein lost all track of distance and time. They passed one intersection after another, three, four, five, each one emptying from either side into their channel, deepening the water and increasing the pressure against their backs. Maybe Abbott had missed his turning and the tunnel would suddenly empty into the Gulf of Mexico. It couldn't be that much further. The idea appealed to him. Sorry, Devlin, sorry guys, swimming to New Orleans instead. Vera Cruz. Rio. The going got hard and Klein found himself panting, sweating torrentially, blinking away the leached filth that trickled down from his scalp and stung his eyes. Up in front Abbott was still only waist deep and gaining distance with each stride. At times Klein lost sight of him in the torch beam he held waveringly above the water and the fear seized him that The Word would instruct Abbott to abandon them, or simply forget about them, and leave them fuck knew how many feet underground, up to their necks in sewage with a pack of Bloods on their tail. Heading west for Christ's sake. An intense claustrophobia seized him. He glanced backwards. Galindez's sweating, pock-marked face toiled a yard behind him. The claustrophobia waned. He wouldn't die alone then. The water was halfway up Klein's chest and each step sapped more of his strength, made it more likely that he would lose his footing and go under again. This time he knew he would inhale and swallow the poisonous waste. He didn't have enough breath not to. Behind them he heard a shout and a splash, then more splashing, voices and oaths, then quiet again. The Bloods had gained on them. He scoured the tunnel ahead with the flash beam.

Abbott had disappeared.

Easy, Klein instructed himself. Just keep moving. You're a cool guy. Have some pride. This is chickenshit. Your father celebrated his twentieth birthday with the First Marine Division on Guadalcanal, waiting to be shipped out under fire with six inches of Jap steel in his gut. This is chickenshit. His father had died from two packs of Pall Malls a day a long time before Klein had been sent up. Maybe Klein felt that he shamed his memory by being here. His Dad had fought three months in the jungle whilst he'd spent three hours strolling around a prison in the dark. It's chickenshit, Klein. But even if it was chickenshit he hoped it made some difference, to somebody, somewhere. Maybe even his father, wherever he was. Klein still couldn't see Abbott, but he didn't feel so badly about it any more.

A new tunnel opened to the right up ahead. As Klein splashed towards it he heard Abbott's humming. This tunnel was the same size as the first one and its floor was maybe four feet above that which Klein was walking on. Abbott appeared in the mouth. Behind him the tunnel ran from the main conduit at an acute angle. Klein passed Abbott the flash and found the edge of the tunnel. He placed his hands and hauled himself up and crawled in. His fingers sank into some unspeakable jelly on the bottom and he knelt upright and scrubbed them in the water. Galindez clambered up behind him.

Klein took the flash back and they trudged on, upstream now, behind Abbott. The water here was only six inches deep and they were able to treble their pace. On the bad news side of things their movement was much noisier and the empty tunnel provided greater amplification.

After a few moments Galindez said, 'They're still with us.'

Abbott stopped. Klein's torch fell on a hole in the wall about four feet in diameter. Abbott shrugged the bag of cement from his shoulder and dumped it in the mouth of the hole.

'This is it,' said Abbott. 'This is where the River ends.'

Klein aimed the beam up this, the last tunnel. It sloped upwards at a forty-five degree angle. Its walls were smooth, the channel at the lowest arc of its circumference coated with brown slime. Despite the flashlight Klein could not see where the tunnel ended.

'You're kidding,' said Klein.

'This will bring you out in a manhole under the basement of the infirmary. It's thirty yards long.'

'That's a hundred fucking feet.'

'Almost,' said Abbott.

If Klein had felt claustrophobic before, he had no word for

what he felt now. 'It's too fucking steep, it's covered with slime. We'll never make it.'

'You'll have to. This tunnel ends at the main wall.'

Abbott pointed into the darkness ahead. Klein aimed the flash beam. In the distance he could just make out a grille of thick steel bars set into a granite wall. The water flowed through the grille. There was only backwards, into the Bloods, or up the sloping conduit.

The sounds splashing towards them were getting louder. Abbott pulled the brick hammer from his belt and with half a dozen strokes with the bevelled edge split the bag of cement across the middle. He took one end of the bag in each hand and tore it in half. He tossed the halves, open ends upward, a yard into the sloping tunnel. He took Klein by the shoulder and bent his face close to Klein's.

Excepting those of his lovers Klein had considered Abbott's eyes as closely as any he had ever known. Their unvarying opacity had led him into speculations across the length and breadth of his imagination and always they had remained flat and dulled and empty. Now, in the beam of the torch, Abbott's eyes were alive with an extraordinary, piercing intelligence, an unfathomable internal power without fear or reckoning, beyond good and evil. A tremor ran through Klein from head to foot. His mouth was too dry to swallow.

Abbott had become The Word.

And Klein was looking into the eyes of God.

The pre-religious deity, the ruler of the vast universe that embraced the cells and molecules, the instincts and impulses of this human brain and of this body towering above him, had made good the cleavage between man and God. And Abbott had become The Word.

'Listen,' said The Word. 'You are going to crawl up the tunnel. You will use the cement dust for grip. You are going to crawl up the tunnel. And you are going to do what you are here to do. Just as I, too, will do what I am here to do. Do you hear me?'

Klein couldn't speak. He nodded. Abbott let go and turned to Galindez. Galindez looked at the hole.

'I'm smallest,' he said. 'I go first.'

The sounds of the gang down the tunnel were loud. The first light of their flash glimmered in the blackness. Galindez clambered up into the tunnel, shoved one of the half-bags of cement forward and crawled after it. Klein turned to Abbott. He suddenly felt a vice of emotion crushing his chest.

'You're not coming then,' he said.

'They are many and I am one. But the River is mine.'

'I'll miss you, goddamn it,' said Klein.

'Klein,' said Abbott.

It was the first time he had ever called him anything other than 'Doctor'.

'No man has loved me more than you,' said Abbott.

Klein wanted to look away but the fiery eyes held him.

'No man has had a greater friend. You came to me when I was down and you stayed. You healed me.'

Klein felt Abbott's fingers wrap around his hand and squeeze. He still couldn't speak. He squeezed Abbott's hand back as if he would hold onto it forever.

'Remember that, always,' said Abbott.

Klein's throat was constricted.

'Always,' he said.

Abbott smiled and again Klein realised it was the first time. He'd never seen a smile on that slab-like face before. His heart felt like it was cracking in pieces. Abbott nodded, as if he knew what was happening inside Klein's chest.

'Now go,' said Abbott.

There were yells of triumph in the conduit and a wavering beam danced over Abbott's face. There was a dull whistling sound and a thud and Abbott blinked. Klein looked down and saw the hilt of a shiv quivering in Abbott's left chest. Abbott looked down. He pulled the knife free and dropped it in the water. He hefted from his belt the ball-peen hammer and stepped out into the centre of the tunnel. He turned and Klein looked into the eyes of God for the last time. Abbott nodded, once, and Klein nodded back. Then he tucked the flash into his pants and scrambled up into the mouth of the tunnel.

As he hauled himself up the first yard Klein remembered asking himself: what sound would echo like the crack of doom from Abbott's chest if he ever became the God that was himself? A barrage of shouting and taunts, indecipherable, reached him from the conduit beneath. The Bloods were here to collect their debt. Klein fought the impulse to slide back down the tunnel. He told himself he had to go on, to the infirmary, to Devlin and the Frogman.

Then another sound, echoing and vast, suddenly shook the granite stones wedged against Klein's back.

'*One.*'

The word was followed by a whomping sound and a scream of pain. Klein shivered and pushed the bag before him and crawled on. Galindez had scattered the cement across the slime-coated bricks and left a trail of gritty mud behind him. Klein struggled to find the best way of moving. The gradient was too steep and he was too heavy for the friction offered by his hands and knees. He had forty pounds on Galindez and now Galindez had forty feet on him. The torch in his belt dug into his groin and ribs. Klein wriggled over, flat on his back. He bent his legs and shunted himself upwards on his ass. His heels slipped away from under him. He looked down past his toes. He'd made barely six feet. He cursed the stone-masons who'd built these walls with such perfection.

'*Two!*' boomed Abbott.

Another scream reverberated around Klein's head. This cement shit wasn't working. He braced the soles of his training shoes and the palms of his hands against the sides of the tube where the bricks were dry and pushed. His ass slid upwards six inches in the slime. Again. Six inches. He pushed and slid, pushed and slid.

'*Three!*'

The fucking cement bag wedged into the small of Klein's back. He hoisted his ass up, pushed, sat on the bag. He pushed again. The bag was under his legs. He remembered climbers using talc and reached his hands down and scooped cement powder onto his palms, rubbing them together to dry up the slime and sweat. He scooped another handful and heaped it on his belly. Down below he heard a flurry of cries and blows, then a great splash and a massed yell of triumph.

Klein knew Abbott was down.

In his mind's eye he saw the Bloods, ten to one, swarming over Abbott, puncturing him with screwdrivers and shanks. Down below he heard a scuffling and panting and the sounds of combat grew muffled.

There was someone in the tube with him.

Klein's first thought was to shit in his face. That would have been easy. His weight was braced across the narrow walls between his back and arms, his soles against the bricks lower down. He pulled one hand free and pulled out the torch. He yelled as a sharp pain pierced his ankle. Another, jagging agonisingly into the bone. He snapped the light on. Beyond his feet a young black face screwed itself up in the dazzling beam. The guy had a shiv and was sticking it into Klein's left leg. Klein thought: the gun. Blow his fucking face off. But with the torch in one hand he couldn't let go with the other. The guy raised the shiv to stab him again. Klein pulled the foot away. His heel bumped into the cement bag. On an impulse he pushed the bag with the flashlight, rotating it to face downwards. The guy below opened his eyes and squinted for a target. Klein got his foot to the bag and stomped downwards. The bag shot down the tube and exploded a cloud of grey powder into the guy's eyes and mouth and nostrils. The face disappeared. A bank of dust drifted towards Klein. He coughed, wheezed. The guy beneath him was squirming and choking in panic. Suddenly the guy was yanked down with a strangled wail, his fingertips clawing the bricks. The bore of the tube opened again. The guy clung to the edge, his face ghostly with dust, blinded and terrified. A ball-peen hammer clenched in a huge blood-stained fist rose and fell.

'*Four!*'

The young guy lay slumped motionless over the rim of the tube. After a moment a red web trickled down the powdered cheeks from the shattered vault of his skull.

Klein shoved the head of the torch, still lit, into his pants. Through the cheap cotton the beam cast a faint, comforting light. Klein went back to his shunting ascent of the tube. The sounds of combat grew dim and as Klein got into a rhythm his technique got better. With each shove of hands and feet he reckoned he made nine inches. His mind flitted to the Robbie Burns poem 'Nine Inch Will Please A Lady'. Even in that stinking tunnel he couldn't help smiling. Devlin would have to be happy with somewhat less than that. Especially after he'd taken all this trouble to deliver it. He killed time calculating nine inches into ninety feet. There was ninety times nine, then ninety times three inches left which was thirty times nine, a total of one hundred and twenty shoves. He couldn't help cross-referencing the implications of this statistic to Robbie Burns's lady. A hundred and twenty full-blooded strokes, call it a hundred and thirty, and the lady would have enjoyed ninety feet of cock. Klein chortled to himself with a touch of hysteria. Better than submitting to the panic-stricken claustrophobia that he knew simmered in his gut. He kept on pushing. So this is how a spermatozoon feels, he thought, fighting its way along the fallopian tube. And that bastard

Galindez was there before him. And if this was a fallopian tube
the prison was a cunt and uterus. Someone had to have been
fucked for him to get here. He thought of his ex-lover, now
dead, and the amusing metaphor turned sour on him. He
noticed that the heels of his palms were bleeding. He stopped
and rubbed them with cement dust from the heap on his belly.
The palms didn't hurt, nor the punctures in his ankle and calf.
Too much adrenaline zipping round his system. He carried on
shoving. His shirt tore open and the skin started to come off
his back over the spine. His breathing got raw and laboured.
The sounds of the fight, if it were still in progress, were now
far below him. All he could hear was the splutter and wheeze
of his own panting bouncing back from the walls into his ears.
He realised he had a raging thirst and with that realisation it
promptly got worse. He hadn't had a drink since leaving D
and had been sweating his balls off ever since. Cramps started
in his calves, his forearms, his ribs. His triceps and pecs burned
with fatigue. He began taking five-second rests between each
lift. It helped. If he lost his footing and started to slide down
he couldn't see how he'd be able to stop himself. Think about
the lady instead, he told himself, think about the lady.

Klein felt a breeze on the back of his neck.

Breeze was perhaps too strong a word. He felt a brush of
air slightly less foetid than that he had become used to
breathing. He stopped, braced himself and bent his head
backwards.

'Galindez!'

A few seconds later a hollow, distorted voice reached him,
surprisingly loud – maybe even close.

'Where the fuck you been, Klein? You been giving Abbott
a blow job while I wasn't watchin'?'

'You spic cocksucker,' bellowed Klein. He experienced a
sudden elation. 'I've been savin' my jissom for you.'

He laughed crazily and his foot slipped off the wall. His ass started to move. His other foot juddered down the bricks. His guts were already back at the bottom of the tube. His finger-nails popped off as he clawed for a hold. Suddenly he was enraged.

'*Fuck*,' he roared.

With all his strength he crammed his shoulder and back into the wall, pushing with one raw hand. He slowed and stopped. He got the soles of his feet back in place. When he felt secure he took some deep breaths.

'You okay, Klein?'

'Fuck you.'

He dusted his hands a last time and started again with angry shoves. A dozen shoves later he felt Galindez's hand grabbing his sodden shirt collar. Klein got his hands over the edge of the hole and hauled himself up and out, and sat on the edge with his head on his chest, eyes closed, gasping. A tremor of intense weakness swept through him and then was gone, leaving him merely exhausted. He clambered to his feet and pulled out the flashlight. They were in a brick-lined culvert. The floor sloped from all sides into the tube they'd just crawled up. From the walls a number of pipes at different heights opened out onto the sloping gully, ready to gush forth a torrent of infected waste the next time someone flushed a toilet. A series of steel rungs bolted to one wall led up to a manhole cover.

Klein glanced back down at the tube then looked at Galindez. 'Glad that bit's over,' he said.

'Me too, but I've seen worse.'

'Oh yeah?' Klein ground his teeth into a who-the-fuck-do-you-think-you-are-type smile. 'How come everyone I meet in this fucking place has always had a worse time of things than I have? Every fucking one. This is the worst day of my fucking life. No one I ever knew in the world had a day this bad. But no, I got to end up in a fucking toilet with a guy – a fucking screw, mind you – who's seen worse. Goddamn if that doesn't make me feel like an asshole.'

The speech somehow made Klein feel like a million dollars. He smiled again.

'I'm sorry you feel that way,' said Galindez. 'What about Crawford, or Bialmann? They're not doing hard time.'

'Bialmann is dead and Crawford, if he survives, is going to lose his leg.'

'Hmm. Can't think of nobody else. That must make you the most fortunate guy in the whole joint. You even got your parole.'

'Yeah,' said Klein. 'I even got my parole.'

He shone the torch onto the rungs of the ladder.

'After you,' said Klein.

Galindez climbed up towards the manhole. At the top he pushed off the iron cover. Blackness gaped beyond. He crawled into the blackness and disappeared. Klein looked back at the tube and sent a prayer down for Abbott. Then he climbed the ladder and stuck his head through the manhole. And it occurred to Klein for the first time that they'd made it.

They were in the infirmary.

TWENTY-EIGHT

REUBEN WILSON TURNED from the peep slot in the steel plate door and called over his shoulder to Devlin.

'They're through the gate,' he said.

Devlin was rolling an oxygen cylinder on its end through the wooden doorway. As she manoeuvred it down the corridor she looked up and saw a giggling, one-eyed face dart up to the peep slot.

'Look out!' she said.

A shower of corrosive liquid scattered through the slot. Wilson's reflexes were quick enough to protect his eyes but the liquid drenched the side of his face and neck. He slammed the slot shut, cutting off the giggles on the other side.

'Shit, man,' said Wilson. He looked around for something to wipe his skin.

'Go and run water over it, lots of it, now,' she said. 'The dispensary.'

Wilson rushed past her as the pain began to bite him. Devlin lowered the cylinder to the floor a few feet from the steel door. As she watched a grey-blue spot appeared in the steel plate a couple of inches from the lock. Grauerholz and his men had cut their way through the gate and were starting in on this the last really solid barrier left between them and the besieged inhabitants of the hospital. After this there was only the wooden door to protect them. Devlin put the thought behind her. The grey-blue spot expanded and grew paler. At the centre it started to glow red. A black, sputtering hole appeared, dripping blobs of molten metal that solidified in lumps as it cooled. She heard the high-pitched hiss of the oxyacetylene flame. Coley appeared behind her with a second oxygen cylinder. This one had a gauge screwed into the neck.

'This one's only half full,' he said.

He started to unscrew the gauge. From the ward came a shattering of glass and a chorus of fearful shouts. She looked at him.

'They using that girder shit to smash the windows in, keep us busy both ends.'

There was another crash from the ward. Coley threw the gauge on the floor and placed the cylinder alongside the first one. From his pocket he took a spanner key and fitted it to the neck of the cylinder.

'You sure this'll work?' he said.

'It'll work,' replied Devlin. 'We might kill ourselves in the process but it will work. I need the key to your cupboard.'

Coley took out his ring of keys and unhooked one. He looked at it wistfully for a beat then handed it to Devlin. She could smell burning steel now. The hole in the door was an inch long.

'Wait till I get back,' she said.

On the way to the dispensary she made sure all the doors in the corridor, to the TV room, the bathrooms and the store-rooms, were shut tight. In the dispensary Wilson was standing over the sink. His head dripped water but the tap wasn't running.

'I said lots of water,' said Devlin.

'We been cut off, remember? Only a pint left in there.'

'Any idea what he threw?' she said.

'Smelt like battery acid. Feels like it too.'

Devlin found a bottle of sodium bicarb solution in a cupboard and broke the seal. There was a rash of blebs and vesicles down Wilson's cheek, neck and shoulder. She sat him down and poured the solution over the affected area to neutralise the acid.

'Painful?' she said.

Wilson shrugged, 'I'm okay.'

More sounds of destruction echoed from the ward. Vinnie Lopez staggered through the dispensary doorway. His eyes fell on the scalpels on the bench. He walked over and grabbed one. His eyes were bright with excitement.

'How you doin' man?' he said to Wilson.

'Pretty good,' said Wilson.

Lopez raised the scalpel. 'I jus' want one, man. One of them big-bearded fuckers. They stick their fucken head through that window, fuck, it's gone, man.'

'I always told you go for more than you think you can get, Vinnie.'

Lopez hitched up his pants around his skeletal waist. 'Both them bearded fuckers dead then.'

Lopez walked out. Devlin went over to the padlocked cupboard and opened it. She carefully took down Coley's big bottle of ether and checked the label. $(C_2H_5)_2O$. She carried it to the door. Wilson stood up and joined her.

'Chemical warfare, eh, Doc?

'You want to throw toilet rolls at them instead, go ahead.'

'What is that shit?'

'Ether. It's an anaesthetic, distilled from sulphuric acid and alcohol if I remember.'

'We gonna put 'em to sleep then?'

'No. It's very volatile, turns to gas on contact with air. Mixed with pure oxygen it makes an explosive combination.'

She looked down at the bottle again. She realised what an

appalling thing it was that she was contemplating. When she'd learnt this stuff in med school it hadn't been with this end in mind.

Wilson, reading her expression, said, 'They could be throwin' toilet rolls at us too, they wanted too. But they ain't.'

Devlin nodded and said, 'Let's do it.'

In the corridor the flame of the cutting torch had two inches to go before it separated the lock from the door.

Devlin said to Coley, 'Go ahead.'

At the far end Coley crouched down by the cylinders and twisted the spanner key, opening wide the neck of the first cylinder. A loud hissing drowned out the sound of the cutting torch. The burning metal at the door glowed a brighter orange. He fixed the spanner to the second bottle.

Devlin said, 'They open the door away from us, right?'

'Right,' said Coley. He opened the second cylinder. Pure oxygen blasted out into the enclosed corridor.

Devlin said, 'Go and wait for me. When I come out slam the door as fast as you can.'

'Here they come,' said Coley.

It was happening. The door was juddering as impatient hands heaved on the handle on the other side. The last half inch of steel spluttered and flared. Coley walked past Devlin and pushed the wooden door almost shut behind her. She was alone with the hissing cylinders and the juddering steel door. On the other side were men who would rape her and kill her friends. Remember that, she told herself. No one invited them. She hefted the bottle of ether above her head in both hands. It didn't feel right. She changed to a shot-putter's stance, the base of the bottle in her right palm against her shoulder. Better. Her stomach was knotted so tight she could hardly breathe. She glanced at the wooden door behind her which kept in the oxygen. It was still open a crack.

The steel door was wrenched open.

Devlin threw all her weight into the bottle, tossing it the length of the corridor, then blasted her ass and shoulder backwards into the wooden door. As the door swung open she lost her balance and started to fall.

Crouching in the open doorway at the other end a man holding a roaring welder's torch stared at the brown glass bottle arcing towards him.

Arms grabbed Devlin from behind as she fell and dragged her across the threshold. As Wilson slammed the wooden door shut in front of her she caught a last glimpse of the ether bottle shattering against the oxygen cylinders.

There was a tremendous double explosion, one blurring into the other, the first a great thumping roar, the second higher pitched and sharper. The stout wooden door shuddered against its hinges with the shock wave. The blast was followed by a deafening silence. Coley hefted Devlin to her feet. She fought down a bolt of nausea.

'Okay?' said Coley.

She nodded, staring at the door. After a moment she said to Wilson, 'Open it.' Her voice was hoarse. Wilson pulled the door open.

The corridor between them and the far steel gate appeared scoured of life. The first explosion, of ether and oxygen, had detonated the oxyacetylene equipment and caused the second. Four corpses, scorched in an instant by combusting gases and torn apart by flying fragments of metal, lay in tangled heaps. A fifth man had been crushed against the cage door by the trolley which had carried the gas bottles, propelled into him by the blast.

Devlin felt her lips trembling. She put the back of her hand to her mouth. She felt the eyes of Coley and Wilson on her but didn't look back. She was glad that Grauerholz and his crackers were dead. She was glad she'd slaughtered the bastards. And she didn't want Wilson and Coley to see that in her face. She suddenly felt disgusted with herself and the gladness vanished. At least it was over, she thought. Now, without Grauerholz to egg them on, maybe the rest would give up. The steel door with its missing lock creaked forward a few inches. After a moment a ragged figure crawled out from behind it into the corridor.

It was Grauerholz.

His skull was coated with frazzled tufts of burnt hair. His clothes were scorched against his skin. His right hand was missing. He stumbled to his feet and fell against the wall, smearing it with blood.

'Hec!'

Horace and Bubba Tolson appeared at the far end of the hallway and gaped at the damage. They stepped cautiously through the gate and stepped over the bodies towards Grauerholz.

Wilson stepped up beside Devlin. 'You crackers want some more we got plenty,' he said.

Grauerholz slowly raised his head to look at them. His one eye seemed as bright as ever. He opened his mouth but no sound came out from his blistered lips. He tottered back a pace from the wall. Then he raised the bloody stump of his arm and pointed it straight at Devlin, staring obsessively into her eyes, and she knew that it wasn't over after all and that he wouldn't let the others give up until he was dead. The Tolsons took hold of Grauerholz with as much gentleness as they had between them and carried him away down the corridor.

'That sucker'll be back,' said Wilson.

Devlin nodded. She walked down the corridor towards the bodies.

'Where you going?' said Wilson.

Coley already understood and was following her. Together they checked the five bodies. The man crushed at the gate and one of the others were unconscious but still alive. They dragged them back and Wilson locked the wooden door.

'How long you reckon 'fore they come again?' he said.

'You oughta know these fuckers better 'n I do,' growled Coley. 'You tell me.'

'Grauerholz is in shock,' said Devlin, 'and he's burned and bleeding. Even he will need fixing up, something for the pain. Maybe he won't be fit to come back at all.'

Wilson and Coley stared at her dubiously.

'If he can walk up to this door and knock on it within two hours I'll open it for him myself.'

'You see, Frog, it's okay,' said Wilson, drily. 'Hec won't be back for least two hours.'

'One thing I'm grateful for,' said Coley.

'What's that?'

'Least you tried to be a boxer an' not a comedian.'

Coley winked at Devlin and walked through the door of Crockett ward.

'Tried?' said Wilson. 'What the fuck you mean, "tried"?'

In the ward the glass in two of the reinforced windows had been smashed out but the assault had bated. They laid the two injured men out on the floor. Vinnie Lopez offered to cut their throats but Wilson told him that was cheating. As Devlin knelt down to examine one of the wounded a vile odour drifted into her nostrils. She looked up. Wilson and Lopez were also wrinkling their noses. She turned.

Standing in the doorway in a small pool of stinking water was a grotesque figure, bleeding from a dozen cuts and smeared from head to toe with foul-smelling slime. Behind him stood Victor Galindez, not as wet as Klein, but just as dirty.

'Hi,' said Klein. 'Anybody know how the Knicks got on?'

Devlin's stomach contracted. Too many different emotions assailed her at once for her to be able to speak. While the others gaped Lopez walked across the room, proud to show Klein he was up and about.

'They lost. How you doin', man?'

He pumped Klein's hand and Klein grinned at him. He turned the grin on Devlin and her heart melted. She walked over and kissed him on the lips.

'Hey.' Klein backed off. 'I'm on the shit list.'

'I don't give a fuck,' she said.

She threw her arms round his neck and tried not to cry. She heard Klein speak to Lopez over her shoulder.

'What was the score?'

'Ninety-three Lakers, eighty-eight Knicks.'

Klein pulled her head back to where he could see her. He saw the tears she was holding back and smiled.

'Damn. Must be my lucky day,' he said. 'Won me two new pairs of Calvins just when I need 'em.'

TWENTY-NINE

WHEN KLEIN HEARD that the water supply had been cut off he was none too pleased. He didn't fancy spending his time shouting across the ten-metre distance people felt inclined to keep from him to protect themselves from the smell. After he'd suffered the thought of this prospect long enough to drink a litre of vile prison cola, Frog reminded him that the showers were supplied by an old-fashioned water tank. Klein belched mightily and dragged Galindez through the dispensary into the shower room.

Klein stood under the hot water and leaned against the wall with his eyes closed. When the worst of the slime was washed away he scrubbed himself with a liquid iodine soap from top to bottom, rinsed himself down, then started again. He did this three times. Each time he discovered a fresh crop of cuts and abrasions. The only ones that troubled him were the three knife wounds on the inside of his left ankle and calf. They were already an unhealthy red at the edges and had to be infected with a cocktail of unpleasant life forms he preferred not to think about. He just hoped the blade hadn't given him an osteomyelitis of the bone. He'd stuff some antibiotics down his throat after the shower.

Next door Galindez climbed out of the shower and towelled

himself down and left. Klein stayed on. He wondered – he hoped – that Devlin would pay him a visit. The thought provoked a ranging hard-on and Klein washed his genitals and ass for a fourth time to be on the safe side. A man, after all, never knew when his luck might be in. He squirted a jot of soap into his mouth and rubbed it into his teeth with a finger. After the sewage he'd been swallowing all night it tasted surprisingly good – artificial, chemical, man-made, clean. He'd experienced enough organic products to last a lifetime. Better than the cola too. He opened his mouth under the sprinkler and rinsed it out. He felt good. He slapped his belly, a taut, satisfying sound. He was a fine figure of a man, by God, and he was alive. Devlin was a lucky woman, goddamn it. He wondered what was keeping her. Caring for the wounded was all well and good, noble even, but what about hail the conquering hero comes? He admitted, magnanimously, that they'd done a terrific job of withstanding the siege so far. But there was only one door left, the windows were almost down and only the shotokan warrior stood between them and oblivion. And Galindez. But Galindez was a guard and it was his fucking job, so he didn't really count.

There were times, Klein reflected, when he regretted being an asshole and others when it gave him a certain amount of pleasure. This was one of the latter. Beyond the shower curtain he heard the door open. Klein thought about breaking into a nonchalant whistle but the only tune that sprang to mind was Doris Day. He refrained.

'Klein?'

It was her voice. Indecision seized him. Should he whip the curtain aside and stand there quivering, a sullen sneer on his face? The memory of a zillion shower scenes in every tenth-rate movie he'd ever seen swilled across his mind. Show a little style, man. Be cool. He coughed and lowered his voice.

'Yeah?' he said.

'We need to talk,' she said.

Few words struck more dread into his heart, or, he reckoned, any man's, than these when uttered by a woman he had the horn for. His erection started to wilt. As if on cue the shower above his head spluttered a couple of times and stopped. The tank was empty.

'Is that okay?' she said.

'Sure,' said Klein, without enthusiasm.

'I'll wait for you in the office.'

What? What the fuck? Didn't she want to watch him towel himself down? He heard the door open and shut again. Devlin was gone. So what? Come on, forget it. She's probably peeking through the keyhole. Except women didn't do that except in porn vids, and only then when there was more than one guy to spy on. Even so just in case, square those shoulders, sullen sneer. Good. He stepped out through the curtain and almost slipped on a glob of slime. He started to dry himself. Be cool, Klein. Don't be in a hurry. Be a man for fuck's sake.

After all it was three years since a woman had seen him naked. As it happened, what with his morning karate routine and working out in the yard, he was in the shape of his life. When he got out he'd have to get down to the waterfront in a body shirt while it lasted. He should have got himself some tattoos. He'd always felt it would have been inappropriate in here given he wasn't considered a real con. Now it was too late, especially as he recalled that Colt Greely was reputed to draw the best tats in the prison. Might put Devlin off too, although the kind of woman he wanted would be turned on by them. Maybe that was it: she was just embarrassed to watch him. His raw hands stung against the towel. Maybe all that tough cocksucking talk was a front. He seemed to remember she was some kind of a Catholic, an all or nothing religion. Mortal sin and all that shit. When they were uptight they were a nightmare. When they were wild they were wild. Sometimes the wild ones needed just a little boost to get them over the line. Klein wrapped a dry towel around his waist and combed his hair with his fingers. There was no mirror in here in which to check himself. Probably a blessing. He sucked his belly in and went into the office.

Devlin was pacing the mustard yellow room smoking a cigarette. She glanced at his body, smiled at him nervously, then stared at the end of her cigarette.

Klein's heart sank. He couldn't help thinking it was typical that, despite the fact it was he who hadn't been laid in what felt like several decades, and he who had spent the night playing the part of a butt plug in the anus of God's creation in order to be here, it was nevertheless he who would have to be duly sensitive to her, the woman's, sexual anxieties. Maybe she'd changed her mind since that morning. It was a long time ago. Maybe she'd spent that time dwelling on the rank stupidity of getting involved with a bum like him. But hell, he'd never felt less like a bum in his life.

Hold on, Klein. The flower of Texan psychopathology was out there trying to kill them all and gang rape her. Give her a break. He took a deep breath. He was the shotokan warrior. He was cool. At last, he really was. He could deal with anything. Just a question of saving the sullen sneer until later. He smiled back at her.

'You look great,' he said.

Terrible line. Fuck.

'All things considered,' he added.

'So do you,' she said.

Klein felt that she could have put more feeling into it but it was a start. There was an awkward pause.

'I've got something to tell you,' she said.

Terrible didn't even begin to describe that one. Alarm bells rang in his head. He wanted to say, 'Can't it wait till later?' but that would've required raising his voice an octave. The wife of a friend of his had once confided to him that a deep, confident voice was the best way to convince a woman that you had a big dick.

Without thinking about it Klein said, 'Is that, "I've got something to tell you" or "Have I got something to tell you"?'

'I guess it's a bit of both,' she said.

She pulled a pack of Camels from her pocket and shook one into her mouth. She offered him the pack.

'You want one?'

For once he wasn't tempted. He shook his head.

'You see,' she paused to light the Camel and inhale. 'I'm in love with you.'

'Goddamn,' said Klein.

Suddenly the depth of his voice no longer mattered. He wasn't a bum after all. He was the shotokan warrior and she was in love with him. He felt his cock rise majestically against the rough cotton of the towel. He quashed the urge to whip the towel aside and dance a jig. His cool was too hard and recently won to abandon it just yet. Sullen sneer, yelled a voice in his head, it's the perfect moment. He resisted. Instead, he settled for stupefaction.

'But there's something else,' said Devlin.

Klein's hard-on held firm but the urge to dance withered inside him. Before his mind could stampede into further speculation the door opened and Coley lumbered in. Under his arm was a bundle of prison blues. He took in the scene with his yellow, bloodshot eyes. He nodded at the desk.

'I wanna get on with my readin' while I got the chance.'

'Reading?' said Klein.

As far as he knew Frog didn't even read the sports pages. Coley tossed him the bundle.

'Clean clothes.' He glanced at the bulge in Klein's towel. 'That is you got any use for 'em.'

Klein twisted the bundle in his hands. His palms burned and the burning made him feel better.

Devlin, who seemed glad of the interruption, said to Coley, 'What do you think so far?'

Coley raised an eyebrow as he walked to the table and dropped into the chair.

'I'll have to finish it before I can give a proper opinion.' He looked at her. 'But so far I have to say it's a goddamned masterpiece.'

Devlin grinned properly for the first time since Klein had seen her. He felt vaguely excluded.

'What goddamn masterpiece we talking about exactly?' he asked.

Coley opened the desk drawer and pulled out a copy of *The American Journal of Psychiatry*. He flicked it open, his chest swelling as he laid it open where Klein could see it.

'This masterpiece, asshole.'

Klein leaned over and read the title. Then the list of authors. Juliette Devlin. Ray Klein. Earl Coley. Klein swallowed and looked up at the Frogman.

Coley's froggy yellow eyes, looking back, were full and for the second time that night Klein's heart almost cracked. He knew Coley better than any man alive. And vice versa. If anyone could know what this meant to the black sharecropper, cast into hell twenty-three years before, Klein knew. He knew. And if the Tolsons had come through the door right then and hacked Klein's head from his shoulders, it would have been worth it all, right then, to see what he was seeing now in Coley's eyes and to feel what he was feeling in his chest. Coley clenched his hands together into a huge trembling fist. Klein put his hand on top of it.

'We did it, man,' whispered Coley.

'We did it,' said Klein.

'We told those fuckers out there,' said Coley.

'We told 'em,' said Klein.

'We told 'em the goddamned truth,' said Coley.

'We told 'em the truth,' said Klein.

'And she wrote it down,' said Coley.

'Every word,' said Klein.

They heard movement and looked up in time to see Devlin disappearing through the door. Klein looked back at Coley. Coley relaxed his fist and stood up. He put a big hand, surprisingly soft, on Klein's bare back.

'Listen to me, man. She's had a day like you wouldn't believe, and she's done right. Wasn't for her you wouldn' of found nothin' in here but corpses. She special, man.'

'I know that, Frog.'

'You jus' treat her gentle, hear me? Gentle. Or your ass answer to me.'

Klein swallowed. He nodded. Coley fumbled with his keys, pulled one off the ring.

'Now you take her to my billet. I already put some clean linen down. Under the bottom left-hand foot the bed they's a loose board. You look in there, find a bottle of wine, best in the house. From that mad Irish fucka I tol' you 'bout. Drink it. And treat her right.'

He pressed the key into Klein's hand.

'Thanks, Frog,' said Klein.

'I reckon the crackers lay off a while. Anything happens you'll know. Now leave me to my readin'.'

Klein, a little confused, grabbed his bundle and went out into the corridor. Devlin was standing with her back to the wall and her eyes clenched shut. Klein took her arm and she opened them.

'Okay?'

She nodded, smiled awkwardly. 'It was your moment, yours and Coley's. I didn't want to intrude.'

'You heard him,' said Klein. 'You think "we" didn't mean you too? You wrote it down. Every word.'

She nodded. 'I'm sorry.'

'Don't be.'

Klein remembered Coley's instructions. His own high spirits in the shower now seemed juvenile. Or maybe just out of place and he hadn't known it. He put his arm round her shoulders and she put her arm round his waist and he led her up the stairs to Coley's room.

Klein unlocked the door and they went in. The room was small and as spartan as a zen monk's cell. No books, no music, no pin-ups. Just the bed, a small table and a single framed photograph on the wall by the bed. Coley had left two candles burning on the table and a heap of incense homemade from sawdust and charcoal and deodorant smouldering in a metal tea-strainer. The bed was narrow but freshly made-up, the sheet turned down.

'That Frogman is something, you know?' said Klein.

He leaned across the bed and looked at the photo in the flickering light. It was in colour and depicted a broad-shouldered, grave-faced farmer standing next to a strong-featured, lighter-skinned woman. The woman held a baby and before them stood three children, two boys around ten years old and a girl around six.

'He hasn't heard from any of them for a dozen years,' said Klein. 'Won't hear a bad word said against them.'

He turned. Devlin was dipping her finger into the wax of one of the candles. She looked like she hadn't heard him. She turned.

'I want you to sit down and listen to me for a minute,' she said. 'And if you speak I won't be able to get through it.'

Klein sat down crosslegged on the bed, his back to the wall, and waited. And while she smoked three cigarettes and paced up and down in the candlelight she told him what had passed between her and Reuben Wilson and tried to make him understand what it had meant to her. And Klein listened without speaking. When she'd finished she stubbed out her cigarette and hovered by the door with her back to him.

'You want me to go now?' she said.

'I want you to stay,' said Klein.

The fact was nothing that she'd told him changed the way he felt about her, except maybe to increase both his lust and his admiration in roughly equal measure. He didn't even worry about the size of Wilson's dick. He had something else on his mind. Devlin looked at him.

'I think what you did was great,' he said, quietly. 'I want you to stay.'

'Really?'

'I may be an asshole, a big asshole, but I'm not that particular category of asshole that would find this a problem. Wilson's a hero. I'm flattered.' He smiled at her. 'On the other hand if you'd fucked Gimp Cotton I might've had a problem.'

Devlin wiped something from her eye. 'I meant what I said downstairs. I love you.'

Klein nodded. There was nothing for it but to get his own business over with too. He'd never actually decided to keep it from her, it was just that he'd never had a good reason to talk about it. Now he did.

'While it's time for dark secrets I'd better tell you mine. It might change the way you feel.'

'I doubt that.'

'I was sent up for raping my girlfriend.'

There was a long pause as she looked at him, searching his face. Within him Klein felt a stirring, the impending eruption of feelings he'd hoped he'd buried and ploughed under with his work, his discipline, his pursuit of survival. He'd buried the feelings out of fear for they were composed mainly of bitterness and rage.

Finally Devlin said, 'I think you owe us both a bit more background than that.'

'Do I?' said Klein.

Devlin breathed deep. 'I'm staying whether you tell me any

more or not. I don't believe you could do anything I couldn't live with. But I'd like to know.'

Klein stared at the flame of the candle.

'We'd been going together four years and it turned sour way long time before the finish.'

'How?'

Klein kept his eyes on the candle. The rest of the room became invisible, including Devlin.

'Usual shit. Trivia, I guess. Stuff keeps divorce lawyers and therapists in clover. No grand crimes or betrayals. Kind of things that always seem trivial from the outside and make your gut bleed like ground glass when you're on the inside. We were very ordinary. Just another fucked-up couple working their variations on an old theme. Mutual torture. It was compelling enough while it lasted, then we both outdid ourselves and it ended.'

Klein glanced at Devlin and saw a fear in her face. He returned to the candle.

'It wasn't physical torture, if that's what you're thinking. Too straightforward. Too simple. You can stretch out mental punishment for a lot longer. In the end all we had left were what we called hate fucks, you know what I mean? They're good while they last. When they're over you can't bear the sound of your own breathing.'

'I know,' she said.

'One night we had our last great hate fuck and afterwards I told her I didn't want to see her any more. I was through. She told me if I walked out on her she'd fuck me up so bad I'd . . .' He shrugged. 'I'd heard all that stuff before and didn't want to hear it again. I got up and left. Next morning the cops arrested me at the hospital and charged me with rape.'

'Did you rape her?'

'She said I did. That's all that it means isn't it?'

'No it isn't. You know it isn't.'

'I fucked her as hard as I'd fucked her a hundred times before. I left her with a carpet burn on her back. She came three times. You wanna read the court transcripts it's all there. She said she'd told me to stop. She didn't. A bunch of her PC friends testified that I'd bad-mouthed them in restaurants, I had a violent personality, I was a martial arts freak, blah, blah, blah. Most of it was true and at the same time most of it was bullshit. Everything was twisted out of context. The whole thing was just a move up from middleweight to heavy but it was the same stupid game, cutting each other's noses off to spite our own faces. I made it worse for myself by going to see her to try talk it through before the trial. Of course it turned into an instant replay of the same old tapes, four years of cat-scratching squeezed into two hours. My lawyer nearly wept and he was right. By the time I got to trial the episode had become me threatening and harassing her.'

'She wouldn't withdraw the charge?' said Devlin.

'How could she?' said Klein. 'The ball was rolling. A three-ring circus. Papers, women's groups, lawyers. And the DA licking his lips at the thought of the votes a conviction would win him. Until my trial that bastard probably thought *The Female Eunuch* was a bible story. Suddenly he's dug up two female PAs, a woman on the bench and appears on the news waving a copy of *Backlash*.'

Devlin smiled involuntarily, stifled it. 'I'm sorry,' she said, mortified. 'You just . . .'

'I know, I know,' said Klein. 'It is a big fucking joke. That's what I thought. The trouble is I was right. My lawyer, who now owns my house, told me not to testify. He said the burden of proof was theirs and if they got me on the stand they'd make me look like Hannibal fucking Lecter. When she testified for the prosecution I knew I'd won. Anyone could see her heart wasn't in it. Then, in the cross examination, my asshole lawyer virtually raped her for me, tried to make her

out to be a slut on the make, which she wasn't, and left her
sobbing into her blouse. By then even I thought I'd done it.
They found me guilty by a majority verdict. The judge sent
me up for five to ten.'

Klein paused and scrubbed his hands over his face.

'What was her name?' asked Devlin.

Without taking his hands from his face Klein said, 'I don't
care to remember.' He swallowed the bile in his throat and
took his hands down. He kept his face turned towards the
wall. 'If rape means using the act of sex to inflict pain on
another then I raped her many times,' he said. 'But no more
often, and no less, than she raped me.'

'Sometimes the line between love and hate is very fine,'
said Devlin.

Klein didn't answer.

'To hurt each other that badly you must have loved each
other very much. At least for a time.'

'Yeah,' said Klein. 'Heaven hath no rage like love to hatred
turned, and all that stuff. We were both guilty.'

He turned and looked at Devlin in the candlelight. Her
face was haunted with pity.

'You didn't appeal?' said Devlin. 'She didn't change her
mind even after you came here?'

Klein smiled and Devlin turned a little paler.

'Maybe she would've done, in time. But the week I was
sent up she went one better than me and plugged herself into
an insulin drip.'

Devlin flinched.

'By the time they found her body her brain was as dead as
a peeled egg. A week later they switched off the life-support
machine.'

There was a silence. Devlin sat on the edge of the bed. She
raised her head and opened her mouth.

'Don't say anything,' said Klein. 'And don't misunderstand

me either. As far as I'm concerned, every day I've served I had coming to me. No one's innocent in the River. One way or another we all wanted to be here.'

Klein sat there against the wall and watched the candle flame, as still and pure as the light in Henry Abbott's eyes, and for the first time since they'd switched off the machine he felt a grief untarnished by anger and with the grief, peace. It was as if his heart had finally come to rest. And he wondered how Henry was doing and if he too had found his final resting, face down in the Green River waters. And Klein thought of Devlin's quotation and wondered if by dawn all of them, just and unjust alike, wouldn't also be cast back into the aimless chaos of matter from which they had come. He looked at the back of Devlin's head.

'We that were able to believe ourselves the final end of creation,' he said.

Devlin laid her head on his lap without speaking. Her finger-tips gently brushed the wounds in his ankle. The pain was reassuring. The weight of Devlin's head against his thighs gave him a hard-on and that was reassuring too. In the end maybe these were the only things you could really count on. And he wondered, if nothing matched the rage of love to hatred turned, then what was the vice versa? Suddenly he could find neither peace nor hatred in him and he wondered where they had gone for without one or the other he felt comfortless and frightened and lost.

Then somehow Devlin did the one thing in the world that could comfort him and if she hadn't done it he wouldn't have known what it was, and he wondered how it was that she did know. She reached up under his towel and put her hand on his cock.

Klein stroked her hair, the short, soft bristles on the back of her neck rippling against his fingers. She pulled the towel open and took his cock in her mouth and stroked his balls and Klein trembled at the tenderness of it and he did not come for it was not yet sexual and he swore he would not cry and he did not.

Devlin sat up and pulled her shirt off over her head. Her nipples stuck out through the white cotton of her bra. She pulled her boots off and then her Levis. And as she knelt over him in her white bra and black G string he put his raw, scabbed hands on the ass he would have died for and in an instant it was more sexual than anything he'd ever known. He got up to his knees and kissed her and tasted the tobacco on her tongue. He ran his hand down her belly and into her hair. His finger found her clitoris, like a small marble rolling in oil, and she bit his face and his neck. Klein pushed her over onto her back and pulled the G string aside and licked her. She came quickly, her body arcing in a bow, the muscles on her abdomen shivering with tension. He pushed her down and made her come again, and would have kept on except she was grappling for his cock and told him to fuck her. So he did, his cock sliding in alongside the G string and it was neither a hate fuck nor a one-last-fuck-before-I-die fuck. He pulled one of her bra straps down and sucked her nipple. He didn't try to delay his orgasm, he just went with it, fucking her with long slow strokes, and when he came he wasn't aware of how long it had taken and he did not care, he was only aware that he loved her and that all the hate in him had gone. He lay on top of her shuddering, for a moment. Then he smiled, for he even lacked the strength to take his weight on his elbows, like the gentleman he hoped himself to be.

So Klein lay there with his eyes closed, breathing softly. He felt himself drifting off and made himself open his eyes. Devlin's face was half-turned away from him, chiselled into fabulous planes by the amber light, and he thought he saw the glistening trail of tears on her cheek. She was intensely beautiful. More beautiful than anything he'd ever known. He wanted to keep on looking forever but his eyelids bore down on him with the gravity of ages. He fought against them but it was beyond him, it was beyond the last vestiges of his strength. Her face slipped from sight. Her nipple was still pressed against his lips. He opened his mouth and mumbled into her breast, so low and slurred he knew she couldn't have heard him.

'I know this isn't very gentlemanly,' he said, 'but I'm going to go to sleep.'

And Klein smiled again because he was kind of an asshole and knew it and because he really didn't care. And then he went to sleep.

THIRTY

HOBBES LAY ON his divan and stared up at the bare bulb hanging from the ceiling. In recent months he had taken to spending his nights here, in a small box room adjoining his wood-panelled office. He had not slept for more than an hour at a stretch in weeks and since the lockdown not at all. He had a wife and home to go to but those moments in which he could find a sufficiently compelling reason to do so had become progressively less frequent and then had ceased altogether. If his wife found this disturbing, Hobbes had not been inclined to notice, much less care. These days he sometimes had difficulty recalling her name and the image of her face rarely crossed his mind. He had no photos of her in his suite of rooms. It seemed to him that she had had at least a fair deal and probably the best of it. She had spent the bulk of his life's earnings on herself and her house; and so to her frequent bleatings on the theme that her life lacked love and fulfilment Hobbes had turned at best a deaf, and at worst a contemptuously unsympathetic, ear. Jane Hobbes – Janet Hobbes? Rebecca? – wouldn't have recognised love and fulfilment if those very qualities had broken into her bedroom at the dead of night and gang raped her. Hobbes smiled to himself at the thought, and then wondered why at this of all times he was thinking of her at all. Perhaps his mind was clearing itself out in preparation for its exit. For the exit was drawing near and he sensed, if he could not yet see, the dazzling light that burned on the other side.

He had surrendered his machine – and Klein had been right, the panoptic machine was his – to a historic spasm of paroxystic violence. Historic. He, John Campbell Hobbes, had made history. He had surrendered his creation in the hope that the feverish nihilism thus released might be subordinated to an end beyond itself. And it had failed. The panoptic experiment had failed as surely as the love he once had felt for his wife. The evidence was there: in the flames of B block, in the mindless bloodlust unleashed against the unprotected wretches in the hospital. He had given them a chance to demonstrate a higher sensibility and they had spat on it. He had dreamed that they might raise themselves above the parapet and cry 'We are more than this! We are more than this filth that you have made of us!'

The room around him echoed like a vast, vacant tomb and Hobbes realised that he had spoken aloud. The time for dreams was over and the time for despair was arrived, the oceanic despair against which he had flung himself in this one last unflinching stand. Now he prepared himself to embrace it. Despair was after all the ultimate transcendence of the ego and his ego had been mashed into embers by a cosmos committed to ruin. Despair was hubristic, not humble; a radical unknowing; an abandonment; a lone voyage with no conceivable destination. He was freed at last to travel and yet a single obligation remained – to begin his journey from the only apt embarkation point: to make himself visible at the very centre of the panoptic machine he had made his own.

There was a knock at the door which Hobbes recognised as Cletus's. He rose from the divan and brushed the creases from his suit, straightened his tie. He opened the door on the Captain's bulky face. Cletus was dressed in the black SWAT suit that made him look more obese than he was. A wire ran from a transmitter plugged into his left ear to a radio in the front of his jacket.

'Excuse me, sir,' said Cletus.

Hobbes walked past him without speaking and sat down behind his desk. The desk moved him, had always moved him. It had stood in this room since 1882. Underneath its glass top was an original architectural drawing, in plan, of the penitentiary. Hobbes was stricken as never before by the awesome beauty of its symmetry. He had walked every inch of the prison's physical reality, he knew every passageway and cell. Yet it was here under the glass on his desk that its perfection lay, in the conception rather than its execution. To Hobbes the drawing embodied the glorious endpoint of the Cartesian project, the attempt to know God and Man through the application of pure reason. Those times were now over and the project was shipwrecked on the rocks of irrationality. Next to the drawing was a fragment of those very rocks: a wrinkled sheet of cheap, blue-lined paper torn from a small notebook. Hobbes had found it wrapped in plastic and wedged between the granite blocks of the wall in a cell in segregation. Scrawled upon the paper in green ink by a laborious hand was a number: 1057. Below the number were these words:

> Every morn and every night,
> Some are born to sweet delight.
> Some are born to sweet delight,
> Some are born to endless night.

Hobbes did not know who had written the verse down, nor if the verse was original or a quotation. It held for him a power and a fascination, all the greater now as he waited through this darkest hour for the light of his final dawn. Endless night. Sweet delight. He had known both sides of the coin and at last he knew that his destiny lay with the one rather than the other. At least he had not lain down with mediocrity. He slid the plate of glass to one side and pulled out the wrinkled paper, folded it along its original creases and slipped it into the breast pocket of his jacket. Cletus coughed. Hobbes had quite forgotten his presence. He looked up.

'Sit down, Captain.'

'I'll stand, sir, if I may.'

'As you like.'

'I just been speaking to the Bureau of Corrections in Austin.' Cletus rolled his shoulders uncomfortably. 'I've been instructed to assume temporary command of the penitentiary, sir.'

This was a humiliation Hobbes had not expected. Now that it was here he was mildly astonished by its irrelevance.

'Go on,' he said.

'The Governor was kind of surprised you hadn't seen fit to inform him of this situation we got. Frankly, sir, so was I. He feels that you are not well enough to continue your duties at this particular time.'

'The Governor.'

'Yes, sir.'

'You have been in contact with him.'

Cletus stiffened his jaw. 'Yes, sir.'

'And on what evidence does the Governor base this assessment of my health?'

'On the evidence and concerns I voiced in my report to him, sir.'

Hobbes nodded silently.

'The Governor has dispatched a National Guard unit to back us up. Your replacement will be flown in by helicopter by morning.'

Again Hobbes nodded. Again he felt no emotion at the news. Another hour was all he needed and the help of Cletus and his men he needed not at all. It had been ordained before the Captain had knocked on his door. This merely added a modicum of urgency. There was no reason not to conduct himself with dignity.

'Have I time to collect my possessions together?'

'Of course, sir.' Cletus shuffled. 'I'm sorry it had to be this way.'

Hobbes walked around the desk. 'I have always found you loyal and utterly dependable, Captain. It's been an honour to serve with you.'

He held out his hand and Cletus shook it. His face was puffy and red with emotion.

'Thank you, sir.'

A muffled sound came from Cletus's earpiece and he pressed a thick index finger against it and squinted. He clicked his radio on and bent his head towards it.

'That's not possible,' he said.

The earpiece hummed again. Cletus looked at Hobbes.

'The lights have come on in the cellblocks,' said Cletus.

Hobbes strode across the room to the north window, Cletus close on his heels. The ridged glass vaults of the four cellblocks radiated a green-tinged glow into the night. At the centre of the glow the great dome capping the hub of the building was dark. Hobbes immediately understood.

'I didn't order this,' said Cletus, bewildered.

'Dennis Terry,' said Hobbes.

Cletus nodded. 'Shit, that old bastard must've got to the emergency generator. Prob'ly was him blew the main power lines this afternoon too. Excuse me, sir. I'd better get going.'

But Hobbes wasn't listening. He stood staring at the dark glass dome. It was more than he had any right to expect. The dome: the supreme cockpit from which to launch his voyage.

And yet it lacked a nimbus, the incandescence necessary for it to fulfil its function. Hobbes turned. Cletus had gone. He was alone. And exwarden Hobbes realised he no longer had any time to lose.

THIRTY-ONE

DEVLIN SAT UP in the corner of the bed, with the picture of Coley and his family just next to her on the wall, and she let go of all that she'd been holding in. She let it go quietly because she didn't want to wake Klein and because she didn't want to have to apologise or explain or stifle her tears yet again. She wasn't even sure for what it was that she cried, but she cried for a long time. She was glad of the weight of Klein's sleeping arm wrapped round her waist, and of the flickering candles. She was glad to be here, in this awful place, where abstraction finally failed her and she could surrender to raw emotion. After a while there were no more tears to come and she wiped her face on the sheet and lit one of Wilson's Camels. Her mind wandered and it wandered a long way. When she tried to recall where it had been she found she couldn't remember. Eventually there was a tapping on the door and she jumped. It took her a second to realise that if it had been Hector Grauerholz he wouldn't have bothered to knock.

'Come in,' she said.

The door opened an inch. 'It's me, Coley.'

Devlin wrapped the sheet around her. 'It's okay,' she said.

Coley came in shyly. He looked at Klein sleeping, then at Devlin.

'Things okay?' he asked quietly.

Devlin smiled and nodded. From the mattress beside her came a grunt and Klein's muffled voice.

'What do you want, you old bastard?'

'Came to kick you out into the yard, muthafucka. Grauerholz could do with some help and we sure as hell don't need yo' sorry ass.'

Klein raised his head and rolled over. He grunted and flinched as various injuries made themselves known. On his chest was a large bruise. Coley held up a pair of scuffed training shoes.

'Figured you'd need these for when you decide to do us a favour and run.'

'You are a fucking old woman, Frog, I ever tell you that?'

Coley threw the shoes on the floor. 'They were Greg Garvey's but he won't mind you wearin' 'em if you don't. We've moved all the guys that would go up to Travis.'

'You should've asked us to help.'

Coley ignored him. 'Found this too, I was bagging your shitty gear.'

He held out a snub-nosed revolver. Klein sat up on the edge of the bed and took it.

'Where did you get that?' said Devlin.

'I took it off Grauerholz this afternoon,' said Klein.

Coley glanced at her and Klein caught it. He jabbed the revolver at Frog's belly.

'That's right. I've been saving your black balls bein' cut off all fucking day and you won't even let me grab some Z's.'

'The lights just went on over in the blocks. Like Christmas. Thought you oughta know.'

'Dennis did it,' said Klein. 'Goddamn.'

'What does that mean?' said Devlin.

'It means all the blacks and Latinos locked down in C block are free,' said Klein. 'That doubles the odds, more, against

Agry. Plus Agry's crew've been getting ripped for hours. The guys from C are fresh and mad as hell. If Stokely Johnson gets it together they should be able to staple Agry's balls to the hot plate, and he'll have to pull Grauerholz out to back him up.'

Coley went back to the door and pulled it open. 'Well, ole Stoke better be quick,' he said. ''Cause Grauerholz out there right now with 'bout thirty new guys, an' they don't look so ripped to me.' Coley fixed Devlin with a heavy stare and pointed up at the ceiling, to the old mental ward above. 'Just 'cause the good doctah back in town don't mean I forgot that deal we made. You still got them keys?'

Devlin nodded.

'Use 'em.'

Coley left and Klein stood up and started to drag his pants on.

'How much is Frogman chargin' you?' he said.

'What for?' said Devlin.

'To turn tricks in his hidey hole.' He grinned and bent over towards her. 'Listen, you want me to pimp for you I'm back on the street and lookin' for work as of today.'

'You bastard.'

She punched him in the bruise on his chest and Klein, pants around his knees, yelled, lost his balance and fell to the floor. Horrified, Devlin leapt from the bed and hauled him to his feet. She searched his face. It was utterly pathetic, she knew, but she was looking for some sign that she meant as much to Klein as he did to her. Given that his affection for Coley was generally demonstrated by insults and threats she wasn't sure what she was looking for. Maybe the offer to be her pimp was such a demonstration. Klein put his hand to her face.

'Do what Frogman says,' said Klein. 'If they break through go up to his hole, lock the doors behind you. I'll get Vinnie to give you his radio. Don't come down till you hear the riot's over on the news.'

The prospect of sitting alone in the roof filled her with horror. Klein saw it.

'I know you won't like this, and I know how much ass you've kicked today, but if it gets hand to hand me and the guys will do better if we don't have to look out for you over our shoulder.'

Klein was right. She didn't like it. But she could see that he was right too about the fighting. She nodded. Klein picked up the revolver.

'You done much pistol shooting?'

She shook her head. He swung open the cylinder.

'Me neither. Look, there are five bullets in here and one empty chamber. I've had the hammer resting on a live round. That means four shots in a row and then a blank. When it clicks on the blank you'll know you've only got one left.'

'I never went for that stuff about shooting yourself rather than getting captured by the Apaches.'

'Once you start shooting it's easy to empty the gun in one. The blank's just a reminder. What you do with the last slug's up to you.'

He handed her the gun and she took it. It was lighter than she'd expected.

'Save it for Coley's hideout. If they do get through they'll have to climb through that hole one at a time.'

'I know what to do.'

'And shoot them in the head from close range. That isn't a Clint Eastwood piece.'

'I said I know what to do.'

'I just want you to survive this thing.'

Klein turned away and started to put his shirt on. Suddenly she loved him very much and with that a terrible anger surged through her.

'You were safe,' she said. 'Why the fuck didn't you stay there?'

Klein looked at her. 'I tried to, but things turned out different.'

'Did you come because of me?'

At the same time as she wanted him to say 'yes' she dreaded having to live with his death on her conscience. Klein sat on the bed and pulled on Garvey's trainers.

'You made it more important to get here, but I was already on my way.'

'Why?'

'I don't know.'

Klein laced up his shoes. She couldn't see his face.

'Maybe this is just where I belong.'

Without needing to he undid the knot on his left shoe and tied it again, keeping his face down. Devlin walked over and ran her fingers through his hair. Klein put his arms round her hips and pulled her against him and she felt the stubble on his face against the skin of her belly. After a moment Klein let go and walked to the end of the bed and knelt down, still trying to hide from her the emotion on his face. He hauled the bed aside and pulled up a board. A minute later he held up an old Jack Daniels bottle filled with clear liquid.

'Best in the big house,' he said. He grinned, back in control. 'Doherty's Legendary Poteen. IRA guy, gun runner, brewed this up years ago. This must be the last of it.'

He stood up and walked past her to the door.

'Come on,' he said. 'We've got a lot to celebrate.'

As she looked him in the eyes her heart squeezed. 'Yes,' she said. 'We have. I'll be along in a minute.'

Klein twisted his lips into a grotesque shape and winked at her.

'What's that for?' she asked.

Klein looked hurt. 'That was my sullen sneer.'

He arched one eyebrow. Devlin burst out laughing.

'Wet between the legs yet?'

Devlin, still laughing, made a circle with her thumb and forefinger and held it up before Klein's face.

'I know,' he said. 'I know.'

He opened the door and left.

Devlin got dressed and stuck the gun into the rear right-hand pocket of her Levis. She left her shirt tails hanging over the butt. Then she blew out the candles and went downstairs. On the way she passed Gimp Cotton hobbling down the steps on his plaster cast. His swollen, tattooed face twitched into what he probably imagined was an endearing smile. She gave him a wide berth.

'All hands to the pumps, eh, Doc?' he called after her.

Devlin ignored him and went into the sick bay office. It was empty. She cut through into the shower room and stopped. The door to the dispensary was open. There Klein, Coley, Wilson and Galindez stood around the far end of the long lab bench drinking Doherty's poteen from a variety of pharmaceutical flasks and specimen jars. Vinnie Lopez's head popped into view, his emaciated face smiling as he held out his glass for a refill. As she watched Klein leaned over and said something into Wilson's ear and Wilson laughed a big deep laugh and Klein punched him lightly in his bandaged belly and laughed with him. Then Coley pointed at Klein and said something with 'this white muthafucka' in it and Klein responded with something else that included '. . . looks like ten pounds of shit in a five-pound bag . . .' and they all laughed, even the dour and quiet Galindez. As Coley recharged their glasses Devlin found herself crying again: because she loved these guys. All of them. These fucking men, demented one and all, incomprehensible, savage and tormented and profane, and laughing like crazy fools, a ship of fools adrift on violent seas. She loved them. And as they raised their glasses together she turned away and hid behind the door so that she might not spoil their moment with her tears.

Footsteps approached the shower room. She retreated further behind the door and scrubbed her face on her shirt sleeve. Galindez came in without seeing her and with his back towards her unbuttoned his flies and pissed in the wash basin opposite the showers. Devlin breathed quietly. She noticed that Galindez's hair was scorched down to his scalp. He finished pissing, buttoned himself and washed his hands. As he turned, looking for a towel, he saw her and started.

'Doctor Devlin.' His dark face flushed with blood. 'Excuse me. Coley said this was the place to . . .'

'I'm the one should apologise. Please. It's okay.'

She smiled, stupidly she felt. Galindez wiped his hands on his shirt. The handle of a screwdriver stuck out from his belt.

'I owe you another apology,' he said, 'for leaving you in danger.'

'That was my fault.'

He shook his head. 'I broke regulations. I'll report it all . . .'

His voice trailed off into an unspoken, 'if we ever get out of here.'

'When no one came for me I was afraid you'd been killed,' she said. 'I'm glad you're okay.'

Galindez nodded towards the laughter next door. 'They've already toasted you three times. Wilson reckons you should have your own crew.' He smiled and raised his hand in a flourish. 'And Klein calls you the Warrior Queen.'

This time she felt her face flush. At the same time she could hardly breathe.

'They're waiting for you.'

She reflexly jabbed her fingers through her hair. 'I need to wash my face,' she said. Why was she such a dork?

Galindez shook his head. 'You can't imagine what it means

to them, you being here. Of course they'd rather you were safe and sound somewhere but . . .'

'I wouldn't be anywhere else on earth.'

Galindez looked at her with his black eyes. He hesitated, then pulled a folded sheet of paper from his pocket. He handed it to her.

'If I don't make it, and you do. To my wife. If you could . . .'

'Surely.'

Devlin took the letter. Her hand trembled as she put it in her pocket.

'Thank you. With your permission.'

Galindez offered her his arm. Devlin's stomach fluttered and she stepped forward and took it. They walked through into the dispensary.

A ragged cheer and a burst of clapping greeted them as they emerged. As they walked the length of the room Devlin grinned foolishly through blurred vision. Klein opened his arms.

'Is this the face that launched a thousand ships, and felled the topless towers of Ilium?'

'Fuck you, Klein.'

She punched him in the chest and Klein fell against her, his arms around her neck.

'Give her a drink, Frogman!'

A 200ml test tube two-thirds full of clear liquor was thrust into her hand. Klein unwrapped himself and kept one arm round her waist. She braced herself and took a slug of Doherty's brew. On the way down it was as smooth as a single malt. She waited for it to blow her away but when it hit her empty stomach it sent a warm tingle rippling through her limbs. There was a strange, caramel after-taste. She looked at Coley.

'Sweet potatoes?' she said.

Coley nodded. 'This woman is everything you say she is, Klein.'

'Let's hear a toast, Devlin,' said Wilson.

There were calls of approval and a silence descended on the crew. Devlin's head was already swimming a little from the alcohol. She looked at Klein an inch away and he nodded, his eyes flickering up and down her face. She looked at Coley, who was watching her gravely, and Wilson, who winked, and Galindez, standing quietly by the door. Finally she looked at Vinnie Lopez, sitting on a chair to preserve his strength and looking from one to the other of the older cons with a young man's awe. His skin was like parchment, and over his ribs and clavicles it was almost transparent.

'My toast is to Vinnie,' she said.

Lopez's face contorted with horror. 'No way, man.' He hauled himself to his feet. 'You can't do that! You can't waste your fucken toast on a fucken scumbag!'

There was a murmur of reprobation.

'You're right,' said Devlin. 'You're a scumbag.'

Vinnie wavered on unsteady legs. He glanced at Klein for understanding. Devlin pulled herself away from Klein, because she couldn't say this while he was touching her, and she wanted to say it. She took a breath and looked at Vinnie.

'You're a worthless scumbag, shitting your life away in the toilet of the world,' she said. 'But this man came back when he didn't have to.'

She pointed at Klein, but she didn't look at him.

'He doesn't know why. But something inside him does, and so do I. It's because . . .'

She paused as she felt her voice breaking up. They were waiting. She pulled it back together.

'It's because only if the most worthless shitting scumbag in the world is worth everything – everything – are any of the rest of us worth anything at all.'

She felt Klein's arm loop round her waist and pull her hip against his. She still couldn't look at him.

'So my toast is to Vinnie Lopez. And all you other fucken scumbags.'

There was a pause and for a second she was convinced that she'd said something appallingly inept. Then Galindez raised his glass.

'Scumbags,' he said.

'Scumbags.' Coley's voice reverberated with feeling.

'Scumbags,' said Wilson.

Klein clinked his glass against hers. 'Scumbags.'

Glasses clinked all round and they drank. There was a sombre silence as each of them retreated for a moment into his own thoughts.

Then Lopez said, 'The toast was for me too, you faggots, not just the fucken scumbags.'

The silence broke into laughter and jeers.

'She might be fool 'nough to waste a toast on you but we sure as hell ain't.'

'Fuck you, Coley, you black fuck.'

Devlin felt Klein's mouth near her ear.

'Love you,' he said.

Before she could look at him there was a crash and a whomping explosion from the ward. Glasses clattered to the floor. Galindez span through the door. Wilson grabbed the poteen bottle. Klein kissed her on the cheek and was gone. She followed them into the corridor. The wooden door shook as something crashed into it from the other side. Through the gate to the ward she saw the dancing light of flames then came another explosion and a flash, and close on its heels another. Before she could get into the ward Coley's big belly shoved her from behind and sent her down the corridor towards the stairs.

'*Go!*'

Coley dived through the flames now billowing from the gate. In each of his ploughman's fists he gripped one of the steel bars dislodged earlier from the windows. Vinnie Lopez hobbled across the corridor and plunged after him.

Devlin was alone.

The door juddered with frenzied blows.

Devlin pulled the gun from her pocket, cocked the hammer and walked back up the corridor and into the ward.

Inside pools of flaming gasoline threw up clouds of oily smoke, and amidst the smoke and flame men fought each other like wild animals. Up and down the aisle between the beds, pinned to bloody mattresses, beneath the gaping window frames where the foemen scrambled through, men slashed and kicked and coshed and battered each other in a struggle without quarter.

Wilson smashed the bottle across a bearded face and rammed the jagged stump of glass into the man's crotch. As the man doubled over Wilson tipped him into a pool of fire. The alcohol in his beard caught light and he squirmed across the floor with his head wreathed in flame.

Galindez raised his arm to block a crowbar and she heard his bones crack as he stepped in, sharpened screwdriver rising, and with three frenzied thrusts perforated the guy's gut.

An inmate in hospital pyjamas grabbed a man in blues round the knees and took him down and Deano Baines fell on him with a pair of scissors, punching holes through his chest. Then someone split Deano's skull and Klein grabbed the guy's head from behind and snapped his spine and snatched the meat cleaver from his hand. And two guys, with knife and chain, leapt from the windows and came at Klein together, and he took the one with the knife first, blasting a kick into his bladder so the knifeman bodily left the floor and crashed into a bed. The other's swinging chain missed Klein's bobbing head but ripped across his shoulder. Bleeding flesh gaped through his torn shirt. Klein half-stepped and kicked the chainman's legs from under him, bearing down, roaring, the cleaver in his hand rising and falling above the chainman's flailing arms to carve away his scalp and one ear and one whole side of his face which hung in an obscene flap from his exposed and bloody teeth. The knifeman staggered back in and his blade pierced Klein's bicep from one side to the other and the cleaver clattered to the floor. Before he could feel the pain Klein backfisted the cocksucker in the face and ruptured his nose. Like a dancer Klein grabbed the guy's wrist and whirled him into an arm lock and bar and cracked the elbow asunder across his knee. Then he took the guy's knife off him, and showed him the blade, and plunged it down behind the left clavicle bone and into the mediastinum. Devlin turned away.

She saw Galindez go down in a curled ball as two cons showered him with blows from stumps of timber. Then Reuben Wilson darted in and let go with the fastest five-punch combination Devlin had ever seen: left hooks to the liver and neck, right overhand bomb to the head, another left to the balls, and a final blurred right uppercut to the chin that extinguished the con's nervous system. But as the last punch landed Wilson spasmed forward as something popped inside him and the second con axed a length of two-by-four across the back of his skull and Wilson fell to his face beside Galindez, groping the floor with shuddering arms. As Coley raised his cudgels to take the guy out Horace Tolson grabbed the steel bars and plucked them from Coley's grip. Lopez flung his frail body against Tolson's monstrous bulk, a scalpel darting for his throat, and Tolson swatted him aside like a bug. As Coley turned to face him Tolson brought the bars of steel down on Coley's collar bones and battered him to his knees. Coley's arms hung limply by his sides. Tolson raised the bars again. Klein flung the knife and charged after it. The blade thunked into Tolson's breastbone and dropped out. Devlin found herself looking at Tolson down the barrel of the gun. Before she could fire Klein tore into him, his right-hand fingers plunging into Tolson's eyes, his forearms locking around his neck, his knee pumping frenziedly in and out of Tolson's groin and belly. Tolson, his eyes hanging out down his cheeks by the strings, dropped the bars and wrapped his huge arms round Klein's body and heaved. Klein arced backwards as his ribs crackled like stale breadsticks and his spine threatened to snap. Tolson's massive neck was too strong for Klein. The giant threw his head back and bellowed with the rage and pain of his blindness. Klein's arms fell limp as Tolson jerked him savagely from side to side and Devlin couldn't shoot for fear of hitting Klein and she ran over the sprawling bodies to reach him. Then Vinnie Lopez jumped on Tolson's back, his legs wrapped round Tolson and Klein both, and the three of them waltzed and staggered down the smoking aisle, a grotesque mutant life form with three screaming mouths. Vinnie's hand coiled round Tolson's neck. A scalpel glinted. Then a red tide cascaded down over Klein as Tolson's throat parted, his severed trachea bubbling in the flood as one last furious howl escaped from his lungs and the mutant toppled in a long slow parabola to the floor.

From the yard came a ripple of gunfire and a series of dull thuds. A cloud of vapour erupted outside the windows. A convict silhouetted in one of the broken frames jerked and screamed and toppled from view. A blinding pain threw Devlin's head to one side and she heard the word 'bitch' and a fist smashed into her belly. She staggered into the wall. There was warm salt on her lips, blood streaming from her onto her shirt. She recovered her balance and through the smoke saw Gimp Cotton stumping on past her in his cast, his tattoos writhing in a spasm of hate. Fixed in his sights was Earl Coley, who was lumbering to his feet with his useless arms, his back to Cotton. The Gimp's hand slid into Coley's pocket from behind and whipped out his keys. He threw them across the room to the con with the two-by-four. Klein struggled to haul himself from under Tolson's corpse. Gimp spun Coley round and stabbed him in the belly.

'You fat nigger fuck! You fat nigger fuck!'

On each 'fuck' Gimp stabbed him again and Coley just stood staring at him without blinking and wouldn't back off. Devlin lunged, stumbling through the flames. A gas bomb landed at her feet in a fountain of blinding smoke, a blast of heat against her leg. She hurdled it, reeled on.

'You fat nigger fuck.'

Devlin swiped a handful of tears and blood from her eyes and shoved the muzzle of the gun into Cotton's ear. Cotton started to turn, his hate turning in an instant into panic. Devlin squeezed the trigger and blew his brains out. There was more gunfire outside. Coley started to fall. Suddenly Klein was beside him, taking his arm across his shoulder, squinting in the gas. Through the ward gate Devlin saw the con fumbling at the lock with Coley's keys. She pointed the gun at him and fired. The con ducked as splinters exploded from the door into his cheek. Devlin ran towards him. Her foot caught a sprawled leg and she fell on her hands, the gun skittering towards the gate. She dived after the gun, grabbed it, up on her knees, her feet, her lungs were scorching, through the gate, the con had the key in the lock, was twisting it. As Devlin put the gun to his head and shot him the door burst inwards and sent her reeling down the corridor. She threw out a hand and grabbed the doorframe of the dispensary and held herself up. She blinked desperately to clear her vision.

Through the wooden door came Bubba Tolson. Under his arm ducked a hairless, blistered waif with a single glittering eye.

'Hope your cornhole's tight, Doc!'

Blue-shirted convicts loomed in the hallway behind them. Her vision blurred over again. Lopez staggered blindly from the ward and bumped into Bubba. Bubba grabbed hold of Vinnie's face with one hand and stove the back of his skull in against the wall. As Vinnie hit the floor Devlin turned and ran.

'Bring her back to papa, Bubba!'

A crashing, heavy-footed gait echoed behind her. She slipped and stumbled her way up the first flight of stairs, her breath whistling through raw lungs inflamed by gas. The gate to Travis ward, locked, anxious faces yelling inside. Heavy steps on the stairs. The corridor. Her eyes blurred again. Up ahead: the door. The keys. She dug in her pocket and pulled out the two keys, forced her brain to remember to choose the right one. She threw her shoulder into the door, it opened, she was through. Shut the door and lock it, she told herself. Charging footfalls, a bearded red face, she slammed the door on it. The door exploded back into her. She fell back on the steps, scrambling up the narrow stairs on her ass as Bubba sprawled below her, his thick fingers groping for her ankle. She twisted over and sprinted upwards. She swopped the keys in her hands. The gate above was open. She went through, swung it shut. She inserted the key into the lock, turned it, prayed. The tumblers clicked into place. She glimpsed a fist coming through the bars.

Her brain cut out.

She woke up on the floor, dazed. She turned. Bubba had his hand through the bars of the gate and was turning the key. He must have punched her out for a second. As Bubba pushed the door open Grauerholz appeared behind him. Devlin climbed to her feet. She still had the gun in her hand, down by her side. Bubba lumbered down the ward towards her. Devlin blinked and backed away. She was still concussed. She had two bullets left. Or one. She couldn't remember if she'd heard the click of the blank. No, two. Bubba got closer. Enormous poundage. Only a head shot would stop him. She stopped backing away and concentrated on not firing until she knew she wouldn't miss.

'Ain't gonna shoot Old Bubba with my gun are ya, Doc?'

She ignored Grauerholz's wheedling voice. Bubba looked

at the gun in her hand and slowed. Grauerholz sneaked up behind him.

'She ain't gonna use it, Bub. Look at her eyes. Look at them tits. Mmm!'

Bubba stretched his hands out towards her and speeded up again. At two paces Devlin cocked and raised the gun and shot him through the forehead. Bubba took another step and she felt his hands clamp onto her breasts, pushing her backwards. The light went out in his dull eyes and he exhaled a last foul breath into her face. Her back crashed into the wall and Bubba's face flopped onto her shoulder. Over his back she saw one frantic eye in a blistered face, the other eye moving underneath its glued lid. Bubba fell into a heap at her knees. She felt a sharp pain in her wrist, brutally twisting her fingers.

Grauerholz stepped away from her holding her gun in his left hand. He wiped his nose on the crudely bandaged stump of his right.

'Now,' he said and giggled. 'Let me see ya take them panties off.'

Two choices flashed through her mind: humour him or humiliate him. She heard a sound on the stairs. The choirboy in Grauerholz made her mind up for her.

'Why, what you gonna do, Hector? Fuck me with your stump?'

Grauerholz blinked and stepped back.

Behind him Klein appeared in the gateway. He was limping and his eyes were shot with blood. In his hand was a steel bar. He started painfully down the aisle.

'It'd feel a whole lot better than your stubby little dick,' sneered Devlin.

She stepped over Bubba's corpse towards him and Grauerholz backed off another pace.

'Come on. Hector. Let me see that cute little dick. Mmm!'

Grauerholz licked his lips nervously. 'You sure got a bad mouth on you fo' a doctah.'

Klein hadn't made a sound but suddenly Grauerholz stepped to the side and turned. He pointed the gun at Klein's chest. Klein froze. Grauerholz stared at Klein as if a ghost had walked in. Klein nodded towards the revolver in Grauerholz's fist.

'I gonna have to take that away from you again, Hector?' said Klein.

Grauerholz's lips quivered and Devlin thought he was going to shoot Klein on the spot. Maybe that was Klein's intention, to take the bullet. In the space of a second a thousand possible interventions raced through her brain, a thousand phrases that might swing Grauerholz's attention back to her – or by the same token make him pump the trigger. On instinct she chose silence. The endless second stretched out into two. Then three. Then Grauerholz giggled. He glanced back at Devlin.

'Look who's here, Doc. Mus' be my lucky day.'

Klein laughed. 'You looked in a mirror recently?' He clutched his ribs and groaned and staggered two steps forward.

'Cut that shit.'

Grauerholz cocked the revolver and Klein froze. She could see his eyes judging the distance. It was still fifteen feet.

'I'm gonna shoot you in the gut, Klein. Then while you lyin' there laughin' an' shit, you can watch me shoot yo' girl-friend in the cunt.'

Klein's body relaxed and she knew he was going to move and she knew that if he charged him Grauerholz would pump the trigger more than once.

'The gun's empty, Hector,' she said. 'No more bullets. Bubba got the last.'

He giggled at her. 'I may have a stubby little dick but I ain't a fool.'

She started casually towards him. 'Take your time, Klein, and finish him,' she said. 'The gun is empty.'

Grauerholz squeezed the trigger and the hammer snapped down with a bright, empty click. Klein walked towards him without rushing. Grauerholz looked at the gun then grinned at Devlin stupidly. He started to back away from them.

'Well whaddya know,' said Grauerholz. 'You got me.' He shrugged and put the gun against the side of his head beneath his ear. 'Guess it ain't my day after all,' he said.

Then Grauerholz pulled the trigger and blew away the lower half of his jaw.

He staggered, then caught his balance. His one eye wobbled, staring down in disbelief at the smoking gun in his hand.

'No,' said Devlin. 'I guess it ain't.'

Grauerholz dropped the gun and fell forward on his face and lay gurgling with what was left of his tongue. There was a clang as Klein dropped the steel bar and bent forward in pain. She went over to him and put a supporting arm round his waist.

'Lucky I got here in time,' he gasped. 'If you'd fucked Hector Grauerholz I really would've started to get jealous.'

There was a clattering of feet on the stairs and a pair of rifle barrels jutted through the bars either side of the gate.

'Klein? Is that you, you smart son of a bitch?'

Captain Cletus came through the gate. He saw Devlin and did a double take.

'Jesus.'

Klein straightened up. 'Where the fuck have you been?' he said.

'Watching a Doris Day picture,' growled Cletus. 'You okay, Doctor Devlin?'

She nodded.

'We'd known you were here we'd've got you out hours ago. I'm very sorry.'

Cletus ripped open one of the pockets covering the front of his suit and pulled out a sealed paper bag. He tore the bag and produced a sterile gauze dressing and handed it to Devlin. For a moment she didn't realise what it was for. Cletus gestured to her cheek. 'Your face,' he said.

She'd forgotten she was bleeding. She took the dressing and held it to her cheek. There was no pain.

'Thank you, Captain.'

'Where's mine?' said Klein.

'Fuck you, Klein. You're lookin' at ten years in seg for this.'

He winked at Devlin, then glanced at Tolson and the charred, gurgling figure on the floor. He motioned to his men.

'Get rid of this shit.'

As they dragged the bodies away Cletus glanced around the deserted, cobwebbed ward. 'Christ,' he said. 'Let's get outta here.'

As they left Devlin palmed the key from the lock.

THIRTY-TWO

WHILE THE GUARDS put out the fire in Crockett Ward, Devlin and Klein helped evacuate the men from Travis. Watched by riflemen in the west tower a thin stream of refugees wended across the yard in the beams of the searchlights towards the main gates. On the steps of the infirmary as they left Klein and Devlin found Earl Coley, sitting, watching his patients go. His whites were covered by a thick apron of blood and he breathed in short gasps. His left arm was buttoned in the crude sling of the front of his shirt. Clasped tight in his right fist was the rolled-up copy of the green journal. Klein looked at him. Coley blinked wearily.

'That the last of 'em?' asked Coley.

Klein nodded. 'You should've been the first.'

'They needed the stretchers. Thought I'd wait, make sure they all okay.'

Coley glanced at Devlin, at her bloody face, and Klein knew he'd been waiting for them too.

'You make it to the gate or do I have to carry your black ass?' said Klein.

Coley let out his breath very slowly to control a spasm of pain. He shook his head. 'I ain't been across that goddamn yard in years. Couldn't find no reason to make th' effort.' He grinned through another spasm. 'Think I'll just set here for a while.'

Klein knew he couldn't move Coley against that ornery will, especially now he was dying. Especially now that Coley knew he was. Before Klein could start fighting about it Devlin pointed at the far wall beyond the cellblocks.

'Looks like dawn,' she said.

Klein looked hard. There was the merest lightening of the indigo sky.

Coley narrowed his eyes in the direction of her arm. 'I do believe you right,' he said.

'See it a whole lot better without that wall,' said Devlin.

She and Coley looked at each other. Whatever it was that passed between them Klein couldn't follow it, but after a moment Coley turned to him and said, 'Well? Is a helpin' hand too much for a old guy with broken arms to expect these days?'

They got him to his feet and Coley gritted his teeth and they shuffled together along the concrete path that wound in the shadow of the main wall. Three times they had to stop while Coley dealt with a spasm and each time Klein thought he was going to die, but Coley cussed and fussed like the fucking old woman he was and they continued. And eventually they shuffled through the main gates and into the tunnel.

Inside a milling chaos of wounded and sick men were watched over by a number of confused, heavily-armed guards. Three ambulances were on the scene and paramedics were working on the injured. Up ahead the sliding steel door was open and a fourth ambulance was nosing its way through. Beyond it the final set of huge iron studded gates were tight shut.

'I stop now I ain't never gonna start agin,' wheezed Coley.

Devlin spotted Galindez smoking one of Cletus's cigarettes and nodding as the Captain spoke to him. She ran across the reception area while Klein and Coley went on. Coley was leaning heavily on Klein's arm now and his breathing was rattling in his chest. Klein felt a terrible need to tell Coley all the things he'd never told him, a terrible haste that at the same time felt unseemly.

'I've been meanin' to tell you, Frog . . .'

'Don't,' said Coley. 'I know. I know.' He lacked the strength to lift his head and look at Klein. He grinned at the concrete ahead of him instead. 'I'm a fucken old woman, right?'

Klein swallowed. 'Right,' he said.

They passed through the open steel door and Klein glanced over his shoulder. In reception he saw Devlin glaring at Cletus and mouthing something Klein was glad he couldn't hear. Cletus scratched the back of his neck with a pained look on his face, then nodded and spoke into his radio. Devlin started back towards Klein. Klein turned back. The wooden gates were twenty feet away.

'Got somethin' to tell you too,' said Coley. 'Might matter.'

'What's that?'

'Nev Agry's got the virus,' said Coley. 'He's positive.'

'What?' said Klein.

'Had me test him, good five years ago, long before you came up.'

'You never told me.'

'Wasn't your fucken business.'

'Is Claude positive too?'

'Far as I know he never been tested.'

As Klein digested this an electric motor droned and the gates in front of them started to creak open towards them. Devlin caught up with them. As the gates opened the sound of a chorus of birds drifted in on a sweet-smelling breeze. Damn, thought Klein, there were birds out there after all, and not gulls either. Coley quickened his pace, his head leaning forward. Three steps later they were outside.

They were outside.

The gates were at the tip of the southern apex of the hexagonal wall. From here there was an uninterrupted view across the bottomlands, to the trees lining the bend of the Green River. Above the horizon beyond the trees a strip of pale red sky shaded into purple and grey and finally into the indigo blackness over their heads.

'Red sky at morning,' breathed Coley. 'Goddamn.' He shook off Klein's arm. 'Think I'll take me a walk.'

Klein let go of him and watched with his heart in his throat as his friend took three unsteady paces towards the rising sun. As Coley took a fourth his leg gave way beneath him and his big, lumbering frame crumpled into the ground. Klein and Devlin rushed over.

'Sit me up,' wheezed Coley.

They lifted him up between them. Coley buckled with pain. He was panting now, barely conscious. His eyes struggled to focus on Devlin. He raised the journal still clutched in his fist and pressed it into her hand. Its pages were bloody.

'Like mah fam'ly t' know, I ain't just a . . .' He broke off as he threw up a mouthful of blood and shuddered and heaved for air.

Tears tumbled unchecked down Devlin's face. 'I'll find them,' she said, 'I promise.'

Coley looked at her and smiled and nodded. Devlin glanced at Klein. Then she bent forward and kissed Coley on his bloody lips and stood up and walked back towards the gates. Klein and Coley were left alone, looking at the sun.

'Pea Vine Special callin' all aboard,' said Coley.

He grabbed Klein's hand and squeezed.

'Glad we both of us catchin' it th' same day,' he said.

Coley's face grew misty before him and Klein nodded. He couldn't speak. His jaws ached with clenching them. Coley's yellow, bloodshot eyes blinked their long slow blink for the last time. He took a great breath through flared nostrils.

'Damn, smells good,' he said.

Then the great black rock that was his head fell forward and the Frogman was dead.

When the sounds in Klein's chest grew quiet and still he laid Coley out on the ground and stood up. A convoy of vehicles was rumbling up the road towards the prison. National Guard units. Klein didn't much care any more. He looked down at Coley, the craggy face restful in death, then he turned away and went back through the gates.

Devlin was waiting for him.

'Thanks,' he said.

She nodded. The tunnel was swarming with guards, yelling at them and at each other as the National Guard trucks roared towards the gates. They walked back into the chaotic reception hall and Reuben Wilson grabbed Klein's arm. Behind Wilson stood Victor Galindez.

'Cletus is sendin' the army in, man.' Wilson held one arm across his midriff and stood slightly bent forward. There was blood clotted into his hair.

Klein looked at Galindez. 'Cletus? Where's Hobbes?'

'Relieved of duties,' said Galindez. 'Ill health.'

'Great. Why the army?'

'Stokely Johnson got Agry and fifty or sixty his diehards bottled up in D block. They gettin' ready burn 'em down. I know Stoke.' Wilson tapped a finger to his temple. 'Ain't nothin' up there but smoke. He'll do it.'

'If I tried really hard,' said Klein. 'I could probably care less. Just.'

'Agry has taken all the hostages in there with him,' said Galindez. 'Twelve men.'

'Then I'm sorry for them,' said Klein.

'Johnson won't back down 'less Agry does,' said Wilson, 'and even then only maybe. That muthafucker did some things.'

'I know,' said Klein. 'I was there.'

Galindez said, 'If Johnson burns down D block Cletus will have no choice. He'll have to send in the guard.'

'Be a bloodbath, man,' said Wilson.

Klein said, 'What's this got to do with me?'

'I can maybe talk Stoke down,' said Wilson, 'but only if Agry surrenders first.'

'You're not going back in there,' said Klein.

Wilson looked at him. 'My people, Klein.' He glanced at Devlin. 'Or maybe they just scumbags.'

Klein didn't speak. As he realised what was coming he looked at Devlin for moral support. She stared back at him with fear then turned to Galindez and Wilson.

'I don't get it,' she said. 'Agry has no more reason to listen to Klein than he does to either of you.'

Wilson read the distress in her eyes and nodded. 'Guess you're right.' He glanced at Klein.

As the meaning of the legacy Earl Coley had unwittingly bequeathed him dawned on Klein's brain he knew that Wilson saw it in his face. And he knew that there was no way out.

'That's not strictly true,' said Klein. 'I don't know if I ever told you this, but Coley was a fucking old woman.'

Devlin looked at him with dread. Klein nodded to Wilson. 'I'll be with you in a minute.'

Wilson glanced at Devlin. Guilt flitted across his features as he saw the anguish in her face. He and Galindez left.

'You really think you can make a difference?'

'Before he died Coley told me that Agry is HIV positive.'

Klein sighed and rubbed his hands over his face. The raw nerve-ends in his palms no longer registered. His ribs and back were a blurred mass of pain. The knife wound in his calf had turned stiff and tight. And he was tired.

He said, 'If Agry's people knew about that I don't think they'd be so keen to go down with him.'

Devlin touched his face and she was with him. She was with

him. Looking at her bloodshot eyes and dirty, knife-scarred face Klein reckoned she'd never looked more beautiful.

'Don't speak,' he said.

She kissed him and he kissed her back. After a moment he found himself grinning stupidly and she pulled back and looked at him.

'What's wrong?'

'You just gave me a hard-on,' he said.

And Devlin grinned too. 'Bring it back in one piece. Even if you don't bring anything else.'

Then Klein collected Reuben Wilson and they walked out through the giant wooden gates and back across the yard towards the prison.

THIRTY-THREE

As HE AND Wilson limped towards the entrance to General Purposes, Klein saw three white cons hanging by their necks from the upper bars of the gate. Closer still, Klein saw that one of them was naked from the waist down and had had his cock and balls hacked off. Wilson avoided Klein's eyes. They entered the wing.

This time the lights were on and had Klein chosen to inspect the carnage and detritus, he could have done so more closely than the last time he made the walk, with Hank Crawford on his back. But he did not so choose. He kept his eyes straight ahead and Wilson at his left shoulder. They passed a bunch of blacks and Latinos squabbling dangerously with each other. As Wilson walked by some of them murmured his name. At the far end of the corridor a mass of men milled around the central watchtower. As Wilson and Klein got closer the frenzied, excited yells of the men sounded familiar to Klein's ears. Since the previous afternoon the identities of the men had changed and so had the colour of their skins, but the impulses remained the same. Klein remembered Boltzmann's Constant: disorder always increases in a closed system. He wondered what the converse was. Now that total disorder had triumphed, what was next?

As more and more men recognised Wilson and the word

spread ahead of them there was a ripple of fresh excitement. Faces grinned, called out greetings, fists were raised in salute. Where Klein caught a man's eyes, and he tried not to, he found anger and suspicion directed against him. They reached the atrium and the crowd parted to form a passage for them. Above their head arced the glass dome and its encircling balcony. The lights in the atrium weren't working but the wasted light falling from the gates of the six radiating blocks provided illumination. There was a strong smell of fuel. A few yards from the sallyport to D block were several drums, buckets of heavy dark liquid, one of the stainless steel cooking vats from the kitchen: all full of fuel oil. Throughout the crowd, here and there, men were smoking joints and cigarettes. If they didn't incinerate themselves first, they were going to pay Agry's men back in their own coin. The gate to D block itself was shut and behind it Agry's crew had heaped mattresses up to chest height against the bars. As Klein watched he saw the men inside flinging water onto the mattresses by the cup and bowl and bucket. Their faces were pinched with the resolution of the doomed.

'Stoke!'

Klein turned at Wilson's shout. A space opened in the crowd. Sitting on a swivel chair lashed in place on the back of a laundry trolley in the gateway to B block was Stokely Johnson. His nose and face around the bullet wound were hideously swollen. Above the swelling his eyes glittered with malice. He saw Wilson and the malice moderated, but not by much. Klein stopped at the edge of the circle and Stokely looked at him briefly without reacting. Wilson held out his hand. Stokely nodded and gave it a short hard squeeze.

'Got the muthafuckas on their knees, Stoke,' said Wilson.

Stokely nodded again. He opened his mouth and spoke slowly.

'Back gate D is sealed. They got nowhere to run.'

'Where'd you get the gas?'

'Tank in the generator shed.'

'You done good, man.'

Stokely nodded. There was a pause. The men in the crowd watched expectantly. Wilson took a step back from the trolley. 'I want you to let 'em go, Stoke,' said Wilson.

The crowd muttered. They waited. Stokely shook his head.

'We got most of the ofays stuck in A, shittin' out their lives. I gave 'em a chance to come out and stand trial. That's mo' than they gave us. Only muthafuckas left in D is them that wants to die.'

There was a bellow of support from the mob. Klein felt the hairs on his arms prickling. Wilson waited for the noise to die down.

'They got the National Guard out there.'

'Fuck the National Guard.'

'You try burn down the screws Agry got hostage in there they'll ice our guys on the rear gate like that.' Wilson made a brief jerking-off gesture with a hollowed fist. 'They'll spring Agry's people to save the hostages, then they'll come in here and put the fire out with our blood. Ain't a single peckerwood in them army trucks out there who ain't spent his whole life dreamin' 'bout this. Niggers in a barrel and a reason to kill.'

Stokely Johnson raised his voice: 'We ain't scared of dyin'! But 'less we make a stand now, no one ever know who we are!'

Wilson walked to the edge of the mob and grabbed a razor from someone's hand. He slashed the tape around his belly and ripped it open with both hands. He displayed the huge scar running from his sternum to his crotch.

'*This* is who I am!' said Wilson.

There were a number of gasps and exclamations.

'You all know where I come from.'

Murmurs of assent.

'Those muthafuckas burned us down. They beat us down.

They pissed in our faces when we was chained on our fuckin' knees. And they'll do it again tomorrow, and nex' week, and nex' year and the year after. I know. I know it better than you all. But they're only men. We just gotta be more men than they are.'

He turned back to Stokely.

'That's who we are.'

Stokely's eyes scanned the men's faces around him. They came to rest on Klein. This time a grudging recognition flickered in them. Klein looked back.

'You gonna send the Doc in there?' said Stokely.

'He can get Agry's guys to surrender. To us. They started this. We finish it. We finish it right, the way they don't expect us to. The way they don't know how to. We let 'em walk out.'

Wilson paused and looked around the circle of faces. They were his again. He nodded to Stokely.

'You want to go in later and cut off Agry's dick I'll come and hold him down for you.'

It was enough. Stokely nodded. And Klein found the faces turning towards him. Thanks, guys. He glanced over to D block. White heads were craning over the barricade, trying to listen. He turned back.

'Pull your people off the rear sallyport,' said Klein.

Wilson nodded and beckoned someone over, gave him instructions. Klein walked over to D block.

A tall, rangy face in wire-rimmed glasses appeared over the piled mattresses. If it was possible to be pleased at all at that moment Klein was pleased to see Tony Shockner. Maybe he wouldn't have to talk to Agry at all, or about his fucking infection. Shockner looked anxious but pleased to see him too.

'Tony.'

'Klein,' said Shockner. 'What's the score, man?'

'You're about to get wiped out in the fourth quarter.'

Shockner nodded. 'I reckon. We got any plays left?'

'Concede,' said Klein. 'Wilson will let you through, screws first.'

'We trust him?'

'You trusted Agry,' said Klein. 'Can't do any worse.'

Shockner looked at him through the bars for a long time and Klein saw the debate raging in the younger man's head.

'Semper fi,' Shockner said.

Klein thought of his father and Agry's perversion of the Marine Corps motto suddenly angered him.

'Semper fi my balls,' said Klein. 'Agry fucked you all. He doesn't give a shit for you or Claude or anyone else.'

'Nev's a hard ass and maybe he was wrong 'bout this, but he's a right guy. He'd take a fall for any of us.'

'Agry's dying,' said Klein.

Shockner looked stunned.

'You understand?' said Klein. 'He's gonna die anyway. Soon. That's why he doesn't give a shit.'

'What's he dyin' of?' asked Shockner.

'Does it matter?' said Klein.

'Cancer?' said Shockner.

Looking at his face Klein realised how much Shockner needed to preserve just a little of the loyalty and admiration he'd invested in Agry. If Agry's brutish charisma had willed and battered Claude into being his wife, then Shockner was his son. Klein didn't really care what Shockner needed or believed. He just wanted to go home. He nodded.

'Yeah, the Big C. One too many Luckies,' he said. 'But remember, Semper fi's supposed to work both ways. He owes you.' Klein nodded at the pinch-faced figures hovering behind Shockner's back. 'And you owe them.'

The balance swung in Shockner's mind. He stepped back from the bars and called instructions to his men.

Klein leaned his forearms agaisnt the gate and his forehead on his arms and listened to his pulse beating through all the holes and bruises in his body. Then he thought: it's over. He could walk away and no one would stop him, not even his fucking conscience, and all of a sudden he was bone weary. He heard the damp mattresses being dragged away from the gate. He would've liked to lie down on one right then, damp or not, and sleep. Just for a while. The main gates were a long way away. His legs were too weak to walk. A little power nap and he'd be right.

He jerked awake, dazed, as the gate was wrenched open. For a few minutes or seconds he'd been out on his feet. He moved over, resting his back to the bars, as a line of ragged, bloodstained khaki uniforms emerged from D block. Grierson, Burroughs, Sandoval, Wilbur, the other hostages, glancing at him uncertainly, still fearful. Then Agry's crew started out in furtive ones and twos. They looked even more fearful, knuckles white on their weapons as they defiled towards the narrow passage that had opened through the mass of angry black faces. Klein dug his fingers into his eyes, still gritty with gas and smoke and bacteria and God knew what other shit, and rubbed them. He could do it, fuck, he'd come this far. He was the shotokan warrior. He could walk back to the main gates before collapsing into a coma. If he did it over there Devlin would be on hand to soothe him. Yeah. She'd had a tough day too but he'd had to travel farther than she had, over rougher terrain, so that was kind of fair enough. He just needed to snap out of it and start putting one foot in front of the other.

There was a gunshot.

Even that didn't make him jump. But he was awake enough for his gut to clench with nausea.

'Klein!' Agry's voice, belligerent with drink. 'Let me see you, you cocksucker!'

There was a flurry of diving bodies all around him. Klein wasn't up to that stuff any more. And it wouldn't have helped. He turned slowly and looked through the bars. Shockner's body was sprawled face down in the walkway. There was a bullet wound in his back. Klein stepped out into the gateway and held onto the frame on either side with his hands. He wanted to keep standing at least until Agry shot him.

'What's wrong, Nev? Run out of faggots to kill?'

Agry stood facing him thirty feet down the walkway. In his right hand, pointing casually at Klein, he held a heavy-looking, short barrelled automatic. Klein didn't recognise the make. In one of those stupid reveries that crossed his mind at inappropriate moments he told himself he should look into that sort of thing when he got home. Yeah. He could become a gun freak.

'Still got your little piece, Doc?' called Agry.

'No,' said Klein. 'I gave it back to Grauerholz.'

'Yeah? How is Hector?'

'It hasn't been his day. How 'bout you?'

'Me?' Agry laughed, his drunken voice echoing up into the vault. 'Well you know, Doc? I have had me a ball.'

'Enchantment strange as the blue up above,' said Klein.

Agry's face sobered. 'Yeah. I guess it was at that.'

His hand holding the automatic fell to his side. He beckoned with his other arm. 'Come on in, Doc. I'll buy you a drink.'

Before Klein could compute that he had no choice anyway he found himself walking as steadily as he could down the walkway of the wrecked cellblock. A good holocaust was just what it needed to finish the job. Agry threw his arm across Klein's shoulders. Klein managed not to fall. They strolled towards Agry's cell.

'Christ, man, you really look like you need it.' Agry's breath was saturated with bourbon.

'Thanks, Nev,' said Klein. 'It was good of you to let me get fucked up like this.'

Agry bellowed with laughter. 'You should be on stage, Klein. Say that's some kind of a kike name, ain't it?'

'Kind of.'

'Don't get me wrong, I like the kikes. All the best comedians are Jewish. Make damn good doctors too.'

Klein, the shotokan warrior, lover and hero of the Great Infirmary Siege, suddenly felt a profound depression. Agry had reduced him down to a bag of abominable clichés. From the door of Agry's cell Claude Toussaint, in red underwear, suspender belt, the works, peered out towards them.

'Hey, Honey,' called Agry. 'We got a visitor. Get some clean glasses out.'

'Is he staying for dinner?' asked Claudine.

Klein's head whirled slightly. But maybe Claude was right. Join Agry in his fantasy and you were safe. For a while. The rear sallyport creaked open a foot and a group of Agry's men, huddled at the back of the block, rushed towards it. Agry brought up his gun and fired indiscriminately three times. The men scattered and two of them fell, squirming and shouting out.

'Cocksuckers,' muttered Agry. He turned back to Claudine and smiled. 'That's real nice, honey, but I don't think we'll have time. Come on in, Klein.'

They went in and sat down around the table and Agry put a tape on. Bob Wills and the Texas Playboys swung into the intro to 'San Antonio Rose'. Claudine poured Maker's Mark into empty fruit jars. Agry offered Klein a Lucky. If Klein ever was to have a last smoke, he didn't want it to be with Agry. He shook his head.

Agry dropped the automatic on the table and swigged a gulp of liquor. He gestured towards the door.

'Those cocksuckers don't know what this is all about. But you do, don't ya, Doc?'

Klein sipped his drink. It was good, but not as good as Doherty's. The gun was a foot closer to Agry's hand than to Klein's. Across the table Claudine was closest but she wasn't looking at the gun. She stared at Klein with frantic eyes and fractionally nodded her head as if to say 'Humour the mad muthafucka.'

Klein shrugged. 'I'm not sure what you mean.'

'Let's put it this way. Look at you. You went through hell and high water, just to be with that lady of yours in the infirm'ry. Didn't even think you'd get out alive, but you had to be there. Am I right?'

Klein nodded. 'Yeah. You're right.'

Agry slapped the table with his hand. 'I knew it. We're just the goddamned same. You and me. Only guys in the whole fucken joint understand what it's about.'

> '. . . It was there I found, beside the Alamo,
> Enchantment strange as the blue up above . . .'

As Agry heard the song his eyes crinkled at the edges. His voice was getting more slurred with each gulp of whiskey. 'Love, Klein. The real thing. All this,' he waved his hand to indicate the destruction all around them. 'All this for love. She never really believed me before.' He looked at Claudine. 'Did you, babe?'

Claudine didn't dare answer. Agry stroked her cheek, turned back to Klein.

'You heard of the Taj Mahal, Doc, in India? Sure you have.'

Klein nodded.

'Well it ain't no palace or castle like most folk think. It's a love gift some guy built for his lady. It's a box of fucken chocolates. Now ain't that somethin'?'

Klein nodded again and took another sip of his drink.

'This is my Taj Mahal, for her.'

He leaned over and kissed Claudine. Klein glanced again at the gun. No way. And he could not fight Agry hand to hand. Not in the shape he was in. He had to take a chance on Claudine. Or better, Claude.

'The face that launched a thousand ships,' said Klein.

Agry pulled away from Claudine. 'Say, that's good,' said Agry. 'Real good. Kind of grand.'

'I'm glad you like it,' said Klein. 'When did you first meet, Claude?'

Claude glanced at him.

'Ain't no Claude round here,' snarled Agry.

'When?' said Klein.

'I'd been up six months,' said Claude, in his own voice. 'So it was just under four years since.'

Klein looked Agry in the eye. 'Then you already knew you had the virus.'

'What virus?' said Claude.

'Why didn't you tell her?' said Klein.

There was a long pause while Agry stared at Klein, his drunken face lurching from one emotion to another as he struggled to cope.

'He was just another long-legged nigger with lips,' blurted Agry. 'What did I care?'

He turned on Claude. 'And you were gonna run out on me, you bitch. With your fucking parole. I gave you . . .'

'Did Hobbes tell you that?' said Klein.

Agry barely looked at Klein as he backhanded him across the face. Klein plunged to the floor. The floor felt marvellous, the flagstones soft as goose down. Unconsciousness lured him with a sweet lullaby of buzzing in his ears. Above the buzzing he vaguely heard Agry bleating on in a whiney voice.

'I gave you everyfuckenthing I had, I gave you the best, I gave you my life, I made you, you bitch, and you pay me back by running out. You didn't even fucking ask . . .'

Klein was dropping off. He felt like he was trying to sleep in a fleabag motel with a noisy couple in the next room. Suddenly a piercing voice, all woman, a shriek of inchoate fury, penetrated his somnolence more effectively than the gunshot had.

'You gave me Aids you cocksucking faggot muthafuckaaa!'

The last vowel was drawn out into an incredible screech of outrage. Agry's bleating response was swamped by the sound.

'You knew! You knew and you still pumped me with your stinking jissom. For years. You faggot. You faggot.'

Klein crawled to his knees. He grabbed the bars to haul himself up. Behind him was a scraping of chairs, a bump, then the sound of Agry blubbering with remorse. Klein turned. Agry was on his knees, his hands clasped before him. Above him stood Claudine, definitely Claudine, her eyes blazing. In her hand was the fat automatic, pointed at Agry's tear-stained face.

'But I love you, Claudine!'

Claudine shot him three times in the chest. In the enclosed space the sound was deafening. Burnt cordite drifted into Klein's nostrils. And that was it. It was Claudine after all, and not Claude as he had thought, that had found the necessary rage. Claudine threw the gun onto the table and sat down, staring into space. After a moment Klein started to hear things again. And Claudine started crying. Klein went and held her head against his chest.

'The thing of it is,' said Claudine, between sobs, 'he really did. Love me. No one ever did before.'

'Yeah,' said Klein, 'it's a bitch.'

She looked up at him to see if he was serious and he shrugged and smiled.

'What the hell, Claude. Let's go before the National Guard shoot our nuts off. You still got a pair, remember?'

Claudine sniffled and wiped her nose and in a twinkle she was gone forever. Claude ripped off his red brassiere.

'Shit. Brothers see me like this they won't need the National Guard. Muthafuckas'll die laughin'.'

He started to peel off his panties and stopped, embarrassed.

'You go on,' he said. 'I'm gonna get changed.'

Klein picked up the gun and ejected the clip and jacked

the shell from the chamber. He put the ammo in his pocket and left. The block was empty. Agry's men had deserted him. In the gateway stood Wilson and three of his Bloods.

'Fuck, man, we was just about to come in and get you.'

Behind them Stokely Johnson had been wheeled up on his laundry trolley to where he could see into D. Back of Johnson the atrium was still crowded with several hundred men. Klein pulled the ammo from his pocket.

'Agry's dead,' he said. 'Your man Claude blew him away.'

He threw the ammo at Stokely's feet. Stokely's eyes hooded with grudging respect.

'I guess it's Miller Time,' said Wilson.

Klein grinned. Then something caught the periphery of his vision from above. He looked up.

'Not yet,' he said.

On the balcony that encircled the base of the glass dome Warden Hobbes came out of a door at the corner where the great walls of B and C blocks came together. Without looking down Hobbes made his way around the balcony.

'Warden!' shouted Klein. 'It's over!'

His voice was drowned out by the jeers and catcalls of the convicts. Hobbes was carrying something in his left hand, Klein couldn't see what, a briefcase maybe. At least it wasn't a machine gun. In the dim light it was hard to make out Hobbes's face. He circled the balcony until he was almost above them and stopped. Wilson held up his hands for quiet but the inmates still had a lot of anger in them aching to be vented. The yelling and jeers continued. Hobbes raised his hand and rested the case on the balcony rail: it was a black plastic two gallon container. Without speaking Hobbes unscrewed the cap and started to pour the contents over his own body.

Gasoline bounced off Hobbes's suit and showered down onto the men below. They shoved backwards out of the way, into the press of bodies. Klein felt a flutter of panic in his belly. The panic was reflected in a wave through the crowd. The catcalls changed to exclamations of fear. Hobbes was drenched in gas. Klein glanced down and noticed what some of the others had. Johnson's stockpile of fuel oil was stacked on the floor beneath where Hobbes was standing.

'Better get 'em out of here,' said Klein

Wilson raised his voice, 'We movin', muthafuckas! Every which way! Come on now!'

There was a blind surge towards the General Purposes wing.

'I said every which way! Use the block gates!'

No one seemed to hear him. At the edges a few men peeled away into the mess hall, C block, B, but most of them were caught up in the press towards the General Wing and the main gates. Wilson was sending men down D. Stokely Johnson's laundry trolley was pushed over in the crush. Stokely jumped from his chair and crashed into Klein.

'Use A,' said Klein.

As Stokely fought his way towards the gate of A block, directing men to follow him, Klein looked up at Hobbes. Hobbes had set the gas can down and was making a speech to the inmates. Amidst the tumult Klein couldn't hear a word he was saying. Hobbes all of a sudden appeared incredibly frail and old, withered inside his own skin. With his sodden, dripping clothes and his speech that nobody could hear he was a pitiful sight. Hobbes wiped his hands on a white handkerchief and dabbed his brow. Then from his inner pocket he pulled out a book of matches.

'Let's go, man,' said Wilson. 'Back down D.'

If Hobbes immolated himself now and ignited the fuel oil there were still a lot of men going to get killed or badly burned.

'*Warden!*' bellowed Klein. '*Hobbes!*'

Hobbes glanced towards him. For a moment Klein caught

a glimpse of the implacable despair carved into the warden's features, then Hobbes turned away. He ripped a match from the book.

As Klein turned to make a run for the rear gate of D he froze.

A second figure was moving along the balcony towards Hobbes.

The figure was so huge he had to stoop under the panes of the great glass dome. He dripped blood from a dozen wounds and was caked from head to toe in slime and filth. On his head was crammed a baseball cap crested with a white X.

Henry Abbott had risen from the prison's deep to join Warden Hobbes at its height.

Klein's heart stuck in his throat.

Hobbes scraped the match along the scratch paper. The match did not light. Again, again he scraped. Nothing. He ripped off another match, tried again. He turned as Henry Abbott's shadow fell across him. As the match flared Abbott reached out, as delicate as a bird, and snuffed the flame between his thumb and forefinger. Hobbes leaned backwards over the balcony in terror. Abbott took Hobbes's arm and pulled him back. Then he bent his head forward and whispered something in Hobbes's ear. Hobbes froze, staring into Abbott's face. As if hypnotised Hobbes slowly raised his hand and pulled something from the breast pocket of his jacket. A piece of paper. He opened it and glanced at it in his palm. Henry Abbott opened his arms and enfolded Hobbes into his breast and squeezed. There was no struggle. As Klein watched Hobbes's final embrace Abbott stared down at him with his bright new eyes and Klein shivered but did not look away.

When Hobbes was no longer breathing Abbott bent down and hoisted him over his shoulder, like a sack of cement. Hobbes hung there, his eyes staring. Abbott looked down at

Klein and raised his hand. Klein swallowed and raised his own hand in return. Abbott turned and walked away. From Hobbes's limp fingers the piece of paper fluttered down into the emptying atrium. Then Abbott and his burden dipped into the dark rectangle of the balcony doorway and disappeared into silence.

The evacuation was almost over. Klein walked across the atrium and picked up the folded scrap of paper that Hobbes had dropped. It was soggy with gasoline. He opened it. The gas had dissolved the ink of the writing inside into a muddy green blur. The only words Klein could make out, and only then with uncertainty, were:

'. . . sweet delight.
'. . . endless night'

Klein put the paper in his pocket and joined Wilson at the back of the queue.

The yard was crowded with convicts and the air was thick with the baying of loudhailers, one minute Captain Cletus, the next some fool Colonel in the National Guard, each giving different instructions. The main gates were barred by a line of soldiers with fixed bayonets.

'This gonna take hours,' said Wilson.

Klein nodded. The idea of a few hours' sleep on the concrete seemed like all he could ever wish for. Through the milling crowd he saw Devlin approaching. With her came Galindez, his arm in a sling, and a fresh-faced guardsman nervously clutching a nightstick. Relief came over Devlin's face as she spotted them.

'You're okay,' said Devlin.

'Go home,' replied Klein 'It's still dangerous in here.'

'You don't know where my home is,' said Devlin.

'I'll find it,' said Klein.

She nodded and smiled. 'You'd better.'

She turned to Wilson. 'I wanted to say goodbye to the Whirlwind.'

Devlin held out her hand, a little awkwardly, and Wilson shook it. Whatever it was she palmed to him, she didn't make the best of jobs of it. Klein glanced at Galindez. He was staring conspicuously in the opposite direction, at a soldier of no interest at all on the other side of the yard. The young guardsman was too busy controlling his bladder to notice anything. Wilson pulled Devlin towards him and kissed her on the cheek. She stepped back. Wilson held his hand out to Galindez. His palm was miraculously empty. Galindez shook.

'Good luck,' said Galindez. He offered his hand to Klein. 'You too.'

There was an awkward pause. Klein wanted to bed down on the concrete with Devlin, but there were more perfect settings for a love scene. Instead he kissed her on the cheek. To his astonishment, she blushed.

'I'd better go,' she said.

Klein nodded.

To Wilson she said, 'If I were you I'd consider a change of career. Being a hero's bad for your health.'

Wilson smiled. 'Maybe I'll give it some thought.' He jerked his head at Klein. 'You take care of this joker. For a white man he's a pretty cool guy.'

Goddamn. Klein felt blessed. He was a pretty cool guy after all. He pulled his shoulders back and inflated his chest, then wheezed with pain as his ribs crackled.

'Christ,' he said.

'Don't worry,' said Wilson, 'I'll give him a few more tips.'

Then Devlin squeezed Klein's hand and turned away and walked back towards the gate with Galindez and the soldier on either side of her.

Wilson and Klein watched her until they could no longer

see the sweet rolling movement of her ass and until the back of her head disappeared into the crowd.

'Damn,' said Wilson. 'My health I ain't too worried about, but my balls, man I'd forgot exactly how much pain those mothers could give me.'

'You're absolutely right,' said Klein.

Wilson pulled a pack of Camels from his pocket and shoved one in his mouth.

'You got one to spare?' said Klein.

Wilson felt inside the pack. There was one left. He gave it to Klein and they lit up. Klein inhaled.

'No matter what they say, these bastards still taste good.'

Wilson nodded in agreement. They smoked.

'Listen,' said Klein, 'there's something I been wondering about and I kind of feel better asking you about it than I would asking Devlin.'

'Oh yeah?' said Wilson, guardedly. 'What's that?'

'Well,' said Klein. 'How big, I mean, you know, in general terms, is your pecker? That is, your dick.'

Wilson looked at him. 'You really want to know?'

There was a pause.

Then Wilson smiled and Klein started laughing.

And Wilson started laughing too.

And the two of them stood in the shadow of the cellblocks, with the light of a red dawn finally cresting the high granite wall, and they laughed their fucking guts out.

And amongst all that teeming and penitent crew in the concrete prison yard, they were the only individuals who laughed.

EPILOGUE

ALL TOLD, THIRTY-TWO men perished in the great rising at Green River State Penitentiary which, for want of a single extra fatality, and to the disappointment of all who survived, made it only the second worst such riot in the annals of US penal history.

On the afternoon following the riot, the National Guard surprised no one by accidentally igniting the fuel dump in the central atrium, thus causing more serious structural damage than had the inmates themselves. After the fire was extinguished the authorities searched the prison high and low for two weeks, with tracker dogs and infra-red heat detectors. They discovered a phenomenal quantity of drugs, distilling apparatus and illegal pornography, and five decomposing corpses in a far-flung sewer conduit, but no trace of the body of Warden John Campbell Hobbes was ever found. With the eager complicity of the State Bureau of Corrections, which sought to absolve the system itself of all culpability, the press turned in a vulgar caricature of Hobbes as a corrupt and racist despot whose aberrant practices were the sole cause of the riot, and such he remains in the popular imagination.

Three hundred and forty-eight men were wounded badly enough to require hospitalisation and it remains a tribute to the paramedical and trauma services of East Texas that more men did not die.

Stokely Johnson had the bullet removed from his maxillary sinus and was transferred to Huntsville Prison. There his sentence was later extended by a total of eighty-four years for offences committed during the riot at Green River.

Hector Grauerholz also called upon the facio-maxillary surgeons to perform heroic work in the reconstruction of his lower face. They did not fail him and though Hector was left with a severe and irremediable speech impediment he was at least able to chew and swallow soft foods. He was sent to the Federal Maximum Security Facility at Marion, Illinois, where he was kept in solitary under permanent lockdown. As Hector could no longer pronounce a wide range of consonants and diphthongs the lack of conversation was no great loss. He took a creative writing course by correspondence, learned to type with his left hand and produced a novel about a gun-toting female crack-dealer called Deveraux. The novel was published to poor reviews but became a cult hit in paperback. A legendary New York novelist has mounted a campaign to get Grauerholz released to a halfway house, but Grauerholz himself is too busy working on the sequel to care.

Myron Pinkley was discovered crying in the chapel with a fracture dislocation of the fifth and sixth cervical vertebrae and the dread 'Custer's Sign' – a ferocious, but temporary and final, penile erection that indicates total transection of the spinal cord. He survived, but suffered permanent loss of function in all four limbs.

Hank Crawford, to his delight, required an above-knee amputation of his left leg. This enabled him to sue the State for criminal negligence and violation of his constitutional rights. They settled out of court for a figure believed to be in excess of one and a half million dollars. When the lawyer who so ineptly handled Crawford's original trial developed pre-senile dementia, Crawford also successfully sued the law firm in question, for an even greater sum. Each year, on the anniversary of the riot, he sends Klein a case of The Lagavulin malt whisky plus a recent polaroid of his prosthetic limb being rubbed between the legs of a different bathing-suited beauty.

Victor Galindez was investigated by the State Bureau of Corrections and received a reprimand for a breach of emergency procedures likely to endanger life. He subsequently left the Correctional Service and now works, more contentedly, as a probation officer out of Brownsville.

Dennis Terry, who escaped without injury, finally applied for, and was granted, the parole he had so long avoided. He opened a diner on the outskirts of Wichita Falls and married a part-Navajo waitress half his age who is expecting their first baby.

Bill Cletus transferred to Huntsville where, unable to collect the retainers he'd been used to, he suffered a catastrophic drop in income. He eventually learned to live within his salary and lost thirty pounds in weight as compensation. In a short and rather florid memoir of the riot serialised in a local newspaper, 'The Great Uprising At Green River State' was subtly transformed into a battle of wills between the mad criminal genius of Nev Agry and the iron-jawed resolution and unflinching valour of a figure modestly referred to in the text only as 'the Captain'. 'Okay, so they're faggots,' barked the Captain, as he defied the craven Warden Hobbes prior to his heroic lone rescue of the infirmary, 'but that don't necessarily mean they deserve to die!' Movie rights were optioned and Cletus alienated his small circle of friends by repeatedly asking them whether they thought Schwarzenegger or Stallone would be better suited to play him on the silver screen. The option, however, was never exercised and with its lapsing Cletus fell into a dark and enduring bitterness from which he has yet to emerge.

Claude Toussaint was given a life sentence for the murder

of Neville Agry and never got to drink One Hundred Pipers through a straw in Alfonso's. He too ended up in Huntsville, where he shaved his hair, took to wearing wire-rimmed glasses and started an HIV support group. Because he was the man who'd iced Nev Agry no one fucked with him and this did his cause a world of good. He also became Stokely Johnson's lover again, though this time out of choice. Klein writes regularly and visits when he can and Claude remains well and in his letters claims to have discovered a sense of self and purpose that had eluded him in his previous incarnations as a transvestite and a pimp.

Eight men escaped during the chaotic evacuation of the penitentiary. Seven were recaptured within a week. The eighth, Reuben Wilson, was reported as last seen fleeing the prison on the day of the riot by Dr Juliette Devlin and Sgt Victor Galindez. He was never recaptured but remains on the FBI's wanted list.

Juliette Devlin never finished her projected research and she never expanded on the pilot study she'd authored with Ray Klein and Earl Coley, though it formed a model upon which others based work of their own. In fact Devlin abandoned Forensic Psychiatry altogether, arguing that she'd got whatever it was she'd needed from it, and she took what some saw as a dramatic side-step into Child Psychiatry, though this seemed logical enough to her. She proved to be particularly gifted at this work, of course, and was appointed to a two-year Research Fellowship in Chicago. One day a package found its way to her postmarked Paris, France and containing two old door keys. A note inside read: '*Hero no longer. Balls blue no more. Thanks for the use of the room!*' It was signed 'W.' There was no return address but one day Devlin plans to drag Klein over to Paris to track the Whirlwind down, though whether she will get to reap it again depends on too many imponderable factors to predict.

Earl Coley's body remained unclaimed and seemed destined for Potter's Field until Klein claimed it himself and shipped it back to New Jersey where he buried the Frogman next to his father. Both tombstones carry the names and dates of the dead men and beneath each the inscription 'The Bravest'. Devlin did find Coley's family and sent them each a copy of the paper, but received a reply only from his daughter, who thanked her for her kindness.

The only other funeral Klein attended was that of Vincent Lopez. Indeed Klein was the guest of honour and as night fell on the trestle tables laid out in that shabby back street in San Antone, many tears were shed and many chests were swollen with pride, as Klein told the story of how Vinnie had saved Klein's life in the terrible final assault and of how, in the end, Vincent Rodrigo Garcia Lopez had given himself for his compadres and died like the man he was.

After the riot Klein spent ten days in hospital, under prison guard, with a raging cellulitis of his left leg as the microbes he picked up in the Green River finally had their way. In the same ward, game rooster that he was, was that same Sonny Weir whose impromptu left arm amputation had initiated the violence. In the next bed to Klein, recovering from burr holes and a reconstruction of the knee, was Colt Greely. Colt figured he owed Klein because if Klein hadn't fractured his skull and crippled him and dumped him in a toilet on B block, Stokely Johnson would've strung him up with the other guys who'd helped cut off the nigger's head. After a certain amount of persuasion Klein agreed to Greely inscribing a tattoo on his left shoulder with a sterile needle and syringe. It showed a dark tower struck by lightning and in a semi-circular scroll beneath it the words VIRESCIT VULNERE VIRTUS. Despite the initial horror inspired by her better judgement Devlin found that Colt's artwork further inflamed her desire to take Klein home and fuck his brains out. Klein thinks it's the coolest thing he's ever done for as he never tires of reminding her, it's the genuine prison article and – at least in principle – the last tattoo ever to be done in the Green River State Penitentiary.

So Ray Klein and Juliette Devlin did get together and even in the darker moods that afflict him Klein has to admit that it's pretty goddamn good. Whilst it remains a theoretical possibility he has given up hope of ever getting back his licence to practise surgery, though he sometimes fantasises about taking off to some war zone with his tools. When Devlin moved to Chicago he upped and followed her and on the strength of his martial arts and convict credentials got a job as a bouncer in a jazz club. To his surprise he enjoyed the nocturnal life and eventually approached millionaire Hank Crawford for a loan to set up a little bar and blues lounge of his own. Crawford was delighted to come in as a one-legged sleeping partner, as he put it, and enjoys showing up unannounced from time to time with a tall Texan girl on each arm like some latterday Alfonse Capone. Klein called the club 'Nine Below Zero' and its reputation in the Windy City continues to grow. Occasionally one of the many itinerant graduates of the riot shows up and sits with Klein into the wee hours, smoking Klein's Camels and resurrecting the ghosts of times past. One of them, Albert Myers, who lost the sight in his left eye, stayed on at the Zero as a bartender.

And speaking of ghosts the prison itself was abandoned and sealed and was never used again for any purpose, disciplinary or otherwise. It stands there still in the bottomlands of the Green River and for all that anyone knows is home only to rats and bindweed and a few vagrant families of nesting birds. Anyone, that is, except Ray Klein.

For now and again, when his heart is heavy and he can't shake off the blues, Klein makes the long drive south and spends the night alone, wandering around those high stone walls whose granite roots are sunk so deep in earth. And sometimes, when a warm wind blows in from the Gulf and makes the empty watchtowers moan, he hears a voice within: of The Word. And Henry Abbott. For Klein believes, and no one will convince him otherwise, that the Man and his God, Man and God both, still roam those empty walkways hand in hand, of the universe they've chosen for their home. And as Klein sits in the starlight, with his back against the iron-studded gates, he listens, enthralled, as The Word beckons Henry from the dark and tells him one more time: of the things that were done, and the tortured and incomparable race that fought and died, in the tale of the Green River Rising.

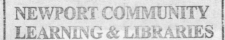

ALSO AVAILABLE IN ARROW

The Religion

Tim Willocks

Malta. May 1565.

From the shores of the Golden Horn, Suleiman the Magnificent, Emperor of the Ottomans, has sent the greatest armada since antiquity to wipe out Islam's most implacable foe, the Knights of Saint John of Jerusalem, in their stronghold on the island of Malta. To the Turks the knights are known as 'The Hounds of Hell'. The knights call themselves 'The Religion'.

Meanwhile, in Sicily, a disgraced and exiled Maltese noblewoman, Carla La Penautier, has been trying to return to the doomed island in an attempt to find the bastard son who was taken from her at his birth. The Religion have refused her every plea and a tormented Roman Inquisitor, Ludovico Ludovici, seeks to imprison her. But Carla recruits a notorious adventurer and arms merchant – Mattias Tannhauser – to help her evade the Inquisition and to escape on the last galley to run the Turkish blockade. As the ensuing apocalyptic conflict between Islam and Christianity becomes the most brutal and harrowing siege in military history, Tannhauser and Carla must survive the bloody inferno and track down a twelve-year-old boy whose face they have never seen and whose name they do not know . . .

'Macho, sexy, profoundly bloody and concerned with spiritual salvation. This wonderful adventure story is also an unavoidably resonant meditation on the power of religion to incite war.' *The Sunday Telegraph*

'*The Religion* is a novel for our times, dealing as it does with the clash between the Christian West and the Islamic East . . . as his epic tale unfolds, he examines, through the reactions of his cast of characters, all of them caught up in extreme circumstances, the phenomenon of religion.'
Independent

arrow books